His heart of sto...

Atop his marble base, the statue towered above her, making Katie feel wonderfully small in comparison. Unable to stop herself, she climbed the marble steps until she stood at the very top, placing her eye-to-eye with the giant warrior. She blinked incredulously. She would swear those eyes truly *saw* her, but she shook off the uneasy feeling.

Kiss me, his expression said. The words pounded through her mind, intense and demanding. Her gaze moved to the warrior's immobile lips, and her fingers soon followed, tracing the lush outline. Well, I could kiss him this once, she thought dazedly, but only this once.

Carefully, cautiously, Katie closed her eyes and took his cheeks in her hands. Her lips met his. Ribbons of heat and passion and hunger traveled all the way through her, and all she could think was: This is what a kiss should be like. A breathy sigh slipped past her throat. "If you were real, I'd gobble you up in one tasty bite."

Then a voice clearly said, "I believe that can be arranged."

sel

the Stone Prince

gena showalter

HQN™

ISBN 0-373-77007-3

THE STONE PRINCE

This edition published by arrangement with Harlequin Books S.A.

® and TM are trademarks of the publisher. Trademarks indicated with
® are registered in the United States Patent and Trademark Office, the
Canadian Trade Marks Office and in other countries.

www.HQNBooks.com

Printed in U.S.A.

To my agent, Deidre Knight.
I am blessed to know you. You stood in my corner
every step of the way and believed in me
when I didn't believe in myself.

To my editor, Tracy Farrell.
A thousand thank-yous wouldn't be enough. You rock!

To the soon-to-be-published authors who helped me
on this journey: Elizabeth Branham, Kelli McBride,
Sheila Cooper, Donnell Epperson, Betty Sanders and
Nancy Cochran. And to published authors Amanda McCabe
and Jill Monroe. I would not be here without all of you.

To Mickey Dowling. You inspire me to write.

To Debbie Splawn-Bunch. I'll never forget the
loving kick in the butt you gave me—or the fact that
you wouldn't let me title this book *The Stone Erection*.

I love you all.

the Stone Prince

CHAPTER ONE

KATIE JAMES COASTED HER fingertips across the muscled chest before her. Warmth tingled through her arm, a drugging warmth more intoxicating than expensive champagne and moonlight kisses. Her lips parted on a wispy catch of breath as images of silk sheets, entwined bodies and slow, delicious caresses filled her mind.

How could this man affect her so powerfully, almost *magically?* How could he affect her at all when he'd never spoken a word to her? His face was beauty personified, yes, but that wasn't enough to entrance her like this, to leave her weak and shaky every time she glanced at him.

There had to be something more to him, something elemental. Something beyond physical beauty that lured her every feminine desire. At the moment, though, she could not think past his physique, and slowly, so slowly her gaze moved over him. He was granite-hard, his abdomen ridged with sinew, his shoulders wide and firm. All of this gave his tall, sculpted frame a dangerous aura—dangerous and utterly sensual. He belonged in the woods with raw, naked branches surrounding him. Yet he stood outside among a brilliant crimson and yellow drapery of azaleas, somehow the absolute essence of masculinity.

"Mmm," she sighed, her eyelids fluttering closed. Her hand dropped to her side. "If only you were real...."

But he wasn't. He was formed entirely of smooth, gray stone—a beautiful statue, nothing more. This was one of the ironies of fate, she supposed, that the first man to ever truly captivate her belonged in a museum and not in her bed.

Why was she surprised by her infatuation with a beautiful, silent, unreal man, anyway? Having grown up with five older brothers, she knew just how annoying real men could be. They burped and scratched in public, cracked derogatory jokes, and somehow managed to charm the pants off women before losing interest and moving on to other conquests.

Her stone warrior could not offend her. He couldn't choose someone else if he thought her unattractive or too tall, because he was permanently mounted to the colored marble base that stood in her garden gallery. A marble base she now stood upon.

Another sigh slipped past Katie's lips, and she fought a deep, primitive urge to touch him again, to hold him, to discover some sort of comfort or acceptance she'd never gained with the procession of men she dated.

This is wrong. I should walk away.

But she didn't.

The cool Dallas breeze ruffled the tight constraints of her ponytail but did little to cool her ardor, and with each passing second the stone warrior's stare unraveled the very fabric of her reservations. Finally, Katie gave in to her craving. She dragged her fingers across his jawbone, loving the slightly bearded texture that reminded her of a man just before his morning shave. She traced the curved outline of his ears and imagined what he would feel like had he been the flesh and blood man she so desired.

Fiery heat rippled across her nerve endings.

Of their own accord, her fingertips wandered lower, caressing his neck. His shoulders. His chest. She even circled his small, puckered nipples. A soft moan of pleasure wafted to her ears, the timbre low, raspy and masculine.

Katie jerked back in surprise. After a moment she relaxed, even experienced a twinge of disappointment when she realized her imagination was simply running wild. Again. Hadn't she sometimes felt his breath upon her face when she drew close? Hearing him moan was no more fantastical than that.

Gravel crunched as a car meandered along her driveway.

Katie jerked around and watched wide-eyed as a black sedan halted just in front of her dilapidated, Victorian-style mansion. Tendrils of mortification raced up her spine, heating her cheeks. She'd been so lost in her scrutiny of the stone warrior, she'd forgotten about prying eyes and midday sunlight.

Just what had this intruder seen?

She scrambled from the dais. The moment her feet hit the soft grass, she counted to ten, using the time to calm her racing heart. She should have resisted the statue's allure; instead she'd acted like a teenage girl kissing her favorite rock star's poster. *Well, no more,* she thought, determination stiffening her spine. *There will be no more touching the statue. In fact, there will be no more looking at him, and absolutely, positively no more thinking about him.*

She watched a handsome, familiar male emerge from the sedan. Never one to back down from conflict, she maneuvered around the bushes and flower beds of her "pleasure garden"—so dubbed by the previous owner because the entire enclosure was littered with naked sculptures similar to *the warrior she wasn't going to think about ever again*—and marched to the driveway.

"Damn it, Gray. What are you doing here?"

Her visitor grinned, not the least put out by her brusque tone. Above them, the sun breathed peacefully, its powerful rays illuminating his tall frame and wide shoulders with an orange gold halo. "You owe me a quarter for cussing, little sister."

Frowning, Katie dug into her pocket, snatched out a quarter and tossed it to him. "I only cursed because you surprised the shi—" Thankfully, she stopped herself in time. "You startled me, okay. For God's sake, call before coming over."

"I called. You didn't answer. You were supposed to be home."

"So you started to worry," she said. For some reason, all of her brothers still thought of her as a delicate flower in need of twenty-four-hour, seven-days-a-week protection. So what that she was now six feet tall and in top physical condition. So what that she'd attended numerous self-defense classes.

Gray shrugged, sheepish. "Yeah. I started to worry."

"Did you consider I might have just stepped out?" She flashed him an exasperated but loving grin. "Don't answer that. Just tell me what you need."

"I wanted to see your newest acquisition. From out here it looks like a dump, by the way," he added good-naturedly, motioning to the house with his chin. "Why aren't you painting or laying tile or doing something to fix the place up? That's your job, isn't it?"

At that moment, Katie's tense muscles relaxed. Gray hadn't seen her with the stone warrior. Otherwise he would have been cracking jokes at her expense instead of inquiring about her activities. "I worked on the upstairs bathroom all morning and needed some fresh air."

He gave the mansion another once-over. "Fresh air? I don't think so. My guess? You feared the walls were about to cave in and got out while you could."

"Ha, ha."

"Honey, I sure hope you knew what you were doing when you signed the deed."

"I've been buying, fixing and selling houses for four years. Give me some credit." She might have chosen an unusual career for a woman, but she loved what she did. Even better, she had an instinct for real estate, knew when and what to buy, knew when to sell, and she almost always made a profit.

A dedicated skeptic, Gray remained unconvinced. "Please tell me you negotiated a good deal. I seriously doubt anyone will ever snap this baby up."

"I'm willing to bet I sell this house for more money than you make in an entire year."

"I'll take that bet." Grinning, he stroked his fingers over his jawline. "To even the odds, you only have to make five thousand dollars over the purchase price and restoration costs."

Katie didn't hesitate. "Deal."

"If you win, I'll wear a dress to the next family luncheon. If I win, you have to have dinner with Steven Harris. He's a new detective in my unit," Gray rushed on before she could protest. "Everyone likes him."

She groaned. Her brother meant well, he truly did, but she wasn't going out with any more of his friends. The last cop he set her up with had spent the entire night discussing—in minute detail—the way a bullet had once pierced his chest cavity. All of the fascinating details were delivered while she tried to suck down chopped tomato spaghetti.

"I've changed my mind," she said succinctly. "The bet is off. I'd rather be staked to an anthill wearing nothing but a bologna bikini than go on another blind date."

Her brother remained undeterred. "Are you seeing someone?"

"No." She didn't elaborate, knowing it would only encourage him. In the last year, she'd endured endless evenings of bad food, bad movies and even worse company. She had finally come to the conclusion that she suffered from a severe case of First Date Syndrome.

The only symptom—which was proving fatal— was that she always found something wrong with her love interests within an hour of meeting them. Richard ate his peas one at a time. John's voice had a high, nasal pitch. Quinn walked with his knees bowed out. Mitch was too clingy. Worse, all of them were shorter than her own six-foot build, and she hated, *hated* looking down at a man. That was how she'd made it to her twenty-fifth birthday without a single male ever making it past the getting-to-know-you stage.

That was also how she'd made it to her twenty-fifth birthday without a single male getting inside her pants.

Deep down she truly desired a man to cuddle with, a man she could look up to (literally) and share her hopes and dreams with. A man who would kiss and lick every inch of her naked, quivering body. But how could she find such a man when she turned away the few who wanted her?

Maybe she *should* go on another blind date.

Gray uttered a long, drawn-out sigh. Thankfully, the sound whisked away her foolish musings. "If you're holding out for perfection," he said, "I'm afraid you're doomed for disappointment."

"Are you kidding me?" Though she was amused by his assumption, she sounded properly disgusted. "I already know there's no such thing as a perfect man. My brothers taught me that lesson very well."

"Smart-ass."

"I'll take my quarter back, thank you very much." Grinning smugly, Katie held out one hand, palm up. She only had four quarters left, and she didn't think they'd last through the day, much less another five minutes with Gray. Earning a little money back was an unexpected boon.

Her brother crossed his arms over his chest. "I'm

not the one who's trying to quit cussing, therefore I owe you nothing more than an apology for soiling your pretty little ears with my crudity."

Her grin quickly faded. "You have the worst potty mouth ever, and I swear you're the one who taught me every dirty word I know."

He shrugged as if to say, *You damn well shouldn't have listened.*

"There's a patch for smoking," she grumbled. "Do you think they make one for cussing?"

"Absolutely not. Soap is the only cure." The tinge of amusement in his voice told her Gray was recalling the many times during their childhood that he'd washed her mouth with soap. "So, when do I get the official tour?"

Though she longed to wash *his* mouth out, she said, "Now, if you've got time."

"I do."

"Then let's get started. Since we're outside, I'll show you the garden first." Oh, he was going to love this, she thought, suddenly bubbling with anticipation. "Come on."

They walked the distance, playfully arguing over whose morning had been worse. He won, of course. Who could compete with being accosted by a delusional psychotic intent on ruling the world? When they reached the garden's entrance, Katie stopped, gave Gray a moment to absorb the ambiance, then splayed her arms wide.

"Welcome to my playground," she said.

Silence greeted her. Impatient, she tapped her foot and waited for some sort of reaction from him. One minute passed, then two. He hadn't moved an inch, hadn't emitted a single sound. Finally, she could stand it no longer. "So...what do you think?"

"Holy sh—"

"Don't say it," she ordered with a laugh.

"But those statues are—" His eyes widened with incredulity as he studied one statue, then another. "They're getting off."

"I know."

Seven statues guarded the entrance. Three were male; four were female. All were nude and posed in different stages of self-gratification. Though he stood just around the lush, green thicket unobservable from where they stood, Katie knew *her* stone warrior had his hands at his sides. He wasn't pleasuring himself, but he was obviously aroused. Magnificently aroused. His body as beautiful as any Greek statue. What he offered a woman, however, could not be covered by a fig leaf.

Why am I thinking about him? Stop!

"I take back my comment about the house being a dump." Gray strolled to a female sculpture whose expression of utter rapture complemented her I'm-ready position. He ran his hand along the curve of her spine. "Hell, I'll even buy the place from you."

Katie's chuckle floated across the daylight, mingling with the sudden eruption of her brother's beeper. He checked the number. In less than a heartbeat of time, his shoulders tensed and his facial features hardened. He was no longer her teasing older brother; he was now a seasoned detective, distanced and in control. "I've got to go," he said, his tone dark with secrets. "I'll visit later this week, and you can give me the grand tour then."

She barely had time to nod before he placed a swift kiss on her cheek, said, "Be good," then raced away. Just like that she was alone again.

With nothing else to do in the garden, Katie strolled to the house, allowing herself only one backward glance. Inside, she blinked away the orange and red specks clouding her vision. Thick cobwebs filled each corner of the dining room, both high and low. Dirt stained every wall and the white paint was yellow and peeling. As she moved into the kitchen, her shoes crunched on the broken shards of what once must have been a magnificent chandelier.

The house needed major renovations to be considered even halfway livable, and at that moment, all the work required threatened to overwhelm her. One task at a time, she reminded herself. One task at a time. Earlier, she'd finished tiling the bathroom walls, so the only chore left on today's To Do list was stripping the kitchen floor. First she had to remove the layer of carpet, which covered a layer of linoleum, which covered a layer of God knew what else. Tomorrow she would replace the wood trim and baseboards in the bathroom.

With a sigh, Katie punched play on her CD player and "Born to be Wild" rocked from the speakers. Two hours ticked by unnoticed as she pulled up and discarded the thin, dirty shag and matting. When she finished, she settled herself and her toolbox on the lime-green linoleum. In her position, a large bay window loomed in front of her, and she had a perfect view of the pleasure garden. Katie couldn't shake the feeling that a pair of intense, observant eyes—his eyes—watched her, waiting and hoping for…something.

Her hands began to shake, but she continued working. After a while, she found it impossible to concentrate and had to stop altogether before she chiseled a finger instead of the floor. Not knowing what else to do, she nailed a sheet over the window, then drove home, cursing her wild imagination the entire way.

For the next three days, she worked from dawn until evening without difficulty. But all the while, a need to see her stone warrior was growing inside her. Even her palms began to ache for him, for a chance to glide over his hard, sculpted muscles.

So far, she'd broken only one portion of her resolve. She'd thought of him. Over and over again. But what about the rest? Not see him? Not touch him? Surely she could remain strong enough to resist his allure.

Her will broke completely the fourth day.

Early that morning she began fantasizing about *his* hands traveling over her body, his breath fanning her ear, his hard, naked *human* body pressing against hers. Those images haunted her, consumed her. When dusk painted the landscape, perspiration dotted her brow and her breath came in short, erratic pants, a condition that had nothing to do with manual labor.

Finally, she strode to the bay window, reached out with a shaky hand and removed the sheet. Moonlight spilled inside at the same moment she felt those invisible eyes upon her. All right, so she'd ignored another part of her decision. She was gazing at him, unable to look away. Big deal. She hadn't touched him. And she wouldn't. But even as she thought the words, Katie found herself strolling out the back door and into the twilight as if an invisible cord tugged her closer.

A chilly April breeze caressed her cheeks and danced several long, pale strands of hair across her shoulders. Spring was a versatile time in Texas. In the matter of a single day, a cool wind could mutate into sizzling heat or bone-numbing cold. The closer she came to the stone warrior, the more her blood threatened to overheat, and she was immensely grateful for the chilly air.

Up ahead, paper lanterns flickered, the bulbs within giving the illusion of actual flames. Crickets chirped a lazy tune. Colorful flowers bloomed in every corner, some yellow and pink, some purple and blue, but each filled the air with a sweet, floral fragrance. Katie worked her way around the winding bushes and soft petals that swayed in her path. When she faced the object of her torment, she came to an abrupt halt and drew in a deep breath.

At last.

Atop his marble base, the stone warrior towered above her, making Katie feel wonderfully small in comparison. As she had many times before, she studied the long, thick length of him—but only in the name of observation, of course. Lord, what would he feel like if he were actually real? What would he say and do to her? A shiver raced through her.

His muscled chest, arms and legs gave him a powerful aura very few men possessed. Long strands of bright green ivy stretched around his left leg, the only color to his form. He was so blatantly masculine, so wonderfully detailed. His eyes seemed heavy-lidded, sleepy, as if forever beckoning a woman to bed. The beautiful sculpted lines of his face reminded her of a movie star. Or someone equally unattainable.

"Damn it, you've invaded every aspect of my life. My dreams. My fantasies. My work. I don't understand how I can want you, *need* you this much."

Touch me, those mouthwatering lips of his seemed to say.

"No, I can't," she answered, but she was already reaching out. She traced her fingers over the cold, hard ridges of his abdomen, trying to absorb his essence. Maybe if she touched him enough, her obsession with him would wane. Entertaining that glimmer of hope, she moved her hands higher and circled his nipples. Just as before, a moan reverberated in her ears and the sound caused warm tingles to liquefy her bones.

What would happen if… She gulped and tentatively moved her palms downward. Her fingers wrapped around his penis, an action so utterly insane, but entirely necessary for her peace of mind. Another bolt of pleasure shot through her, this one so hotly intense she was nearly incinerated.

Katie jumped, startled. Surely she had just imagined such a forceful electrical charge. Brow wrinkled, she clasped his rigid length again. Shivers swirled and danced through her, just as intense and just as arousing. No, she had imagined nothing.

Unable to stop herself, she climbed the marble steps until she stood at the very top, placing her eye-to-eye with the giant warrior. Katie blinked incredulously. Once. Twice. She would swear those eyes truly *saw* her. The thought made her swallow with trepidation, but she shook it off. Statues, no matter how eerily real, were simply inanimate objects.

And yet…

Kiss me, his expression said.

The urge to do just that besieged her. Thankfully, her common sense reared its head. Touching a work of art she could somehow justify; kissing a work of art she could not.

Kiss me.

"No," she said. "No, no, no."

Kiss me! Kiss me! Kiss me!

This time, the words pounded through her mind, insistent, intense and demanding. Her gaze moved to the warrior's immobile lips, and her fingers soon followed, tracing the lush outline. *Well, I could kiss him this once,* she thought dazedly, *but only this once.* Twilight offered a shadowy sort of protection, so no one would ever have to know.

That thought provided all the incentive she needed. Carefully, cautiously, Katie closed her eyes and cradled his cheeks in her hands. That invisible force pulled her, hard, and she moved closer, closer still. Then her lips met his. Ribbons of heat and passion and hunger traveled all the way through her, and all of her thoughts tapered to a close except one: This is what a kiss should be like.

Her hands slid from his cheeks and into his thick, silky hair, holding him captive. His lips were softer, warmer, than she imagined, and she lingered far longer than she should have before laying her head upon his shoulder. Her nostrils filled with the clean, male scent of him.

She could almost feel his hands caressing down her back, cupping her butt and guiding her even closer against him. She could almost feel his breath against the curve of her neck and the hot wetness of his tongue as it glided along her collarbone. Could almost feel the slow, rhythmic beat of his heart.

"I truly am insane," she whispered, but Lord, she liked the feeling. Another breathy sigh slipped past her throat. Crickets began another leisurely tune while fireflies flickered and danced overhead. "If you were real, I'd gobble you up in one tasty bite."

Then a deep voice whispered next to her ear, "I believe that can be arranged."

CHAPTER TWO

THE VOICE WAS pure unadulterated sin, like warm brandy on a cold night, and so suggestively sexual Katie thought she had imagined it, that her fantasy life was hitting a new level. But then she came to realize two startling facts. One, her inner voice had never spoken with a raspy, masculine accent before. And two, the strong, bracing arms she had visualized around her waist were actually there.

Shocked, she snapped to attention...and found herself staring into the most beautiful pair of eyes. Eyes that were pale blue, almost crystalline, and aglow with knowing, wicked promise.

Eyes that belonged to a man, not a statue.

Katie gasped with a combination of disbelief, fascination and mortification. Where was the gray stone? *Where was the freaking gray stone?*

Breath snagged in her throat, and she squeezed her eyes tightly closed. When she refocused, everything would be back to normal. She was sure of it. She was, after all, a mostly sane person. Yes, she experienced moments of madness—like kissing the statue, for instance—but those moments always passed.

Please, Lord, let *this* moment pass.

Very slowly, she cracked open her eyelids.

The warrior's image remained the same: human.

Damn, damn, damn, she thought desperately. How could a flesh-and-blood man with bronzed, completely kissable skin be holding her in his embrace, the heat of his body seeping through her clothes, his heartbeat pounding against her chest? Oh, God, the moon suddenly seemed brighter, the air thicker.

"You're…you're…" Mystified, she struggled to form a coherent sentence. There was an explanation for this. She had only to ask. But when she opened her mouth, only one word formed. "How?"

He withdrew his arms from her waist. Looking bewildered, he slowly moved his body this way and that, stretching and twisting each vertebra of his back as if for the very first time. And then—Lord above, he smiled, a devastating smile that revealed even white teeth and sent waves of sexual heat straight to her core.

"I've owned this property for two and a half weeks, and I've walked through this garden almost every single day. You've been right here, hard and cold and stone. You're a statue," she babbled. "I know you're a statue."

"Nay, *katya.* I was a statue." Just then his eyes widened with—joy? Awe? Disbelief? She wasn't sure which. Whatever the emotion, he appeared as if he had just realized the full extent of his proclamation.

What the hell was going on? Katie's confusion grew with lightning speed. She needed to hear something intelligent and rational. Something believable. Not "I was a statue."

Still grinning in that luscious way, he closed his

eyelids and muttered a long string of unfamiliar words, his tone urgent. When he refocused, he paused to catalog his surroundings. One heartbeat passed. Two. Fierce disappointment pulled at his lips, eradicating his smile. He uttered the words again. Again surveyed his surroundings.

"Explain how this is possible," she said, a pleading quality in her voice. "How you were stone, and now you're a man. A trick of the light, maybe? Or a hallucination? That makes sense, right?"

"Nay." He shook his head, causing dark locks of hair to sway at his temples. "It makes no sense whatsoever." He reached out then and touched her cheekbone, as if he needed to reassure himself that she was real.

Perhaps it was that gentle caress, or maybe even her own wits finally sparking to life, but Katie suddenly realized that she had no idea what this very real, very muscled man planned to do to her. Battling a surge of fear, she slapped at his hand, pushed at his chest and spun around, ready to dart to her truck and speed away. But she had forgotten that she was perched on a ledge several feet above the grassy foundation. She teetered precariously on the edge, trying to regain her balance without actually reaching behind her and grabbing hold of the stranger.

A second later, she hurtled face-first toward the ground. She twisted midair and managed to land on her butt with a painful *thwack*. The impact knocked the air from her lungs and whisked several strands of hair over her eyes.

Once she found her breath, she jumped to her feet. She didn't run as she'd first intended, however. Be it shock or fascination, Katie remained firmly in place. The man had stepped down from the dais and stood just in front of her. *He's taller than I am,* she thought, her eyes widening. So tall, in fact, she was forced to look up, up, up. The realization caused her common sense to melt like ice cream in a hot summer sun. Amazingly, the top of her head barely peeked above his shoulders, and for the first time in her life, she felt breathtakingly feminine and surprisingly vulnerable.

"Were my muscles not so stiff," he said, his ice-blue gaze sliding suggestively down her body, "I would have caught you." He took a step toward her.

What am I doing? Retreat! "Stay where you are," she said, inching away.

He sighed. "I mean only to ascertain you are unharmed. Women are weak, delicate creatures, and you collided quite forcefully with the ground."

Katie stopped, her eyes narrowing as everything clicked into place like a lightbulb inside her mind. She scanned the garden. Her brothers were behind this and were most likely hiding in nearby bushes, having a good laugh at her expense. No one except her family spouted that "women are weak" crap.

Lord, the man standing before her was probably Steven Harris, the detective Gray wanted her to date.

"Gray, Nick, Erik, Denver…you can come out now," she called, spinning around to make sure her voice carried. "I know you're here."

Steven, aka the statue, crouched down in attack position, scrutinizing the garden. His muscles tightened and strained. "These enemies await you?" His voice was almost imperceptible.

"Not enemies. Idiots." Katie shouted for her brothers again. "The joke is getting old. Come out. I know this is Steven." She rammed a pointed finger into the hard warmth of the man's chest.

"I am not called Steven."

He said it with enough conviction and disgust that a small kernel of unease slithered along her spine. "I mean it," she yelled, her voice sharper than before, "come out or I'll give this guy the Tae Kwon Do Kick of Death you taught me."

"So there is no danger to you?" the man asked.

Only to my sanity. "No."

His stance relaxed and he turned away from her. He began stretching again, this time rolling his shoulders and ankles. All the while the words *I am not called Steven* echoed in her mind. If he wasn't Gray's friend, who—and what—was he? The direction her mind veered just then scared and confounded her all the more. Had he…was it possible…could his transformation have happened supernaturally?

No. *No, no, no, no, no.* The guy wasn't Steven Harris. Fine. That was easy to accept. But he *was* simply a man. A man who had a lot of explaining to do, be he a psycho killer or a practical jokester sent by her brothers.

She chewed on her bottom lip. Psycho killer? "Maybe I should go," she said, trying for a nonchalant tone, but sounding more like a buzz saw grinding against wood. She began hedging backward again. He didn't offer a word or glance of protest, didn't act as if he cared, and after a moment's thought that brought her to a halt. Surely a killer would have tried to stop her.

She stood there, curiosity battling with prudence while she silently observed this man who had appeared from nowhere, taking in every detail, searching for answers. He was just so…big. One flick of his wrist, and he could snap her neck like a twig. There was a gentleness to him, however, that belied any menacing intentions. A walking contradiction, he was. She must have blinked or lost focus, because she didn't notice any sudden movement toward her, yet suddenly he was just in front of her, looking at her, into her.

"I thank you for breaking the curse," he said, tracing a finger along her nose. "But now I must go." Without another word, he slipped around her and strode away.

Curse? "Where are you going?" The man had materialized in her garden, wearing nothing but a smile, and thought he could leave without any type of explanation? Oh, that just pissed her off, made her forget any lingering hint of fear. He was big enough to hurt her, yes, but she was mad enough to inflict some major damage of her own. "I demand you tell me who you are and how you transformed from stone to man."

In a graceful motion at odds with his size and previous inflexibility, he spun around to face her. His eyes possessed a wistful quality. In a mere snap of time, his soft expression mutated into potent fury, like fire across a night sky, both hot and cold at the same time. "A woman has no right to issue such a demand."

Had a sword been strapped to his waist, she felt certain he would have unsheathed it just then—and used it on her! He was tense and ready, like a vengeful hunter inspecting cornered prey.

Unexpectedly, he turned and again strode away.

Just let him go, she thought. But Katie found herself calling out, "Wait!" She jolted after him and latched on to his arm. A puny action, really, but he stopped all the same. "You can't leave. You're naked."

He took his time facing her this time. When he did, he arched one brow in an insolent salute and gazed down at her. "You know not your place, woman."

His words expressed displeasure. But his voice was husky and richly intent, and resonated a secret, carnal meaning meant only for lovers. Did he realize what his tone had just suggested? He stared down at her, his eyes heavy-lidded and erotically inviting. Her nerve-endings sparked with renewed life. Oh, yes. He knew. He knew exactly what he'd suggested, and if she gave him the slightest encouragement, he'd strip her down and put her "in her place."

Katie gulped, feigning ignorance. "I own this land. *This* is my place."

"'Tis not what I meant and well you know it. Someday a man will show you exactly where you belong by giving you the savage bedding you silently asked for each time you passed through this garden."

Hearing the actual words proved more potent than the veiled innuendo, and she jerked her fingers from their tenuous hold on his bicep. What stung was that there was nothing she could say to discount him. Only five minutes ago she had caressed the stone man's nipples, wrapped her palm around his penis (twice!), and kissed his lips.

This wasn't any friend of her brothers'.

The truth of it danced through her, undeniable now

in every way. Her brothers would never allow a man to intimidate her like this. Or even invite her to participate in a night of debauchery. Not even for a joke.

"Only a proper bedding will teach you proper respect for a warrior," he said. "Unfortunately, I have not the time to instruct you. Now, I thank you once again, *katya,* but I must return home." Then, for the third time, he tried to abandon her.

In this instance, however, he stopped without her urging.

He glanced left then right, studying the horizon. He cursed in a language she didn't understand, then spun around to face her. A scowl marred the perfection of his features. "I have just realized you are a necessary burden, for I know nothing of your world beyond this enclosure."

Her brows knit at "necessary burden." Her nostrils flared at his next words.

"Take me to the nearest sorcerer."

"No way in hell," she shot back.

He crossed his arms over his chest. The stubborn stance said that he was a man used to issuing commands and receiving instant compliance. Normally she wouldn't even think twice about confronting someone with an overabundance of testosterone. But the way this guy was looking at her, as if he was a king and she was his royal subject headed for the guillotine, almost made her jump into action.

"You will do as I say or—" He stopped abruptly. His eyes widened. "Curse it! There is something else I had forgotten in the excitement of returning to my homeland." He bared his teeth in a scowl. "'Tis something

I would as soon forget again, but cannot, for my continued freedom depends upon it."

"What?"

"To begin, I must bed you."

Katie stifled a gasp of alarm. Or maybe it was a gasp of anticipation. Maybe even anger that he'd said he would rather forget her. Whichever the reason, she'd already lost all claims to sanity. Any other woman would have run screaming for help before he'd finished his last sentence. Bed her, indeed.

Silence stretched between them. With each passing second, she became increasingly aware of his nakedness, of *him*. She smelled his warm, masculine scent, felt the caress of his gaze over each and every part of her body as if *she* were naked. Her blood heated, and her hormones raced into overdrive, calling out, *"I'll take you, I'll take you, and I'll do anything you want."*

"I won't discuss bedding you," she said, cutting through the silence, "but I will tell you that there are no sorcerers."

For a moment his expression became unguarded, revealing pain and fury, but also desolation, a desolation that tied her stomach in a thousand tiny knots. "We do have psychics," she added, willing to say anything to wipe away such bleakness.

"Psychics?"

Was he purposefully acting perplexed or did he truly not know? "Psychics are people who claim they can tell the future with supernatural powers. You know, through magic."

He paused, considering her words. "I seek someone who wields magic, so aye, your psychic will do nicely." Despite his now amiable tone, cold determination claimed the lines of his jaw. "Now, take off your clothes. When both our bodies are sated, I will allow you to take me to the psychic."

He would allow her? Gee, thanks. "My answer is no," she said firmly. "On all counts."

The blue of his eyes sparkled like ice chips in a winter storm and was the only warning she received about his intentions. Before she had time to blink, he was on her, pinning her back against a statue. She knew she should have been scared, but she wasn't. She was strangely aroused.

I don't know anything about this man, she reminded herself. She didn't know how he liked his coffee, or if he kicked little puppies when no one was watching. Her long-ignored body sprang to life, anyway. Her nipples strained for contact, and her hips arched forward, arched into him. Bedding him didn't seem like such a bad idea at the moment.

"I did not ask you, *katya,* I commanded that it be so." The low timbre of his voice held the steely edge of a sword.

She gulped, unsure whether she was still turned on or if she was deathly afraid. The man oozed power and authority and if she didn't get his mind out of the gutter, hers would be joining him there. "Uh, about the psychic. All business establishments are closed until tomorrow morning."

He paused. "When the sun rises, you will take me to see this man of magic. I will have your word on it." His lips parted as he awaited her answer, giving a hint of the pearly whites beneath. "As for the bedding—"

"If you finish that sentence, I swear to God I'll never take you to see a psychic."

His mouth tightly closed, and he remained quiet, though anger seethed just below the surface of his skin.

Wow. She hadn't expected the threat to work, but now that it had… "I want you to answer some questions for me."

His expression darkened. He surprised her by barking, "Ask."

So she did. "How did you make the stone disappear?"

The fine lines around his mouth pulled taut.

She waited, hoping to hear words like *new next-door neighbor, trap door* and *silver paint*. Instead, she heard only silence, and as minute after minute dragged by, her sense of unease grew. Finally, she could stand it no longer. "You're starting to frighten me here. I mean, I know what I'm thinking isn't possible, and yet…" She peeked up at him through her lashes.

Again, silence. She thought her nerves would completely frazzle before he answered.

"Magic," he finally snapped, as if she was the meanest woman in the world for making him answer. "The stone disappeared through magic."

She opened her mouth to question him further, but his arms snaked around her waist, halting the words in her throat. Unbidden, a shiver moved through her, and she leaned into him. Her body was reacting all on its own, heedless of her will. Lusting after a man was natural, expected even, but having sex with a stranger journeyed beyond her realm of acceptable.

That didn't stop her mind from imagining his hands roaming down her stomach, slipping inside her pants, under her panties, and...another shiver racked her. Damn it, she had to get away from this man, had to think clearly before she did something crazy, like actually throw herself at him and demand he "put her in her place." But when she tried to dart away, his arms tightened around her, keeping her still.

"Let me go," she demanded. Her arousal mingled with another spring of fear.

His hold only tightened further.

"I'm warning you. Let me go before I show you the skills of Master Kai's best student."

"I know not this Master Kai, but neither he nor his finest student are a match for me." To prove his point, he brought Katie more snugly into him, hardness to softness. Cotton to flesh.

Far from cowed or charmed, she was now furious. Eyes narrowed, she bit out, "We'll just see about that, won't we?" She was just about to knee him in the groin when he squeezed her butt, startling her.

"Allow me to give you a demonstration of my persuasive skills." He pressed the juncture of her thighs against his growing erection. Despite her best rational intentions, Katie found her blood becoming molten lava, an inferno of need. While his lower body rhythmically brushed against hers, he palmed one of her breasts. So unexpected and new, these touches electrified her, moved across every fiber of her being with the intensity of lightning. Her knees weakened, right along with her will.

She licked her lips and prayed he didn't notice her mounting desire.

He noticed.

A dark brow rose, taunting her. "Have you, mayhap, changed your mind about the bedding?"

Yes, yes, yes. "No," she forced out. "I want you to let me go. Now."

He didn't look convinced, but he said, "Know that I consent to your will because it is *my* wish to do so." With those magical, deft fingers, he kneaded each rounded curve of her buttocks. "Otherwise such a demand would go unheeded." Then suddenly, he released her.

She darted away. "Touch me again, and you'll be sorry."

He gave a husky chuckle that rumbled deep in his chest. "Sweet *katya,* arousal burns bright in your eyes and your body trembles when I touch you. You could run from me, but do not. When I touch you again, you are the only one who will be sorry…for your denial."

She gasped at his implication—even though he spoke the truth. "That's not arousal in my eyes, that's fatigue." Lie. "I tremble because I'm cold." Bigger lie. "And for your information, I haven't run away because I'm waiting for a chance to pummel you." The biggest lie of all.

"Is that what your world calls mating now?" His half grin slowly and deliciously lifted into a full-fledged smile. His gaze raked over her tall frame in a bold scrutiny, somehow making Katie feel as if he'd removed every stitch of her clothing. "Then much do I look forward to your pummeling, *katya.*"

She scowled. "My name is Katie, not *Katya.*"

"You are a *katya* to me. A—" he searched for the right words "—little witch."

Her jaw opened, then closed with a snap. Instead of being pleased that the endearment didn't mean "pleasure slave" or "easy lay," she was insulted. "How would you like me to call you giant bastard?"

"Call me whatever you wish." His grin remained in place. "Be warned, however, that I will make you kiss the sting of such a sharp sobriquet away. A woman's duty, after all, is to pleasure her man."

He was acting as if he controlled the fate of the universe—her universe most particularly. Well, there was one fact he would soon learn about her: A woman she might be, a doormat she was not. "Look," she told him, "I'd appreciate it if you'd stop with the pleasure talk. I'm a woman, not a one-nine-hundred number."

His brow puckered with confusion. "I know you are a woman. Did I not hold your breast in my hand?"

I will not scream. "You have five seconds to help me understand what happened or—" Nothing sounded quite brutal enough, so she finished with, "Or you'll regret it."

"What is there to understand?" As if he couldn't tolerate going without human contact, he began closing the distance between them again, this time at a steady, predatory pace. "You broke the curse, *katya.* You set me free. Now you must give yourself to me body and soul so that the curse will be broken forever."

As if that explained everything. There was no time to ponder his words. He was getting closer by the second. *Naked man approaching. Naked man approaching.* She darted to the left. He followed.

"I warned you not to touch me." Now she darted to the right. He followed. And then he was in front of her, once more so close she could feel the heat of his body. Her back pressed against the tall, rising column of a prickly bush. She gazed up at him, the scent of raw male virility wafting to her nostrils, carnal and sexy. Without pausing to think about her actions, she gave a sharp twist and placed her foot behind his knee. That knee collapsed and brought him propelling in her direction. She latched on to his arm and sent him all the way to the ground, face-first. When he hit, he hit hard, all that muscle and brawn weighing him down. But he didn't pause, didn't stop to take a breath. He was back on his feet almost instantly and facing her with a look bordering on murderous.

"Do not attempt that again." From his expression to his tone, his need to retaliate shone brightly. Yet he didn't. He remained in place, glaring and huffing instead. "Next time I will not be surprised and you will find yourself my prisoner."

"Just maintain your distance and there doesn't have to be a next time."

His lips thinned with displeasure, telling her without words he would rather throw her over his shoulder and spank her—her treacherous heart gave an anticipatory leap at that thought—but he nodded stiffly. "How did you learn such a trick?"

"Hard work." At last she was able to draw in a steady breath, and she forced her heartbeat to slow. Getting her eyes to peer away from him was another matter entirely. Thick battle scars formed a random pattern across his abdomen. Somehow, each one added to his appeal. A whorl of hair surrounded his navel, then dipped enticingly—*Do not look down,* she commanded herself. But she did anyway and prayed he didn't notice.

He gave her a slow, knowing perusal in return.

Katie cleared her throat. "Tell me more about the curse."

Bitterness hardened his features, and she felt a twinge of guilt for mentioning what was so obviously a painful subject. However, that twinge was not strong enough to make her revoke the question.

"That need not concern you," he said.

Oh, really? "Do you want my help or not? With the psychic," she added quickly, dispelling any notion she meant the bedding.

His eyes narrowed. "Percen de Locke is a powerful sorcerer, as well as my half brother. He cursed me, locking me inside stone, able to hear, see and feel everything around me, yet unable to respond. Until a fair maiden's kiss set me free. Temporarily."

Well, she thought, she'd wanted a rational explanation, and this was a far cry from rational. The guy had been locked in stone and her kiss had temporarily set him free. Yeah, right. That kind of thing only happened in fairy tales. Besides that, she was no princess charming. Katie drummed her fingers along her crossed arms and thought to expose his lie for what it was. "You wouldn't, by chance, have powers of your own?" she asked. "Magical powers that can prove your story?"

He arched a brow. "What of my transformation?"

"I need something more."

Eyeing her thoughtfully, he said, "Would you willingly invite me to your bed if I possessed these magical powers?"

She wasn't sure, but she thought she detected a note of resentment in his tone. Katie studied his masculine features. Not a flicker of emotion betrayed him, however. "No," she said, "I wouldn't. And don't change the subject yet again. Can you prove your story or not?"

He blew out a breath of frustration. "Though this garden is remote and not many have passed through over the ages, I have had centuries to study your world. You are a race that relies on the seen, the explainable." A pitying light entered his eyes. "Your people fear magic because they cannot control it. Where I hail, both Great-Lord and peasants laud mystical abilities, and before you ask again in your strange way, aye, I wield magic. Magic that I can prove."

A sense of impending doom slithered along her spine. "You said you have studied my *world.* By that you mean another state or country or continent, right?"

"Nay. World means celestial body. Planet. Star." His eyes glazed with sadness, giving him a vulnerable aura that touched her. "For me, world means Imperia. My home."

He held up one palm and closed his eyes. A look of intense concentration etched his expression. As she watched, a small, colorful globe materialized in the air above his skin, spinning slowly. Three smaller globes circled above it. Every inch was exquisitely detailed, making each orb appear solid, and yet colorfully translucent.

She tentatively reached out and touched the largest globe, surprised to find the sphere firm and warm. At the moment of contact, vivid pictures flashed in her mind like the click of a camera. She gasped. Crystal castles stretched to the violet-and-pink skyline. Majestic, dragonlike creatures soared from cloud to cloud. Trees arched in every direction, heavy with brilliant sapphire and diamond-colored fruit. Most beautiful of all were the blankets of white grass that billowed with a gentle, dew-kissed breeze.

His expression tightened, as if he were using every ounce of his strength to maintain the image above his palm, but the globes began to waver, then disappeared altogether. His hand dropped to his side.

Oh. My. God. He'd been telling the truth. Magic. A cold shiver raked her, freezing her limbs. No mortal man could conjure such a wondrous apparition. And no earthly man could change from stone to flesh in less than a heartbeat.

"You have magic powers, and you're an alien." She blinked, then blinked again. Images of spaceships and bedlam danced through her head. "You're an alien, and you have magic powers." Maybe if she said it a thousand times, her shock would melt away. "You're an alien. An alien with magic powers."

When he didn't respond, she added, "You don't look like a creature from another planet." Really, what else could she say? Her mind had yet to return from hiatus.

"Just what does a creature from another planet look like?" he asked.

"Green skin, a long, slimy body and large black eyes that look at you as if you need to be laid out flat on a table with a probe slowly working its way toward parts of your body that don't bear mentioning."

"I have encountered one race who looks as you've described." He shrugged. "They travel from world to world searching for knowledge and enlightenment."

"On spaceships?"

"Aye."

She shivered, never wanting to come face-to-face with the "enlightened" race. But Lord, had she ever thought to come in contact with any otherworldly being? NO! "How did *you* travel here?" Katie mentally patted herself on the back. Here she was, conversing quite rationally with an alien, not lying on the ground in a dead faint.

His lips thinned. "My mother sought to aid me," he replied tightly, "and opened a vortex that sent me from my world to yours."

Her gaze darted around the maze, cataloging the other statues. Had they all been sent from another world? Were they all aliens just waiting for her kiss so that they could come alive?

The warrior in front of her chuckled, as if hearing her unspoken question. Or maybe she'd spoken it aloud. At this point, Katie wasn't sure what she was doing, saying or thinking.

"I am the only one," he assured her. "The others are merely stone."

Her shoulders slumped with relief. Lord knew her body systems couldn't take another male like— She drew a blank. "What's your name?"

"I am Jorlan en Sarr. Once the first in command of Great-Lord Gui-en Sarr's army." With a proud tilt of his chin, he crossed his arms over the solid wall of his chest.

"Well, I'm Katie James, first in command of James Real Estate."

"Katie." He said her name differently than she'd ever heard it, halting over each syllable and prolonging the *a* and *e*. Kaay-tee. He nodded with approval. "Similar to *katya*. Such a name well suits you."

For some insane reason, she was pleased that he thought so.

Just then, a night wind drifted by, causing his nipples to pebble. Katie was proud of herself for noticing because that meant she hadn't been looking down south.

"You know," she said, "it's just occurred to me that we can continue this conversation inside the house. You must be cold." The best thing about going inside was that she could cover his nakedness with a sheet. That, in turn, would stifle her growing attraction to him.

Good God, she was lusting after an alien.

At least he isn't a psycho killer, whispered beneath her thoughts.

"You are not cold," he said, "and yet you are wearing practically nothing."

"I'm wearing a tank top and jean shorts. Perfectly decent attire."

"I am attired as *Elliea* intended."

"But—"

"Lest you forget, I would have your word that you will help me locate a sorcerer at tomorrow's dawning."

Another breeze blew by, and this time she was looking down south. Her cheeks heated.

"Well?" Jorlan asked. Obviously patience was not one of his virtues.

"It's hard to concentrate when you're—" she searched her mind for the proper word "—waving around like that. For God's sake cover yourself."

He glanced down at his nude form and shrugged, completely unabashed. "The male body is nothing to be ashamed of, *katya*. Best you become used to mine very quickly."

Just what was he implying? That he would never wear clothes in her presence? Or that he planned to make hot, dirty monkey love to her whether she granted permission or not, so she should become accustomed to his size? Either way, he would damn well put on some clothes!

"I give you my word I'll take you to a psychic tomorrow. Happy now?"

"Nay." His chin tilted to the side, and he worried one hand over his jawbone. His eyes were guarded, waiting. He resembled a man about to encounter a dangerous storm. "Women cannot be trusted to honor their word."

Katie snorted. She wanted to ask him why he'd sought her promise at all since he never intended to believe her. She rolled her eyes instead. "You're lucky I'm feeling gracious, Jordie. I'm going to allow you to live after making such a chauvinistic remark."

He frowned.

She grinned. "Now let's hustle inside. Unless, of course, you plan to break *your* word."

"Only a dishonorable man would do so. Not I," he ground out, his tone iron-hard.

"Really? Well, I believe the deal was that if I gave you my solemn oath to take you to a sorcerer tomorrow…which I did…you would go inside…but there you stand. Hmm, what can that mean?"

His frown became a fierce scowl.

Good. She'd made her point, though why she was goading him, she didn't know. She did know she was beginning to feel safe in his presence. Odd, but true.

"After you." She waved him ahead, partly to watch the way his butt moved as he walked, and partly because she didn't want him behind her. Although, as she followed behind him, she realized she didn't like the submissive implication that scenario provided.

He threw her a glance over his shoulder, a wicked gleam darkening his irises to a smoky blue. "Mayhap next time you can return the favor and stroll naked in front of me."

Not even if he was dying and that was the only way to save him.

The closer they came to the house, the more she realized this man was her responsibility. He might taste sweeter than chocolate ice cream on a sizzling hot day. He might be planning to seduce her so she would learn her "proper place." (That one still had the power to infuriate her.) And he might be a warrior used to control. But she had kissed him. She had set him free, and that meant his well-being, for a while, at least, fell on her shoulders.

Inside, she watched Jorlan dart about, inspecting the splintered wood, wallpaper samples and tools that were scattered throughout. Katie snatched a paint-splattered sheet from the floor and wrapped it around his shoulders. He didn't acknowledge her action. Fortunately, his lack of attention didn't dislodge the sheet.

Unfortunately, the colorful linen did little to detract from his masculinity. He could have held a box of tampons in one hand and a purse in the other and still she would not doubt his virility.

"If we're from different worlds," she asked, "how do you know my language?"

"Think you I could not conquer your primitive language whilst I whiled away the last few centuries?" He sounded angry, offended and amused all at once.

She opened her mouth to explain she hadn't doubted his intelligence, that she'd merely wondered if that, too, was through magic, but she said instead, "If you're smart enough to learn an entire language, what kind of mental block kept you from learning about women's liberation?"

"I learned about equal rights and other such nonsense, but what I learned was not what you would like. I learned that your world order began to decline the moment your men lost their warrior instincts."

"Well, maybe you just didn't have the right teachers." Her fists clenched. "Let's go into the living room and I'll teach you a thing or two about feminine power."

At last he turned those startling blue eyes to her. "When I go into this 'living room' with you, it will not be for conversation."

Change of plan. "Are you thirsty?" she rushed out, then didn't wait for his answer when she said, "Of course you are. You've been unable to drink since the Stone Age. I'll get you something. I have a cooler in my truck." With that, she raced into the cool night air.

He softly chuckled, and his whispered words, "There is no escape from me this eve," followed her the entire way to her vehicle.

CHAPTER THREE

JORLAN EN SARR FELT his lips kick up in a smile as he watched the little witch scamper away. And she was a witch, whether she denied it or not, for she had heard his voice, had felt his urgency, while he resided inside the stone—something no other woman had done during his thousand spans of confinement.

His smile continued to grow as he imagined her doing to his flesh what she'd done to his stone casing. He was a male, after all. A healthy, lusty male, at that, and it had been too long since his last coupling. But then, suddenly, his amusement faltered. His expression went flat. As distracting as little Katie was with her flashing amber eyes and touch me/do not touch me demeanor, she could not overshadow his primary focus: total, complete freedom. Total, complete vengeance.

Many centuries had passed since the eve his curse had been spoken into existence, yet his need to rid the galaxies of Percen de Locke, to punish his brother in the most painful way possible, had only grown and festered until it became a bone-deep wound. Over the spans Jorlan had stroked the wound like a lover, embracing his need for vengeance with single-minded intent. Release.

He did not care why his brother, the most powerful sorcerer in all of Imperia, had cursed him to a life of misery and desolation. Nay, he cared only about striking the bastard down. Under the right circumstances, a sorcerer could live for eternity, sustained by magic. Jorlan's own mother was a former priestess of the Druinn and had seen over fourteen centuries.

Besides that, time flowed differently upon each world. A thousand years had passed here, yet how many eves, seasons, or spans had passed on Imperia?

It didn't matter. De Locke was still alive. Jorlan knew it, *felt* it.

Vengeance *would* be his.

Just thinking about the cries of mercy he would incite and ignore brought a sense of anticipation that released his muscles from their viselike clasp. Even more than the joy of revenge, however, was the joy of returning home. Tomorrow Katie would lead him to a sorcerer—psychic, her world called them—and he would use that person's power to send himself through the cosmos. *Home.* By *Elliea,* had he ever thought to return a free man? Dreamed, aye. But never had he truly believed. Until now.

Upon first realizing the stone had dissipated, Jorlan had forgotten all thoughts but those of home and had attempted a spell to open a vortex. That spell had promptly failed, for his powers were, and had always been, unstable. He was glad, though, that he was still here, for he had yet to accomplish the second requirement of his brother's spell. Katie might have set him free with her kiss, but his freedom lasted only a short while. Only fourteen days. Unless and until he made her fall in love with him. 'Twas a cruelty on his brother's part, and the only way to forever free himself.

I will not return to stone, he vowed darkly. Nay, he would do whatever was necessary to prevent the curse from claiming him once again. Even seduce and leave the lovely Katie, for how else to win a woman's heart than to bed her?

Jorlan knew Katie desired him, and he did not think it would take more than this one night to woo her. He would simply give her the greatest sensual pleasure she'd ever known. No woman, save those with no heart to give, could guard themselves against such an assault. He had experience with the heartless variety, and knew from watching Katie these last cycles that she was nothing like Maylyn, a heartless wench to be sure, and the only woman he'd ever been foolish enough to love.

Drawing in a deep breath, he imagined the air laden with the majestic scents of Imperia. There was no other land that branded its essence onto a man's innermost being, almost as if the very foundation was an old, dear friend. There was no other land that filled the void inside him. No other ruled by mystical principles, where magic was lauded and male domination accepted.

In that moment, Jorlan was filled with a sense of desperation, of longing more intense than a bolt of lightning. No doubt this night would stretch the length of eternity. Scowling now, he whipped away the cloth that draped his shoulders. The soft material whooshed to the floor. Using physical activity as an outlet for his emotions, he worked the lingering stiffness from his limbs. At first his movements were clipped and unsure.

But as blood rushed through his veins, reminding him that he truly lived, his riotous emotions calmed, as did his gestures.

"I'm back," Katie called a bit later, her tone hesitant, yet laden with forced gaiety. She marched into the unfurnished chamber holding two red containers.

Jorlan stilled. Through half-lowered lids he watched her legs close the remaining distance between them. She had the legs of a warrior maiden: long, slender, firm, the kind that wrapped around a man's waist and held on till the end of the ride. The thought caused every inch of him to harden. Seducing her would be no burden. In fact, he was more than ready, more than willing, to begin. Human contact had been denied him for far too long.

When Katie had strolled in the garden for the first time, he hadn't been curious enough about her to truly notice her. Aye, he had desired her kiss to set him free, yet he hadn't cared about the woman herself. Too many females had passed and ignored him for him to place any hope on another. But this one *hadn't* ignored him, and he realized now that he was all too interested in the woman herself. She truly was a vision, and as he continued to study her, something long forgotten stirred within him. Something…tender.

He mentally cursed himself. By all that was holy, he would not feel anything tender for this woman. Nay, he would allow himself to feel nothing deeper than arousal. When a man allowed himself to feel anything more, he opened himself up to hurt and betrayal.

Looking nervous and unsure, Katie flipped her ponytail to one side. The action reminded him of how she'd tossed him to the ground as if he were an insignificant pest, a feat no other woman (or man, for that matter) had ever done. What skill she possessed! What strength. He imagined all that energy beneath him. Above him. Beside him. Around him. Yet she claimed she wanted nothing to do with him sexually. Well, he would just have to use every ounce of his seductive prowess to make her forget her misgivings. He grinned slowly. Her seduction, and subsequent avowal of love, was a much-needed challenge and would most assuredly help the night pass more quickly. Also, her seduction would aid him with his vengeance quest, for what man could think clearly when his cock begged for attention?

She came to a sudden halt, no longer appearing nervous. Nay, she appeared furious. "What are you staring at?"

"You." And he continued to do so. She did not have the boyishly slender hips he'd seen on other women of her world. Katie's body was curvy, sweetly rounded in all the right places, and inherently female. The succulent swells of her breasts and the generous curve of her waist fit perfectly with her unusual height.

"Stop that right now," she demanded. "You're staring at me like I'm a candy bar, and you haven't eaten in a year."

"I will stop when I am finished and not a moment sooner." Right now she wore a thin top covering and a pair of cropped blue *drocs*—jean shorts, she had called them. The luscious skin of her neck, collarbone, arms and legs was left uncovered for his perusal, and peruse her—all of her—he did. So thoroughly, in fact, that he counted eighteen freckles atop each shoulder.

Did she have freckles hidden elsewhere?

Most of her hair was scraped back, yet a few pale tendrils spilled free like warm shimmers of sunlight. Not a single curl or wave marred the straight perfection of each strand. He suddenly longed to comb his fingers through the thick, silky mass, to spread its heaviness across his pillow.

Her features were not beautiful in a traditional sense. Nay, they were different, exotically sensual, carnally alluring. She had high cheekbones, a pert, up-tilted nose, and large amber-colored eyes framed by thick, sooty lashes. Those eyes slanted upward, giving her a permanent take-me-to-bed expression. And her lips…by *Elliea*, the more he studied them the more he imagined them all over his body. Her lips were lush, pink, and full enough to launch an army into war for a single kiss.

Just then that mouth parted with shock. She stepped directly in front of him, her face becoming a comical etching of incredulity, awe and embarrassment. "I thought you understood that you absolutely must wear the sheet." Even her voice appealed to him, sweet and husky. "You can't just go around naked. You'll be arrested for indecent exposure."

Unconcerned, he crossed his arms over his chest. The woman seemed to think it was her right, nay, her duty, to snap retorts and issue orders. While he applauded her spirit, he certainly resented her lack of respect. He was a warrior first and foremost, and a warrior did not take orders. A warrior gave them. "I am still waiting to hear you utter the word *please*."

She surprised him by shouting, "Just put on the damn sheet before I drop you on the ground again!"

He scowled. Best she learn now with whom she dealt! "You will ask me nicely, woman, and mayhap if I am feeling gracious, I will wear the *damn sheet*. If I am not feeling gracious, there is no power strong enough to force me to wear it." 'Twas not the way to seduce a woman, he knew, but it was becoming more and more clear to him that this particular woman was in dire need of masculine guidance—his guidance—before the actual loving could begin.

Surely the males of her world would thank him.

She bared her teeth in a scowl of her own. "I will not ask nicely. You will simply bend down, pick up the sheet, and wrap it around your waist because it is the polite thing to do. You are, after all, standing inside *my* home."

He ignored her. She stomped her foot. He almost laughed aloud, then, for who would have thought an inability to manage him would cause such a purely feminine reaction in one so warriorlike? "I hope you enjoy the view, *katya,* for you will be seeing it all night."

Silence.

Then, "Nicely," she ground out.

His lips twitched. What an amusing little imp she was. "With such a sweet concession, how could I refuse?" He retrieved the linen and, just to provoke her, secured it low on his hips—low enough to hint at what stirred underneath.

"Here, drink your strawberry soda and shut up." Mutinous, she tossed him a container.

He easily caught it, though he never removed his gaze from her. He had won their contest of wills, and yet she still issued commands. How was one supposed to react to such a tyrannical disposition in a female? If Katie were a man, he knew exactly how he'd react: talon slicing downward to silence the offender. "If you speak to me that way again, little witch, I will personally silence you—with my tongue."

She gasped.

He nodded, satisfied she'd been properly intimidated. He thought now she would act as she ought. Mayhap he should have known better.

"That's the second threat you've made about your tongue," she growled. "Just so you know, if you come near me with it, I'll bite it off."

Instead of reprimanding her yet again, Jorlan remained silent, deciding instead to pretend she hadn't spoken. She was obviously confused and upset by his sudden appearance in her life, and knew not how to handle her emotions. But this was absolutely the last time he would allow her to speak to him so insolently without punishment.

That decided, he scrutinized every angle of his "soda" thoughtfully. The metal was a shiny alloy unfamiliar to him. Not knowing how to drink from it, he waved his hand in a circle above the container and uttered a spell. "Open now, this you will. Open now, and be unsealed."

Bang.

Katie screamed and clasped a hand over her heart. Red liquid rained upon them like a summer storm. Several droplets clung to his face and neck, while others latched onto the hairs under his navel. Most of the liquid splattered atop Katie's head, streaking her hair.

"Why did you do that?" she demanded, running a hand through the now reddish-blond locks.

"I was thirsty." Using the linen's hem, he tamped down his irritation and quickly wiped away the evidence of his spell gone awry. All of his life, magic had swirled within him. However, he should know better than to attempt any type of spell, for he'd learned at an early age that he held no control over the force of his power—a fact that bothered him greatly and sorely bruised his pride.

"Next time ask me to help you, okay? My heart can't take another scare tonight." Katie popped the top of her container and handed it to him. "Here. You can have mine. I'm not really thirsty, anyway."

He set his decimated beverage aside and accepted what she offered. Tentatively he sipped. The delicious elixir moved down his throat, and he relished the taste. "'Tis worthy enough for a king's table," he said, awed. "What other culinary wonders does this cursed world possess?"

"Lots of things." She hooked errant strands of hair behind her ear. "Chocolate. French fries. Cheesecake."

Jorlan's stomach rumbled. He knew nothing about the items she had named, yet each one sounded like ambrosia to his overly starved body. Their lovemaking could come after he'd eaten. "You will prepare each item for me."

Her sandy-colored eyebrows drew together. "Is that so?"

"Aye. 'Tis so." He nodded to assure her he meant what he said.

"Well, guess what? I promised to take you to a psychic tomorrow, nothing else."

"I am hungry, woman."

She rolled her eyes, something she did often in his presence. "I'm really not in the mood for whine this evening, thank you very much, so just stop. I'm not your personal chef and that's the end of it."

"Seeing to a man's needs—all of his needs—is a woman's only purpose in life."

"You're kidding me, right?"

"Nay. I would never jest about a woman's duties."

"I'm just sure you wouldn't." She lost her look of amused tolerance, looking instead like a determined woman on a mission: death to every male within sniffing distance. "Let me explain something to you, Jordie. You're—"

"Jorlan." He did not like it when she shortened his name and used that impertinent tone, making "Jordie" sound like something she would call a bothersome child.

She continued on as if he hadn't spoken. "You're out of luck, *Jordie,* because I don't cook, and even if I did, there are no supplies here."

"You will provide me with a weapon to hunt our food, or you will provide me with your world's cuisine. Nothing else is acceptable."

Arms akimbo, she dug her fists into her sides.

She had to relent, he assured himself, for he, a fierce Imperian warrior, had just issued a direct order.

"How did you survive as stone if you couldn't eat?" she asked calmly.

"'Tis no concern of yours."

"You want to eat?"

A muscle ticked in his jaw. "Magic sustained me."

"Then cast another spell. *I'm not cooking.*"

How had he ever thought her antics amusing? "Since it is your hope to starve me," he replied sharply, "at least take me to another domicile. Long have I been without the comforts of home, and you have nothing here save linens for us to slumber upon."

"Us?" she sputtered. "There is no us when it comes to sleeping. I thought I made that clear."

Would she contradict everything he said? "Where you sleep, so, too, will I."

"You haven't gained my permission to stay with me, much less share my bed."

"Why would I be foolish enough to ask your permission? You might say no." He was not a stupid man.

Her lips stretched tight. "I'll let you stay in my home tonight because you have nowhere else to go, not because you decreed it. And for your information, *this*—" her arms swept about, indicating the chamber around her "—is where I work, not where I sleep. My house is a few miles away and very comfortable."

"Then why are we still here? Let us be off." Impatient now to arrive, he didn't wait for her agreement, but simply headed for the door.

"I have rules, though," Katie rushed on.

He stopped midstride, then slowly turned to face her. "Rules?" he said, his tone deceptively soft.

"Three rules I expect you to obey if you want to stay with me." She held up one finger. "Rule number one: no telling me what to do. I've noticed you're a give orders kind of guy. Well, I'm a take-your-orders-and-shove-them kind of girl. That isn't productive. Therefore, while staying with me, you obey me. And that's not negotiable."

As she spoke, Jorlan slowly unfolded the multicolored cloth at his waist. His nakedness had disconcerted her earlier, and he knew it would do so now. He wanted no talk of rules and regulations unless he was the one issuing them.

Katie's mouth formed a small O, but far from silencing her, his action seemed to propel her onward. "Two," she said. "No touching me without my permission."

That one he liked even less than the first. "And the third?"

Another finger. "From now until I'm rid of you, you will always, *always* wear clothes."

Jorlan crossed his arms over his chest. He actually preferred wearing his garments. When not coupling, of course. But the little witch sought to place him under her control, and that he did *not* like. The warrior in him rebelled, for not even the Great-Lord had dictated his actions to such a degree.

Yet how did one deal with such a brazen female?

The answer came to him in a flash; he almost smirked.

"Well?" Her hands anchored to her hips.

"I agree to your terms, *katya*."

A genuine smile of relief lifted the corners of her lips, a smile that softened her expression and lit her features with radiance. The effect was devastating, and his breath hitched in his lungs. No woman had a right to possess such a grin. He resisted this newly discovered allure, vowing to remain impenetrably guarded against that captivating smile.

"That was easier than I expected," she said, still smiling.

"I agree to your terms," he added as if she hadn't spoken, "with a few minor adjustments."

That wiped the grin from her face, and he was once again able to breathe. "You have nothing to bargain with, Jorlan."

He arched a brow. "Do I not?"

"If you're planning to use your magic—"

"No magic, I promise you."

"Well, then, you're screwed, because I'm not changing the rules." Her satisfaction rang loud and clear.

Pretending to mull over his next words, he stroked his jaw. "We must journey to your dwelling this night, must we not?" He didn't give her time to respond. "I can do that clothed...or I can do that naked."

She gasped. "Now wait just a damn minute. I can leave you here by yourself, you know."

"If you think to leave without me, you will find yourself over my knee getting the spanking you so rightly deserve."

"If you think to spank me, you'll find yourself getting the beating *you* so rightly deserve!"

"You will listen to my adjustments or I will break every one of your rules. Beginning now." With purposeful strides, he closed the distance between them.

"I agree," she blurted out, her hands raised to ward him off. "I agree."

He stopped only a heartbeat away. "Number one: I

will give you no *unreasonable* demands, as long as you do the same for me."

The tension in her shoulders relaxed a little. "That's fair enough."

"Number two: I will touch you only if you touch me first." Now enjoying himself, he propped his arm against the wall beside him. "Or mayhap I will wait until you ask me, very sweetly, to put my hands on you."

At first she looked as if she might snort. But then, her gaze raked over him, and her cheeks reddened. "I'll maintain my distance," she said, averting her eyes, "because there's no way in hell I'm asking you to touch me."

"You did before. In the garden."

"That was different." Her cheeks burned all the brighter. When he made no comment, she burst out, "It *was* different. The stone appealed to me. You do not."

"Say no more, little witch. I would not have you regret more words than you already shall."

She leveled a glare at him, but didn't deny his claim.

He pushed his advantage. "Number three: I will wear clothing when the situation warrants it, and only then."

Silence.

Stubborn woman. "These are the adjustments I wish. If they are not acceptable…" His voice trailed off, allowing her to assume whatever she would.

A sigh pushed past her lips with enough force to cast a sweet ripple of air upon his cheeks. "I accept them, okay. Are you happy now?"

"Not nearly as happy as I would like to be." He

reached out, intending to brush a fingertip across her cheek. Then he recalled her rule and his own stipulation. Unless she asked, he could not touch her. With a muttered curse, he dropped his hand to his side.

She grabbed the sheet and shoved it toward him. "This situation warrants clothing. Since you know nothing of my planet's customs, you'll just have to take my word on that."

Frowning, he once again covered his lower body with the linen.

"Thank God we only have to put up with each other until tomorrow morning," she muttered. "I might die from stress otherwise."

More amused than irritated, he said, "Are you usually this surly with your guests?"

She swatted at the air with her hand once, twice. "I am *not* surly."

"Aye, you are, and argumentative, too. But mayhap by tomorrow's dawning you will be too sated to bicker with me."

Her jaw clamped together with so much force he feared the bone would snap. But with a visible effort, she managed to relax. "Let's go home," she said. "I'm too tired to deal with you anymore tonight." With that, she turned on her heel and headed toward the door.

"If I break one of your rules," he called behind her, "I will allow you to give me a severe tongue lashing all over my body."

She nearly choked on that one, and it required all of his strength to smother his laughter. Ah, life had never seemed so ripe with promised pleasures. For now, he was free from de Locke's curse. In a matter of hours, he would lose himself between a woman's soft thighs. And he would return home on the morrow. What more could a man possibly want?

CHAPTER FOUR

I'M IN SOOOOOO MUCH TROUBLE, Katie thought.

She eased into her truck, but she didn't start the ignition; she just sat there, clutching the steering wheel so tightly her knuckles turned white. Jorlan climbed inside and perched beside her in the passenger seat, oblivious to the riotous sensations dancing through her. Lick him all over? The idea held more appeal than swimming in a giant vat of melted Hershey's Kisses, yet also went against every ounce of common sense she possessed. Contrary to what Jorlan might think, hopelessly chauvinistic men did not heat her blood in a good way.

Well, not usually.

His "you will do this" and "you will do that" *did* irritate her to no end, but that irritation failed to obliterate her attraction to him. He was just so wickedly masculine, so unabashedly male. He knew his appeal and wielded an entire seductive arsenal, which he didn't hesitate to use to his advantage.

With his words, his glances, and his soft touches, he'd made his plans to have her quite clear. So many times during their interaction, she'd wavered, wondering if she should just give in or continue to resist.

And if she did resist, was she simply postponing the inevitable?

Intuition told her this man could not only give her the wildest night of her life, he could also cure her of First Date Syndrome. He didn't walk bowlegged or speak with a nasally tone. No, he strode with the gait of a hunter, strong and assured. His husky voice produced shivers of delight, not shivers of revulsion. She hadn't seen him eat, but she doubted he ate his peas one at a time. He just didn't have the patience to be a nibbler.

He wasn't patient, period.

Yet, that didn't turn her off as it should have.

"How do you force this vehicle into motion?" At her side, Jorlan opened the car door, but he didn't get out. He simply closed the door again, then opened and closed it, the hinges squeaking with each movement.

"Keep trying it that way," she muttered, still lost in thought.

When one overlooked his impatience, his chauvinistic demeanor and his penchant for disobeying, Jorlan was nearly perfect. And he *did* excite her in a way she'd never experienced before.

So what if she did it? What if she took the pleasure he was offering?

One simple brush of his body against hers had almost caused her to experience her very first orgasm. No telling what full-body, skin-to-skin, plunging-deep-inside contact would do to her. Kill her, most likely, but what a way to die! However, despite his I-can-give-you-a-mind-numbing-climax sexual magnetism, he truly annoyed the hell out of her. In attitude, he was too much like her brothers. Katie's brows drew together. Okay, so had she just talked herself into sleeping with him? Or had she talked herself out of it?

Time to regroup. Pros: 1. She had desired him, both stone and flesh, for the past three weeks. 2. He could whip her body into a pleasure soufflé. 3. He was leaving the next morning.

Cons: 1. He was leaving the next morning. 2. His arrogance grated on her very last nerve. 3. She would be nothing more than a momentary convenience to him—a necessary burden, at that.

Did she truly want to be a momentary convenience for her first time?

No.

She wanted hearts and candy, flowers and music. She wanted words of praise and acceptance, maybe even a whispered, "I simply have to have you. I can't live without you. If I don't touch you soon I'll die. Please. I'm begging you."

Okay, maybe that was a little extreme. But she knew, *knew* she wanted more than Jorlan would give her.

So the cons won. The man beside her, with his lose-yourself-in-me eyes and his to-die-for muscles, would be nothing more than a boarder. A nonpaying boarder, at that.

"Shut the door and buckle up," she told him with more force than she'd intended. "We're going to move now."

His expression clouded with confusion, as well as a bit of indignation, and he closed the passenger door with a final snap. "On Imperia, we travel atop horned stags very similar to your horses. This is my first time inside the belly of your enchanted transportation, so I know not of what you speak. Buckle up?"

She demonstrated what needed to be done.

He followed her example. A moment passed. He tried to scoot left and right, yet the belt hindered each motion. Frowning, he ripped himself free. "I will not trap myself inside your transportation."

Here we go again. Katie swallowed a sigh and geared herself for another argument. Lord knew if she demanded that he duck in order to protect himself from a bullet, he would only say, "A woman takes orders, *katya,* she doesn't give them," and then promptly be blown away by gunshot.

"The seat belt is there for your protection," she explained. She fluttered her lashes the exact way that made her brothers crumble. Jorlan didn't even blink. "If I come to an abrupt stop and you aren't wearing it, you'll fly into the windshield, crack your head and die." A little extreme, she knew, but she could think of no other way to make him listen.

His frown deepened, but at least he rebuckled.

Once they were properly situated, she started the truck and eased onto the road. Warm gusts of wind whipped through the open window, laving her face, lifting her hair. A horn blasted. Startled, she scanned what little traffic occupied the highway and discovered the honk had not been for her, but for a male driver who was swerving from one side of the road to the other. Accelerating, she quickly passed him.

The faster she drove, the more Jorlan relaxed his stiff posture. "'Tis exhilarating, this speed." His chuckle wafted to her ears, warm, husky and, oh, so inviting.

This man annoys me, she reminded herself.

They lapsed into silence. Unfortunately, that silence worked against her. Instead of concentrating on the oncoming traffic and construction cones that lined the median, her thoughts drifted to Jorlan's circumstances. Her insatiable curiosity soon overrode her good intentions. "How long were you imprisoned in the stone?"

"Nine hundred spans, seventy-two days and twenty-four minutes." He spoke so quickly, so assuredly, as if he'd never stopped counting.

"A span is a…"

"Year. A span is a year."

"That means you're over nine hundred years old." The truck swerved as she jerked to face him. He'd mentioned that several centuries had passed, but she hadn't given it any thought until now. "Surely you don't expect me to believe that. Most people never reach the age of one *hundred,* and those who do absolutely do not look like you. A thousand-year-old man would be buying Depends, drinking Ensure and worrying about osteoporosis."

He regarded her strangely. "Most of what you said escapes me, *katya,* yet will I strive to reply. Once the curse was spoken into existence, I stopped aging."

"But you'll age now, though. Right?"

"I will not age at the rate of your world, nay. I am part sorcerer, and sorcerers are eternal beings sustained by magic. Immortal. Aye, we can be killed with physical weapons as any flesh-and-blood creature, but if unharmed, our magic will keep us alive for eternity."

"But that's imposs—" She clamped her lips shut. On

top of everything else she'd witnessed and heard tonight, what was so unfeasible about a thousand-year-old alien who resembled a Calvin Klein underwear model and would live forever?

"Oftentimes, the myths and legends of one world are the facts of another. Over the spans," he said, "many people came into the garden at twilight, whispering of vampires and werewolves, creatures who do not age. Is it so unfathomable, then, that like these creatures, sorcerers can live forever?"

Unfathomable? No. Not anymore. Frightening? God, yes. "I believe you, Jorlan. I do. I was just taken by surprise, that's all." She paused as a thought occurred to her. "You said you're only part sorcerer. How long will *you* live?"

The corner of his eye twitched. "That does not concern you."

"I can easily drive you back to the garden, you know. In fact, I'm turning around right now." She jerked the steering wheel to the left, just to make a point.

"Because you're so obviously fascinated with the workings of my world," he said, his tone stilted, "I will answer this one last question. I am the first and only halfling born between a mortal and a sorceress. My path is uncharted. Mayhap I will live half of forever. Mayhap not." He paused. "Now you answer a question for me."

"Okay."

"What think you of love?"

She blinked at such an odd change of subject. "I'm not sure I understand what you're asking. Do you want to know what I think about a man and woman falling in love with each other?"

"Aye."

"Well, I think it's great." Her brows knit together. "Why?"

Instead of answering her, he turned and faced the window with a satisfied smile. Though slight, the movement caused his sheet to part, revealing a portion of his left thigh. Katie's chin snapped forward. *Watch the road,* she commanded herself. But her gaze repeatedly returned to Jorlan, and every time she glimpsed him, her mouth watered for a nibble of that golden thigh. *He's not a bucket of chicken.*

He shifted in his seat, exposing more…more… please God…oh yes! The sheet was completely split down the middle, revealing the entire length of his leg.

"What are you thinking about?" he asked suddenly. "Your face is flushed and your eyes look hungry. Starved, actually."

Katie's cheeks reddened, and she jerked her attention to where it belonged. "I'm not going to bed with you, okay?" Oh my Lord, she thought the second the words escaped her mouth. She might as well have asked him if he wanted to finger paint her naked body with caramel-and-chocolate ice cream and lick it off.

A knowing, masculine chuckle filled the small cab.

Thankfully, he didn't reply and the rest of the ride passed in silence, a silence she was now grateful for.

At home, she found Jorlan a Dallas PD T-shirt and a pair of sweatpants Gray had left behind. While Gray had always looked relaxed and cozy in the clothing, like a man spending a lazy day at home on the couch, watching TV and eating Twinkies, Jorlan looked eatable. His rock-solid build stretched the material and showcased every inch of his brawn. Had any other man ever looked so *indecent* in sweatpants?

Note to self: Write Hanes a very stern letter about what's appropriate in leisure wear.

P.S. Never invite Gray over again. His clothes are obscene.

Katie ambled into the living room, her newly clothed alien not far behind her. His gaze scalded her back, causing heat to percolate just underneath her skin. She stopped, whipped around, ready to demand he glance away. She froze instead. By the sparkle in his eyes, she knew he was planning something naughty—like removing her clothing piece by piece. Far from angering her, the thought made her heart leap with anticipation. Damn him! The man was too appealing for his own good, and at the moment he was standing way too close for her peace of mind.

She needed space and some sort of brain enema.

She stepped away.

He followed. Their gazes were locked and the space between them crackled with awareness. "If you ask, I will massage my hands in your hair, *katya,* and set each strand free from confinement."

Unable to help herself, she gazed at the hands in question. They were blunt, hard hands, clean yet well-worked. The hands of a warrior. Yet, she thought, under the right circumstances, they were probably capable of extreme gentleness and unending tenderness—a massage being one of those circumstances.

Before he could sense her growing willingness, however, she planted her hands on her hips and strove for a flippant tone. "The day I ask you to touch my hair is the day I cook you a seven-course meal." Which meant it would *never* happen. She wasn't his slave, and besides that, she hated, *hated* to cook.

But *never* was such a strong word. She probably wouldn't cook him a meal. No, that didn't work either. She might not cook him a meal. Damn, damn, damn. If only the sexual tension between them didn't generate enough electricity to light the entire state of Texas.

Jorlan inclined his head. A dark eyebrow arched and his expression was amused, as if he'd somehow listened to her internal deliberation. The corners of his mouth rose in that knowing grin she was beginning to despise. "Now I will not just make you ask for my touch, *katya*. I will make you beg for it. Over and over again."

His raspy tone suggested he possessed a sexual knowledge that went beyond the Kama Sutra. When most men spoke, their voice rated no higher than an Encyclopedia Britannica on her Knee Weakening Radar. But Jorlan's sensuality blared like a cataclysmic force of nature, and he definitely tipped the scales.

The crux of Katie's problem was that she didn't have much experience in dealing with such a sex-minded, eager man. Such blatant, in-your-face masculinity had certainly never been present in any of the men she'd dated. Plus, her intimidating height and take-charge attitude kept most advances at bay.

Most of all, she just didn't possess the soft, angelic beauty that inspired ardor. She knew it. Everyone else knew it, but that didn't seem to bother Jorlan. And maybe that was why he affected her so strongly. Why every moment she spent with him caused her fortitude to wilt a bit more. He was the first man ever to look at her as if she were a succulent morsel to be devoured in one tasty bite.

What if she was never able to find this type of chemistry again? Never find a man who made her *feel* like a woman, a woman with needs and desires? If she didn't grab onto Jorlan while she had the chance—

Wait! Good God, what was she thinking? He wasn't even touching her and already she was about to beg for his embrace. She needed to douse the budding fire within them both before the flames spread and became unstoppable.

Time to begin "Spending the Night with Katie Orientation."

She motioned for him to sit on the couch. He shook his head no.

Why am I surprised? "Would you *please* sit down?"

He did, grinning all the while.

"Now," she began. "I believe I've already mentioned this in the rules, but it bears mentioning again. Except while bathing, you must remain dressed, both inside and outside of this house. Otherwise you will be arrested and thrown in jail for indecent exposure." Or magnificent exposure if the arresting officer was female.

"After you broke the spell, I was not taken prisoner while I stood unclothed in the garden," he pointed out. "And I think you know that bathing is not the only time clothes are a hindrance. What about a long bout of pummeling?"

"As you won't be getting pummeled in this house, I feel no responsibility to respond to that statement."

He crossed his arms and gave her an amused look. "Your denials grow tiresome."

His self-assured pitch irked her, so she placed her hands on her hips and glared at him. "Did you ever consider the fact that I could have a boyfriend? Someone I'm in love with and committed to?"

One minute blended into two, and still he didn't answer her. She knew he'd heard every word she had spoken, though, because she'd shouted them so loudly her neighbor's dog was barking. "Well? Did you?"

Something dark, intense and desperate kindled in his eyes, but was quickly masked with indifference. His voice was anything but indifferent, however, when he said, "If you have a man, you should not have touched me as you did. You should not have kissed me."

Her gaze skittered guiltily away, and she noticed the light on her answering machine was flashing.

"So do you? Do you have a man?" Now his tone was as pleasant as if he'd asked, "This jelly doughnut is delicious, would you like a bite?"

Her motions clipped, she hooked a lock of escaped hair behind her ear. For some reason, she just couldn't lie to him about this. "No, I don't have a man." *Her* tone was as incensed as if she'd said, "You ate my doughnut, you dirty bastard."

"I see no problem, then." This time he spoke with a husky drawl any true-blooded Texan would have been proud of. "You desire me, and I desire you. We can give each other pleasure...and mayhap even love."

Love? She sucked in a breath. "You don't even know me." She paused as a thought occurred to her. "Oh my God, you're one of those losers who tells a woman he loves her simply to get her into bed."

"I have said nothing of loving you, *katya*." His features pulled tight, revealing just how much she'd offended him. "Sometimes honor is all a man has, and I would never dishonor myself by lying about my emotions. I wished only to inform you that I would not be adverse if you offered me your heart."

And that was just so much better, she thought dryly. "You're a romantic at heart, Jordie. You truly are. And now I'm done with this conversation." Katie strode to her coffee table and jabbed the play button on her answering machine.

"Hey, sis. I'm going out of town for a few days and wanted to know if I could borrow your—"

Her brother's voice jammed to a halt when Jorlan leapt across the room and pounded the little black box into a thousand tiny pieces.

"Joorlann," she drew out. "Why did you do that?"

"I sensed no magic from the box and yet it spoke." He stared down at the shattered box as if expecting the pieces to somehow reattach themselves and attack. "The device must be mighty indeed to hide such power."

"Voice recording isn't magical."

He made no reply, no body movement to indicate that he'd heard her.

"From now on, if you don't understand something, ask me about it."

Now he gave her a you-silly-little-girl frown. "Taking time to ask questions can give the enemy an opportunity to attack."

"My answering machine is not your enemy!"

"Not anymore," he answered smugly.

"Damn it, Jorlan. You can't just destroy my things. You have to—damn it," she said again. "You made me cuss." Katie reached inside her pocket and handed him two quarters. At his questioning eyebrow lift, she explained her quest to speak more like a lady.

He chuckled. "You owe me more than this." He pinched the change between his fingers and held it up for inspection. "Since the moment you first kissed me, your many expletives have nigh singed my ears."

Do not think about kissing him. Do not think about kissing him. "Anything I said in the garden doesn't count. I was in the middle of a crisis situation."

"Crisis situation or no, I still recall your words to me, just before you wrapped your palm around my—"

"That's enough." He wasn't speaking of curses now; he was speaking about her midnight confession. *Damn it, you've invaded my fantasies,* is what she believed she'd said. "I'm sure you misheard. And for your information, touching your… Well, it was an accident." Before he could add anything else, she said, "Look how late it's gotten." Katie pretended to study her wristwatch, only to realize she wasn't wearing a watch. "Are you ready for bed?" Wrong question.

"I have been ready for some time." His gaze raked over her with enough heat to incinerate her. "I am still ready."

Yes, you are, she thought with a sigh. But this situation called for direct negation, not you-have-a-beautiful-body-and-I-could-lick-you-all-over remembrances.Before she could make a caustic remark, Jorlan spoke again.

"I would like to bathe ere I…sleep." He hesitated over the word "sleep" long enough to make her anticipate "make love to you."

Gulping, Katie led Jorlan to the bathroom and showed him how to work the knobs. "Place a small drop of shampoo into your hand and lather the bubbles through your hair. If you get it into your eyes…" Her voice tapered to a close, for as she spoke Jorlan gripped the hem of his shirt and pulled the material over his head. "Uh, don't get any suds in your eyes or they'll burn so badly you'll want me to pluck them out. And I might just accommodate you."

The shirt whooshed to the floor.

She'd seen his chest before—and a whole lot more—but that didn't seem to matter. Each time she saw his beautifully tanned skin, she had the same reaction. Heat. Fiery heat that erupted into flames. Self-preservation kicked into gear this time and kept her hormones under control.

I have to stop reacting to him like this.

"I would willingly place these suds in my eyes," he said low and honeyed, "if I knew you would kiss away the pain."

"And I will forcefully put suds in your eyes if you don't stop that."

His chuckle swam over her like a caress, soft and wonderfully erotic. "This I might allow did you press your body against me to do it."

She ignored that comment, as well as the fluttering in her stomach. "When you're finished, turn the water off and put your sweats back on. And if you didn't understand that, let me put it another way. Do not leave this bathroom without getting redressed." All the basics covered, she raced to the door.

"You do not have my permission to leave." With the stealth of a trained military man, he moved in front of her, halting her just before escape.

Her back went ramrod-straight. "I don't need your permission for anything."

"You are a woman," he explained.

"You're very observant, aren't you?"

He sighed. "You must wash my back."

"Wash your own back." Katie inched forward another step. Another. And another. Almost there. If he would just move out of the way...

"As it is clear to me that you do not understand, I will explain another way. My muscles are still stiff from my confinement and require the gentle touch of a female."

"I'm not touching your back for any reason because I know you'll consider that part of your rule adjustment. I'll find myself naked and in the tub with you."

His long, spiky lashes swept down in a slow, alluring appraisal. "Would that be so bad?"

"Yes!"

He leaned against the door frame and smiled. "I can promise you that you will enjoy every moment."

"I'm sure you can, but I'm still not interested." She pushed past him and closed the door firmly behind her.

Alone in the hall, she tried not to imagine all that glorious skin covered with glistening soap bubbles.

She failed.

He emerged half an hour later on a cloud of steam. A clean and fresh floral scent enveloped him. Fortunately, he was wearing his pants. Unfortunately, he was not wearing his shirt, and he was, without a doubt, one hundred percent pure Imperian beef. Droplets of water trickled from his hair and down his rippled chest, pooling in his navel. Her mouth went dry, and she wanted so desperately to lick the moisture from his skin.

Lord, when had she become such a sexual creature?

"All of your 'shampoo' was scented for a woman," he accused.

And for seduction, she silently added. "Are you still hungry?" The words emerged as a croak.

He perked up. "You will feed me?"

"Sure. Why not?" They adjourned to the kitchen, and Katie used that time to cool her mounting desire. All the while doing subtle, deep breathing exercises, she gathered the necessary items for a turkey sandwich. She knew how to cook, very nicely, too. But she hadn't actually baked a meal since leaving her father's home at the age of eighteen. A small rebellion, she supposed, for all the years she had slaved over breakfast, lunch and dinner for the men of the house.

"I'm not your personal chef," she told Jorlan, "so pay attention. Next time, you're on your own. Are you watching?" Before he could answer, she began, working as she spoke. "Bread. Mayonnaise. Cheese. Turkey. Lettuce. Tomato. Bread. Got it?"

He nodded, and she handed him the sandwich. He

ate the blasted thing as if he had never tasted anything so delicious in all his life. Definitely not a nibbler. In fact, he somehow made the simple act of chewing a passionate feat. His strong jaw moved quickly. Potent and intense.

Damn it! She needed to find something about him that turned her off. First Date Syndrome was preferable to Obsession Disease.

Jorlan fixed himself three more sandwiches.

"What are the houses in your world like?" she asked, sitting beside him.

He spoke in between bites, his eyes warm with remembrances. "They are much bigger than those offered here. The stones are more colorful, the chambers open and easily accessible. At times, it seems the sky dusts the floor." He drained half a carton of milk, then leaned back in his chair with a satisfied grunt.

"Sounds beautiful."

"'Tis indeed."

"Come on. I'll show you where you'll be sleeping. Alone."

"Your continued rejection humbles me." The wry comment was delivered with an equally wry grin.

"Something needs to," she muttered.

Walking through the hall, a sweet vanilla scent drifted to her nostrils. That was the only thing she liked about the place. The smell. Decorated with a contemporary slant, the interior was too bold, too modern, and lacked character. Instead of wood, the walls were trimmed with silver metal. Instead of carpet or paneling, the floors were covered with mosaic tile. Ceramic animal paws showcased all the light fixtures. She would have preferred a chandelier lit by hundreds of crystal prisms.

Katie knew she'd bought this home for all the wrong reasons. Her dad, who would have a fit if he knew a strange alien male was staying the night with her, believed only men could earn a living as home renovators—or anything else, for that matter. She'd wanted to prove to him that she, a woman, was a success at her business.

To this day, he refused to believe she earned her money on her own and hadn't borrowed from her brothers.

Ryan James had been raised by the "old school" of thought. Men worked and earned money while women baked cookies, raised the kids and devoted their entire lives to pleasing their husbands. (Much like Jorlan's perceptions.) Maybe that was why, sixteen years after becoming a widower, her dad still had yet to remarry. No sane woman would take him. He barked orders like a drill sergeant and expected total compliance from those around him.

As a child, that type of ideology could have easily crushed her spirit. Yet her brothers had sought to protect her from their father's low expectations. They'd made her one of the boys, helped her don jeans and tennis shoes instead of lace and bows. She'd trailed their every step. She'd helped them catch frogs, stood by their sides and fished in a nearby pond, and held her own as they wrestled in the mud.

She and Jorlan reached the guest bedroom. "This is it," she said, flipping the light switch. The room instantly brightened. "The bathroom, or chamber pot, or whatever you call it, is through the side door. It's nothing as grand as what you described, but it's comfortable and private."

Entranced by the origin of light, Jorlan barely registered her words. With the tip of his finger, he lowered the silver switch. Darkness flooded the small area. When he raised the switch, light once again sprang from the overhead source.

"Again I sense no magic, and yet..." Up, down, up, down he continued to move the switch. "I would not have guessed your world capable of such things. First a talking box and now instant lighting."

Katie chuckled, charmed by his bedazzlement with technology. "What does your world use for light?"

"*Lamori* gems."

"Are they magic?"

"Nay, they are alive."

She did not even want to contemplate living stones.

"Even on Imperia, a world of highly developed mystical abilities, no one has yet mastered magical lighting."

"We haven't either. We rely on electricity."

"I am unfamiliar with this word." He flipped the light switch several more times.

How best to explain... "Electricity is a fundamental entity of nature consisting of negative and positive kinds composed respectively of electrons and protons." She spouted Webster's definition with ease. "This is observable in the attraction and repulsion of bodies electrified by friction and in natural phenomena." Wires and power circuits were part of her business, after all, and God knows how many classes she'd taken on the subject.

On and off the light went.

"Does the room meet with your approval?"

"It will suffice. For now." Jorlan released the little switch and surveyed his new chamber. The room offered ample space, but better yet, it provided the most important item in a man's life beside his talon, his *horri* and his food. A bed—a bed Katie did not plan on making use of in the way *Elliea* had intended, he thought dryly, but a bed all the same.

"What do you mean 'for now'?" she demanded.

He hid his amusement behind a bland expression. He had expected such a reply from this woman who continued to refuse all pleasures; he simply had not expected the reply delivered with such force. What a little vixen she continued to be, commanding and impudent.

Puzzling, too.

Since reaching his fourteenth season, women of every age, size and color had flocked to his bed, ready and willing to please him. Almost all had offered him their love, something he had humbly accepted without actually giving any of himself. Nay, he realized, that was a falsehood. He'd given Maylyn everything he had to give, including his heart. He'd been entranced with her dark, mesmerizing beauty, her willingness to please. Only later had he learned that she felt nothing for him in return, that she had merely done his brother's bidding.

Still, Jorlan had always understood what drove Maylyn. Katie, he did not. Why did she grow more and more skittish each time he drew near? Too many possibilities sprang to mind.

A former unpleasant lover?

Misplaced modesty?

A need for commitment?

Which of these applied to Katie? All? None? If he knew, he could figure out how best to approach her. As it was, he was making no progress, and his body's desire for contact, any feminine contact, was growing by the second, growing intense and all-consuming. All of his long repressed needs, needs that had nothing to do with at last breaking the curse, were hammering through him.

The smart thing to do would be to satisfy his body's demands on his own, *then* pursue Katie. Mayhap he should even cease all talk of bed sport and concentrate this night on winning her friendship. He could always drown himself in a bevy of available female bodies once he returned to Imperia, a place where women were accommodating and willing to give of themselves without qualm. Willing to strip him naked and take him into their mouths and bodies while their own pleasure mounted.

His gaze slid down the length of Katie's curves. In the chamber's glorious light, her creamy skin glowed with health and vitality. Her shoulders sloped with captivating elegance, and her hips swelled with tempting allure. Nay, he decided. The way to win her was to pleasure her as he'd originally planned. Besides, he did not want to experience his release alone. He did not want to wait until reaching Imperia to have a woman. Right now, he wanted *this* woman, from *this* world. *This* night. Having all of Katie's warriorlike passion at his disposal would nigh burn him alive, and he longed to burn. Burn, burn, burn.

Mayhap he could convince her to sleep beside him, for no female could resist the silent, seductive presence of a man during twilight. He grinned with anticipation. Just how would Katie respond to an accidental touch, a caress of warm breath, or a whisper of erotic promises?

She must have sensed the direction of his thoughts because she blurted out, "I have another rule!"

His hands tightened into fists. These rules were going to be the death of him. "You cannot add rules at your convenience, woman."

"I can and I will. I'm in charge here."

"*That* is debatable."

"No, it isn't."

She glared up at him.

He glared in return. "I have decided to hear this new rule. You may speak."

Katie absolutely did not like him when he used that I-am-male-therefore-I-decide-the-fate-of-the-world tone. She obeyed anyway and spoke. "Rule number four: no sharing beds."

Surprisingly, he didn't balk. Instead, he crossed his arms over his bronzed chest and said, "My adjustment to this rule is simple. I will not share your bed, but I will slumber in your room. And if this is not agreeable, I will simply knock down your door and share your bed without your permission."

Argh! Far from being frightened by his threat, or even intimidated, Katie was infuriated—and just a bit aroused. "I'm not comfortable sharing a room with you."

"Nevertheless, you will." He arched a dark brow in challenge. "Or are you afraid of your reactions to me?"

Her eyes narrowed to tiny slits, and she stared at him, unflinching. "I'm not afraid of anything."

"Then why not allow me inside your chamber?"

"Because I don't trust you to stay on the floor!"

His shoulders puffed with indignation. "I have given you my word."

"Well, I want a blood oath."

Scowling, he ground out, "I vow to you here and now that I will not join you under the bedcovers this night. That does not mean you cannot join me on the floor."

Why did he have to go and put such an idea into her head? She pointed a finger at his chest. "Do you swear by all that is holy that you won't try anything?"

His nostrils flared, but his tone was quiet. Too quiet. "This I have already answered."

No, he hadn't. Not really. He'd promised only to stay on the floor. An image of his glorious body splayed out on her bedroom carpet filled her mind. Would she feel his heat? Hear the soft whoosh of his breath? Smell the clean scent of his skin?

She had lied to him a moment ago. She *was* afraid of her reactions to him. Very afraid. But despite her fear, she was going to let him stay in her room. Lord, she was. She was going to let him stay in her room.

Keep your friends close and your enemies closer, her brother Erik always said. Jorlan might not be her enemy, but he was damn sure on his way up her hit list. The man wouldn't climb into her bed, but he'd issued a brilliantly orchestrated invitation: *Join me.*

If he thought for one minute she was giving in to that invitation, he'd soon find out that his erection was the last thing on her mind. Well, almost the last. Okay, she couldn't stop thinking about the damn thing. It was *huge*.

I'm an idiot, she thought. "Just in case you get any ideas, know that I'll be sleeping with a can of Mace in one hand and pepper spray in the other."

His expression turned mocking. "Just in case *you* get any ideas, know that I'll be sleeping with a feather in one hand and massage oil in the other."

With those words ringing in her ears, Katie knew she wasn't going to get much sleep. She massaged her temples in a vain effort to ward off the oncoming ache.

I'm in more trouble than I realized.

CHAPTER FIVE

"I'M IMAGINING EVERYTHING I long to do to you, *katya*. Are you imagining what you long to do to me?"

Oh, yes. Yes, she most definitely was imagining.

"In my mind I see my hands cupping your breasts and gently squeezing while my tongue lightly traces a path from one waiting nipple to the other."

As it had for the past hour, Jorlan's husky voice slid like a rasp of silk, low, sleek and honeyed, touching Katie in the darkness, leaving a sultry haven in its wake. Toasty warm, she lay in bed, a thick, downy comforter covering her. But it was the man sprawled on her floor that was responsible for her overheated blood, not her covers.

Katie tried to recall why she was so determined to resist him. She did have reasons, right? She just didn't know anymore, and she wasn't sure how much more she could take before she locked caution inside her panty drawer and caved. Jorlan's passionate assault, which had begun long before he'd ever spoken to her, was quickly eradicating all of her defenses.

"Would you like to feel the heat of my tongue?"

To keep herself from blurting out YES!, she pursed her lips together so tightly she probably incurred permanent wrinkles. Why had she let Jorlan inside her room, anyway? And why for the love of God was she still in bed and not on the floor with him?

"Your back arches, a silent plea for my touch between your legs," he continued mercilessly. "But I do not touch you there with my fingers. Nay, I kiss my way down your stomach and taste you with my mouth, letting my tongue flick left and right, then circle around, creating a hot, wet friction."

"You promised you wouldn't try anything!"

"I never promised I wouldn't speak or imagine. And what I'm imagining right now is so very naughty. You're lying—"

Dropping her can of Mace and pepper spray onto the mattress—which, in actuality, were a can of hairspray and a water bottle—she placed her palms over her ears, muffling his voice. She began snoring like an old man with a foghorn stuck in his throat. All the while she pictured bathroom tile and drying grout—anything to keep her mind from thinking about naked bodies and potent pleasures.

You never give me what I want, her body complained, *and I want Jorlan.*

Shut up, her mind demanded. *You've gotten us in enough trouble!*

Tile. Grout. Tile. Grout. With Jorlan's voice blocked and her mind picturing drying tile grout, slowly, so slowly, her overly sensitized nerves calmed. The tingles of anticipation faded. When she felt enough time had lapsed, she let her snores taper off and removed her hands from her ears.

Blessed silence greeted her.

Then, as if he was acutely attuned to her every action, every feeling, every thought, Jorlan said, "Just say the words, *katya*. Say the words and I will give us both release."

"I'll say the words, all right." Her nails dug deeply into the sides of her legs, leaving half moon crescents. "I'll say shut up or get out. Please! We have to get up early, and it's two in the morning already. After I take you to the psychic, I have to go to work. I *need* to rest."

Five. Ten. Fifteen minutes passed. He didn't speak again. She didn't even hear him breathe.

In the mounting silence, Katie's eyelids began to grow heavy. She gripped her hairspray once again, ready to leap off the bed and whack him over the head with it if he so much as whistled through his nose. After a while, her grip relaxed, and she rolled to her side. The last thought to drift through her mind before she ultimately succumbed to darkness was *That man needs a muzzle, and I need a bare-assed spanking for letting him in here.*

MORNING DAWNED bright and early. "Way too early," Katie muttered. Then she groaned. Her eyes burned, and her head throbbed. She needed a protein shake or she would soon sink into a take-me-to-the-hospital-for-a-caffeine-IV coma.

Normally she jogged five miles a morning. Today, however, she was going to make an exception. At the moment, she couldn't have jogged to the bathroom if her bladder depended on it.

The sheets and blankets were tangled around her like a butterfly's cocoon. She grumbled under her breath as she battled her way free. Something thudded to the floor, but it wasn't a protein shake, so she didn't bend down to retrieve it. Rubbing her eyes, she stumbled into the bathroom.

She washed her face then brushed her teeth and hair. The features that looked at her from the mirror were glazed with…something. Tired. Very tired. Hoping hot, steamy water would help, she climbed into the shower. When she emerged, she tugged on her robe, feeling less groggy, but still craving a sweet fruity shake. Once her veins ran with enough B-12 to energize the retirees at Shady Meadows, she would be alert enough to deal with Jorlan.

Jorlan!

Katie's eyes widened with dismay. How could she have forgotten about the sexy, six-foot-six-inch alien sleeping in her room? Heart pounding, white terry-cloth robe flying, she darted out of the bathroom; her gaze scanned the floor, but she saw only a can of hairspray.

Jorlan was gone.

The only reminder of his presence was the rumpled pillow and blanket tangled together in a hcap at the foot of her bed. She grabbed some clothes from the closet and hastily pulled them on as she raced out of the room. She'd barely managed to zip her jeans when she stepped into the living room. No sign of her alien.

What if the mother ship had beamed him up? Worse, what if he was still here, in her house, going through her things? Katie's stomach knotted as she envisioned laundry strewn across the floor and broken knickknacks scattered about. Through the dining room she went, as if hot coals simmered under her feet.

Then she saw him.

He stood in the kitchen, humming a song she didn't recognize. His back was to her as he rifled through the contents of her fridge. A sigh of relief pushed past her lips when she noticed he was wearing the clothes she'd given him last night. Except now the shirt looked lumpy, and the pants were hanging low on his waist, teasing her, tantalizing her, because a slight brush of air might slip them to the floor….

It was dangerous to become so enflamed at the mere sight of him. Yet she didn't know how to temper her reaction.

Katie cleared her throat.

In one fluid motion, Jorlan whipped around and unsheathed a knife strapped to his ankle, ready to strike. The action so startled her, she could only blink up at him, unable to run, much less breathe. He stood there with the deadly aura of a man who knew exactly how to fight, how to kill and maim, each of his actions as terrifying as the weapon itself. When he realized who she was, he relaxed his stance and returned the blade to its makeshift holder. Even though the knife was now hidden, her heartbeat didn't slow. No one should be able to move that fast or that lethally.

"Good dawning, *katya*." He gave her a half grin that erased the hard lines of her mouth. "Sleep well?"

"No. I didn't." She chewed on her bottom lip, still staring at the sheathed blade. "What are you doing with that knife?"

"I was in need of a weapon."

"Why?"

With a negligent shrug, he turned back to the refrigerator. "'Tis of no concern to you."

"It is when you're wearing *my* weapon."

"If you must know, it is for my protection. If—" he faced her again, this time shooting her a narrowed glance as if everything depended on her "—if I travel to Imperia this day, I must be prepared ere my enemies come upon me."

He'd said before that he was going home after she took him to the psychic, but she hadn't really considered how far away that was until this moment. For a reason she didn't understand, the thought of his leaving Earth suddenly saddened her. She wanted him gone, of course, just not light-years away.

What was his rush to return, anyway? Did he have a family—translation: a wife and children—that were awaiting his presence? Katie almost uttered a string of the foulest words she knew. Here she was, lusting for Jorlan, sad that he was leaving, and he could very well be married.

She wasn't going to ask him, though. They didn't have any type of relationship, and as he liked to point out, it wasn't any of her business.

"Are you married?" Damn it! The question emerged before she could stop it. The man had tried to seduce her, after all.

"Married is life-joined, aye?"

"Aye. I mean yes."

"Then nay." He suddenly looked offended. "I would not have touched you otherwise."

"Oh." *I'm not relieved,* she thought, curls of an emotion she didn't want to name floating through her bloodstream. *I'm simply happy the man has some morals.* "So you're really going all the way home?"

"Only if we find a true mystic and only if—" He stopped and looked away.

"What? Only if I bed you?"

"Nay. Only if you fall in love with me," he answered flatly.

She blinked. "I don't understand."

"'Tis part of the curse. You freed me. Now you must freely and truly offer me your love or I will be returned to stone. Forever, this time."

"You're kidding me, right? Trying to get me into bed again?" She laughed, the sound weak and unsure.

"Do you truly think I would tease you about my freedom?" The absolute conviction in his voice rang loud and clear.

"No," she said softly. "I guess you wouldn't."

"My brother planned for another to kiss me—a woman I despised. He thought 'twould be amusing were I forced to pursue a woman I so loathed. But 'twas you, *you* and not she, who became my savior." Jorlan pushed out a breath. "'Twas not my plan to tell you all of this, *katya.* Yet you are being so stubborn, I felt there was no other way. Can you try, at least, to help me?"

"I don't know how to answer that." The enormity of the situation hit her like the weight of a jackhammer. Jorlan's fate rested with her. Good God. He might as well have asked her to weave her hair into fourteen-karat gold. "I mean, if I told you I loved you, it would be a lie."

"This I know, but I can make you love me." He took a step toward her. "Just give me a chance and I will give your body untold pleasure."

"How would *that* make me fall for you?"

"Bodily pleasure often leads to love for a woman."

For the briefest moment, Katie hesitated. Oh, she didn't doubt his claim, and if anything, that was what scared her the most. "If I said yes and ended up giving you my heart, would you stay here with me? Even for a little while?"

He gave one stiff shake of his head. "Nay."

She uttered a shaky laugh devoid of humor. "You're asking for a lot from me, but giving little in return."

"This I know, as well." While he sounded properly apologetic, he didn't offer a single concession. "I can make the pleasure worth it."

Lord, what was she going to do? She couldn't tell him no; she'd ruin his life. She couldn't tell him yes; she'd ruin *her* life. "You'll have to give me time to think about this."

He frowned. "Time is my enemy."

"Well, it's all I'm offering right now. Take it or leave it."

He drew out a long breath. "I will take it."

They lapsed into an uncomfortable silence.

"You know," she finally said to cover the mounting tension, "you're going to need a little bit of magic to sharpen that knife you stole from me." This line of conversation seemed safe enough. "It's used for cooking, not killing."

"It was not used for killing *before*."

Great. Just freaking great.

"I have commandeered other weapons from your household, as well," he added. As if he were speaking about something as tame as bunny slippers, he nonchalantly turned back to the fridge.

Dread slithered down her spine, chilling and oppressive. The morning had started off badly and was now progressively growing worse. "Want to tell me exactly what else you've commandeered?"

He'd found an old pair of Gray's shoes, she saw as he showed her the pair of scissors strapped to his left ankle, the knife on his right ankle, the metal spatula at his hip and the rolling pin at his back, anchored by the waist of his pants.

"What are you going to do with that?" She motioned to the rolling pin with a wave of her hand.

"Do the talons fail me, I will strike my enemy into submission."

"And the spatula?"

"I am not sure, but surely such a design is intended for severe torture."

Torture was right. "You can't just go around killing and torturing people, no matter what planet you're on." She said the words with enough force to let him know she meant business. "Put everything back right now."

"Nay." A hard glint darkened his eyes, and he shook his head. "In this I will not relent. When entering an unknown situation, a man must be prepared for the worst."

He's right, Katie thought, but she would never make such an admission aloud. Being prepared for the worst was the first lesson in self-defense. Yet none of her classes had mentioned defeating an attacker with a spatula. A pencil, maybe. Even keys.

Really, though, what harm was there in letting him have some of the "weapons"? She never used them, anyway. And if they made him feel safer, well, that was all that mattered. She couldn't fathom being stuck on another world, alone and destitute.

"Why don't we compromise?" she suggested. "You can keep the scissors and the spatula—" and look like an idiot, she silently added "—but the knives and rolling pin stay here."

Silence filled the room as he considered her proposal.

Finally, he nodded. "I accept your compromise. Do you not see how reasonable and willing to negotiate I am?"

"Yeah, you're a regular kiss-ass." His face brightened, and she added, "You're not getting a quarter, nor are you kissing my... Well, you're just not!"

His eyes twinkled with mirth, making the pale blue irises sparkle like diamonds in the night sky. "I will not take you to task for your impertinence—unless, of course, you desire punishment in bed. There is still time ere we visit the sorcerer."

She rolled her eyes, trying to appear cool and unaffected on the outside. On the inside, however, her body was screaming *hip, hip hooray, there's still time.* "Make sure the weapons are hidden when we leave the house, okay?"

"I am not an untrained youth." His mirth was quickly replaced with ire. "I know weapons must remain concealed when not engaged in battle."

O-kay. With every word he'd spoken, his irritation had grown. Right now he looked ready to attack her with the knives for daring to insult his intelligence. Time to change the subject. "Did you find anything good to eat?"

"Nay." His expression lost most of its heat. "You did not show me how to prepare *this*." He held up a Tupperware bowl filled with pasta. A thin layer of mayonnaise and cheese coated the surface.

Ew, she thought. He'd tried to make a sandwich out of it.

"'Tis unseasoned and tasteless and hard and quite the worst morsel I have ever eaten."

Katie noticed several bite marks around the corners of the bowl. Laughter threatened to bubble past her throat, but she swallowed it back. "That's the container, silly. The real food is inside." She pried the bowl from his fingers. The action caused her palm to brush his, sending a jolt of electricity up her arm. Shaky now, she set the plastic aside. "You don't want what's inside that for breakfast, anyway."

"But I am starved, and you have no more supplies." He stroked his fingers over his jaw.

Geez, housing an alien was more expensive than she had envisioned. "I'll take you to this little café about fifteen minutes away. They make the best protein shakes. We can be in and out in less than an hour."

Delight glimmered in his expression a split second before panic settled there. A heartbeat later, he grew pensive. He gave a small shake of his head. "Nay." His tone held no hint of his emotions. "We will go to the sorcerer first. I am eager to meet the one who will take me home. After that, I will concentrate on you. And I will win you, *katya*. Doubt it not." The last was added with an ominous edge, daring her to contradict him.

She gulped. "You may be willing to skip breakfast, but I'm not. The café has a cheese omelet that—"

"Nay. I have decided."

"But—"

"Nay, *katya*."

"Fine." Grumbling under her breath, she grabbed the phone book from the shelf under the microwave. "We have time to visit *one* psychic. *One*. If this *one* doesn't work, you're out of luck for today. I'm hungry and have work to do, and I only promised to take you to *one* place." She just prayed he understood how many one equaled.

"If you wish to convince me to dine first, such antics are not necessary. I have decided I will allow you to convince me…in bed."

Always he returned to this subject. "You know, there's a chance you could give me a million orgasms and I still wouldn't fall in love with you. For your own sake, you might want to rethink your strategy." Ha! Take that, she thought, flipping through the yellow pages.

"The only way to know for sure is to let me give you one million orgasms."

Without glancing up, she answered, "No."

How had he ever been foolish enough to think of a challenge as fun? Jorlan wondered. The woman was driving him insane with her denials. *Do not touch me. Do not please me. Do not make me quiver with delight.*

If only he wanted her simply because of the curse, mayhap hearing her say "no" wouldn't bother him so much. But nay, each time he saw her, spoke with her, thought of her, Katie raised emotions inside of him he'd rather not encounter. She was slowly but surely worming her way under his skin, and he did not like it. *She* was supposed to fall for him, not the other way around. He knew only too well that romantic sensibilities were dangerous.

He could not fathom how she was getting to him so quickly and so expertly. Did she wield some sort of magic he could not sense? Mayhap. Aye, mayhap. 'Twould explain many of his feelings for her. Curse it, he'd thought his defenses were in place, both magically and emotionally. Yet here he stood, wanting her, needing her, as he'd never wanted another. Well, he had to do something to prevent further softening on his part. But how was he to fight against her and win her at the same time?

"Here's one," Katie said, her honey-rich voice cutting into his thoughts. "The House of Mysticism. A place where deepest desires are realized." She paused. "Sounds like a hoax to me, but you're the expert. It's only five miles away, and the ad says—" Katie's voice became mocking here "—the owner possessed the ancient power of the Druids."

Druids? Jorlan's back straightened, and he shot to attention. Though he could not read Katie's language, he snatched the thick yellow tome from her hand and searched the pages. Druid. Druid. Druid. The name pounded in his head, an echo of his salvation. Surely this was no coincidence. His mother's people were known as the Druinn. Mayhap they were one and the same.

"Well, what do you think?" Katie asked, gazing up

at him through the thick shield of her lashes. "Does it sound like the kind of place you're looking for?"

He nodded. "'Tis exactly the kind of place I am looking for. Let us waste no more time. We leave immediately."

KATIE DECIDED TO ACCEPT that the day was only going to get worse when she found herself standing in front of an old, crumbly building with a neon sign that winked I KNEW YOU WERE COMING in bright pink letters.

Sunlight glinted harshly upon the fading yellow, blue and gold paint decorating the splintered wood. Several shingles were missing from the roof, and some, she noticed, were strewn across the front lawn and embedded in the weeds. She cringed at such an atrocity and fought the urge to offer her services, free of charge, simply to rid the world of such a visual blemish.

"Are you sure this is the kind of place you want to deal with?" she asked Jorlan for the third time.

His gaze scanned the perimeter, taking in every detail. "Is this the home of the Druid psychic?" It was the same thing he'd said each time before.

"Yes."

"Then this is exactly the kind of place I want to deal with."

Katie remained unconvinced. "Instead of relying on someone else, why don't you just click your heels together or something and send yourself home?"

A muscle ticked in his jaw, and seconds dragged by in silence.

"Well?"

Nothing.

I don't need this aggravation, she thought darkly. Every time she asked him a personal question, he turned mutinous, as if she had no right to know anything about him. He'd take her heart, sure. But share the tiniest bit of information about himself? Hell, no.

"Come on," she snapped, angry with him—and with herself. "Let's get this over with." The man was too secretive, too stubborn, and she was better off without him. If this psychic had the power to help him, Katie decided then and there to lie and say she loved him just to get him out of her life.

Holding her head high, she marched to the front door. She reached out, clasped the knob, then stopped, waiting. Jorlan never approached her side. Frown deepening, she spun around. Her alien stood in the exact same place she'd left him, his chin angled to the side, his legs braced apart.

"I sense no magic here," he said. His own frown deepened. He closed his eyes and drew in a breath.

"You didn't sense magic in my answering machine, either, and look where that got you."

"'Twas different."

She wanted to ask how it was different but knew she'd get no answer. "Do you want to leave?"

"Nay." He still did not join her on the porch.

Was he simply nervous? Anticipating success? Failure? Or was he right? There truly was no magic here. She believed the latter and decided to point out the obvious. "If there's no magic here, they won't be able to help you."

"The most powerful of the Druinn are able to disguise and hide their power." He didn't seem convinced that that was the case here, however. In fact, every emotion except assurance played over his features: doubt, hope, determination.

In that moment, her demeanor softened toward him. He wanted to go home; she couldn't blame him for that. Were the situation reversed, she would desire the same thing, and would do anything, use anyone, to gain what she wanted, and she probably wouldn't share her personal information with aliens, either. At least he was honest about his intentions.

"Let's go inside and give it a try," she said softly.

"I need but a moment more."

"All right. Take as long as you need."

Jorlan jerked a hand down his face. Though everything inside him screamed to leave this place, he couldn't walk away. If there was a chance, even a minute chance of discovering what he needed, he had to go inside.

When he tried to move his legs, however, they refused to obey. He scowled. What was keeping him locked where he stood? Doubt? Mayhap. Yet he knew that was not the whole of it. As questions swirled through his mind, a foreign emotion uncoiled inside him, an emotion he couldn't identify—or mayhap did not want to identify.

How much time had passed on Imperia? If, like here, a thousand years had passed, how many of his friends had possessed enough magic to survive the ages? How many had suffered in death? How many still lived? How would his family receive him? Would he be welcomed with open arms or looked upon as a stranger? Jorlan dragged in a harsh breath. The sweet, gentle scent of the air was almost foul in his nostrils.

"I'll be with you the entire time." Katie's voice wrapped around his body like a soft, comforting cloak.

His gaze sought hers and he watched a gentle smile play across her mouth, that mouthwatering smile that lit her entire face. A man could get lost in the sensual web she wove and forget all about his troubles. Forget his impatience to leave.

Jorlan shifted from one foot to the other and forced himself to glance away. The woman was in desperate need of a keeper, he was coming to realize, and 'twas a job that appealed to him more each second he spent with her.

Mayhap when he left, he would take her with him; he would instruct her in the proper ways to interact with a man, all the while winning her affections as the spell stipulated. He could make love with her—many, many times—with the mystique of Imperia surrounding them. Better still, Katie could serve as a seductive distraction did he have no family left.

As quickly as the idea formed in his mind, Jorlan discarded it. He would get what he needed from her, and then he would leave her here. He did not have room in his life for a woman from another world, especially one that made him feel things he was better off not feeling.

"When we finally come together, *katya,* many worlds will shake."

"Yes, well…" Katie paused. Not knowing what else to say—which only happened in Jorlan's presence— she pivoted to face the door. The knob turned easily, and she stepped inside, sinking into plush burgundy carpet. Jorlan was close behind her this time. The fine hairs on the back of her neck stood at attention, as if reaching for him, desiring his touch.

Why did she have to respond so easily to *this* man?

As the door closed with a *thwack,* a bell jingled to announce their presence. They stood in silence, waiting, yet no one greeted them. There were no employees in the small room. No customers.

Curls of smoke rose from jasmine-scented incense, floating up then dipping down and expanding throughout the cluttered space. Dim lighting and glittery walls gave a mystical ambiance, compounded by the soft, lyrical music that played in the background.

Finally, a dark-haired woman who looked to be in her midfifties stepped beyond the decorative fringe. With her large hazel eyes and prominent cheekbones, her features were attractive, if somewhat dulled by time. She wore black slacks and a tailored white blouse completely at odds with her new-age business. Gazing at her, only two words entered Katie's mind: professional and legitimate.

Suspicion instantly grew in Katie's mind.

Jorlan knows best about magic, she reminded herself. He said there was a chance this psychic had the power he needed, and she had to allow him time to discover the truth, be it good or bad.

"Hello," the woman said. "Welcome to my humble establishment." She had the cultured accent of an English gentlewoman. "How may I help you?"

Jorlan dispensed with pleasantries. "Do you possess the power to open a vortex?"

The woman folded her hands together and drummed her perfectly manicured nails against each other. "Exactly what type of power do you mean?"

Quickly Katie placed a hand over Jorlan's mouth. "Why don't *you* tell us the answer to that question." Surely a self-professed "seer" could answer so simple a question.

Jorlan pried her hand from his mouth, but didn't release his grip. He kept her palm captured in the warmth of his own. "Do not silence me again, *katya*," he growled softly, the words meant only for her, "unless you use your tongue."

"Ah, young love," the woman sighed.

Fat lot you know, Katie almost blurted, her doubts increasing all the more.

The older woman gave her a faint smile, deepening the crinkles at the corners of her eyes. "You do not believe in the supernatural, do you, dear?"

"I believe in facts," Katie replied, trying to ignore the *rightness* of holding hands with Jorlan. There was just something so gratifying about having her hand linked with his, a subtle reassurance and a tangible action of affection. Even though he felt nothing for her— nothing substantial, anyway—the action made her feel needed.

"I believe in facts, as well," the woman answered.

"Then you'll understand why I demand proof of your abilities," she said. Her alien knew nothing about Earth, knew nothing about scams people often attempted on unsuspecting individuals. If this woman truly was the sorceress he sought, she was going to have to prove it.

"Of course I understand. Sit, sit." With a delicate wave of her hand, the Englishwoman motioned to a small table at the back of the room. "Would you like something to drink? Coffee? Tea? I even have a wonderful herbal elixir that promotes brain activity."

"No, thanks," Katie answered, shaking her head. While the herbal elixir piqued her interest, she wasn't going to relax her guard. "We're fine."

Jorlan tugged her to the table. After she scooted to the middle, he squeezed the long length of his legs underneath the too-short surface. The woman took the seat just in front of them. "Give me your palm," she immediately told Jorlan.

His lips thinned, and he sliced his gaze to Katie. "Do all the women here command a warrior thus?"

"You better believe it. Now give her your hand."

Storm clouds of fury filled Jorlan's eyes, but he did as instructed.

The woman hunched over his palm, tracing each line with a long, oval-tipped nail. "You wish to find a way home. Am I correct?"

"Aye."

"You cannot do it alone." A statement, not a question.

That muscle in his jaw was ticking again.

"All that is needed is someone to guide you," the woman said. "Do I speak the truth?"

"Aye."

The hard tone of his voice, like a hammer hitting a brick wall, caused Katie's toes to curl, and she was immensely glad his attention was not directed at her. Intent, she watched and listened as the interaction between Jorlan and the woman continued. Every time the Englishwoman spoke, Jorlan shifted uncomfortably in his chair. He appeared both furious and sad, as if he had just accepted this wasn't going to work, but was holding on anyway just in case a miracle happened.

"Someone can help you," the woman was saying. "Someone *will* help you. Someone whose name is... I'm getting an impression of the letter *K*. Yes, yes. Someone whose name begins with the letter *K* will guide you home. Do you know someone whose name begins with *K*?"

"Aye." He didn't look happy about it either.

"Good, good." She continued to study his hand. "I predict much—"

"I do not need your predictions, woman." Suddenly, his fury overcame his sadness and hope. "I need to know if you can open a vortex so that I might leave your world and enter mine. Can you do this or not?"

"You have the power within yourself to go wherever you wish."

Jorlan's eyes narrowed to tiny slits. "I do not have the power within myself. This I know for fact."

"You *do*. You have a power that, if properly nourished, can grow to a powerful force."

Hope grew in his eyes again. "How do I nourish my power?"

"I have developed a potion that binds with the magic inside of you, causing your flesh to weaken and your inner spirit to flourish. After you drink this powerful elixir, I will chant a spell of strength and courage over you."

Katie had heard enough. There was no way in hell Jorlan was drinking anything this woman had prepared. "What you're looking for isn't here, Jorlan," she said.

His only answer was a slight, almost undetectable nod.

"Now wait a secon—" the woman began.

"For God's sake," Katie shouted, cutting her off. "This is a bunch of crap and you know it. Most of what you said is so ambiguous I'm not sure whether you're talking about a tour through Disneyland or if you were singing the alphabet." She smacked her hand upon the hard wood of the table. "You can't help him any more than a Keebler Elf could. Admit it."

The woman's lips thinned. "Everything I said is true," she ground out. "Only the heart can guide a man home. That, and one of my potions."

"But you just said someone whose name began with *K* could help him," Katie pointed out.

Weathered cheeks bloomed with color, from embarrassment or anger, Katie didn't know. "I meant—"

"I know what you meant." Katie didn't mean to sound so harsh, but damn it, she hated that Jorlan was so upset. "He called me *katya*, therefore you get an impression of the letter *K*. And the thing you've—" She stopped herself, debating whether to confess Jorlan's true origins. Her gaze gravitated to him. He looked so lost, and wanted to go home so badly, she decided that confessing his alien status was worth the risk of sounding like a nutcase. "The thing you have failed to divine is that we're not talking about an emotional home here; we're talking about *another planet*."

"So you're aliens, are you?" the woman asked without missing a beat, as if she'd heard that claim a million times before. "I knew it the moment you stepped inside." She pulled a small, dark bottle from her pocket. "Drink this and you will—"

Argh! Katie jolted up, fist clutched tightly. "You can take your potions and stuff them up your as—"

"That is enough." Jorlan's voice echoed off the walls.

Everything instantly quieted.

"'Tis time to leave, *katya*." He didn't wait for her reply. He simply pushed to his feet and strode quietly from the building.

CHAPTER SIX

EVERY MAN POSSESSED one fear, a fear that consumed him, could drive him to the brink of madness. Jorlan had just discovered his. Being trapped on this forsaken world for all eternity frightened him to the marrow of his bones. He'd known the possibility existed since the beginning of his curse. Yet now the realization weighed him down, more potent than ever before because he was finally free.

Free, but yet, not free.

He couldn't go home until he won Katie's love; that he accepted. He had only thirteen more days to win her; that he accepted, as well. But what he could not accept, did not want to accept, was the fact that no true sorcerer might dwell here, that there might be no means to return home when the time came.

He stood outside the false mystic's dwelling, his legs braced apart, his arms locked behind his back and his muscles clenched. It was a warrior's stance, one normally used just before battle as plans and strategies were formed.

This seemed the greatest battle of his life.

His first instinct had been correct. No magic resided in the House of Mysticism. He had known it before stepping inside, and he'd known it after. Yet he had foolishly clung to hope. Now he was forced to face the truth.

What manner of mystic studied a man's hand to open a vortex? One without any true magic or ability, he answered darkly. The irony was that the fraud inside that shabby building had actually spoken some truth. He *should* possess enough power to take himself home. Magic dwelled inside him, so much magic—but 'twas a force he could not control, therefore, 'twas a force he could not reply upon. Curse it! A simple spell was all that was needed. A simple spell, yet hopelessly beyond his grasp.

He tried again, anyway. He closed his eyes, raised his arms high in the air, and uttered the needed words. As he spoke, the air around him swirled, swirled around and around, faster and faster, and then…stopped. He tried again. Nothing. Again. Nothing.

Each of his failures—with Katie, the psychic and his own powers—weighed heavily upon his shoulders. His arms dropped to his sides. Why did the magic and spells that came so easily to his mother's people prove so difficult and oftentimes disastrous for him? Why? Did he possess too much *physical* strength, mayhap? Did his supernatural ability to hunt and destroy his enemies somehow weaken his magical ability? If so, he would gladly relinquish the gift, for what good did it do him when he could not even initiate battle with his *greatest* enemy?

Jorlan's teeth ground together, and his breath scalded his throat. Pride demanded he at last avenge his loss of time, companionship and pleasure. Pride demanded…and yet still he could do nothing.

He uttered a dark, humorless laugh. The curse welcomed his frustration like an angry storm cloud welcomed a raving wind, both ever ready to unleash a torrent of sorrow and pain. Fists clenched, he fought for some measure of inner peace. One minute stretched to another, yet his struggle proved fruitless. He needed an outlet, something, *anything* to soothe the razor-sharp edges of his emotions.

A soft, gentle hand touched his shoulder. "Are you okay?" an even gentler voice asked. "I know that didn't go the way you planned, and I'm sorry I brought you here, but we'll find someone else. There were tons of names in the phone book, and I promise we'll visit another psychic in the morning. I would take you now, but I'm afraid another failure would…" Katie's words drifted to quiet. "I just think it would be better to wait until morning."

He gazed down at her beautifully tapered fingers, at her pale skin against his own deeply tanned. For one raw moment, that touch made him feel as if he'd harbored his hate and resentment too long, as if he had nothing to fear. Yet he still craved an outlet, and she had just provided him with one. He drank in her loveliness, letting it soothe his inner wounds like a caress. "I warned you of the consequences did you touch me, *katya*," he said, his tone deceptively soft.

She snatched her hand to her side. "Wh-what do you mean?"

"Touch me first, and I have the right to touch you in return. *That* you agreed upon."

"You looked so upset—I didn't mean—that was not an invitation!"

"Wasn't it?" He spun to face her, took her forearms in his hands and hauled her to him. Chest to chest. Hardness to softness.

"Let go of me," she told him heatedly, but she made no move to pull away. Nay, she sank more snugly into him. "Let me go," she said again, this time with breathless surrender.

He didn't want to let her go; he wanted to hold her so tightly against him she could only part her lips and cry out his name. She must have sensed his needs, for her gaze collided with his, amber eyes locked with blue. Neither glanced away.

"You will thank me for my refusal in just a moment." He didn't give her time to deny him. His fingers journeyed upward and tangled in her hair; he tugged her closer until not a breath of air separated them. Then he ravaged her there in the morning sunlight where anyone could see them, where anyone could hear them. Over and over he pushed his tongue past Katie's teeth, stroked inside, took. Demanded.

For a moment, he thought she meant to resist, but Katie surprised him by uttering a low and needy moan. She opened for him completely, then moaned again. The sound washed over his body, fueling his need. Her ragged breath fanned his nose and his cheek as their tongues danced and sparred. The carnal fragrance of her filled his head, and he thought to hold her in his arms for all the days of his life.

Last eve he had wondered at her taste, and now he knew she tasted sweet and female, part soothing balm, part kindling. Would she taste the same between her legs? Just the thought of laving her there caused the fire inside him to rage—a fire that had nothing to do with his pain, his sorrow or his duty. Nay, he burned only for Katie, for her passion. Burned to take her breasts in his hands. Burned to suck her nipples into his mouth.

"This is what I wanted last eve," he whispered hotly. "This is what I craved while I lay upon your floor, tightening my hand upon my cock, all the while imagining your touch instead."

She whimpered.

He placed his hands upon her buttocks and lifted. She wrapped her legs around his waist, pressing her woman's place against his erection. Up. Down. Up, he urged her, mimicking the motions of sex. She willingly arched back and forth. He ached to shove her *drocs* down and push deep inside her. He ached to feel her inner walls clench as she searched for release. He ached so fiercely, in fact, he decided not to wait, to take her now, inside the enchanted transportation. Aye, he had to feel her body surge with pleasure, had to watch her face light, watch her lips part. Give her one peak after the other.

Her tongue moved against his in sync with the motions of their bodies. He was shaking, oh, how he was shaking. His control was tethered on the brink of elimination. He'd never experienced anything quite like this, never experienced anything quite so intense. Jorlan told himself it didn't matter that she affected him so strongly, but he was not foolish. Something was happening between them, growing. Something he needed to deny, but could not.

"I don't think I'm ready for this," she muttered into his lips. "But you feel so good it's hard to think clearly."

"If you must think," he said, maneuvering them both to the vehicle, and tugging at her shirt all the while, "then think of how much pleasure I can give you."

"I have," she whispered. "I really have. I tried not to, but last night…"

"I've imagined, too. In my mind I pictured your nipples pink as little berries. Pictured the soft, pale curls that guard your essence." As he spoke, he played with the areas in question.

"Jorlan, I—" Katie paused. Closed her eyes. Opened them.

In an instant of time, a mere heartbeat, the passionate haze evaporated from her features, leaving an expression that read: *I'd rather burn in the fires of Hel la Fir than continue.*

"No," she said, pushing away. Her breath was ragged and unsteady. "No. We have to stop."

Sweat beaded on his brow. "Is that truly what you want?" He knew it wasn't and reached for her. One more kiss, one more touch, and he could send them both through the corridors of paradise.

With a squeal, she swatted his hands away. "Stop. We have to stop." There was still a breathless, husky quality to her tone. "We're outside in full view of the world, for God's sake."

He flashed his teeth in a scowl. "Did I not please you?" he demanded. "Did I not make your body hunger for more?"

Instead of answering his question, she said, "I'm sorry, but I'm not ready for this."

"Give me two minutes, and I will make you ready."

He let his voice drop to a seductive whisper, a feat that required his full concentration. "Let me, *katya*. Let me have you, and I swear to *Elliea* you will enjoy every moment of it." He'd never begged for anything in his life, but he was perilously close to dropping to his knees and pleading with her to accept him.

"I know I'll enjoy every moment," she breathed. "Believe me, I do."

He thought he had her then; he even reached out and wrapped his palms around her waist, but she shook her head, darted away, and said gently, "No." Then with more force, "No. Not here. And not now."

He cursed under his breath. "Why do you fight so hard against what you feel?"

She glanced away. "I don't think you truly want to hear my answer."

"You will tell me anyway."

"You want to know. Fine." Anger sparked in her eyes, and she faced him again. "I'm not sure I even like you. You're bossy and arrogant, and you refuse to answer the simplest questions about yourself unless I nag you."

"Whatever you wish to know about me, I will gladly tell you. After."

"No! Yesterday I was a necessary burden to you, and now I'm supposed to melt at your feet because you're a great kisser? No!"

Jorlan shoved a hand through his hair. Women had their place. And this one belonged directly under him. Katie might deny her attraction to him, but he would spend every one of the next thirteen days overcoming such false resistance. And false it was, he had no doubt.

The woman came alive in his arms, like a molten river erupting from a mountain.

But by the holy laws, such a contrary female annoyed him. Why couldn't she be like the complacent, unassuming women he was used to? A woman who rarely strayed from what she was told? Jorlan knew how to deal with that type of female. But this one...

"You want me, *katya*. Think you I cannot smell your desire?"

Her jaw dropped. Closed with a snap. "What you're smelling is last night's turkey sandwich," she growled. Then her face flushed with embarrassment, as if she couldn't quite believe what she'd just said.

"If you use your tongue as expertly in bed as you do to turn me away, a man would die quite happily in your arms." With barely a breath, he added crossly, "You do realize, do you not, that your stubbornness punishes us both?"

The golden amber of her eyes hardened with anger. "I could very easily toss you on your ass. Again! How's that for punishment?"

"You are most welcome to try and fight me." He almost wished she would, so that he could allow her to win. The thought of her standing over him, chest heaving... He sliced that image to a close, knowing it would do him no good now.

"Look," she said, rubbing her temples. "I haven't had my protein shake this morning, so I'm in a bad mood. Let's just forget this ever happened and go eat breakfast. Like I said, we'll find you another psychic tomorrow."

Forget? Long would the image of her passion-glazed features remain in his mind. Long would the sweet taste of her linger in his mouth. Forgetting their kiss wasn't an option for him, and it infuriated him that the little witch thought she could so easily push him from her thoughts. He almost ripped the clothes from her body then and there so that he could brand his touch upon her as she had done him—an eternal brand that would haunt her long after he'd left her.

"Nay," he finally said. "We will search for another sorcerer now."

"If you give me another day, I can do some research and hopefully we'll bypass all the frauds."

He watched her through lowered lids for a long while. "Very well. I will go with you to find nourishment, but do not think for one moment that I am finished with you. Next time, I will not release you until we are both weak with pleasure."

UNTIL I'M ALONE, I will not think about our kiss. I will not think about our kiss.

Katie made her way through the restaurant, muttering those words under her breath with every step. Crackling voices and the tantalizing aroma of fresh, gourmet coffee wafted around her. Lights were dimmed for effect and the walls were painted a rich toffee brown.

She'd discovered the place the day she closed on the Victorian. She'd come here every morning since. The food was decent, the protein shakes divine and the employees entertaining.

She adored the place.

Frances, a middle-aged waitress who liked to bash

the male species with anyone who would listen, was Katie's favorite.

"Hey, doll," Frances called when she noticed her. "I'll be right with you."

Katie slid into the only available booth. The shiny purple vinyl squeaked with the movement. Jorlan folded his long legs beside her, and scooted until their sides were touching. His weapon—aka: the spatula—had to be digging into his skin, but he was too entranced with the goings-on around him to notice the discomfort.

A family of four sat to their right, arguing over the need for chocolate this early in the morning. Katie agreed with the kids; there was never a bad time for chocolate. A silver-headed man was just in front of her, trying to eat his eggs and read his paper at the same time. It wasn't working. To her left was a young woman who was a regular patron of the place. The girl was in her early twenties, had rumpled red hair, two dimples in her cheeks and breasts the size of watermelons. Katie's own sun-ripe tomatoes paled in comparison, and she resisted the urge to slump her shoulders.

Today the girl wore a pair of baggy jeans and a plain, oversized T-shirt. Every couple of seconds, she shivered as if a block of ice surrounded her. Delicate and pretty, she should have radiated happiness. She didn't. The lines of fatigue and sadness around her eyes and mouth made her appear ancient.

As if sensing her scrutiny, she sparked a glance in Katie's direction. Their gazes collided. Dark-brown eyes narrowed a split second before the girl looked away. Then that chocolate gaze swung back to Katie, this time with purpose, and moved pointedly on to Jorlan. Something exotic and knowing flashed in the girl's eyes, making her appear fresher and utterly beautiful. A foreign emotion swam through Katie as she turned in time to see Jorlan return the silent greeting.

Katie fisted her hands and stayed the urge to launch over the table, a catapult of kicking legs and swinging arms. Deep breath in; deep breath out. *This isn't jealousy,* she assured herself. Jorlan was her responsibility, and she had to look out for his best interests.

"Do you know her?" Jorlan asked, indicating the brown-eyed girl.

"No. Why do you ask?" Katie's hands flexed more tightly. A muscle cramp, nothing more.

Jorlan scratched a hand over the dark stubble covering his jaw. "She seems unhappy. Lost, even. I was thinking that mayhap she is in need of a good pummeling." He paused, then glanced back at Katie. "What think you of that?"

Katie stiffened as though her entire body had turned to stone. "You can get those thoughts out of your head," she snapped. "For all you know that girl charges a fee to get naked and pummeled." Which Katie highly doubted, but still!

Intrigued, Jorlan looked from the girl to Katie, from Katie to the girl, and then back to Katie. "How much do you think she charges?" he asked, continuing to stroke his chin as if he were picturing the scenario and liking it.

"How much doesn't matter, you pervert. You have

no money, and I'm not giving you any. Besides, I said she *might* be a hooker, not that she actually is."

Instead of sputtering with indignity as she'd hoped, he chuckled. "You sound jealous, *katya.*"

"Jealous?" She snorted, doing her best impression of a carefree woman with hundreds of lovers. "I'm not jealous. Jealousy is for those who actually care romantically about the other person. What I feel for you is similar to what I feel for my brothers."

Jorlan's quirky, confident smile faded. His features grew hard and cold, like ice freezing the ocean. "I am not, nor will I ever be, your sibling. And if you think otherwise, 'tis time we finished what we started this morn. You *do* care for me romantically, and I can prove it in front of all these people. You usually require proof, do you not, *katya?*"

Those words were all too true. True enough to make her shiver with a mixture of fear and anticipation. Yet his confidence in her capitulation annoyed her. He acted as if he had only to touch her and she would sink into him. Well, she might have allowed him a few liberties during *that moment that she wasn't thinking about until she was alone,* but that wouldn't happen again anytime soon.

"You want your usual, doll?" a gruff female voice asked, preventing Katie from tossing Jorlan a stinging retort. She settled for giving him a this-isn't-finished glare then turned her attention to the waitress. "Yes, thank you. I'll have my usual."

Frances set two glasses of water on the table with a clang. Her black slacks and tailored white blouse hugged her generous curves. Her sherry-colored hair, which had probably come from a bottle, was twisted in a bun atop her head. "What about the big guy? He want a protein shake and an omelet, too?"

"The big guy can speak for himself," Jorlan growled.

Far from being intimidated, Frances rolled her eyes and gave Katie a get-rid-of-this-one look. "So what'll it be? I'm just dying to hear what you want." Her droll tone stamped over Jorlan's stiff shoulders.

Frowning, he raised the menu and studied the words. A minute passed, then another. Impatient, Francis tapped her shoe. (She wasn't a favorite with the male patrons. But her boss was female, which was the only reason she still had a job.) "Sometime today, big guy."

With a kingly, I-am-too-good-for-this air, he dropped the menu onto the table. "I have decided Katie will choose for me."

Katie almost laughed. She did sigh. The man didn't know how to read her language, but he refused to admit such a weakness aloud. Such an action almost made him seem—dare she think it?—vulnerable.

"Let's see…" She grabbed up the menu. Besides Tupperware and turkey sandwiches, what did extra large aliens eat for breakfast? "He'll have the mushroom omelet with peppers and ham. Two bagels with strawberry cream cheese, an English muffin and three blueberry tarts."

Frances looked up from her notepad, wearing an incredulous expression. "Anything else?"

"Yes. A pecan waffle."

Though neither woman spared him a glance, Jorlan said, "Two pecan waffles."

"You're gonna have to roll him out of here. You know that, don't you?" Just then, a devilish light entered Frances's hazel eyes. She smiled, crinkling the wrinkles around her eyes, and clasped the menu in one hand. "I got a new one for you, doll. Heard it just this morning."

Katie opened her mouth to tell Francis she'd listen to the joke some other time—Lord knew how a chauvinist like Jorlan would react to man bashing—but Frances continued before she could stop her.

"A young couple was in their honeymoon suite the night of their wedding. As they undressed for bed, the husband, who was a big, burly man—" this was said with a pointed glance to Jorlan "—tossed his pants to his bride, and said, 'Here, put these on.' Though the wife was confused by his request, she put them on. The waist was twice the size of her body. 'I can't wear your pants,' she told her husband, 'they're too big.' 'That's right,' the husband said, 'and don't you forget it. I'm the man who wears the pants in this family!'"

Frances took a deep breath and continued. "The wife whipped off her panties and flipped them to her husband. 'Try these on,' she said. Knowing he needed to pacify her if he hoped to get lucky, the husband did as she demanded. He tried the panties on and found that he could only get the lacy material up as far as his kneecap. He said, 'Hell, I can't get into your panties.' And the wife said, 'That's right, and that's the way it's gonna be until you change your damn attitude.'"

Katie choked on her water.

Jorlan frowned.

When her air passage cleared, Katie smiled up at Frances. "I'll have to tell that one to my brothers."

"I thought you'd like it."

"If you ever need a break from the café," Katie said, still grinning, "come talk to me. I'm restoring the old house on Gossamer Lane and could use the help. And the entertainment."

"Really? Seriously?"

"Absolutely." Katie usually hired outside help for renovation and restoration when she purchased a new house. For some reason, she'd been reluctant to hire anyone for the Victorian, wanting instead to do the work herself. But the sheer elation in Frances's eyes convinced her to stick with her usual method. "You could start anytime."

"I might take you up on that." Frances beamed. Then, with another meaningful glance to Jorlan, she sauntered away, leaving behind the echo of her happy whistle.

Jorlan's features darkened with ire. "That woman needs a keeper."

"You think every woman needs a keeper," Katie replied dryly. Her gaze flicked to him, observant and narrowed. "Did you ever consider the possibility that your men-are-superior views are stupid?"

"Nay." He answered with absolutely no hesitation.

"Figures." She had anticipated such an answer, yet had hoped he would surprise her. "Look, some men are not honorable and often mentally and physically abuse a woman in an attempt to break her will. Is that the kind of keeper you would have for Frances?" Caught up in her speech, Katie leaned into him, even pointed a finger in his chest. "Just because a woman has spirit, does not mean she needs a man to guide her."

"Aye, it does." Jorlan, too, leaned forward. Their noses touched, sending a jolt of awareness through her system. He grabbed her finger and held the appendage captive in the warmth of his hand. "If a woman pushes a man beyond his control, she risks physical injury."

"And a guardian would keep her safe?"

"Aye."

Katie let out her breath sharply. "Even from himself?"

"Aye. Even from himself." The blue of his eyes clouded with silver and gray. "A warrior trained in the art of battle will save a woman from the very danger she herself creates."

The noise of the café faded from her ears as she concentrated on the man before her. "But, Jorlan, with your logic, a woman wouldn't need a keeper if a warrior simply controlled himself."

Jorlan paused, considering her words. When their meal was delivered, Katie's voice still echoed in his mind. *A woman wouldn't need a keeper if a warrior simply controlled himself.* There was truth to what she'd said, though such ideology contradicted the entire Imperian way of life, a way of life that suggested men were men and women were weak.

He had much to think on.

A wondrous aroma drifted into his nostrils. Frances, the aging servant, tossed numerous plates in his direction. Several pieces of food flopped to the table. His stomach rumbled. Ravenous, he made short work of every bite, nibble and crumb, relishing the taste, texture and color. The light-brown squares filled with dark-blue spheres were his favorite. Katie, he noticed, ate only a plain omelet and drank a mug of light green, clumpy liquid. With each gulp, she closed her eyes and uttered a wordless exclamation of ecstasy. He considered dousing his body in the murky-looking concoction.

"Now that one need is satisfied, I need only a nice, leisurely pummeling to feel complete," he said. "Mayhap the girl would be interested."

Katie scowled.

He almost laughed. 'Twas the action of a possessive woman, and one that filled him with hope. Soon…oh, aye, soon Katie's love would belong to him.

"Keep in mind," Katie bit out, "that you have no money. Women do not sleep with poor men."

"Then I shall acquire riches."

"As if it's that easy! First of all, no one but me will hire you. Second, any money you make belongs to me to reimburse me for your food and shelter. I'm not a woman who will support a man while he does nothing except watch TV, lay on the couch and drink beer."

"So you wish to hire me?"

"Yes," she said after a moment's hesitation.

"Do you, by chance, wish me to labor in the bedchamber?"

She threw her hands into the air. "No! The work I'm offering you has nothing to do with being naked, getting naked, or getting each other naked."

Her dictate left many wonderful possibilities, for at times, clothing offered just as much, if not more, stimulation than flesh. Aye, he could very well imagine her with a long, shimmery blue gown draped over her curves, covering every inch of her. Slowly he would raise the gown's hem. Higher. Higher still. Not ever making her naked, but slowly revealing the succulent skin of her calves, her thighs, and then her—

"You can get that perverted gleam out of your eyes," she ground out, slapping her hand onto the table with a thump. Glasses clanged together. "You'll paint, put up siding, lay tile, shingle or whatever I happen to need done. To the house," she added, "not to me. And I don't want to hear any complaints."

Complain? About physical labor? When his body already hummed with excitement, vibrated with too much energy? "Exercising my muscles holds great appeal, *katya*. I will do whatever needs to be done, no matter that you are impudent in the asking of it."

For a long while, she said nothing. Then she sighed, a long drawn-out sigh. "Look, I don't mean to be so snappy, Jorlan. I really don't. I just don't know what to do about you." She tossed green paper onto the table surface. "Come on. We've got a lot of work to do today." She slid across the seat and stood.

He pushed easily to his feet.

Their gazes locked for one heartbeat before she turned away and headed for the exit. Jorlan had only taken four steps when someone grabbed his forearm. He spun, clutching the weapon at his waist without actually removing it.

The redhead smiled up at him.

He relaxed his warrior stance.

"Hey," she said, her voice throaty and seductive. "I'm Heather."

'Twas the type of reception he was used to receiving. He returned her smile. "'Tis my pleasure to meet you, Heather. I am called—"

"I know who you are. You're Hunter Rains, the self-help guy. Twelve steps to a better you, and all that. I recognized you the moment I saw you." She looked down at her feet, suddenly shy. "Anyway, what I'm trying to say is that I've read your book and I know you're from Australia. I'd be glad to show you around Dallas. I'm—"

Katie had spun around at Heather's first words and now stood directly beside Jorlan. Her eyes went molten, then icy. "He's not available."

Heather never even glanced Katie's way; she just blinked up at Jorlan. "Are you? Unavailable, I mean?"

He didn't answer right away. Too much did he enjoy Katie's jealousy.

"I'll be waiting in the truck," Katie snapped. She swirled on her heel and strode outside.

Jorlan faced the little redhead again. Here was a woman like those of his world. Willing to please. More than likely, she would do whatever he asked if he showed the slightest bit of interest. Yet he felt nothing, not even a faint stirring of lust.

"Though I may come to regret these words," he said when his body failed to respond to the girl's nearness, "I am indeed unavailable."

"But the woman you're with is so…tall and plain."

"Plain?" He chuckled. "Her beauty is endless."

Heather gave a disappointed shrug of her shoulders. "It was worth a try, I guess."

With nothing left to say, he followed the path Katie

had taken. As she'd said, she was waiting for him inside the belly of her transportation. Her limbs were stiff, her expression cold.

He slowly grinned. The day was indeed ripe with promise.

CHAPTER SEVEN

Imperia

PERCEN DE LOCKE HOBBLED across the ancient sands of Druinn, a haven situated in the heart of Imperia and invisible to mortal trespassers. Moonlight spilled upon the crystal grains, creating an illuminating sphere of mystique. The fragrance of *gartina* and *elsment* ghosted a cool, moist breeze upon his cheeks and neck, ruffled the dark locks of his hair, then swirled away. Stars twinkled from their perch in the heavens, so close he had only to reach out to hold their essence in his hands.

What a mockery this beautiful refuge made of his emotions.

His limbs shook with hatred, impotence and rage. He was barely able to move his legs one after the other as he paced. Only yestereve he had cursed Jorlan en Sarr inside an impenetrable wall of stone. The warrior had stood here, the centerpiece of the Druinn sands, yet now he was gone.

Gone!

Percen sensed his mother's magic, smelled the flowery scent of her perfume, and knew beyond a doubt she was responsible, that she had either set Jorlan free or sent him away. Fists clenched at his sides, he closed his eyelids. Using his mind's eye, he searched through the lingering magic for answers. Energy coated the air in layers, each layer a different color, depending on the spell or magic used at a particular time. The most recent spell churned on top, giving off a reddish hue. 'Twas not a spell that worked beside another, but a spell that created and drew on other energies—a spell that opened a vortex.

He knew then that she had sent Jorlan away, effectively saving the cursed warrior from Percen's wrath. The knowledge smoldered inside of him, blistering like a fire raging out of control.

"Why do you torment yourself so?" a soft, feminine voice said from behind him.

Percen halted midstride. Tiny white crystals scattered around his feet as he whipped around. A darkhaired beauty stood proudly before him, a cerulean-colored amulet at her throat. The center of the jewel pulsed with the life of an ocean. The woman's regal shoulders were squared with concern. Feigned concern, he knew, for she cared nothing about him.

"Did you come to gloat?" he snapped.

"Nay." Her expression was unreadable as she reached out to touch his shoulder. His simmering glare stopped her. She waited a whisper of time, then dropped her hand to her side. "It does not give me joy to see you so upset."

"Do not act as if you care what I feel. I know where your affections lie."

Her eyes, pale-blue just like his own, darkened with

sadness. "I am your mother. Why do you think I can care for one of my sons but not the other? Aye, I left you here, but I have always had the same devotion for you that I have for Jorlan. Always."

"Liar!" He closed the distance between them there in the quiet of the white sands. His rage grew hungry, and without warning, he struck her. Hard. Putting all his strength behind the blow. Her head snapped to the side, and a small trickle of blood flowed from the corner of her lip. "You are a liar." He spoke slowly, softly. Harshly.

Silence weighted down like an oppressive shadow, and he watched his mother's cheek redden and swell. *He* had put that mark there, and the knowledge cut deeply, shamefully. He held his breath until his chest burned in agony, for the gentle fragrance of her perfume taunted his nostrils. He waited for her next words, the words that would at last confess her hatred of him.

They didn't come.

Tears pooled in her eyes; her chin wobbled. "Please believe me when I say that I am devoted to you. Not because you are my son, but because I love you."

These words were somehow more offensive than if she'd slapped him in retaliation. For how long had he waited to hear such a wondrous declaration? Forever, it seemed. Yet it meant nothing to him now. Nothing! "Your actions belie your words, Mother."

"'Tis not true."

"You claimed to love me spans ago, and yet you left me, deserted me as if I were garbage when you life-joined with the mortal king."

"I left you with the Druinn *because* I loved you.

How can you not see that? I could not take you from them, knowing you were destined to become high priest."

"What does power or sovereignty matter without love? All I've ever desired is the feel of your arms around me, comforting me. The sound of your voice soothing me to sleep. But you denied me those things as surely as you granted them to Jorlan."

"I'm sorry," she whispered, her voice broken and disjointed like the winds of the third season. "So sorry. I didn't know, didn't think—"

"No." He cut her off, scowling. "You didn't think of me. You have *never* thought of me."

"Percen, please stop this. I love you. I truly do."

Again, those words. How they cut into his soul, making him bleed inside, leaving a hollow ache where his heart had once resided. "As I said, your actions belie your words. You claim to love me now, and yet you sent Jorlan away, preventing me from obtaining my greatest desire."

Her eyes closed; her lips pressed together. "Aye. 'Twas I who sent him away."

A long silence stretched.

"Tell me, Mother," Percen said. "If I give you another chance, will you at last prove your love for me?"

"Whatever you wish, 'tis yours," she said hopefully, though she still did not face him.

He knew exactly what he wanted. "Bring the statue back to me."

"Nay. Not that." She gave a firm shake of her head. "Never that."

"Curse you, why did you take him from me? Why?

A *loving*—" he sneered the word "—mother would have left me to my vengeance."

At last her eyes met his. He pierced her with the full fury of his gaze. She did not look away from him this time, and in fact, held his stare with a proud tilt of her chin. "Jorlan is my son, just as you are, and I would not see him suffer for my sins."

Hearing her words of devotion for his most hated enemy cut deeper than a sharp-edged talon. "By sending him to another world, you punished *me*. Does it please you to see *me* suffer?"

"Your happiness means as much to me as his does, but I could not allow you to sentence your brother to a life of imprisonment." Like a dark angel amid the white sands, she sank to her knees and scooped a handful of the tiny crystals, letting the grains sift between her fingers. One lone tear dripped into her palm, blending and thickening the sand. "Had I the power to break your curse, I would have done so instead of simply sending him away."

Percen's nostrils flared. All of his childhood he had always prayed for this woman's love, had craved it with every fiber of his being, yet he had found only emptiness. Always emptiness. He supposed he shouldn't have blamed Alana for leaving him. What mother could adore a son so hideous to gaze upon? He knew his scarred, haggard exterior was, at times, too much to bear.

'Twas one of the reasons he hated Jorlan so passionately. Jorlan possessed the beauty of ancient legends and the strength of a warrior. With brawn unlike any other, the handsome giant felled his enemies with a deadly determination few possessed. Praise met his every action, unlike the dismal recognition Percen received when his own mystical powers were required. His magic should have been praised, his skills exalted.

"He is your brother, Percen," she said softly. "Set him free."

"He is my greatest foe, Mother. I will see him die first."

Her lips parted on another sigh, and she once again reached to touch him. He backed away. He would not accept comfort from her now.

"You need a woman." Absently, she scooped another handful of sand. "Someone to heal the hurts within you."

"What woman would have me?" He laughed, the sound harsh and bitter in his ears. "What woman would have a man whose skin is marred with so many scars? Whose body is twisted and bent?"

She answered without hesitation. "The woman for you is the woman who can look beyond appearance and see the wonderful man inside."

"This from the woman who not only abandoned her first son, but also destroyed her second—"

Her chin jerked up, and she spoke over his last words. "Do not say it. Do not say those words aloud."

"What? Do not speak your sins aloud for all of the Druinn to hear? I know what you did to the—"

"Percen," she once again cut him off, desperate this time. She stood to her full height. "That is enough."

He paused, considered her plea. "You are right. Your sins against the mortals matter little to me. In fact, I welcomed your deed." His head fell back and he gazed up at the heavens. Twin moons glowed, creating shafts of violet light. Why could life not be simple? A man was supposed to live and love and die. Instead, he lived, he suffered, and he continued suffering. "To what world did you send Jorlan?"

Her eyelids fluttered to a close, but not before he caught a glimpse of her relief. "I sent him far away where a loving maiden will one day set him free. He deserves a life of happiness."

"And I do not?" Percen slammed his fist against his palm.

"I did not say that," she gently assured him. "But your happiness does not lie in Jorlan's suffering."

Aye, it did. Or mayhap…mayhap his redemption lay with another's suffering. "I hardened Jorlan as surely as your neglect hardened my heart," he said, more to himself than to her. "But mayhap I should have hardened *you* instead."

Once the words were spoken, he realized just how much he meant them. If she were stone, she could not say things that hurt him. Could not leave him alone and destitute. Could not choose Jorlan over him once again.

She must have read his intent in his eyes, because she said, "Percen, do not do this," and backed away. She even clasped her amulet to send herself to another plane.

His powers were much stronger than hers; the Druinn had seen to that. By *Elliea*, she had seen to that. With a curl of his fingers, he froze her feet in place, making it impossible for her to move, physically or mystically.

"It is past time you thought upon your actions and your choices. Were even Jorlan here, he could not save you from my spell. We both know he has not my magical abilities, yet you have always chosen the weaker of your sons. Think on that."

"Percen—"

A grin curled at the edges of his lips. "Just remember, 'tis I, and I alone, who can free you from this spell. One of life's ironies, I suppose, is that the same person who hurts you is the very one who can save you." Not allowing himself to consider his own actions, he unsheathed his scepter and raised his arms high in the air. The jeweled hilt glistened in the moonlight, creating shafts of colored light that speared onto the sand.

"Flesh and blood thou may be," he chanted, focusing all his energy onto his mother, "but stone is all the eyes shall see."

"Do not do this," she uttered once more, her eyes wide with horror.

He closed his ears to her pleas. Had she listened to *his* pleas all those spans ago? Nay. She had seemed all too eager to abandon him. Scowling, he finished his curse. "Cold as marble, hard as rock, with this curse I thee lock. The Stone Queen you shall forever be, unless my life's blood sets you free."

Wind suddenly burst forth, beating through the night like a devil's breath. Lightning erupted from the sky and crashed against the sands. Bit by bit, her flesh hardened to silver stone.

There. 'Twas done.

But he did not feel the relief, the ease of suffering, he'd hoped for. Nay, he felt...shame, a trickle of sorrow and need. Deep, abiding need for all that he'd ever longed for, but had never possessed. He reached out, then let his hand fall to his side. She stood so beautifully before him.

His shoulders slumped. "Should I set you free already?" he asked, though he knew he wouldn't. "I am going to search for Jorlan. You know that, do you not? Just because you sent him to another world does not mean I cannot find him."

Overhead, the stars slowly disappeared as thick gray clouds formed. A roll of thunder echoed, then stilled. It was as if the emotions churning inside him were changing the weather. "You and I both know time passes differently from one world to the next. One day has passed in Imperia, but how many days have passed for Jorlan? Is he free? If so, is he old and wasted away? No matter what his age, what his life, I *will* bring him home. Time and distance have no hold upon me."

Percen knew he shouldn't leave Imperia. But he would do it. He would take leave of this world and never return if it meant finding his brother. The Druinn needed him, for something dark hovered just over the horizon. Something the citizens of this land were not prepared for. He did not know what it was, a war, mayhap, but he knew many lives would be lost soon. Yet his vengeance meant more to him than the safety of his world.

Droplets of rain began to fall, splattering upon the sand and stone. Several drops landed on his mother's face and ran down her cheeks like tears. "If I present him to you, will your heart fill with joy and make you at last feel tenderness for me? *True* tenderness, not the empty emotion you professed this day?"

Silence.

Silence so thick it cast an oppressive shadow across the white sands, and at that moment it seemed as if even the rain dared not pitter-patter. Percen dropped to his knees, pressed his forehead against her midriff, all the while craving her arms around his shoulders. "If I give him back to you, will you truly love me? Mayhap even love me more than you love him?"

Again, silence.

He expected nothing different, but could not stop himself from hoping for a sign that she heard him, that she welcomed his need to please her. But as he gazed up at her face, her expression clearly proclaimed: *You are my greatest disappointment.*

And it did not have to be so.

"I will find him," Percen said finally. Purposefully. He pushed to his feet and stroked a hand across her soft white cheek. "I will search the galaxies, if need be, and find exactly where you sent him. And then, sweet Mother, I will bring him back to you."

Broken and destroyed.

CHAPTER EIGHT

WHILE KATIE MANEUVERED the enchanted transportation along the winding roads, Jorlan weighed his options. The woman was obviously in a temper. Her breath was coming in short, shallow pants and her fingers were clutching the steering wheel as if it would fly out the window if she let go. He needed to gently sway her from her pique so that she could at last admit her desires for him. But how?

He could make her laugh with a story of his childhood. He could whisper sweet, seductive words in her ear. Or he could simply wait until her anger crumbled on its own.

"I don't think this is going to work between us, Jorlan," she said.

A dark, primitive blaze uncurled inside him. "It will."

"Of course it works for you. You gain everything and lose nothing."

"So I must lose something to win you? Then so be it. Name it and it is gone."

"That's not what I meant."

"I have less than thirteen days, *katya.* 'Tis a mere flash." He had considered begging before, dropping to his knees and begging her for her affections. His desire for permanent freedom far surpassed any pride he harbored. "You have only to tell me what you need of me and I will do it."

"I don't know what I want from you, okay? I only know I can't give my heart or body easily. Besides that, it's hard to think of you as the love of my life when I know you consider me nothing more than a necessary burden."

"Then I—"

"We're from different worlds," she rushed on, slicing his apology to a halt. "I have enough trouble with Earth men."

"Just because you have trouble with men of your own world," he growled, "does not mean you will have trouble with a man of Imperia."

"No, it just means I have trouble with any man who wants to screw everything female." Katie parked the vehicle, emerged, then strode inside the old house, all without uttering another word. She was beyond angry now, that much was obvious. Her shoulders had been stiff and her chin high and she had never once glanced back to see if he followed. He didn't. He remained within the enchanted transportation.

The day was not fraught with the promise he'd first supposed.

Screw everything female? He had already proved those words for the falsehood they were by declining the girl, but he only now realized the full extent of what had transpired inside the café. He, a man who had been without bodily contact for more than nine hundred spans, had been unable to summon a single shred of awareness for any woman save Katie since obtaining his freedom.

The simple fact was that he was fast becoming obsessed with Katie.

"Katie," he said, wanting to hear her name aloud. "Pretty, courageous Katie James. How can I want you so desperately, yet want no other?" Though he hated himself for it, he did want her desperately. Wanted, if only for a little while, to be the center of her life. Wanted to tear down her resistance and bend her so completely to his will that he could take her whenever, wherever he wanted. More than that, he wanted her cries of love to ring in his ears long after he left her.

For the first time, however, he considered what would happen to *her* if he were to win her. Would she suffer greatly if she fell in love with him and he simply abandoned her? Curse it, she claimed she did not need a man's protection, physically or emotionally. Why should he consider her well-being his responsibility?

Obsessed. Aye, he truly was obsessed, for not even Maylyn had affected him like this. He'd thought of her, but not constantly and she had never confused him. He'd wanted her, but it had been a gentle kind of want, a need to cherish and show tenderness. Now, with Katie, he felt anything but gentle, and all traces of tenderness had already dissipated. He felt an ache, an all-consuming desire that constantly battered against his reservations. He felt a need to dominate, a need to ride her harder than he'd ever ridden a woman.

What did it mean that he simply *had* to have her, whether she returned his affection or not? That he simply had to taste more of her? Her lips were too sweet, her scent too delectable, and her body too ripe. What did it mean that a part of him was willing to wait forever, if need be, to have her?

He didn't want to contemplate the answer.

The air inside the transportation was hot, cloistering, and sweat dripped down his chest. Still he made no move to leave. He needed more time to gather his wits. Closing his eyes, he thought back over Katie's reasons for ending their kiss. They did not like each other, she had said. He liked her all too well. She thought he still considered her a necessary burden. She was necessary, but no longer a burden. They did not know each other, she had said. He did not like discussing his life, but he would do it, tell her anything she wanted to hear.

Aye, he would do whatever was required to gain her favor. In the process, he would do whatever was required to rid himself of his fascination with her.

Resolved, he emerged from the vehicle and followed the path Katie had taken.

KATIE SERIOUSLY CONSIDERED doing a dropkick and punch right into Jorlan's solar plexus, followed by a knee to the groin, and as a finale, taking his rolling pin and bashing him over the head. The man was entirely too confident, too cocky (in every way) and most assuredly a jackass. And to top it off, he was too damn sexy for his own good.

Even the redhead had noticed.

Just thinking about the redhead sent her already heated blood into a serious boil. *Where is that rolling pin?* she thought savagely. *Where is it?* At the moment, she'd even settle for the spatula. Jorlan might need her love, might want to use her body, but he still wanted to sleep with every woman he encountered. Yes, he was a jackass and a womanizer and there was no way in hell Katie was falling for him.

She paced the living-room floor, her movements clipped, jerky. The soles of her shoes squeaked with each step. Her palms were clenched so tightly her nails dug half-moon crescents into her skin, and her knuckles had long since lost all traces of color. Five minutes later, her muscles were still clenched. Somehow, and God only knew how, she managed to paste a carefree smile on her face when the screen door groaned in protest and Jorlan entered the house. His massive frame filled the entrance.

"You are tense," was the first thing he said.

Tense! Tense! She rounded on him, one finger pointed at his chest. "Are you blind? I've never been more relaxed in my life."

One inky brow rose in mocking salute. "Then why is your eye twitching?"

She spun away from him, blocking his view of her face. "There's something in it. An eyelash, I think."

"Then there is no need to tell you that the girl—"

"Girl? What girl?" Katie tried for a carefree laugh, but couldn't quite manage it. Jorlan could do what he pleased, with whom he pleased, and show interest in little redheads all freaking day if he wished. "I have no idea what you're talking about."

"Then allow me to remind you," he said at last. Silently, he moved behind her, placed his fingers at the base of her neck and gave a gentle squeeze. He bent down, allowing his breath to fan her ear. "The girl found me desirable. Had I shown any interest, I could have had her sooner rather than later," he said.

Lord, she both hated and loved his words. "You showed no interest?"

"Nay."

Slowly, she released a breath she hadn't known she'd been holding.

"I *should* have been interested," he added in a self-disgusted growl. "She was a woman who knew what she wanted and was not afraid to try and obtain it."

"Just what are you implying?" Katie spun around to confront him. "That I'm too cowardly to go after what I want?"

He clasped a pale lock of hair from her ponytail and brushed the strands across his lips.

She shivered.

His gaze locked with hers. "That is exactly what I am saying, *katya*. You have been afraid of what I make you feel since the beginning."

"That may be true," she retorted, "but how dare you judge me? You don't know me, not my likes, my dislikes or my past. You have no idea what made me the woman that I am."

"You are right," he said, his voice just as dark. "I do not understand you, nor do I know much about what makes you do and say the things that you do." Then, "But I would like to."

But I would like to, echoed so sweetly in her mind and so shocked her, she could only blink up at him. His tyrannical disposition she could resist. This…gentle caring she could not. Suspicions sparked in the back of her mind, like a candle in a shadowy room. "Is this a ploy to make me fall in love with you?"

He ignored her question. "From the moment I first appeared to you, you have driven me half-mad. I cannot explain the connection between us, but I do know that it is there."

This was everything she'd ever wanted to hear from him, and yet self-preservation proved tenacious, clinging to her with a sharp grip. "What you're saying is wonderful, and I want to believe you. I do. But how can I truly believe that you're interested in me as a person and not just my love?"

"Can I not say the same to you?" he demanded quietly.

He could, she realized then. He really could. Since he first appeared in her garden, she had lusted after him like he was the last piece of chocolate in a PMS survival kit. She probably would have slept with him already if he'd claimed just once to love her or even that he would stick around for a while. But she'd never once stopped to consider the man beneath the brawn.

He lightly fingered her earlobe. "I want you to know about me, and I want to know more about you."

"What do you know about me already?" She didn't mean to sound so desperate, like a child pleading for assurance, but she just couldn't help herself. Things were changing between them with every word he spoke, and she *liked* the changes. Maybe too much.

"I know that you do not smile nearly enough. I know that you were generous to allow me into your home when I had nothing to offer you in return. And I know that I hurt you by calling you a necessary burden." His fingers released her ear, traveled to the base of her neck and lightly massaged. "For that, I am truly sorry."

Katie stilled, absorbing the warmth of his hands and the glow of his apology. But surely she had misheard him. Surely this man, this warrior who took great pleasure in ordering her around, had not just apologized.

"Jorlan—"

"Nay. Say no more. I once thought taking only your body while remaining distanced was best. Not so now."

And yet, she thought suddenly, he seemed more distanced from her than ever before. There was a flat tinge to his eyes that clashed with his honeyed tone. For the life of her, she couldn't make herself care that this might be a ploy.

"You intrigue me," he continued, "and I find myself constantly thinking about your thoughts and actions. Were I home, I would still wonder, and I would regret not knowing. We have this day, and only *Elliea* knows how many others, to learn of each other. If you wish."

If she wished, Katie silently repeated. What did she truly want from this man who had no plans to stay? Just how much of herself was she willing to risk? The answer had seemed so clear only this morning.

"No alliance is one hundred percent secured," he said. "In this, at least, we know the final outcome."

He was right, of course, but that didn't make her decision any easier. "Saying goodbye will be harder if we've initiated any type of emotional relationship."

"Only if we make it so."

So where did that leave her? She truly had tried to ignore her attraction to him, but it hadn't gone away. It had only grown stronger. So strong, in fact, she had only to picture his face in her mind and bam! She desired him. Katie closed her eyes. Opened them. Gazed up at him. "Just give me a little more time, okay? That's all I'm asking."

He lightly pressed his lips to her collarbone. Flames uncoiled in her belly, and she almost blurted her capitulation then and there. But Jorlan pulled back, and said softly, "I remind you that time is our enemy, *katya*. Do not forget that fact."

"How can I?" she answered, her tone just as soft.

A long, protracted moment passed. She stayed exactly as she was, afraid to sever—or perhaps afraid not to sever—the tentative bond growing between them. Then, suddenly, Jorlan stepped back and clasped his hands together, brisk and formal, as if they'd never shared such an intimate moment. "What labor would you have me do? I am eager to begin."

The heavy sexual tension eased with the small distance between them, making her feel as if she had been released from some sort of captivity. "I need you to move the large rocks that line the edges of the driveway to the back fence. It's a tedious and back-breaking chore, and I hate to ask you to do it, I really do, but you're free labor, and I…" She shrugged.

The blue of his eyes twinkled. "Have I not told you before that I welcome the chance to exercise?" He turned and tossed his next words over his shoulder as he strode to the door. "Worry not, for I fully intend to lose myself in whatever physical task you place before me."

With the sexual innuendo lingering in the air, Katie found herself alone.

Alone.

Time to think about the kiss, her mind shouted.

"No. I'm not ready," she grumbled.

Kiss, kiss, kiss.

Realizing she could delay the inevitable no longer, Katie sank onto the scarred hardwood floor, rested her chin upon her upraised knees and remembered. When she'd first felt Jorlan's arms anchor around her waist, smelled his hot, masculine scent, she hadn't wanted to run. She'd wanted to feel and touch him, to allow him to feel and touch her in return.

And oh, how he had touched her. He'd stroked his tongue into her mouth, sending scalding heat all the way through her. The world around her had faded to black, and she'd known only Jorlan. Desire had coiled deep in her belly, tightened her nipples, and pooled between her legs. She'd been completely lost. Lost, as if she no longer existed as a separate being. She'd reveled in every moment and hungered for more—more of the glorious sensations. The consuming ache. The sheer need. Her entire body had come alive, each nerve ending on alert and ready for completion.

She'd been kissed before, but *this* had been different somehow, more than a simple meeting of lips. Thinking back, she realized every other kiss she'd ever experienced had left her cold and hollow, and she had always craved escape. With Jorlan, she had craved forever.

For the first time ever, the chemistry had been exactly right.

I'm going to sleep with him, she admitted then. She could no longer deny the inevitable. Like Jorlan, she would always wonder what could have been if she didn't take what she wanted now, while she had the chance. Besides, she'd played things safe with Jorlan so far and look where that had gotten her. Frustrated and unsure. Confused. Why not dive headlong into whatever pleasures awaited her in his arms? Damn the consequences?

Feeling more lighthearted than she had in days, weeks, even years, Katie gathered her heat gun and putty knife and jumped into her work. Two hours later, she was humming under her breath and tearing up linoleum in the upstairs bathroom when Jorlan reappeared.

"I have finished my task," he said, his pride in his accomplishment evident.

She faced him. He had removed his shirt, and she saw that sweat beaded his forehead and chest. Several scratches from the sharp-edged rock marred his abdomen. Dirt streaked his brow. He looked like a primitive god, strong and confident and oh, so delicious. Knowing she was soon going to have all that strength above her and inside of her made her mouth water.

"What would you have me do next?" he asked.

"Why don't we talk?" she suggested.

His chin tilted to the side, and he watched her for one protracted moment. Satisfaction flittered through the depths of his eyes. He nodded. "We will talk."

Suddenly nervous—she didn't know why—she set her tools aside and pulled her knees up to her chest. "Have a seat. Please."

He eased down in front of her until they were eye to eye. Getting comfortable, he removed the weapons strapped to his body and set them at his side.

"I'd—I'd like us to get to know each other," she confessed.

Whatever reaction she'd expected, he didn't give it to her. He nodded calmly, assuredly, as if he'd known all along she would capitulate. "Why do you not begin?" he said. "Tell me about—"

"No!" Katie hadn't meant to shout the word, but she'd suddenly been overcome with a single fear. What if she told Jorlan about herself, and he didn't like what he learned? She wasn't like most other women; she was lacking in so many of the feminine graces. "I'd rather hear about you. Tell me about your family, about your past. If you want to, I mean."

"I will tell you anything you wish to know, *katya*." He stared at the wall just above her left shoulder, perhaps seeing through it, through the passage of time and galaxies to his "other" life. "Where should I begin?"

"At the beginning, of course."

"I thought as much." He sighed. His muscles smoothed beneath his skin, and he settled his back against the wall. "My father, Great-Lord Gui-en Sarr, a king, you would say, died a few spans before my confinement. He—"

"Your father was a king?" she demanded, incredulous. No wonder Jorlan expected his commands to be instantly obeyed. He was freaking royalty.

"Aye, but the throne will never be mine."

"Why not?"

"I was not chosen."

Her brow puckered with confusion.

"An Imperian great-lord is chosen by the Kyi-en-Tra Crystal," he explained. "Upon the death of the current lord, men journey from all over the world to touch the ancient stone, for whoever makes the crystal burn bright with crimson is known as the one true king until his death."

She could just imagine the impatient hopefuls standing in line, awaiting their turn to touch the stone. "So you didn't give the crystal color?"

He chuckled. "Do not look so sad for me, *katya*. My father's brother, Challann, took the throne. He was a good and just man. The people adored him, as did I."

"You would have made a spectacular king or lord or whatever."

A negligent shrug lifted his shoulders. "The people would not have agreed. To them, my sorcerer's bloodline tainted my royalty."

"That's discrimination."

"But the truth all the same."

Looking away from him, she tinkered with the scraps of linoleum scattered around her. "If you're thought tainted, why do you want to go back so badly?"

"'Tis my home," he said simply. Then shrugged again. "In Imperia, I may not be a great-lord, but I am a man of consequence, a warrior of great ability and power. Here I am only a man who must rely on a woman to see to my needs."

Yes, she could see how that would eat away at his pride.

Stretching out her long legs, Katie leaned back

against the wall. Cool tile seeped through the thin material of her shirt. She felt as though there was something she was forgetting, something she wanted to tell him. When she realized what it was, her eyes widened, and she silently cursed herself for getting so caught up in his story of kings and princes that she hadn't said these words sooner. "I'm so sorry about your father's death."

He nodded to acknowledge her empathy.

"How did he die?" she asked gently.

Jorlan propped his elbow on his bent knee and hesitated only a moment before answering. "He was murdered. I commissioned several sorcerers to aid me in my search for the culprit, yet no one was able to divine the truth."

"Were there any suspects?"

"Many believed my half brother responsible, but Percen did not have the strength to rise from bed that eve, much less thrust a talon into a man's chest."

"How do you know?" She tried to keep her tone light and easy, not wanting him to see how sad she was for him, how she longed to wrap her arms around his neck and take all of his past pain away. "Your brother could have been faking his injury to give himself an alibi."

"'Tis not a possibility. He was recovering from a talon wound. A wound I inflicted."

His words elicited images of blood and war, a side of Jorlan she knew existed but didn't want to contemplate. She preferred instead to think of him as the charming, sexy man before her. A man who was a prince and should have been king. "If you had decided to challenge your uncle for the crown, could you have done it?"

"Why?" His gaze grew cold, like pools of ice in the winter. "Do you have hopes that I will take you back with me and make you my queen?"

"No," she assured him, a little offended that he thought so little of her. "I'm curious, is all. Your mother was—is—a sorceress, yet her bloodline didn't prevent her from becoming queen."

The coldness remained in his eyes, but it was no longer directed at Katie. He seemed lost in his memories. "My mother was never truly accepted. Her sovereignty and the authority it brings were ignored."

"That's awful."

"A marriage between a sorcerer and mortal has always been forbidden." He pushed out a breath and jerked a hand down his face. "Both my mother and my father knew this and accepted the consequences."

"Why is such a union forbidden?"

"Because mortal and immortal have different life spans. While a sorcerer can live forever, a mortal cannot. My mother watched my father grow old, while she remained young. Every day she became increasingly aware that my father was dying, that there was nothing she could do to save him. And then, suddenly, he truly was dead."

Compassion shimmered in Katie's gaze, and it affected Jorlan more than it should have, warming him all over. He had stepped inside this chamber thinking he was guarded against her allure. Yet as he spoke, sharing a part of his life he'd never shared with another, he was somehow making the connection between them grow stronger.

"Did your mother take another husband?" she asked, her tone as gentle as a fifth season breeze.

"Nay. She loved my father with all of her heart, and claims the heart can only love so greatly but one time. Besides, she abandoned her people to be with him; she even abandoned her first son, my half brother. No man of the Druinn would have her, and I doubt another mortal man would have her, either."

"Even though she is a former queen and high priestess?"

"Even then. The Druinn are loyal to Percen now, and would not wish to anger him." Percen… His image flashed in Jorlan's mind. As a child, Jorlan had prayed for a chance to meet his brother. He'd wanted someone to play with, someone to teach him the ways of magic. Yet his mother had always refused to introduce them, saying Percen belonged with his own people and needed no reminder of his mortal ties.

On the eve of his eighth span, Jorlan finally decided to visit his brother on his own. While his parents were too consumed with celebration details to notice his absence, he had sneaked away from the palace. For three hours he traveled, imagining the blessed meeting with every step. Percen's face would light with happiness, and he would take Jorlan in his arms and swing him around with joyful abandon.

His imaginings died a quick death when he entered the white sands of Druinn.

Percen recognized him instantly. Instead of happiness, a dark cloud of hatred had descended upon his brother. Percen had pushed him, ridiculed him, spat on him, all the while destroying his boyhood dreams. Jorlan had never gone back, nor had he told his mother what had happened. He'd merely grieved in silence for the brother he would never know.

"I almost feel sorry for your brother," Katie said, her voice whisking away his bleak thoughts. "I mean, I ache for his loss. Losing a mother is difficult. Mine died of heart failure when I was nine years old, and I still miss her." Featherlight, her exhale swayed on the midday air. "I always knew she loved me. I don't know what I would have done if I'd thought she hated me."

That Katie could hurt for someone she'd never met—no matter that the person was his greatest enemy—touched Jorlan to the very core of his being. Not many people could be so understanding, so filled with empathy. Katie might strive for a hard, warrior-like demeanor, but she possessed the soft, caring heart of a woman.

Curse it. He didn't want to, but he liked this side of her.

Her lips began moving again, but he didn't catch the words. He was staring at her, Jorlan realized. Staring at her lush pink lips while the world around him ceased to exist. Unable to stop the images, his mind entertained pictures of those lips closing over his shaft, her pale hair spilling over his legs. Need uncurled inside of him like a lion awakening from an afternoon rest. His muscles clenched. If he did not distract himself, he would be ripping off her clothes, curse their talk and curse her resistance.

"Tell me about your life," he barked.

A look of panic darted across her expression, but was quickly replaced by determination. Silently, she watched him. He wondered what she was thinking. Heat soon grew in her gaze, hot and consuming, slowly cresting to the rest of her features.

She smiled seductively.

On her hands and knees she crawled to him, not stopping until her nose brushed his. "I was born November sixteenth. Blue is quickly becoming my favorite color, and when I die, I want it to be from pleasure." Then she planted her lips over his, took his tongue inside her mouth and sucked.

His body sprang to life immediately, and he groaned against her lips. Their tongues battled for control, thrusting, darting away, thrusting again. He wanted to howl when she eased back. She traced the seam of his mouth with her tongue, and he wrapped his arms around her waist, lest she decide to end the embrace altogether.

"Did you like that?" she asked instead.

"Aye."

"Want me to do it again?" In that instant, Katie wanted so badly to be naked, wanted Jorlan to be naked, as well. Without conscious thought—Lord, she couldn't think, only feel—she leaned into him, pressing herself more fully against him. Her nipples hardened, her lips tingled and her body came alive.

"Nay," he breathed.

"Nay?" She froze. She craved him with every ounce of her being and *he didn't want her to do it again!*

"This time," he said, "I want to do it to you."

As she sagged with relief, the pink tip of his tongue circled her lips, tasted every corner, nibbled every indentation. She twined her fingers in his hair, losing her breath completely when he shifted to lick her ear. "I want more." *I need more.*

"Then more you shall have."

"But just one more kiss," she whispered, recalling where they were. "One kiss and then we'll stop. If you still want me, we can start again later."

"I want you now, and I will want you later. So I will give you the one kiss you are asking for," he said, "but it will be a kiss that lasts all through the eve and requires our naked bodies to be entwined."

Before she could reply, his mouth reclaimed possession of hers. She opened for him, opened and cried out in pleasure at the same time. With each flick of his tongue, desire slammed into her forcefully, coaxing tremors from her. Hot and eager, mercilessly, he moved his mouth over hers. He slanted across her lips with a savage hunger that caused stars to twinkle behind her eyelids.

Their first kiss had been fiery and wonderful, but *this* was the essence of dreams. Soul-searing, erotic dreams. It made up for every second date she'd ever missed, every evening of bad company she'd ever endured, and every night she'd spent alone, wishing for someone to love.

Lost in his scent, his body, his maleness, she gave herself completely into the kiss, holding nothing back. Giving him every ounce of herself. Had other women ever experienced such bliss? A bliss that eclipsed reason and time? Movies and books lauded such passion, of course, but had anyone ever really tasted it as she was now?

How sad if they had not.

Her arms moved over Jorlan's muscled chest, feeling his skin, jagged in some places, smooth in others, but hot all over. She jerked the spatula from his waist and tossed it aside. His tongue continued to caress her mouth, bold and passionate. She pushed him down until he lay flat on his back. Her knees braced his sides, spreading her legs wide, and she arched her hips, thrusting slightly against his erection.

"Aye, just like that," he praised. "Again."

She arched once more. This time, the contact caused a ragged moan to slip from her throat because he arched, too, making the impact deeper. Stronger. Over and over they continued the motion. Then in one fluid motion, he tumbled her over, taking control and pressing himself between her open thighs. He trailed kisses of fire along her cheek. He swirled his tongue around her ear, dipped inside, pulled out, and dipped again. Had he stripped her naked just then, had he plunged into her body and buried his cock to the hilt, she would not have protested.

She would have thanked him.

This is the wild, wanton woman I've always longed to be, Katie realized. She felt utterly alive. So free. But reason tried to insert itself. *You're lying on the bathroom floor. You've only known this man a few days. You wanted only one kiss.*

Yes, she'd asked for only one kiss, and he was taking far more. In fact, he was *ravishing* her. The thought caused hot, heady moisture to pool between her thighs. How easily she pictured him holding her down and forcing her to face her desires. How easily she pictured…and how easily she wanted the fantasy to come true.

She wanted to be ravished.

"We have to stop kissing," she said, breathless. "We shouldn't be doing this."

"When you stop wanting my kisses, *katya,* then will I stop."

Oh, yes, my barbarian warrior. You're in control.

He pulled back a little, gazed down at her, his eyes smoldering to a fiery blue. He reached under her shirt, kneaded her breast, and decided the contact wasn't enough. He shoved her bra up, let his fingers roll her nipple, and then, suddenly, he froze. His growl echoed loud and long off the walls.

"With much regret do I recall our bargain." Dark emotion etched his expression. "I cannot give you pleasure unless you ask nicely. Or beg very prettily."

No, no, no. She wasn't supposed to beg for anything except mercy, and he wasn't supposed to be chivalrous! That wasn't how a man ravished a woman. He was supposed to take her, seduce her completely, damn the consequences. At this point she'd even settle for a "I know what's best for you, *katya.* I'm only doing this for you."

"This time, however," he half snarled, half moaned, "I will make an exception."

Oh, thank you. Thank you. She almost smiled. She did tighten her hold on his neck, ready for another mind-blowing kiss. Her elation was short-lived, however.

"You do not have to beg," he said. "You do not even have to ask. You only have to push me away if you wish me to stop. I will give you time to decide."

She didn't want time, damn it. She wanted his

tongue in her mouth. Wanted his hands on her breasts. Now. But he was the ravisher, and she was the ravishee, and the fantasy wouldn't work if she forced herself on him.

"One, two three," he counted. "Time is up."

His mouth smothered hers.

Relieved, excited, she leaned up for his kiss. The silky heat of his tongue danced with hers. His body pushed against hers. He smelled so hot, so masculine. So delicious.

"What do you want me to do to you?" he demanded.

"I have no control over you," she breathed. "You'll do whatever you want, no matter what I say."

He jerked back, confused. "No, I—" Suddenly, comprehension dawned. He smiled wickedly. "That's right," he said, his tone heavy with authority. "I'll do whatever I want to you. Your protests mean nothing."

Hallelujah.

For what seemed hours, but could have only been minutes, he worked his hands over her body, learning her every curve, teasing her, tempting her, making her beg.

"Who is in control, *katya?*"

"You are," she whispered. "Only you."

"Do not forget."

"Never."

His big hands closed over her breasts. Intense pleasure rocked through her. He pinched her nipple at the exact moment he pressed his erection against her clitoris. Their clothes added to the friction, and she shot off like a Fourth of July rocket. Her moans became wild cries, a building crescendo, the force of which made her almost incoherent.

When she quieted, Jorlan held her for a long while, his shallow breaths in her ear. He pulled back, searching her face. "Katie," he said softly, "you have already—"

"I know. I'm sorry." How embarrassing. He was still primed and ready; she was all finished. But damn it, she hadn't been able to stop it, hadn't wanted to stop it. Her body had raced toward completion, heedless of anything else. "I truly am sorry. I just couldn't help myself."

"Do not apologize." His tone was reverent. "Simply do it again."

She slowly smiled. "Again? Really?"

"Most definitely. I command you." His lips claimed hers once more.

Her arms wound around his neck, holding him captive. Her ankles locked around his waist. He reached between them, grasped the neck of her shirt, and gave a sharp tug. The cotton split down the middle. She bit her bottom lip to keep from shouting her renewed excitement.

Jorlan was just reaching for her shorts, and she was just arching her back to give him better access, when a voice said from the doorway, "Uh, am I interrupting something?"

CHAPTER NINE

"Nick!"

Cheeks flaming, stomach filling with a sickening combination of dread, embarrassment and horror, Katie attempted to jump to her feet and disengage from Jorlan at the same time. Before she succeeded, he jolted to a battle position, his feet squared apart, his fists clenched, facing her brother with an expression that clearly read, "Prepare to die." The swift motion caused her alien's legs to pound against her knees.

She collapsed with a shriek.

Neither man spared her a glance.

Popping up, she hurriedly tied the torn folds of her shirt together—which barely managed to cover her pink, lacy bra—then shoved her hair back from her face. Jorlan quickly thrust her behind him.

If she hadn't known better, she would have suspected he was actually trying to protect her. From her own brother! The idea was simply too ridiculous to contemplate, and she decided he was simply being his chauvinistic self. Something along the lines of get-thee-behind-me-oh-weak-one.

Then he said, "Stay behind me, Katie. I will eliminate this threat."

Oh, he really is protecting me, she thought, melting. She should have been angry. After all, she'd proven her ability to drop an opponent to the ground. But Lord, this made her feel dainty and cherished.

Reaching up, she moved her fingertips over Jorlan's bare back. She loved the hardness of him, the heat. Her teeth ground together. She'd finally decided to go all the way— Wait! Not wanting to ruin the fantasy she'd created in her mind, she corrected herself: A man had finally been strong enough to ravish her, and a family member showed up to bear witness. If her heart hadn't been racing with desire and her limbs hadn't been trembling with mortification, she would have leapt across the room and slapped Nick upside the head with a flanged plunger.

Men!

Her brother, who seemed more amused by Jorlan's words than concerned, gazed over the giant's left shoulder. "Katie, Katie, Katie," he clicked under his tongue. "I walked through the pleasure garden before coming inside the house— you're missing a statue, by the way—and thought to give my hormones a break. But what do I find? Live porn."

Inwardly cringing, Katie placed her hands atop Jorlan's shoulders and peeked over him. She actually had to stand on her tiptoes! "Nick," she said again, this time more calmly. "First of all, I sold that statue," she lied. "And second of all, just what the hell are you doing here?"

Nick chuckled. "I'll collect my quarter later. 'Hell' is still a naughty word, isn't it?"

Jorlan's muscles relaxed, going slack beneath her

palms. "The two of you are familiar with each other," he said.

"Yes." Her tone managed to convey every ounce of her disgust. "The man standing just out of strangling distance is my voyeuristic brother."

"As he is part of your family," Jorlan announced, "I shall allow him to live."

"Please reconsider," Katie said sweetly.

Nick's chuckle grew to body-shaking laughter. "No reason to be so sensitive, little lovebird. I did you both a favor. The bathroom floor is a killer on the back. Anyway—" he waved one hand through the air, his eyes going from tawny-colored amusement to dark brown steel in less than a snap "—I'd like an introduction."

"The introduction can wait," she grumbled. "I'm too upset with you right now. A loving brother would have left without saying a word."

This loving brother arched a sandy brow, managing to retain his intense air, yet somehow appearing amused, as well. "And miss all the fun?"

She loved this man, but geez! Nick, just two years her senior, had always been the comic, the teaser and tormentor. *Her* tormentor, more specifically. As children, most people had mistaken them for twins. Not only for his constant ribbing of her, but also because they looked so similar. They were both tall, possessed the same straight, silvery-blond locks, and the same light brown eyes that tilted up at the corners. That, to Katie, was where the similarities ended.

Where she was curvy, he was all planes and angles. Where she was soft, he was hard. His expression was permanently etched with a mischievous quality usually reserved for small children and cartoon characters. She possessed more of a serious edge, all work and no play. Or so she'd been told.

"What are you doing here?" she demanded for the third time. "I gave you the grand tour last week."

"Can't a guy visit his one and only sister out of love?"

"No."

"You know me too well." Grinning, he switched his attention to Jorlan and held out a hand. "Since Katie refuses to be polite, allow me to introduce myself. I'm Nick James. Katie's favorite brother."

She snorted at that.

"Jorlan en Sarr." Jorlan regarded Nick's proffered hand.

"Shake it," Katie whispered in his ear.

"Ah, 'tis a form of greeting." He took Nick's hand and pumped up and down with the force of a level eight earthquake. "While in the garden, I watched many perform just such a task."

Nick regarded him strangely, studied his facial features for a moment. His eyes narrowed. "You look familiar."

Katie inwardly moaned. Then she paused. Relaxed. What were the chances of her brother linking Jorlan to the missing statue? Her guess: slim to none. Nick, the co-creator of *Slip Through Time,* a virtual reality game, might have a very high-concept imagination, but aliens, curses and magic spells went beyond the realm of perceived truth.

Still, she wasn't going to take any chances. The redhead at the café had thought Jorlan looked like a self-help guru, but Katie knew her brother would never buy that. So, she opened her mouth to weave an elaborate lie involving an automobile accident, amnesia and psychotropic medication, but Nick's next words stopped her.

"Hey." He pointed to Jorlan's chest. "You're that guy on the cover of those romance novels."

Ahh, even better! "That's right," she assured her brother with a nod. "Jorlan poses naked on book covers."

Suddenly very intent on the conversation, Nick leaned against the door frame. "Do the women pose naked with you?"

Like Nick, Jorlan perked up at the mention of naked women. "Aye," he said. "My women pose naked." As he spoke, there was a hint of longing in his tone. He reached around and circled his hand over Katie's waist. That strong hand slid lower and gently squeezed her butt.

The action sent another round of heat through her. Fighting a moan, she slapped his hand and moved to stand beside him. She slanted him a halfhearted glare that said, *Behave—but only a little.*

Nick barely spared her a glance. "How does a guy go about getting a job like that?"

"You love computers too much to switch jobs," she reminded him.

"Who says I can't do both?" her brother shot back. "Naked modeling *and* creating VR games."

She frowned. "I do and that's final."

"I would do what the woman says," Jorlan interjected. His gaze traveled from brother to sister. "She has a temper that nigh flays her opponent alive."

"Very true, very true." Nick shoved his hands in his slack pockets and jingled change. "Where you from, Jordie? I can't place your accent."

"Anguilla," Katie rushed out before Jorlan could answer. "He's from Anguilla." Surely her brother knew nothing about the place.

"That's an island in the British West Indies, right?" Nick asked.

"That's right." Katie decided then to nip all questions concerning geography. "Let's go to the kitchen," she said. "You can explain whatever it is you want from me over a bottled water." With that, she stepped around Jorlan and pushed past her brother.

Behind her, Nick erupted into laughter. "Katie," he called, "you've got a piece of linoleum glued to your ass."

Of course, the two men were best friends after that. They entered the kitchen chuckling over something Jorlan had said. She was fairly certain that something involved breasts and thighs—and not the chicken variety. Nick had one of his arms around Jorlan's shoulders. When their laughter subsided, her brother fired off a round of questions about Jorlan's job.

"Do you get to hold them against you or are you put together digitally?"

"Do you undress in the same room?"

"Of all the models you've worked with, who has the biggest rack?"

Scowling, Katie hurled a bottled water at each man. Jorlan moved with lightning-quick reflexes and managed to catch the thing midair; Nick wasn't so lucky. The plastic thumped against his stomach, hard, and he sucked in a breath. She sent him a smug smile.

He unscrewed the top and took a long swig. All the while, he gave her a brotherly, time-for-payback glare. Lowering the bottle, he said, "I thought you were dating Steve Harris, the detective from Gray's unit."

Katie had just taken a mouthful of the clear liquid; she spewed every last drop onto the floor. "What?"

"Steve Harris. Your boyfriend." Nick practically sang the words to the melody of *Katie and Steven sitting in a tree, K-I-S-S-I-N-G.*

She slammed her water onto the countertop. "He's not my boyfriend. Our brother would like me to date his friend, but I said no."

"Oh, really?"

"Yes, really."

"The way Gray talked," Nick continued, "you and Stevie boy were already planning the wedding."

Mouth agape, her gaze skidded to Jorlan.

He crossed his arms over his chest, a storm cloud of fury brewing in his expression. Nick continued talking, saying something about flowers and churches, but she barely heard him. She continued to watch Jorlan. He looked ready to pounce on someone—namely her—and he was soaking up every word Nick uttered as if it were gospel.

Her fists clenched, crushing the bottle. Just what kind of woman did Jorlan think her to be? Only moments before, she had kissed him, touched him, almost made love to him, and now he thought her capable of marrying another man?

Did he actually think her so lacking in honor? Obviously. Hadn't he thought her capable of wanting him so that he could make her a queen?

Men were idiots!

"I've never even met the guy," she told both her brother and Jorlan stiffly. "And I have no interest in meeting him, either."

"Good. That's why I came to see you." Nick worried a hand over his clean-shaven jaw. "I wanted to tell you to keep away from Steve. I don't want you to hook up with a cop."

His tone made her suspicious. She placed her hands at her hips. "And just who do *you* want me to hook up with?"

"I was going to recommend a buddy of mine. Nice guy. Girls go wild for him."

"'Tis enough!" Scowling, Jorlan advanced on Nick, willing to rip out the man's tongue to keep him from saying another word. He felt…disbelief? Mayhap. Fury? Most definitely. Katie and her brother spoke so blithely of another man—of her marriage to another man—and *he did not like it!* In fact, the thought nearly drove him mad. He did not believe her capable of making love with one man while being promised to another, yet his fury did not lessen.

He needed her, and he would allow no other man to touch her. Not because the thought of another man feasting from Katie's sweetness sent a cold rage storming through him, but because she belonged to him now, her time, her body, and her heart, and he would not share!

Jorlan had almost reached Katie's brother, his intent to pulverize shining brightly in his eyes. Grinning, Nick held up his hands to ward off the oncoming attack. "I've since changed my mind, Jordie. You're perfect for her. Honest. My buddy pales in comparison."

Jorlan stilled. Nick's retraction mollified him somewhat. Yet that wasn't the reason he had stopped. He had just come to a startling revelation. He did not simply lust for Katie, did not simply need her to save him. He cared for her. Despite his efforts to prevent such a thing from happening, it had taken only a few hours for his obsession to deepen. He'd shared his life with her, had watched her writhe as he gave her body the ultimate pleasure, and now *he* had sunk deeper under *her* spell. The knowledge blistered through him, and he cursed his own stupidity. Why? Why had he allowed himself to care about this woman? Had he learned nothing from Maylyn?

At least he hadn't been foolish enough to fall in love with her. Still, he cared for Katie and wanted her with him. If only for a time. He'd thought before of taking her home with him. He had discarded the idea because he had not wanted to make her his life-mate. But now, the idea held merit. He *could* wed her, not permanently, of course, but a temporary joining of mutual benefit.

On his world, a temporary joining had never been considered before. He was willing to make an exception, however. Katie was mayhap too bold, too outspoken for his homeland, but with the proper guidance such qualities could be corrected.

Never had a solution been simpler. He would wed her. She would confess her love for him, come home with him. Then she would come *for* him, again and again. When he no longer cared for her, he would send her home.

Perfect.

Jorlan grinned, suddenly contented.

No longer the source of his wrath, Nick settled himself comfortably atop the speckled counter behind him. "You do anything besides modeling, Jordie? Like security work? Or military intelligence? I swear to God you've got the same guarded look in your eyes that Gray and Erik have."

"Who is Erik?" Jorlan demanded, his fury bursting forth anew.

Katie slapped him on the shoulder. "What's wrong with you? Erik is my brother."

Jorlan leveled a frown her way. "Just how many brothers do you have?"

"Five. Four are scattered across Texas, and one lives in New Orleans."

"Well?" Nick interjected, obviously not liking that his question had been ignored. "Do you do anything besides modeling?"

Katie answered for him. "He's a handyman. He's taking a break from cover modeling and has become my temporary employee."

Her brother clicked under his tongue. "Exactly what type of services are you paying him for?"

This time, Katie slapped her brother's shoulder. Unlike Jorlan, who had barely reacted, Nick winced. "Say another word along those lines," she growled, "and I'll personally kick your ass."

Jorlan grinned, glad such threats were not reserved for him alone.

"I have a feeling I'm going to leave here a rich man." Nick's brown eyes glistened mischievously.

Katie punched him again, harder this time. "You're not getting any money from me."

Enjoying their byplay, Jorlan settled back against the wall and merely watched the two interact. A twinge of regret and homesickness washed through him. Regret because he'd never thought to tease his own sister in such a way. Grace was his father's only child born by the first queen. After, or maybe because of, her mother's untimely demise, Grace had grown to be soft, skittish and wary of men. Jorlan had always treated her with care. Mayhap teasing her would have helped her.

Mayhap he would upon his return—if she still lived, he thought darkly.

Both Katie and Nick were regarding him expectantly. He must have missed some of the conversation. "I am staying in Katie's house," he said, hoping that answered whatever question had been placed before him.

Katie gasped.

Nick lost his grin, but quickly managed to collect himself. "That's good to know. But for the third time, are you up for pool later? After work, of course. We wouldn't want to piss off the dragon lady."

Most of the man's words confused him, yet Jorlan realized some type of invitation had been issued. Why could these people not speak plainly? "I thank you for the offer, yet I must decline. What time I have left here will be spent with Katie."

Nick's gaze sharpened. "You're going back to Anguilla?"

"Aye." He did not correct Nick's pronunciation of his world, for he did not wish to embarrass Katie with her mistake.

"Soon?" Nick pressed.

"'Tis my hope."

"I see." For some reason, Nick seemed unhappy, even angry, at that fact. "Well, the invitation is open all night if you change your mind. Katie has my number. Call if you want a ride."

Call? By shouting? Jorlan nodded.

"Well, my work here is done." Nick hopped from the counter and kissed Katie on the cheek. "Don't forget the family luncheon on Saturday—and bring your date. Dad'll love him." With that, he tossed a wink over his shoulder and disappeared out the door.

"Oh! Wait!" Katie called. "Stay here," she told Jorlan, then quickly added, "Please. I want to talk to my brother alone for a moment." Without waiting for his reply, she raced outside.

"Nick," she shouted, the sun beating down on her shoulders.

Her brother glanced up. He stood just in front of his dark blue sedan, holding his car keys and wearing a pair of sunglasses. With his light-colored hair and deeply tanned skin, he looked every inch the modern sun god. Hand shielding her eyes, she moved off the porch. A warm breeze blew by, kissing her skin. "I need to ask you a question," she told him.

"Uh, oh. This looks serious. You know you can ask me anything, Katie Kat."

She gulped. *I can't believe I'm doing this.* But she had so little experience, and her brother *was* an expert.

Or so he often claimed. She just wanted to have all necessary information at her disposal in case—*when*—she actually slept with Jorlan. After their explosive encounter in the bathroom, she knew it was only a matter of when and where, and she wanted the experience to be as pleasurable for him as she knew it would be for her.

"What's going on?" Nick asked, more serious now. "You look like you're about to vomit."

"Promise me you won't tell anyone about what I'm about to ask you."

"Promise."

Her steps hesitated. She fought the desire to shout, "Never mind," and rush back into the safety of the house. *Just blurt it out,* she commanded herself. "What do you consider sexier? A woman wearing nothing at all or a woman wearing satin and lace? Or maybe black leather?"

His jaw nearly dropped to the ground. "I am *not* answering that."

"Don't be a baby." She had gathered the courage to ask, so he was damn well going to answer. "I was going to ask what turns a man on most, hand stimulation or mouth, but I settled for the other question instead."

Frowning, appearing lost, he rubbed a hand over his eyes then pinched the bridge of his nose. "I can't believe we're having this conversation."

Neither can I. "I want Jorlan to…you know—when we…you know." When had she become so inarticulate?

Nick's head dropped back, and he gazed at the sky. Then, "Nothing. Always nothing. And that's the only question I'm answering. Got it?"

"I love you!" She threw her arms around him, hugged him with all of her might; she pulled back, grinning. "Now get lost. I've got work to do."

He took her by the shoulders and gave a little shake, looking more intense and grave than she'd ever seen him. "You better protect yourself, do you hear me? And I don't mean emotionally. Use condoms. Not one, but two. And if he gives you any crap about not needing them, don't listen."

"I'm a big girl, Nick. Have a little faith." But she hadn't given condoms or safety a second's thought while lying on top of Jorlan on the bathroom floor. "I'll be careful next time," she vowed.

"Next time!" His eyes squeezed shut, opened. "God help me. I never want this conversation mentioned again." Muttering under his breath, he threw open his car door and dropped inside with a thump. "You're just a baby, for Christ's sake, and you're talking about having sex."

She rolled her eyes, but he didn't see the action because he was already racing away, leaving flying gravel and exhaust fumes in his path. Katie picked the tiny silver rocks from her hair as she strolled back into the kitchen. Jorlan stood exactly where she'd left him.

"Let's grab something for lunch," she said, before he could say a word. She didn't want to talk about their kiss. She didn't want to talk about their encounter with Nick. She just wanted to think, to plan. Everything had to be perfect when they finally made love. "You're hungry, right?"

"I am always hungry."

The words "for you" hung in the air unsaid.

CHAPTER TEN

PERCEN DE LOCKE HAD scoured the galaxies for two cycles. Was Jorlan still frozen inside the stone, he wondered, or was his brother now a free man? That he did not know caused frustration to claw at his insides like the sharpest of talons, yet he also felt the first stirring of hope. He had been unable to locate his half brother so far, but he was close enough that he could sense Jorlan's essence.

Aye, he was close....

AFTER JORLAN DINED on more fried chicken and mashed potatoes than should have been humanly possible, and Katie had consumed a *normal* amount, they worked six more hours at the Victorian. When she finally decided they'd accomplished enough for one day, her muscles were burning with fatigue. As she drove home, her stomach began churning with anticipation and nerves. All afternoon, she'd imagined making love with Jorlan.

Cool air blasted from the truck's air conditioner. Katie kept her attention on the road and off the man at her side. Her body was primed for contact, demanding no less than total and complete satisfaction. If she took her brother's advice, she should drop her clothes the moment she stepped inside her house. Perhaps then Jorlan would take over. He would jerk her into his arms, slam the door shut with his foot, then kiss her into readiness.

The idea thrilled her, brought to mind all the wonderful things they'd done earlier, but once they stepped inside her house, Katie lost her nerve and didn't give Jorlan a chance to embrace her. She clutched her keys in her hand and inched back into the doorway. "I've got an errand to run."

He turned and faced her, frowning. Was he disappointed? "What type of errand?"

"Be good while I'm gone," she said, ignoring his question. "No leaving the house. You might get lost."

His frown deepened, and he opened his mouth to speak.

Quick as a snap, she was on the porch, slamming the door behind her. Quicker still, she shoved her key in the gold clasp, gave a twist of her wrist and effectively clicked the lock in place. Then, she waited. The warm evening breeze penetrated the thin tank top she'd changed into. She watched the high, arching door, praying Jorlan wouldn't follow her. One minute ticked by, two. The cherry wood remained closed. Relieved, she hopped off the porch and glanced behind her. Her house gleamed in dusk's fading light. The white stucco, stained glass windows and crenellated rooftop created a pretty, if flashy, sight upon the hilltop.

The drive to the store required a little more than fifteen minutes. Katie strolled down aisle after aisle. She grabbed a pair of sweatpants, two pairs of black slacks and a pair of jeans for Jorlan, thinking—happily—that he would be with her for a bit longer while he tried to win her over. Plus, they still had to find a true psychic. She scrounged through a pile of T-shirts, picking out the largest ones and praying they'd fit a WWE wrestler-type frame. Shoes came next, but she was unsure about size.

If he's big everywhere else, she thought, *it figures his feet are also large.* Katie didn't want to contemplate the direction her thoughts went after that, but she had to. Boxers? Or briefs? Cheeks red, body overheated, she threw a packet of each in the basket.

Next came condoms. There were so many brands, she simply didn't know which to choose. She reached out to grab a box, any box, then froze. What if her brothers were hiding nearby, waiting to jump out and scream "Boo"? She jerked her chin left and right to make sure no one hovered nearby. Finding herself alone, Katie swiftly gathered up a box of neon-colored ribbed, two boxes of lubricated and a box of nonlubricated. No telling which type Jorlan would favor.

She also snatched up a tube of spermicide and a tube of vaginal lubricant. She wasn't sure if either was necessary, but wanted to err on the side of caution. Beyond a doubt, Jorlan had been with many, many women—all women who were sophisticated and knew exactly how to please him, she was sure. Katie didn't want to rate as the worst lover across the galaxies.

Jorlan had once mentioned massage oil and feathers. Perhaps that was a fantasy of his, a fantasy she could fulfill. After finding the oil, she stumbled upon a rainbow-colored feather duster. Perfect.

Hmm, what next? Obviously, Jorlan liked to get kinky. He'd mentioned spanking her once, not that she planned to remind him of that anytime soon. However, Katie didn't want him to think she couldn't handle a little bondage, so she marched to the toy aisle and snagged a pair of plastic handcuffs and a parcel of rope. (She decided against the straw cowboy hat.)

At the register, a fierce blush spread like wildfire across her cheeks and collarbone. The sales clerk, a tall, gangly boy of no more than twenty, lifted a box of condoms and gave her an I-know-what-you're-doing-tonight chuckle, followed shortly by, "Want me to do a price check on this? I think it's on sale."

"Uh, no. I'll pay full price." Thankfully she would never have to face the guffawing teenager again.

Driving home, Katie wondered just how Jorlan would react to her purchases. Would he give her that slow, bone-melting smile of his, then jerk her into his arms? Oh, yes. That was exactly what he would do, and she didn't need magic abilities to predict what would happen after that.

Katie parked her car in the driveway and hefted the bags from the passenger seat. She practically floated to the front door—which was unlocked, she noticed, frowning now. Hadn't she specifically told Jorlan to stay inside?

Just where had her alien warrior gone?

"He better be here," she muttered fiercely.

Scowling now, she shoved open the front door and marched inside. The first thing she noticed was that the

TV volume was up way too high. She could hear multiple male voices laughing, joking and burping. But Jorlan wasn't in the living room, she soon discovered, and the TV wasn't on.

The voices were coming from her kitchen.

Katie experienced a flash of confusion and dread. Not knowing what to expect, she gulped and slowly stepped one foot in front of the other until she stood inside the kitchen. When she saw the source of the noise, her eyes widened and her jaw almost dropped to the floor.

"Hey," her brother Denver called. He sat on the bar stool at the counter, a beer in one hand and a margarita in the other. His bottom lip was swollen and bloody. "Did you come to join the party?"

Before she could answer, her other three brothers called, "Look who finally got here," in disjointed harmony.

"What's going on?" Katie eyed each one of her siblings through narrowed eyes. "And where are your cars?"

"We parked in back," Erik explained. His sandy-colored hair, which was normally smoothed back from his forehead, was standing on end and in complete disarray.

Nick rubbed his fingers over his black and blue cheek. "When I told the boys what you asked me earlier, they decided to bring the party here."

Katie wanted to stomp her foot. She settled for growling, "You promised not to tell!"

He shrugged. "I lied."

"We wanted to meet Jordie boy," Gray piped in, his voice slurred. Grinning, he threw his arm around Jorlan's shoulder. Gray had a black eye; Jorlan had a cut lip. Both men wavered a bit on their feet. "We sure are glad we met him. Got to work out some tension."

"Worked out some tension," Jorlan echoed. He nodded, swayed. Nodded again.

"You've been fighting?" Her incredulity echoed off the walls, though she supposed she shouldn't have been surprised at all. These were her brothers, after all, and they derived great joy from pounding the hell out of each other.

Nick swaggered to her and planted a kiss on the end of her nose. He darted away before she could slap him. "We had to make some things clear to Lover Boy."

"What kind of things?"

"How to treat our baby sister, for one."

"You're kidding me, right? Please tell me you're kidding." When no one spoke, she gave in to her previous impulse and stomped her foot. Once. Twice. "I could kill you all. I really could." She jerked a hand through her hair. "Besides using Jorlan as a punching bag, what else did you do to him?"

"Nothing." Erik held up his left hand in the Boy Scout salute. "Honest."

Jorlan moaned and clasped a hand to his head. "The chamber is spinning. Make it stop." His golden complexion was slowly turning green.

Concerned he might have a concussion, Katie dropped her shopping bags and raced to his side. His pungent scent invaded her nostrils, and she suddenly knew his condition had nothing to do with a head injury. Good Lord. She waved the air in front of her face. "You got him drunk," she accused.

"Sure did." Gray frowned. "Didn't realize Anguillaers were such lousy drunks, though. The man can't hold his booze worth a damn."

"That's because he's never had any, you idiot." She hadn't meant to scream the words, but honest to God, she was about to surpass her big-brother tolerance level. "Just how many beers did you give him?"

"We didn't give him beer. Precisely," Nick hedged.

"Then what *precisely* did you give him?"

"Tequila. Straight from the bottle." That from Gray, law enforcer extraordinaire.

Jorlan swayed. He almost fell, but she managed to hold him up with her hip. She just couldn't freaking believe this. Her alien warrior was wasted. Totally and completely smashed.

"*Katya*," he said slowly, carefully articulating each syllable. "I think I am dying."

"You're not dying," she replied dryly. She led him to the living-room couch and helped him ease down. With every motion, he groaned. Sitting beside him, she smoothed his forehead. "But by morning, you'll wish you were already dead."

Jorlan slapped a hand over his eyes and moaned. He muttered something in a language she didn't understand, but she knew by his tone that the words weren't pleasant.

"I'm sorry, Jorlan," she said, her voice now soft and gentle. "I don't know what you're saying." She traced his eyebrows with her fingertips, and would have been surprised had she seen the I-told-you-so look Nick gave the rest of her brothers.

Jorlan spoke again, this time in English. "What sort

of devil brew did your brothers give me? I wanted 'lick her,' not death." His voice was slurred, almost incomprehensible, and she had trouble deciphering what he said.

"What the hell is this?" Nick shouted.

Katie whipped around, expecting to find…what? A decapitated body, maybe. Or a ticking bomb about to explode. What she found was Nick holding one of the plastic bags, a dark scowl pulling at the corners of his lips as he rifled through the contents.

Katie jolted up so quickly Jorlan's body bounced on the couch springs. His arm swung up and down as he grappled for something solid to hold on to. She didn't stop to help him.

"Give me that!" She launched herself at Nick.

A split second before their bodies collided, Nick tossed the plastic satchel to Gray. Gray missed. The contents spilled across her carpet.

Tick. Tock. Tick. Tock. The only sound to be heard was the ticking of her grandfather clock. All eyes were fastened on what lay oh, so distinctly on her floor. Instead of diving to the ground and snatching everything up, Katie straightened, angled her chin to a proud tilt. She couldn't control her blush, however, and knew if a fire detector had been nearby, she definitely would have set it off.

"Four boxes of condoms?" Gray shouted.

"Handcuffs?" Erik added, his tone a bit more discreet.

"Rope and a feather duster?" Denver yelled. His eyes sparked with fire.

I am not here, Katie thought. *I am not standing*

*here while my brothers ogle my purchases. I'm swim-
ming in a clear blue ocean with the wind whipping my
hair and the water splashing around my body.*

That fantasy came to an abrupt halt with Nick's next
words. "What kind of kinky shit are you into, Katie
Kat?"

That did it. Her temper exploded.

"Get out. All of you." She jerked a finger to the
door. "Get out right now. I'm not speaking to any of
you for the rest of my life. You invaded my home, got
my—my friend hammered, and now you think it's
okay to go through my things? Have I ever treated any
of you with so little respect?"

They managed to look contrite, but not a single
man made a move toward the exit.

"If I want to have sex with a man while he's tied to
my bed and tickle his entire body with feathers, that's
my business!"

Again, silence.

"I'm old enough to make my own decisions."

"You're our only sister," Erik said, as if that explained and excused everything.

"We just wanted to meet your new boyfriend,
honey." Gray motioned to the now unconscious Jorlan with a tilt of his head. "You told me you weren't
seeing anyone. The next thing I know, Nick is calling
me and going on and on about how you were making
out on the bathroom floor with a romance cover model
from Anguilla."

She shot a narrowed glance to Nick, the tattletale.

He shrugged sheepishly, as if to say, "What else was
a brother to do?" Then he grinned. "Mind if I pluck

some of those feathers from the duster? This girl I'm seeing is really into—"

"Out!"

"Don't be mad, sweetheart." Blinking over at her, Erik stuffed his hands in his pockets. "We love you and only want to protect you."

His apology didn't surprise her. He was the peacemaker of the family. He was also the oldest and a former Army Ranger. His chosen profession was so at odds with his peace-loving nature, she often teased him about being a closet activist.

She sighed. "I will get you back, you know?"

"We know. You always do." Denver lost his intense edge, even managed a half smile. "We wanted Jorlan to know what he'd be dealing with if he hurt you. This is the first man you've ever shown such an interest in, and we didn't want to see you get hurt."

Despite herself, Katie softened. She was still going to get revenge, but she abandoned images of a bloodbath. Even though they drove her crazy, made her wish she'd been an only child, she truly loved each of her brothers. All of her life these four handsome, wonderful men, plus the absent Brian, had protected her. They had guarded her from hurt and pain. They loved her. They would always love her, and she couldn't fault them for trying to keep her safe.

She *could* fault them for being so damn nosy.

"You guys have to realize I'm a grown woman. I can be with whomever I want, with or without your approval."

"Yes, but—" Gray began.

"No buts," she said, cutting him off. "I don't interrogate your girlfriends, nor do I get them drunk and beat them up."

Each masculine face showed its own version of remorse.

"For what it's worth, we think he's an all-right guy," Erik told her.

"He's different. In a good way," Denver added. "I never knew a man could fight with a spatula."

Katie smiled; she just couldn't help herself. Some women had the power to know what a man truly meant when he spoke, and at this moment, she was one of them. Erik and Denver were politely telling her Jorlan was weird. "He may be different," she told them, "but he's mine." At least for now.

Erik nodded. "Why don't you bring him to Dad's on Saturday? We need a chance to make up for tonight."

"We promise we'll be good." Nick gave her his customary if-you-believe-that-it's-time-for-a-mental-evaluation grin.

Did she and Nick truly share the same parents? Perhaps he had been adopted. "I'll think about it, okay? I'm not sure how much more of you guys I can stand."

"Fair enough."

One by one her brothers kissed her on the cheek. "Don't let Gray drive," she commanded.

"Give us some credit," Denver tossed over his shoulder.

Together they all strode outside. Well, every one else strode. Gray stumbled. "Don't forget Saturday," he said, his tone a bit slurred.

"I won't." Sighing, she waved them off.

Alone at last, Katie went back inside and locked all of the doors, keeping predators—both related and non-related—out. She was shaking her head as she ambled back to the couch.

Jorlan was still passed out.

In sleep, his features were relaxed, giving him a boyish quality she'd never associated with him before. Boyish…it was hard to imagine that this hard, strong (drunk) warrior had ever been a boy. His innate sensuality, his commanding demeanor, and the patent stillness he sometimes adopted made her think that perhaps he'd sprung fully-grown from his father's thigh, like an ancient Greek god.

Greek god. Yes, the description fit Jorlan perfectly. His physical attributes were exceptional, from the dark shadow covering his jaw to the iron-hard muscles corded throughout his entire body. More than that, there was something heavenly about the way he smelled. Not the tequila, of course, but the heady mixture of heat, soap and man.

Katie glided her fingers over his jaw, loving the rough texture and thinking that only two days ago she had wished for this very thing. To slip her hands over warm flesh, instead of cold gray stone. Sighing, she covered his body with a downy blanket that didn't quite reach his toes. "Just what am I going to do with you, Jorlan en Sarr?"

CHAPTER ELEVEN

JORLAN AWOKE SUDDENLY.

Sunlight streamed inside the chamber he occupied. He closed his eyes. Opened them. Squinted. Why was the light so cursed bright? Why did his head pound so sharply he thought it might explode? And why in the name of *Elliea* did his tongue feel dry and parched as if a tiny creature had crawled inside and died?

Was *he* dying, mayhap? Had he been ill?

Slowly, the details hazy, his head began to fill with memories, though several pieces of information remained impossibly out of reach. One bit of information, however, pounded in his mind: Katie's brothers were responsible for his torment!

Jorlan jerked upright, intending to collect his weapons and destroy all four of the cursed men who had given him "lick her." But the action made his vision swim and his stomach lurch. He eased back down.

"Lick her" was obviously a poison of some sort. There were many different types on his world and all were used for different reasons, but he was unfamiliar with the toxins of Katie's world. He suspected that the fiery concoction he'd consumed was not only used for incapacitating an enemy, but was also used as a truth serum.

Too well did he recall the many questions Katie's siblings had drilled at him.

"How long are you staying?"

"Why are you leaving?"

"What are your intentions toward Katie?"

Jorlan was unsure how he had responded, but thought mayhap one of his answers caused a battle. Recalling a well-placed jab, he fingered his lip. Aye, there was a definite soreness. He did not recall the exact details, but he knew the fight had been four against one. Who had won, he was unsure. While he had once taken on nine rebel soldiers and emerged the victor, Katie's brothers were a much more imposing force.

A sharp pain lanced through his head and Jorlan grimaced.

He had to get up, had to fight the sickness. There was much to do this day. He stumbled from his bed. The action caused his stomach to gurgle, twist and lurch. He fought it, but soon realized it was a losing battle and raced to the bathing chamber where he heaved into the sink.

After he'd emptied his stomach and scrubbed his mouth clean, he went in search of Katie. His steps were slow and careful as he uttered a prayer that she possessed some sort of antidote. If not, the pain in his stomach and head might kill him before the day ended.

He found her perched at the kitchen counter, flipping through her thick, yellow "phone book" and sipping green liquid from a mug. Even with his senses dulled from pain, she was a sight to behold. Sunlight poured through a nearby window, caressing her with an angelic glow, paying her the glorious tribute she deserved.

Beside her, a soft melody hummed from a magical black box. His first instinct was to attack, but then he noticed how her foot tapped in rhythm to the beat, and he remained in place. 'Twas like her talking "answering machine," he realized.

Today Katie wore short, tight *drocs* and a brown top held in place by thick straps. Though both garments fit her curves like a second skin, neither the top nor bottom garment was truly an alluring piece, yet on her they looked stunning. Breathtaking. He could have gazed upon her exquisite loveliness forever.

Which was strange, he thought, considering he'd judged her merely beautiful before. As he watched her chew on the end of a thin writing instrument, moving those lush lips up and down—mimicking an action he had often fantasized about in the last days—he decided he had the right of it now. The word *beautiful* did no justice to such ethereal perfection.

This woman possessed a splendor beyond any he'd ever known.

He must have made a sound, a groan of need, mayhap, because she swiveled and faced him.

"Jorlan! Good morning." Her gaze raked over him, and her expression clouded with concern. "Not feeling so well, huh?"

He scowled at the reminder. "I long to impale all four of your siblings onto a pike so that hundreds of hungry animals may gnaw upon their flesh. Mayhap then they will learn the proper respect for a warrior."

"You still have yet to teach me," she muttered. Then she flashed her teeth in a wide smile. "Call me morbid, but I like seeing you like this. You're not quite so intimidating."

"When have I ever intimidated you?"

"Oh, you have," she confessed. "More times than I care to admit. Now have a seat before you topple over. I'll get you some coffee and aspirin. They're miracle cures, I promise you. They saved my life every time I overindulged." She hopped to her feet.

Fast losing strength, he sank into the offered chair. "Did those devils once poison you, as well?"

"No." She chuckled, a sound that skipped along his senses with an almost physical pleasure. "I did it to myself."

"Why would you purposefully poison yourself?"

She poured black liquid inside a cup and handed it to him. With deft movements, she opened cabinet after cabinet, searching inside. "The first time, I was mostly curious and didn't know when to stop. The few times after that, I made the mistake of drinking on an empty stomach."

He rested his chin in his hand. "I had no idea you were such a masochist, *katya*."

She stopped and swung to face him, palms on hips. She was frowning. "Just where did you learn that word?"

"Many spans ago, a woman and her lover came to the garden and—"

"Never mind," Katie interjected. "I don't want to know." She threw open the last cabinet. "I'm going to kill Nick," she ground out.

"Not if I kill him first," Jorlan muttered darkly.

"Every time he comes over, he rearranges my cabinets so I can't find anything the next day. This time I'm going to double kick that man's family jewels until he's singing soprano. That ought to teach him."

Jorlan almost laughed. He did grin. The things this woman said could turn him inside out trying to understand, but for once he totally and completely grasped her meaning. And he was instantly glad he was not Nick James. A woman's wrath was one thing, but the wrath of Katie James was quite another.

"Wait!" she exclaimed. "I found it." She whipped a small white bottle from the bottom shelf. After popping the top, she shook two pink tablets onto her hand. "Here." Palm outstretched, she offered him the pills. "Swallow. Don't chew."

He weighed them in his hand, unsure how they could help him. With a shrug, he tossed each tablet into his mouth. He washed them down with a long gulp of coffee, almost gagging as the hot liquid scalded a path down his throat. Strawberry soda he liked; this he did not.

"Are you, too, trying to kill me?" He glared over at Katie.

She shrugged delicately. "Coffee is an acquired taste, I guess. I don't drink it often, but every once in a while I indulge."

Scowling, he wiped the remaining liquid from his mouth. She watched him, following the action of his hand with her gaze. When he stilled, she leaned over the counter and rested her elbows on the speckled surface. A dazed, dreamy look entered her eyes, as if she were lost in some sort of fantasy. Just what was she picturing in that mind of hers? Knowing Katie, she was probably imagining herself swimming in a giant tub of her green liquid. Or mayhap, like him, was she suddenly imagining naked bodies and heart-pounding kisses?

Jorlan's blood instantly kindled. They'd come close to coupling yestereve.

So close.

Two more minutes and he would have had her naked. Three more minutes and he would have been inside her. Four and he would have had her calling his name as wave after wave of pleasure hit her. He loved when she climaxed. When she'd experienced her pleasure that first time, he'd nearly spilled his seed, so intense had his delight been. He'd never witnessed anything quite so sensual.

Curse Nick James!

In the next instant, Katie shook her head, and her dreamy expression vanished. Jorlan wanted to rail at the heavens. Earnest now, she slid a single sheet of paper directly in front of him. "Look here," she said, oblivious to the riotous needs crashing through his body. Her fingertip brushed the side of his hand and he sucked in a breath. "I made a list of all the psychics in Texas. I've called most of them and crossed off the ones that seemed duplicitous. We have time to visit three, maybe four, then we have to go to work."

Only one day ago he would have snatched up the list and demanded they visit each location until they found exactly what he needed. Right now, however, he didn't want to think past bedding Katie (when did he *not* think about bedding her?) and making her his temporary life-mate. Bedding her would have to wait until they had enough time to enjoy each other to the fullest, for he knew now that he would settle for nothing less than long, leisurely loving.

The binding he could take care of now.

Just how would she respond? He watched her, trying to predict the outcome. Her hair cascaded down her back, thick and glossy, like a crown of brilliance reserved only for celestial creatures. Her expression was guarded. Slowly, so as not to alarm her, he pushed to his feet, stepped around the counter, and closed the distance between them. Positioned behind her, he clasped several tendrils of her hair to his nose, sniffed their floral essence, and caressed them over his cheek. His eyes closed in surrender. *"Katya?"*

"Hmm?" She leaned back against him.

"I would like you to go to Imperia with me."

"What?" Katie spun around to face him, all of a sudden at a loss for words.

"When we find a sorcerer, I want you to come with me to my homeland."

He said it so simply, as if it were the most natural thing in the world for her to hop across one galaxy to another. The idea tempted her. Exploring alien homes, eating alien food, and best of all, sleeping in an alien bed with Jorlan. Could she abandon her work, though, for such a vacation? "How long would you want me to stay?"

"However long you like." He propped his hip against the counter's edge, and pinned her with his cool blue stare. "Sorcerers abound in my homeland. When you are ready to depart, we will purchase an open vortex. 'Tis that simple."

"No, it's not that simple. I hate to bring this up, but what if…what if you turn back to stone while we're there?"

A muscle tightened in his jaw. "If you still cannot love me, we will return before the curse takes effect. Now, do you wish to go or not?"

"I don't know," she hedged.

"Would it help to know that you must wed me before you can travel with me?"

Her mouth dropped wide open, and her knees nearly collapsed. "Wed you? I thought marriages between a sorcerer and a mortal were forbidden."

"I am the son of a great-lord. I do what I please."

"So you're really and truly asking me to marry you?" She was smiling, a genuine, happy smile, but she just couldn't help herself. It didn't seem to matter that what he was suggesting was ridiculous, that they'd known each other so short a time, and that he could very possibly be using marriage as a means of getting what he wanted. Joy was traipsing through her at an alarming rate.

"My people would not accept you if you were not my life-mate, so aye, I am really and truly asking you to marry me. For a time," he added.

For a time. The words echoed inside her mind, destroying her elation bit by bit.

"I must warn you," he said, almost as an afterthought, "that I am unsure of the time difference between our worlds."

"What do you mean?"

"I suspect time passes more quickly here," he explained, "but how much more quickly, I know not."

"So I could visit Imperia for five days, but when I return, five hundred years could have passed here?"

His jaw tensed, and she knew he didn't want to answer, but he did anyway. "That is correct. Only one sorcerer has the power to manipulate time. My brother, Percen, the Druinn high priest. Yet he would never do anything to help me."

Probabilities and possibilities drifted beneath her thoughts. If she chose to go with him, she could definitely return to Earth, but the Earth she knew might be very different from the Earth she left behind. She might never see Nick's mischievous grin. Never feel the warmth of Erik and Denver's hugs. Never again know the comforting haze of Gray's presence. Or hear Brian's husky laugh over the phone. All to stay with Jorlan *for a time*.

"I'm sorry," she told him, casting her gaze to his chest. She didn't want to see his eyes, didn't want to see whether they darkened with disappointment or froze with indifference as she declined. "I can't marry you, and I can't go with you. My family is here."

He nodded briskly, as if he understood what motivated her, but didn't like it. "I will give you time to think on it."

Now her gaze snapped to his. "I don't need time. I just gave you my answer."

"That answer is not accepted. You need more time, and I am willing to give it to you."

Part of her wanted to chuckle; part of her wanted

to cry. Lord, this was hard, so very hard. Why did saying no have to be this difficult? She knew beyond a doubt that she was staying here, where she belonged. She knew, too, that he would go on without her and feel no remorse. Perhaps that was what hurt the most.

Damn it! Why couldn't he have been the domineering chauvinist she'd first thought him? But nooo. He turned out to be so much more than a dictatorial tyrant. He turned out to be a Prince Charming. Beneath his "women are subservient" views beat the heart of a mighty yet gentle man whose touch melted her reservations and whose determination was heartening. No, she might not trust him, but she still desired him.

She had to change the subject before she succumbed to tears. "Look, I'm going on my jog—that's a type of exercise where you run a far length," she explained at his confused expression. She *needed* to jog. "While I'm gone, you can change into your new clothes. Yesterday I bought you a pair of pants, some shirts, shoes, and, uh, some underwear. When I get back, we'll visit the locations on my list."

"I must insist I jog with you."

At first, she wanted to refuse him. Then she realized that getting oxygen to his brain might actually do him some good. She found his new jogging shoes and handed them to him. "Sure you can keep up? I run every morning, and you're battling a mighty hangover."

"I will do more than keep up, *katya*, I will leave you far behind."

He would, would he? His confidence helped her forget her sadness. Too, her competitive nature sprang to life. "Why don't you prove it, then?"

"Always you demand proof. Well, this proof I will derive much pleasure in giving, for I long to see the expression on your face when the jog ends and you realize I have passed you. Twice." With that, he pulled on his shoes and led her out the door.

The race was on.

Twenty minutes ticked by, and she held her own. They didn't speak, so absorbed were they in their competition. They ran down a zigzag path a mile from her house. The path circled Earlywine Park and was designated specifically for runners. All around them the trees were radiant with shades of brown and green, and here and there pink-tipped flowers bloomed prettily. Twigs snapped beneath their pounding shoes. Dew kissed the air.

Another five minutes passed under the strenuous pace. Never slowing, Jorlan removed his shirt and draped it over his shoulders. She opened her mouth to complain, but the words froze in her throat. His deeply tanned, muscled chest was glazed with a sheen of sweat, and beads of the liquid were dripping along the ridges of his abdomen. The sight distracted her. She stumbled. Chuckling, he increased his speed and moved ahead of her. Katie glared at his back. He'd done that on purpose, the cheater.

By now, her muscles were burning with every step, but she too quickened her steps until she caught up with him. Another ten minutes passed. She was tiring, but didn't slow. Jorlan showed no signs of slowing, either, damn him.

"Are we going to run forever?" she snapped, huffing and hating herself for it.

"I can," was his casual reply.

"Well, so can I," she growled and called forth every ounce of stamina she possessed. This man was *not* going to beat her!

But damn it all, there had to be a way to end this.

An idea immediately formed, and she wasn't surprised by the speed with which her mind was working. With all the oxygen pumping through her, she could have calculated the atomic mass of an elephant while devising a plan to end world hunger.

"Race you to the house. Last one there has toilet duty." With that, she took off full speed ahead.

He tried to pass her left side, but she veered in front of him, blocking his way. He moved to the right, but she had been anticipating the action and swerved to cut him off once again. Katie beat him to the door by half a second and nearly tripped over the newspaper lying on her porch. She managed to catch herself in time. "Ha! I won." The words left her throat on short, choppy gasps of air. She would have laughed in his face, but her chest felt like a volcano churning with lava.

"You did not play fair, *katya*." He sounded winded.

"Of course I didn't play fair, Jorlan. Where's the fun in that?"

He opened his mouth to reply, but a car eased up her driveway, diverting his attention. Her alien immediately mutated into I-will-save-you superhero mode. Only when the car parked behind her truck and Gray emerged from the driver's seat did Jorlan relax. Her brother, however, looked stony and hard. A little hungover, but ready for battle all the same.

Katie's smile of welcome evaporated. "Gray? Is everything all right?"

He ignored her. Another man exited the car, and Gray spoke to him in hushed, angry tones. The man was an inch or two shorter than Gray, which put him only a bit taller than Katie. He had dark-brown hair and big puppy-dog eyes. Women probably went crazy for him. Had Katie met him a day ago, she might have gone crazy for him, too—at least for the first date. Now her thoughts were consumed with the warrior beside her.

Gray moved to the porch. He didn't make any introductions. He got straight to the point. "I want to talk to you about last night, about some things Jorlan said to me and the boys."

Though her brother was speaking to her, he was watching Jorlan. Katie gazed first at one man, then the other. Jorlan had his arms crossed over his chest; his eyes were narrowed to tiny slits; and his nostrils were flared. They were in some sort of high noon showdown.

"He's leaving you in two weeks," Gray continued.

"I know." Her shoulders sagged with relief. For a minute, she'd thought Gray meant to tell her Jorlan had confessed he was from another planet. "Now that that's settled, you have exactly five seconds to apologize for your behavior," she said, her tone sugary sweet, "or I'm going to snap your neck like a twig."

The handsome stranger at Gray's side laughed. It was the first sound he had made during the entire exchange. "You said she was spunky, Gray," the man said, still laughing. "You didn't say she was homicidal."

Gray decided then to make the proper introductions. "Katie, Jorlan, this is Steve Harris. Steve, this is my sister Katie and her friend, Jorlan. He's a romance cover model." His disgust over that fact lingered long after his words.

This was Steve? Katie thought, surprised.

This was Steve? Jorlan thought darkly. The man Katie's brothers wanted her to wed?

"Nice to meet you," Steve told them.

"You, too." Katie hadn't quite managed to close her mouth yet.

Seething, Jorlan remained silent, though the if-you-touch-her-you-will-die glare he wore said plenty. Just in case Steve did not get the hint, he draped a possessive hand around Katie's waist.

Steve didn't even try to shake her hand in greeting.

"I can't believe you're so calm about this." Gray raked a hand through his hair. "Do you never follow advice, Katie? What am I always telling you?"

"Don't talk to strangers."

"Not that."

"Buckle up or die."

"Not that, either."

"Carry Mace—"

"That you should never spend time with a man who won't stick around."

Katie placed her hands on his shoulders, leaned up, and kissed her brother on the cheek. "I love you, too, Gray. Now get out of here. I've got things to do."

"We're not finished with this conversation." He gazed over her shoulder and pinned Jorlan with an expectant stare. "I'll talk to you later."

Her alien nodded stiffly.

"No, you will not talk to him later," she called.

But Gray didn't hear her. He and Steve had already piled into their car and were racing away.

Jorlan's palms curled around her forearm, tight and menacing. He swung her around. "You will not see that man again."

"My brother?"

"Nay, the other."

What was this? A moment of jealousy? She studied him, watching, gauging. Oh, yes. This gorgeous barbarian was indeed jealous. He fairly seethed with it. Katie entertained a flicker of delight and had to hide her smile. He deserved this after what he had put her through with the redhead. "And what are you going to do to me if I *do* see him?"

The corner of his eye twitched. "Do you truly wish to know the answer to that?"

"Absolutely." Some of her smile peeked through.

Slowly, desire eclipsed his anger. He gave her that cocky look of his that said he knew exactly how to make a woman's punishment pleasurable. "I will—" He paused, as if searching for just the right method of correction.

"Spank me?" she offered helpfully.

He gave a stiff shake of his head.

She tried again. "Douse my naked body with honey?"

His eyes ignited with blue fire. "Nay. I'll prove your desire for me wherever we happen to be, whoever happens to be around us."

"If you're so tough, why don't you just try it?" The

words slipped out before she had time to think about them. She had just issued a sexually charged challenge to a fierce competitor, a man who did not like to lose.

"Do you provoke me?" he said softly. "I shall. I shall indeed."

CHAPTER TWELVE

THREE DAYS AND twelve psychics later, Katie and Jorlan had developed a routine.

Morning: jog, visit psychics.

Afternoon: work at the Victorian.

Evening: talk, watch television.

Twilight: sleep apart and fantasize.

Though his body and mind screamed that he at last tup her, that his time was quickly running out, Jorlan hadn't kissed Katie, hadn't touched her, or whispered erotic words to her. Nay, he was subtly, through pleasantries and courtesies, trying to win her love and convince her to wed him. So far, he had failed. In fact, his solicitous manner had had the opposite effect on Katie, and it seemed as if she retreated a bit more from him each day. The continued failure, both with Katie and with the psychics, was causing his desperation to grow.

Only ten days remained. Ten short days until the curse claimed him once more.

Could he afford to lose another day to her stubbornness? More and more he felt the coldness of stone running through his blood, trying to freeze him where he stood. He had to make Katie love him. Had to force her to fall by whatever means necessary. He couldn't tolerate failure much longer. Soon. He had to win her soon.

But what could he try that he had not already tried?

He'd pursued her sexually, had made her jealous, had shared his past with her, had given her time, and when all of that failed, had pursued her friendship, trying to prove to her that he truly did care for her and desired her happiness. Yet, his efforts had gotten him nothing but lost time.

Curse her. Did she not understand the great honor he was paying her by offering to make her his temporary life-mate? Nay, she did not! With her "No, I will not wed you" and her "You must obey my rules," the woman was quickly eradicating his legendary control. She should know him well enough by now to know that he *would* convince her to come with him, that she *would* give him her heart, and that she *would* belong to him for however long he wanted to keep her.

He would accept nothing less than absolute compliance from her.

If only this day did not seem destined for failure, as well.

After a minor accident involving Katie's transportation and a stationary pole, six jaunts into nonmagical establishments and a bout of stomach sickness caused, Jorlan was sure, by a slab of greasy food Katie referred to as pizza, he was not in a good mood. Plus, the new clothing he wore—the item Katie called underwear— was nigh smashing his man parts.

"Well, that's all of them," Katie said, brushing her hands together once, twice.

They stood outside The Knowing Palm, a small

building that supposedly housed one of the greatest male psychics ever to live. *Ever to live in a delusional world of his own creation, mayhap.* Birds soared high above him, circling and searching for food. The hot sun beat down. A soft wind danced about, carrying a gentle scent, like flowers and rain that reminded him of Katie.

"We've wasted our morning in one shop or another." Katie shielded her eyes with her hand. "We've got work to do, so let's head over to the Victorian. I'll put together another list tonight. The Internet is sure to have more names, and we can visit one or two over the weekend. If they're not too far," she added.

He paid her speech no heed. "We have been to six places, *katya,* yet there were seven left on your list."

Her gaze flicked away guiltily. "We're not going to the seventh."

"Why not?"

"It'll take us four hours to get there and four hours to get back."

"So?"

"So, that's hell on the butt, and I'm not doing it."

"I shall massage away any discomfort you acquire."

She crossed her hands over her chest. "I have to work in order to live, Jorlan, because when I work, I make money and that money pays for my food and shelter. I've gotten behind since you entered my life. I'm not making that drive."

He simply stared at her.

She bared her teeth in a scowl. "Contrary to what you might think, I do not speak to hear my own voice.

I said we could visit more places over the weekend, and we will."

"I do not wish to wait. I will take your transportation and drive myself."

"No. No. No!" Katie fisted her hands on her hips and stood her ground. She wasn't giving in on this and that was final. No way in hell did she want to take an eight-hour road trip. They'd been in and out of the car all morning, and besides that, she really *did* have to work.

But that isn't why you don't want to go. The truth danced within her mind, and Katie stiffened. She hadn't wanted to visit any psychics today. And she more specifically didn't want to visit this next one, not because of work or a sore butt, but because she feared success. If they found someone who could take Jorlan home, he'd leave her sooner rather than later.

Didn't he realize that she wanted him to stay here with her a while longer?

No, he didn't realize, because he was moving toward her with intent shining in his eyes. She backed up. He continued to advance. Then he was on her. Surprisingly, he didn't haul her into the truck, and demand she drive him to Lubbock. He simply reached inside her beige short pockets—an innocent touch that caused fireworks to explode between her legs because it was the first touch he'd given her in three days, the jerk—and pulled out the truck ignition key.

Her body screamed *find more keys!* But she could tell by the irritated look etching Jorlan's face that assaulting her person, pleasurably or otherwise, was not his intent. He turned away. "I will visit this location, and then I will return to you."

In a flash she pictured him stranded on some isolated road, or worse, a populated town demanding everyone obey his every command. Someone would take offense, there would be a fight, Jorlan would win (he had a spatula, after all) and the other person would die. Then Jorlan would be hauled away to jail, where he would await trial. The government would find out that he was from another planet and all hell would break loose.

She couldn't let that happen.

Katie raced behind him, swiped out her foot and tripped him. He crashed onto the hard ground, falling like a condemned home. She moved quickly, rushing to his hands and snatching the key. When she tried to dart out of reach, he latched on to her ankle. The next thing she knew, she was lying flat on her stomach and trying to suck in air.

Jorlan flipped her over, pried the key from her Kung Fu grip and smiled.

Smiled!

She used her hands to push herself upright and watched him practically skip to the truck.

"Wait!" She jolted after him, spitting gravel along the way. She latched on to his arm. "Let's compromise about this."

"I have been a warrior my entire life. I know nothing of compromise."

With those ominous words ringing in her ears, he shook off her hold and strode to the driver's side door of her truck. She hopped in front of the vehicle, arms splayed wide. "You compromised about the weapons, didn't you? You compromised about sleeping on my floor instead of my bed." She expected him to pick her up and carry her to the side of the road, effectively moving her out of his way.

He didn't. He remained beside the open door. "If you are concerned about so long a drive," he said, his tone deceptively soft, "we will not come back until the new dawning."

"No. Absolutely not. I've lost enough time because of you."

"Then I will see you later." He settled himself inside the cab.

"You don't know which way to go." Ha! That should stop him.

The corners of his lips rose in another smug smile. "You have used this map all these many days." He held up the booklet in question. "Think you I cannot do the same?"

"You don't know the names of the highways, and you can't read my language. Besides that, I'll turn you in to the police for stealing my car."

He sighed. "Much do I regret the use of force, *katya*."

His eyes were darkened, and she paused. "You haven't used any force," she said cautiously.

"But I am going to."

Before she had time to blink, he was out of the car and closing the distance between them. With only minimal protest on her part, he scooped her up into his arms. She could have struggled or fought him harder, but she didn't want to hurt him. Without a word, he dumped her into the passenger seat and settled himself behind the wheel.

"Now you will go with me," he said confidently.

Katie made a grab for the key. He easily evaded her, then shoved the jagged metal into the ignition and started pushing pedals. Jerk. Stop. Jerk. Stop. A cold sweat broke over her, and she scooted to his side, trying to take control of the wheel.

He held fast.

If she saw one car, even one, headed toward them, she was going to shove Jorlan out the driver-side door—no matter how many injuries he would sustain. Or, maybe she'd press his carotid artery until he passed out. For now, they were alone on the road and she had time to gently make him rethink this.

"You're giving me whiplash," she shouted.

Unconcerned by her supposed pain, he continued on.

"Do you want to kill us both? If you keep this up, you're going to. And you're going to ruin my truck! This trip is ridiculous. We don't even have a change of clothes. We'll have to come back tonight and then my butt will really hurt and you'll be sorry because I'll take it out on you. I have too much work to do on the house. I'm on the clock, you big jackass, and you're going to pay me for my time."

"Are you trying to make me wish I'd cut off my ears and left them behind?" he growled, still not sparing her a glance.

"Yes!"

He was gripping the steering wheel so tightly his knuckles had long since turned white. The truck inched along the road, doing no more than five miles per hour.

"I could walk faster than this, grandpa."

A muscle ticked in his jaw, and the beleaguered expression on his face was almost comical. "You will clamp your lips together, *katya*, or I will do it for you."

"Then do it for me. I'm not shutting up. And know this. If you try and make me stay silent, there will be no one who can tell you that you're going the *wrong freaking way!*" Before he could respond, she leaned forward and jerked the volume on the radio to full blast. Meredith Brooks belted out "Bitch."

The word instantly hit home, and Katie cringed. He didn't deserve this. He just wanted to go home. Jorlan must think she suffered from permanent PMS. Maybe that was why he hadn't touched her these last few days. He was afraid she'd attack and kill him in his sleep. Sighing, she turned down the radio. "Pull over," she told him.

"Nay." The word emerged like the bark of a caged animal.

"Pull over. I'll drive us there."

His chin snapped around. He faced her hopefully. "You speak true?"

"Yes, damn it. Now pull over."

He would have stopped right there in the middle of the road, so great was his relief. She pointed to the side. "Don't stop here. Stop over there." Once at a halt, they quickly switched places.

"You really owe me for this," she muttered.

"I can very easily pay you once we arrive. I need only a bed and five minutes of your time." The teasing sparkle was back in his eyes, and only then did she realize how much she'd missed it.

"Five minutes?"

"Nay. I have changed my mind." His lips twitched. "I only need two."

Katie shook her head and turned them in the right direction. "You're incorrigible, you know that?"

"Aye. I know."

And she liked him that way.

They drove in silence for about twenty miles, the soft hum of the radio the only noise. Katie felt Jorlan's body heat, keeping her mind in the gutter. Perhaps she was, by nature, more sensual than she'd realized. Or perhaps she was simply carnally addicted to Jorlan, because her brain began to weave ribbons of fantasy through her mind. She saw it all so clearly. Jorlan would scoot closer beside her and trail his hand up her thigh, making her shiver and ache for more. His eyes would devour her as he whispered a provocation she could not ignore. *I dare you to experience your ultimate pleasure, katya.* And she would. Oh, she would. The hot tips of his fingers would push aside her panties and slip easily inside. He would stroke her then, first with leisurely slowness, like a deliberate brush of velvet across steel, then with eager swiftness.

Perhaps he would take his fingers from her and place them in his mouth, as if he couldn't live another moment without knowing the taste of her.

"Katie?"

The voice was real, not part of her fantasy, and she jolted into awareness. "What!"

"Do you purposefully drive like this?"

"Oh, God!" Amid honks and flashing middle fingers, she jerked the truck off the median and into the proper lane. She took a moment to collect her wits, slow her breathing and control her shaking—shaking that had nothing to do with bad driving. Lord, she wanted to explore his body, wanted to allow him to explore hers. She wanted to feel the hard ripples of his muscles, the smooth silkiness of his skin.

"What were you thinking about?" he asked.

Swallowing hard, she forced her attention to remain on the road. "I just can't believe we're doing this. Were you this impulsive at home?"

"Nay." He offered no more information. "What is this place like we are going?"

"Pretty much the same as Dallas." She had to keep him talking, had to keep herself distracted. "You know, you've told me about your family, but nothing really substantial about your world. What are the differences between Imperia and Earth, besides the fact that all of your women are slaves?"

He took exception to that. "Women are not slaves on Imperia. They are merely the responsibility of their men."

She smiled at his set look. "There's a difference?"

"Aye. A slave must obey *his* or her master at all times." He emphasized male slave to the point that the word *his* echoed in her ears long after he'd spoken. "They have no rights of their own. Ever. But a woman under a man's protection is allowed to voice her opinion."

"As long as her opinion isn't different from her man's, right?"

"Not in public, nay."

"Then there is no difference between a slave and a protected woman."

He sat up straighter in his seat, a clear indication he didn't like the direction of her thoughts. "Do you purposely misunderstand? A woman is respected. Revered, even. A slave is nothing more than a possession, to be discarded at will."

"Discarded? Just what the hell does that mean?"

"Just that the slave may be given or sold to another. I did not say I applauded the practice. Just that 'tis the way it is done. You will be happy to know I am beginning to see that not all women should be or need be taken care of."

Before she could reply to such a wonderful statement, the truck swirled and a loud "pop" rang out. Heart racing, Katie quickly pulled over to the side of the road.

"What is wrong?" Jorlan demanded.

"Flat tire, I think."

That's exactly what it was. A little less than forty minutes later, she had the tire changed. She could have done it in half the time if Jorlan had stayed inside the truck as she'd asked him to. But *noooo*. The barbarian had to stand over her shoulder, offering his opinion about everything!

"Are you sure that goes there?" he had asked. "I would put it here."

"I'm sure."

"Are you positive the truck will not flip over? That metal object is holding it at an incline. I would raise the truck from the middle."

"I'm sure you would."

"Are you turning the—"

"I'm sure! I'm sure! I'm sure!"

He began chanting something under his breath.

The flat tire exploded.

A strong blast of air and rubber sent her reeling backward. Jorlan loomed over her. He didn't look concerned for her, though. No, he was frowning down at the slain tire as if it were deadly poison.

"What did you do?" Katie demanded, jumping to her feet. Her pulse had yet to slow.

"A spell," he grudgingly admitted. "I'd hoped to help you."

"For God's sake, never help me again!"

"Not even to wipe the black soot from your face?"

"Not even then!" Her nerves were on edge when they got back on the road a short while later. She was dirty and sweaty and hungry. Worse, she was dismayed. Katie didn't like that Jorlan had watched her do so unfeminine a task. What man desired a woman who could beat him at sports, change her own tire, and kick his ass in a fight? No one, that's who. Plenty of men thought of her as "just one of the boys." She didn't want Jorlan to think of her that way, too, which was a bit contradictory, she supposed, since she wanted him to see her as independent and capable.

He was just so damn sexy, so masculine, and that masculinity needed a totally feminine counterpart. Her hands clenched. She'd just bet Jorlan preferred short, dark-haired women who wore dresses and lace and spoke with soft, angelic voices.

Everything she was not.

He didn't want her anymore, she finally admitted. That he hadn't touched her for three days was telling enough, but she'd continued to hope she was mistaken. If only he'd attempted to seduce her once in the last three days. Just once. She wouldn't feel so...forgotten. Damn him, anyway. Somewhere out there was a man—besides Jorlan—who would accept who she was. This man would play basketball with her, take her to football games. And every moment they spent together, he would look at her as if she were the most beautiful, feminine creation God had ever produced. Not the way her brothers looked at her, but—

Oh, no! Her brothers. She almost groaned. Her family worried more than most, and she knew they would send out a search party if they discovered her truck gone all night long.

"Hand me the phone in the glove box," she told Jorlan. Exasperation dripped from her tone.

"What is this glove box?"

She pointed.

"Ask nicely."

They were back to that again, were they? Frowning, she dug the phone from the compartment herself and punched Erik's private number. He was the most easygoing of the group, and would probably ask fewer questions.

He answered after the third ring. "James."

"I'll be in Lubbock for the night." She didn't waste any time.

"What for?" Erik replied.

"Just felt like getting out of town." *I'm becoming a compulsive liar,* she thought darkly, and it's all Jorlan's fault.

"What for?" her brother asked again.

"I needed a break."

"You going by yourself?"

"No."

"Well? Who are you going with?"

She paused. Then offered simply, "Jorlan." Before Erik could ask any more questions, she said, "Listen, I better go. Aren't you always warning me about the dangers of driving while talking on the phone?"

"All right, all right. Hint taken." His deep, rich chuckle rang in her ear. "Lubbock, you said?"

"Yeah." An eighteen-wheeler whizzed beside them. The driver blew his horn and waved. Katie ignored him. "I'll be fine, so no worries."

"Put Jorlan on the phone for a minute."

"I can barely hear you," she said, then made static noises. "Must—be—" Grinning, she pressed End and the line went dead. Her grin only grew broader as she pictured Erik sputtering into his phone.

A short while later she realized they were running out of gas. Her smile sloped to a scowl. She blamed Jorlan for this newest development. If he hadn't insisted on this trip, a trip she hadn't planned or packed for, she would have been safely ensconced inside the Victorian, not worrying about low octane.

By the time they reached the nearest gas station, the truck was puttering on its last burst of energy. Glaring at Jorlan, she filled up the truck and tallied up another thirty-five-dollar expense. Katie strode inside, gathered up a few necessary items and approached the register. Jorlan owed her big-time for this, and he *would* pay—but not with cash.

A few minutes later, they were once again eating up the miles.

THE FOUR-HOUR TRIP TO Lubbock took them a little over seven, and the sun had long since set when they finally passed the Welcome sign. Katie's rear end hurt, but surprisingly, her bad mood had evaporated. Being with Jorlan gave her a sense of joy that far surpassed any negative feelings.

Right now, raindrops were hurling themselves onto the truck, creating several rivers that pooled together at the bottom of the windshield. As she peered past the wipers making perfect arches on the glass and listened to the storm billow in every direction, she maneuvered the truck into a motel parking lot. Not long after, she and Jorlan were the temporary residents of room number 314.

"For dinner, let's go to a restaurant. I'm sick of fast food," she told him, heading back to the truck.

He fell into step beside her. "What of the psychic?"

"Closed. We'll have to wait until tomorrow morning."

"With you 'tis always tomorrow." He sighed.

They had dinner at Blue Waters, a nearby seafood restaurant. Jorlan devoured his crab cakes with unfettered delight. By the time they stepped inside their hotel room, the moon had crested and slowly dripped a golden glow onto night's shadows.

The first thing Jorlan did was pick up the TV control and start pushing buttons. "What does this do?" he asked. In the next instant, images flooded the small black screen. Of course, her alien didn't try to hack the television to bits as he had her answering machine. Why would he? Old reruns of *Baywatch* were playing—a boob marathon. Watching the show with an intense devotion that did the male species proud, he settled atop the bed, stomach down, elbows propped against his chin.

Before Katie could relax as well, a little girl's screams of "That's my hamburger" seeped through the walls. The high-pitched words were shouted over and over again, then combined with another, more annoying voice, this one shouting, "Mom, Carrie isn't sharing." Soon a sharp ache was pounding in Katie's temples.

"I'm going out," she said. It was either that or stomp next door with muzzles and a stun gun.

Jorlan didn't spare her a glance. "I will go with you." His tone lacked conviction.

"Are you sure you can tear yourself away?" she said dryly. "I'm going to Cahoots—a bar where people drink 'lick her.' There'll be loud music and rowdy people and no women in swimsuits."

"You will not go to this place alone. I will go. Or—" Now he leveled a gaze at her, his eyes suddenly sparking with passion. "Or we could stay inside this chamber. In this bed." He eased to his feet and slowly approached her. "I have tried to give you time, *katya,* but that has not worked for me. Why do I not show you all that you will miss do you not wed me?"

She didn't retreat. No, she stepped closer as relief and happiness pounded through her. He still wanted her! And Lord, she still wanted him. Without another word, their lips met. On a moan, his tongue swept inside her mouth, hot and demanding. Jorlan cupped her breasts in his hands. Pure ecstasy rocked along her body.

"I want to see you," he whispered. He tugged at the straps of her tank top.

"I want to see you, too." She pulled his gray T-shirt from his jeans, and then...

"Mom! Carrie took my shoes." The little girl's voice once again penetrated the walls. "Give those back, butthead. Mom! Make her give me back my shoes."

"Wait." Breath ragged, Katie disengaged from Jorlan. Her first time was not going to be inside a rented room while the devil's spawn played nearby. "We have to stop."

Something dark glimmered in his eyes, eclipsing his passion. "If this is your way to punish me, *katya,* because I forced you to come here, you chose wisely."

His words irritated her enough that she didn't correct him. "If you're a good boy for the rest of our trip, I'll let you kiss me when we get home." She meant it as a rebuke, but realized then that she wanted it to be an invitation.

"Let us go before I no longer care that you have said nay." Movements clipped, body stiff, he adjusted his "weapons."

Her nerve endings were still on fire, and if she didn't leave soon, she was going to forget her reasons for ending their embrace. "Leave the spatula here, okay? Other people might not understand the reasons you carry it."

Of course, he paid no attention to her warning and brought the stupid thing.

Cahoots was a large bar and club situated on the edge of town. Tumultuous rock music assaulted her ears as she and Jorlan stepped inside and meandered across thin, black carpet in search of a table. All around them, bodies gyrated to the fast-paced beat. Cigarette smoke created a thick, choking cloud that enveloped the dancers like a ghostly hand. Katie wanted to play pool, but all the tables were currently occupied.

Jorlan's expression was pained and stoic, though he seemed a bit shocked by the intimate way couples were dancing. They settled inside a booth. Katie set the empty beer bottles onto the nook behind them, clearing the table surface. Then, with a sigh, she settled in her seat and simply absorbed the atmosphere.

"What do you think?" she shouted over the music a short time later.

His nose wrinkled. "'Tis…interesting."

Her lips twitched, but she managed to subdue her grin. "Wanna drink?"

He gave a single shake of his head.

"Well, I do. I'll be right back." Katie worked her way to the bar. By the time she reached the shiny mahogany wood, Jorlan was beside her. Two bartenders were on duty, mixing drinks and popping beer caps. A woman stood off in the corner drying glasses; her bright orange nail polish gleamed from the overhead lighting. Her hair was a deep, rich purple. She had a cigarette clamped between her pink, glittery lips; her eyebrow was pierced, and she had a row of cowboy hat tattoos down her right arm.

Katie purchased rum-and-Coke for herself and a 7-Up for Jorlan, knowing he wanted nothing to do with "lick her" unless it involved a tub full of naked women. Her fingers tightened on the glass at the thought of him with other women. She practically shoved the drink at him. "Here."

One of the male bartenders gave Jorlan a twice over, his eyes growing wide. "Hey, aren't you—holy shit. I can't believe this. Man, you're like Mike Calman, the best lineman ever to play for the Wyoming Wranglers. Will you sign this for me?" He slid a napkin over the bar surface.

At the words *Mike Calman* several people turned and stared at Jorlan. An avid sports fan, Katie had watched Mike Calman lead his team to several major victories over the last two years, and she didn't think Jorlan looked anything like the famed football star. Within moments, however, an entire group was surrounding him, asking him questions like, "Where's your Super Bowl ring?" "Who's going to replace Coach Garedy?" "Are you thinking of playing for the Cowboys?"

Katie had no idea how Jorlan answered, but whatever he said, the people were charmed. To those who bothered to spare her a glance, she tried to explain Jorlan wasn't a professional football player, but her protests were laughed off. Finally, she'd had enough and she tugged on his arm. "Let's go back to the table, Mikey."

He nodded, albeit reluctantly.

She was just turning back to her table when, out of the corner of her eye, she saw the purple-haired woman behind the bar approaching. Her eyes were filled with purpose, and not even her thick, spiky mascara could mask it.

"Anything I can help you with, sugar?" she asked

Jorlan. "We don't get many professional ballplayers in here, but I'm sure I can come up with something to keep you entertained."

Liberated women were a nuisance, Katie decided. "Mr. Calman here just wants to relax. In private."

The woman kept her attention on Jorlan as her gaze darkened with disappointment. Somehow, she was still able to convey hot, sexual interest. "You sure, sugar? I'm real good with…balls."

"What do you have in mind?" he asked.

Katie stiffened. How dare he! She'd brought him to Lubbock out of the goodness of her heart. He owed her a little consideration. And coming on to a starstruck bartender was not her idea of consideration.

"I'm Rinnie, by the way, and a big fan. I swear on the Lone Star Flag that I've never seen a lineman with more power." She squeezed his bicep for emphasis. "Do you mind if I show you off upstairs? The girls are gonna want to meet you."

"I do not mind, nay."

"I didn't know you had an accent. It's so cute." Rinnie grinned, a wide grin that spread from ear to ear and revealed slightly crooked, yet utterly endearing front teeth. "Come on. I'll introduce you to some people. Upstairs is for our VIPs and you, Mike Calman, are definitely VIP. Very Irresistibly Packaged."

So upstairs they went, though from the frown Rinnie shot her, Katie knew she wasn't welcome. Katie's teeth ground together with every step. There was a crowd of people, an equal mix of men and women, situated in one large room, talking and laughing. The entire area looked more like a restaurant than a bar.

Small, round tables were situated around a tantalizing buffet of enchiladas, rice, cheese sauce and chips. Katie's mouth watered, but she made no move to eat. She was too busy guarding her VIP. Not that her death-ray glare was doing any good. Like a pack of bees, everything female swarmed around Jorlan as if he were a pot full of honey and they had to eat him or die.

Rinnie made the introductions. "Hey, everybody. I'm sure you know who this gorgeous man is, so I won't bother introducing him. Just show him a real good time, you hear, so he'll come back and visit us." She leaned into Jorlan. "You let me know if you need anything, anything at all. I'll just be downstairs."

All of a sudden everyone wanted a piece of Mike Calman.

For the next hour, Jorlan talked and laughed with everyone but Katie, soaking up attention as if it was oxygen he needed for life support. Fuming, Katie plopped into a chair that was propped against the back wall. Every once in a while a brave man approached her and flirted, but her snappy retorts combined with the prepare-to-die glares Jorlan sent them caused each man to make a hasty retreat. Once she found herself alone again, Jorlan would turn back to whatever woman he was flirting with and ignore her.

She wasn't sure exactly what he was doing. Teaching her a lesson, perhaps, for ending their kiss too soon? The moral being that if she didn't snatch him up, someone else would? Oh, yes, that was exactly what he was doing, she realized as she looked, *really* looked into his eyes. They were glazed with hard-edged determination, not enjoyment. Lord, how many times had she watched her brothers do the same thing to their women?

Well, *she* could teach Jorlan a lesson. It was about time he learned that Katie James knew how to play the Dating Game! Unfortunately, she had run most of the men out of the room, so her choices were limited. She motioned a short, round man over with an I'm-very-limber smile.

He eagerly joined her.

Jorlan watched Katie interact with the newcomer; she smiled and laughed and acted as if she'd been lost in a desert for an entire span and the chubby man could provide her with water. Black fury surged within him so potently he craved the long, sharp length of his talon. He saw the man latch on to her shoulder—a man who would die if he didn't remove the offending appendage immediately.

Katie said something to the marked-for-death man. Plump cheeks turning red, he huffily marched away.

Jorlan relaxed. Better. Much better. By her own doing, Katie belonged to him. She'd kissed him. Allowed him to sleep next to her bed. She'd even listened while he spoke of his family. No other man was allowed to touch this woman who was to be his life-mate and live.

Something brushed his jaw. He half turned his attention from Katie and frowned. The woman at his side was persistent, tracing her fingertip over his face. She'd offered him the use of her bed three times already, and had even slipped a key inside his pocket. He muttered something quick and impersonal in her direction, then once again went back to fully watching Katie. She was scowling, but she was alone.

Just then, someone thrust a beer bottle into Katie's hand. She set aside her empty rum-and-Coke glass. She wasn't thirsty, but as she continued to cast covert glances in Jorlan's direction, she pictured herself in a boxing ring with each woman present and drank. Deeply. She'd never enjoyed the taste of beer, but before she realized what she'd done, she had consumed four bottles.

A waitress arrived with a tray of Jell-O shots and nachos. "In honor of Mike," she said. Cheers circulated throughout the room and Katie found herself having one shot, then another without giving the nachos a second glance. Jorlan, she noticed, didn't even sip his water. He was too busy watching her. Had he learned his lesson? Not quite well enough, was her guess. Arching one brow, she looked over at him and raised her glass in a silent salute, a salute that said *bite me*. A leggy brunette, who was wearing a short spandex skirt and minitop, playfully jumped onto his lap.

Who did he think he was, anyway? Only an hour ago he'd tried to get into *her* pants. Only three days ago—or was it four?—anyway, he'd asked *her* to marry him. She'd told him no. Big deal. That didn't mean he had the right to flirt with other women.

Before she knew it, Katie had worked up a good steam.

She jackknifed to her feet and propelled over to the snuggly couple. She pointed to the woman with a shaky finger. When had her hands gotten shaky? "Look here," she shouted. The noise level tapered to quiet. "The last woman who made a play for him ended up in the hospital."

"Why?" the woman asked with a little, tinkering laugh. Obviously she thought Katie was joking. She flipped her main of glossy hair over her shoulder. "Did he lick her to death?"

Katie's eyes narrowed. "No. I broke every bone in her body and ate her organs for breakfast." She said it with a lethal seriousness thrummed with icy determination.

The brunette jumped up as though Jorlan had suddenly mutated into nuclear waste.

"Now let's dance," Katie commanded Jorlan.

A wicked gleam entered his eyes, and he stood, holding out his hand to her. She took it, glaring around her just in case someone decided to protest. Together she and Jorlan strode downstairs and stepped onto the dance floor. It seemed like he had to hold her up, though. In the short time she'd been upstairs, the lower level had somehow become tilted, and each time she moved, her head felt fuzzy.

"That was quite a display, warrior woman."

"Are you laughing at me?"

"Aye."

Well, at least he was truthful about it. Sighing, she rested her head on his shoulder. "You're too handsome, Jorlan. Do you know that?" Her lips clamped shut. Why had she admitted that aloud?

His husky chuckle reverberated against her chest. "Tell me more. Tell me what you like about me."

For some reason, that sounded like such a good idea. "Well, you're tall. I think that is *sooo* sexy."

"Hmm. What else?"

"At the house that first night, when you were naked,

I kept looking down and all I could think about was how big you were and how wonderful you would feel buried deep inside me."

He stilled. His arms, which were wrapped around her waist, pulled her closer into his embrace. "'Tis very intriguing, that desire of yours."

"Want me to tell you your bad qualities? They're bad, very, very bad." She didn't give him time to answer. "You're an alien." She rose up and glared at him accusingly. "Why'd you have to be an alien?" Too heavy to hold up, her head plopped back onto his shoulder. She sighed, disappointment and need trickling from her lips in a steady stream.

He arched a brow. "What else is bad about me?"

Her brow furrowed. "I don't remember." Why was the room spinning? "I have a disease, you know?"

"Disease?" The word lashed from his lips with the force of a tornado. "Why did you not tell me before? Should we take you to a healer?" His eyes were the color of a starless night, both blue and black and almost surreal.

"A healer can't help me." Her fingers hooked onto the waist of his jeans. "My disease is fatal."

"Whether you want to or no, you are going to my world, *katya*, and I will find you a healer." His arms held her so tightly she was fast losing her breath. "I will listen not to your protests."

"I know you're just saying that 'cause you don't want me to die before I fall in love with you. But what if I can't? I mean, what if I'm incapable of loving a man? Did you ever think of that? I'm dying of First Date Syndrome, after all. Ever heard of it?"

"You are dying from First Date Syndrome?" he asked, incredulous.

"That's right."

He growled low in her ear. "Do not ever do that again, woman. I thought you were truly sick."

"I am. I'm sick in the head. I've never made it past the first date. Maybe, if you were from here, I'd go on a second date with you. Maybe then I'd love you." Gently stroking her hands up and down his back, she explained about some of the horrid evenings she'd endured. Once she thought he chuckled, but she knew she was mistaken. They were discussing something very serious here, something that affected her entire life. But her head was whirling uncontrollably, and she forgot what she wanted to tell him.

"Jorlan," she whispered. "I think I'm going to pass out."

And she did, sliding down into a liquor-soaked darkness.

SOMEHOW, AND JORLAN HAD no idea how, he managed to drive Katie to a nearby lodging without getting either of them killed. The transportation was not easy to manage, but neither was the snoring Katie. He had to pay for a new chamber with Katie's green paper, since he could not recall where their first lodging was located.

As he carried her to their new room, Katie moaned sporadically. He blamed himself for her condition.

He had watched her consume the truth serum "lick her" yet had done nothing to stop her. Too much had he longed to question her, to discover the truth of her feelings for him. Only, she had fainted before he had the chance to delve too deeply.

He *had* learned some interesting facts, however.

The woman thought of him as her property. The knowledge was more potent than any healing concoction, and he smiled as he recalled the way she had threatened the dark-tressed woman. He had thought Maylyn loved him, but Maylyn had never been possessive of him. She had been content with what time he could give her, unconcerned if he spent time with another female.

Katie's possessiveness was indeed a glorious sight. Watching her face down the brunette had caused need to smolder in his blood, and he'd wanted to strip Katie down and plunge deep inside her right there at the bar, while the music blared around them and the smoke billowed like a hidden alcove.

Such thoughts could do him no good now. The hour was late, and they had much to do on the morrow. Inside their small, private chamber, he stripped Katie of her clothing—except for the black material that guarded her feminine portal. Very pretty. The dark fabric against her pale skin was the most ethereal sight he'd ever beheld. As he gazed down at her, his breath heated in his lungs. Her breasts were the perfect size for his hands. Her waist dipped and flared in all the right places.

He'd once noticed freckles on her shoulders and wondered if she had any elsewhere. He now knew she did. Three perfect freckles dotted her stomach. The sight tantalized him, made his body harden all over. He wanted to curse, for he knew these twilight hours would offer him no release, only a sweet kind of torture.

Carefully he placed her in the bed. After stripping down to nothing except skin, he climbed in beside her.

He smiled the entire night.

IT WAS THE WARMEST PILLOW she had ever owned.

Katie snuggled deeper into the mattress, letting the pillow's heat seep into her flesh. She skimmed her leg upward, found something hard and hot to prop her knee against, and sighed contentedly.

Jorlan's clean, unique scent enveloped her, giving her a little taste of heaven. She felt so safe, so secure, and she never wanted to leave this warm refuge. Her head ached a bit, but other than that she felt absolutely wonderful.

Somewhere in her conscious mind, she heard a loud crack of thunder boom. Heard rain beat rhythmically against the window. Instead of luring her to sleep, the pitter-patter of rain helped clear the sleepy fog from her mind.

She stretched. Smiled. Stretched again. Hmm, such hard, delicious warmth…

She stilled.

Hard?

Delicious?

Katie's eyes popped open. She was practically naked. Jorlan was *completely* naked. And they were in bed. Together.

And it was quite obvious his body liked the contact.

She debated whether to lie back down or run for cover. Finally, Katie scooted away. Just what had happened last night? She knew she and Jorlan hadn't made love because her body felt the same. Still, there was something so intimate about waking in a man's arms.

Her gaze caressed his sleeping form. Biting her lip, she tugged at the sheet, showing more and more—

"Good dawning." Jorlan's sexy voice rumbled through the cover of silence.

He was awake! Suddenly panicked, she jerked to her feet, taking the sheet with her—which left his nakedness in full view. She tried not to look; she really did. But wow! "What are you doing in my bed?" she demanded, more for the sake of her sanity than anything else.

Unfazed by the fact that his muscled glory was bared for her scrutiny, he watched her. His mouth curled up in a lazy smile. The kind of smile that always preceded trouble. "I am not in your bed. You are in mine."

"How did I get here?" She searched the room and discovered totally foreign surroundings. "Where are we?"

"I could not find the place you picked, so I purchased us a chamber in this establishment." Cozy as a kitten, he stretched, eyeing her through half-lowered lids. "Do you not recall?"

Yes, she remembered and suddenly wished she didn't. With that memory came remembrance of the way she'd acted at the bar. She'd threatened a woman for him. She'd plastered herself against him on the dance floor. She'd admitted how sexy he was. Her cheeks warmed. She turned away. "I have to use the bathroom."

Jorlan sat up. "I shall join you."

"No, you won't!" And with that, she slammed the bathroom door shut and clicked the lock in place.

"You did not have my permission to sleep with me," she shouted to the wooden barrier.

"I was protecting you," he called.

She wasn't that stupid. She knew what he'd been doing. Copping a feel, that's what. Gazing into the mirror, she watched her lips lift in a smile. Then she sighed. If she wasn't careful, that man was going to have her begging to go with him to his planet, even though he only wanted her on a temporary basis.

CHAPTER THIRTEEN

THE NEW DAWNING HAD BEGUN so sweetly with Katie in his arms, and now Jorlan almost resented the fact that he had to leave the rented chamber. He wanted to coax her back into bed. But alas, she had balked so adamantly about his taking her from her work that he knew she would not countenance any more delays.

But one day soon they were going to make love and nothing was going to stop them.

He rose from the soft comfort of the bed and dressed. Katie emerged moments later, and they were off. At the new psychic's abode, he discovered what he had been searching for since first awakening to Katie's kiss.

Magic.

Magic enveloped him the moment he stepped inside the shop called Vortex. The name should have made him realize 'twas what he needed sooner. He paused a moment, breathing in the sweet, rain-kissed essence so like the air of his homeland. So like Katie. Yet, as he stood with the wondrous scent in his nostrils, he had trouble believing this much anticipated moment was upon him. How long had he prayed for this? How long had he wished?

Too long.

Squaring his shoulders, he studied the dwelling. The carpet was beige, as were the walls. There were no frivolities or bottles displayed on stands. Incense did not fill the air. Nay, the place showcased only a long, thin counter.

Several people loitered about, talking, laughing, and exchanging information. But Jorlan paid them no heed. He was too intent on the lone man standing behind the counter. The man was short and had thinning brown hair, eye spectacles and high blade-like cheekbones that could have cut glass.

"This is it, isn't it?" Katie asked, suddenly beside him. Those were the first words she had spoken to him since leaving the rented chamber. "This is it," she repeated, her tone laden with a strange pitch he could not identify. "It feels different than the others."

Her observation amazed him, for no magic beat within her veins. She was not a child of the Druinn, nor did she possess the soul of the ancients. Yet she knew, just as he did, that true power beat within these walls. Mayhap he should not have been surprised. She had been attuned to his feelings since the beginning.

"'Tis the magic you feel. Magic that can take me home."

"Home?" She said the word as if she'd never heard it before, then lapsed once more into silence. Her gaze darted around the room. Her features were tense with…what? He did not know. He could not read the emotion shining so brightly in her eyes.

"This magic is not born of your world, but of mine." Jorlan breathed deeply. "The vibration is very strong, the essence quite unique, and almost familiar. Whoever this sorcerer is, he is very powerful."

"I see."

Now he recognized that pitch. Accusatory. She spoke as if she'd just discovered him standing over a dead body, talon in hand. He turned to her, took her chin in his hands. "We could leave today, together, if you would only agree to come with me."

"I've already explained my reasons for staying." Her expression was sad and resentful at the same time.

His eyes narrowed. "I cannot go without you, *katya*. This you know."

"I—"

"Before you again say no, recall that I have not seen my home in a thousand spans. I am…begging you." The words emerged stiffly. "Please. Come with me."

"If it weren't for the time difference, I would. I'd leave with you today, now, this instant." Moisture pooled in her eyes, and he experienced a twinge of guilt for pushing so insistently. But then she blinked and glanced away. "I'm sorry. I can't risk it."

He knew she meant more than just risking a trip to his homeland. She meant love. She couldn't, wouldn't risk loving him. He tasted sickness at the back of his throat, felt the cold edge of stone course through him. He forced himself to calm. Whether she denied it or not, he was making progress with her, and he would continue to do so, even if he had to double his efforts. He refused to even contemplate the fact that her love might spring too late.

"Then we will stay," he relented. "For now."

She gazed up at him with a soft, completely feminine expression. He was potently reminded of their kisses—of all the kisses they'd already shared and of all the kisses they *would* share. "Do you still wish to meet this sorcerer?" she asked.

"Aye. Just because we do not go this day, does not mean we will not go another day." Taking her hand in his, he stepped to the counter.

"I welcome you," the little man said, beckoning them over.

"I have come for—"

"I know why you are here," the man said. He pushed his glasses higher on his nose. "However, I am not the one you seek. I cannot help you."

At that, a sharp sense of dread pulsed through Jorlan. "*Someone* here can help me. I know this to be true."

"Yes. There is someone."

"Where can I find this someone?"

The little man stepped back, out of arm's length. "You cannot. He will find you—if he wants to."

Jorlan's teeth gnashed together. Curse it, something *would* go right for him this day! "For now, I wish only to talk to the man, and I will find him whether he wants to be found or not. I will have your aid, as well. Where is he?"

"Could be anywhere, really."

Jorlan gripped the edge of the counter so tightly the bones of his fingers almost snapped. "Where. Is. He?" His voice slashed out, edged with fury.

The little man blanched. "Whoa, whoa there. You're not the only one who desires a trip home. Mon Graig has many dwellings throughout this world and takes many through the vortex. Sometimes he is gone a few days, sometimes he is gone a few years, but no one, *no one* knows exactly where he is or when he will return."

"How long ago did he leave for this last trip?" Katie asked softly. She placed her hand upon Jorlan's arm, and he felt himself relax.

"Nine weeks or so."

Which could mean anything, Jorlan thought, closing his eyes. *Wait, wait, wait.* The words scorched a path through his body. He was so very tired of waiting for the things that he desired.

Katie's fingers gently squeezed his forearm. She was so close her breath fanned his skin. Just like that, he felt himself relax again. How did she soothe him so easily?

"For all we know, the man could return tomorrow," she said, her tone as gentle as her touch.

Jorlan gave a stiff nod. "You are right."

"Use this time to raise some cash," the little man interjected. "These trips aren't cheap, you know."

"How much is needed?" Jorlan stared down at the clerk so intently that the man began to fidget.

"It's, uh, different for everyone. Mon Graig will tell you when he comes for you."

"I will pay nothing until I find myself standing on the soil of my homeland."

"Understandable."

"Good." Jorlan nodded, satisfied he'd done all he could do. "Then tell Mon Graig my name is—"

"Doesn't matter what your name is. Mon Graig will find you. I'm sure he already knows of your visit."

Frowning, Jorlan wrapped his arm around Katie's waist and strode out the door.

AS HER TRUCK RACED along the highway, Katie glanced over at Jorlan. He had barely spoken a word to her since they'd left Vortex. His entire demeanor screamed "no touch" right now. She knew he was disappointed. She knew he needed time to face the reality of a prolonged stay, but as he was fond of telling her, time was their enemy.

There had to be something she could do to cheer him up.

They soon crossed into Dallas. Twenty minutes later, she eased her truck into the winding driveway of the Victorian. Jorlan loved physical labor, so what better way to keep his mind busy than to put him to work?

Katie placed the truck in Park. Her eyes narrowed. An old, rusty and unfamiliar Dodge Dart was parked in front of the house.

Curiosity tugged the corners of her lips downward. If the car didn't belong to one of her brothers, to whom did it belong?

"Who is here?" Jorlan asked. Each word portrayed a hint of the dark emotions swirling inside him.

"I don't know." There was no one inside the car, and she saw no one loitering on the lawn. "I wasn't expecting anyone."

She found the Dart's owner perched on the porch. Frances, the waitress from the café, jumped to her feet. Another woman—Heather, Katie realized—stood beside her, looking as bored and contemptuous as ever, her arms wrapped around her middle, as if the humid heat didn't touch her.

"What's going on?" Katie asked Frances.

The waitress twined her hands together and gazed

nervously down at her fingers. "Did you mean what you said about wanting me to work for you?"

Katie didn't hesitate with her answer. "Absolutely." She didn't like to acquire help from big businesses, or even temp agencies; she preferred working with people she knew, people who needed the money.

Frances blinked up and smiled, a smile so bright it illuminated her entire face, eradicating wrinkles and making her glow with youthful exuberance. "Then I accept. I can't thank you enough for this, Katie. Really. I owe you a big fat one."

"Yeah," Heather said, her tone dripping with disdain. "Thanks a bunch."

Katie's gaze slid to the girl. Recalling her move on Jorlan, Katie scowled. Heather glared.

Frances uttered a discreet cough. "Uh, Katie? May I talk with you in private?"

"I don't need you to—" Heather began, but Frances cut her off with a muttered, "Shut up." Then, "Please, Katie."

Curiosity rising, Katie nodded. "Yes, of course." But she hated leaving Jorlan and Heather alone together. No matter that Jorlan was free to do what—and who—he wanted, Katie now admitted that she considered him her property. Maybe she should get him a sign that read Owned By Katie—Beware and hang it around his neck. Some women, though, would consider such a sign an aphrodisiac and give chase. So, she'd just have to brand Jorlan another way. A hickey, perhaps?

As she strode with Frances to the side of the house, dodging rain puddles along the way, Katie imagined Jorlan's body and all the places susceptible to a hickey.

She slowly grinned. Her lascivious thoughts ground to a halt, however, the moment she and Frances reached the side of the house.

"Heather is my daughter," the waitress blurted.

Shock reverberating through her, Katie stood frozen. "Your daughter? But that's impossible."

"I'm afraid not," came the sighed reply. "She's really, truly mine."

Katie massaged the base of her neck. She was trying to digest the information, but had trouble meshing the image of the teasing Frances and the mean-spirited, over-sexed Heather. "I was in the café almost every morning for three weeks and so was she, but the two of you ignored each other."

"She's had a really tough life." Frances shifted from one foot to the other. "Her father, my ex, was a bad, bad man. He did things to her, and I didn't know about it until too late. When she turned twelve, she ran away from home. I didn't hear from her until about a year ago. She doesn't like me much, but she's been staying with me, and we're short on cash. And I—I thought," she stammered, "I'd hoped if you hired me, you might want to hire her. I swear on my ex's grave, may he forever burn in hell, that I can get us both here right after my shift at the café. And we'll work seven days a week if you need us."

Most of the animosity Katie felt toward Heather drained away as quickly as if a plug in a tub of water had been pulled. Her imagination filled in the gaps Frances's explanation left out, and the end result wasn't pretty. Her heart ached for the little girl Heather had been. "Why does she dislike *me?*"

Frances's lips compressed. "She's never spoken of it, but I can guess. You've got everything she's always wanted. You're successful and you've got a man that loves you."

"Jorlan doesn't—"

Frances cut her off with a self-disgusted snort. "She hates my guts, too, if that helps. If you don't want her around, I'll understand. But, if it's okay, I'd still like the job."

Katie was probably going to regret this, but she said, "It's yours, Frances. And Heather, too."

Another glorious smile lit the waitress's face. "Really? You mean it?"

"You can start tomorrow."

"Oh, Katie, thank you! Heather's real good with flowers and such, and I'm a real fast learner. Whatever you want me to do, I'll do it."

They discussed what time Frances and Heather should arrive, what sort of things they would be doing, and how much money they would earn.

"I can never thank you enough, doll." Frances's hands shook with the force of her delight. "I swear you won't regret this."

I hope not, Katie thought as they walked back to the porch.

Jorlan and Heather were chuckling over something Heather had said. The girl was standing too close to him. Way too close for Katie's peace of mind, and she felt a twinge of regret for her impulsiveness already. Frances ran to the couple and threw her arms around her daughter. "We got the job," she sang happily. "You and me both." Laughing, she twirled them around.

Heather abruptly pulled away. She acknowledged the news with a half smile.

"There are ten rules I forgot to mention," Katie said. "Well, they're safety tips, really." She threw Jorlan a do-not-talk glare. "There will be no adjusting them." When she had everyone's undivided attention, she began. "Number one, do not attempt to fix anything without checking with me first."

Two female heads nodded in unison. Jorlan crossed his arms over his chest, and she just knew he was waiting for her to say please. "Number two, always make sure a room is properly ventilated before you begin working. Numbers three through ten, Jorlan is off-limits."

"Jorlan?" Heather's nose crinkled. "I thought he was Hunter Rains, the self-help guy."

"You thought wrong. His name is Jorlan, and he's mine."

Frances stared over at Jorlan with horror. "You don't have to worry about me making a move on you. Men are the Black Plague of Death upon the Earth, so why would I want one?"

Jorlan frowned.

Katie just prayed Heather listened to her mother's words of wisdom. "Well then," she said, brushing her hands together. "I'm glad that's settled." She was just about to change the subject when Frances did it for her.

"I've got a joke for you. A husband looks at his wife and says, 'I'm in the mood to try a new position tonight. Something I've never done before.' The wife sends him a flirty eyelash flutter and says, 'A new position sounds wonderful. You can stand by the ironing board and I'll stretch out on the couch, drink beer and fart.'"

Everyone chuckled except for Jorlan, which was to be expected. Yet somehow, the expression tightening his features didn't fit with simple male irritation. This seemed altogether more serious. Frown sharpening, he whipped out one of his "weapons" and scanned the surrounding area.

"I sense trouble," he said.

Katie lost her smile. Her gaze jerked around the porch. "What's wrong?"

With his palm gripping her forearm, he pulled her off to the side until they were alone, but his gaze never ceased its search. "A sorcerer is here."

"Are you sure?" Katie didn't feel anything, didn't feel the faint stirring inside of her that she'd felt this morning. But she had to ask. "Is it Mon Graig?"

"Nay."

"How do you—"

"'Tis a different kind of magic." Jorlan drew in a long, deep breath. "I sense no immediate danger—but one must be careful when dealing with hidden powers." With that, he deposited her back on the porch. Without another word, he slipped away and slowly circled the house.

"Was that a spatula?" Frances asked, her face drawn together with curiosity.

"Yes," Katie answered as if it were perfectly normal for a giant of a man to wield a cooking utensil as though it was a lethal blade. "Yes, it was."

CHAPTER FOURTEEN

PERCEN DE LOCKE GRINNED slowly.

At last, after a seemingly endless search, he had found Jorlan.

He had found Jorlan!

Of course, his brother was no longer stone, but flesh and blood. Percen's first reaction to that fact was fury, but as he watched Jorlan interact with the mortal women, that anger melted away and his smile grew. Jorlan was free, but only for a time. The spell had not yet been broken completely. Its shackles were still wrapped tightly around his brother. How wondrous! Jorlan must be desperate for his savior's love, knowing his deadline fast approached.

Percen wanted to dance upon the grassy plain, but could not, for his twisted leg prevented such an action. He wanted to laugh and shout his success to the world, but could not, for he wished to keep his identity hidden.

At least for now.

Somehow, though, Jorlan had already sensed him. The cursed warrior was now guarded, searching. In fact, he strode about the house, determined to discover who watched him. He passed Percen once, even a second time, but never detected the truth. Percen could not contain a small chuckle.

You can't catch me, he inwardly sang, imitating the happy little boys he'd heard playing earlier that day. So carefree those children had appeared, he'd cast a spell of understanding just to learn their words. Those words now echoed smugly in his mind. *You can't catch me. You can't catch me, I'm the gingerbread man.*

Oh, what a fun game. He himself had never played games as a child. Nay, there had always been a spell to learn, an incantation to perform. There had always been punishments to endure and sorcerers to entertain. *A future high priest must be properly groomed in all facets of life.* His tutor's stern voice resonated in his head—a voice that still caused him to shudder with horror.

Nay, no games for him.

His half brother had led such a charmed life, pampered by the king and all of his servants, coddled by his mother, adored by anything female. Jorlan knew nothing of pain and suffering. *Nothing!* He knew nothing of craving something with every ounce of his being, yet being unable to acquire it.

But I will teach him, Percen thought darkly. *Aye, 'tis past time I taught him.*

His brother rounded a corner and returned to the three mortal women. A frown still marred the perfect warrior's perfect lips. Which of the three women was responsible for breaking the curse? Percen wondered, for he would begin Jorlan's punishment with her. He immediately eyed the youngest one. With her glorious red hair and big brown eyes, she was beyond beautiful, like a finely carved sculpture. The next woman was old enough to be Jorlan's mother, and the last was too tall and plain. Percen meant to study each one, to gauge their reactions to Jorlan and Jorlan's reaction to them, but he couldn't stop his gaze from returning to the young beauty. She was the kind of woman he had always longed to possess. To hold in his arms, to love and cherish.

But her kind never desired him in return.

Even knowing that, need began to churn inside him. Hot, driving need that, for a moment, surpassed and masked his sole reason for being there. He watched her smooth a tendril of hair from her brow. His blood became enflamed. His body hardened. Though her every move was like living passion, there was something almost vulnerable about her. Something sad. Something that pulled at his deepest yearnings.

The girl glanced around her, above her, below her, as if she could sense his scrutiny. Unexpectedly, her gaze connected with his. Blue to brown. Desire to confusion. He was nearly forced to his knees with the intensity of longing that swept through him. She didn't look away. She held his stare and slowly offered him a smile.

He sucked in a breath. Could she see him?

Nay, nay she could not, for her shoulders sagged slightly, and her smile faded. Her gaze moved to the railing beside him.

Was she Jorlan's lover? Had Jorlan touched her, planted himself firmly between her thighs? Percen scowled as those images flashed through his mind. Of course his brother had tupped her. What man would turn away from such loveliness? Not Jorlan, surely, a connoisseur of female flesh. Well, 'twas reason enough for Percen to have her himself.

As his scowl lifted into a predatory grin, Percen tapped a finger against his chin. Just how should he go about winning this girl? His ugliness caused even the staunchest of stomachs to churn. Magic, mayhap? Aye, he could use the same spell he'd used all his life to lure women to his bed, a spell that made others see him as the man he wanted to be, not the man he truly was.

His eyes narrowed when the object of his query brushed her fingertip across Jorlan's arm. Jorlan sent her a questioning gaze, then smiled, as if telling her without words to continue.

Percen's fingers bit into his palms. Oh, this was going to be fun. So much fun.

CHAPTER FIFTEEN

THE DAY PROGRESSED QUICKLY for Jorlan. He worked much, talked little, and always remained alert. By the time he and Katie entered her home, he was at last able to relax, for the sensation of being watched had finally abated. Still, he desired time alone to ponder what had happened. Without telling Katie his purpose, he went into the bathing chamber, stripped, and stepped inside the tub. Warm water rained liquid heat upon his naked body, almost like a caress.

The presence he had felt today...something had not been right. Yet he could not exactly lay claim to what it was that bothered him. He pressed his forehead against the cool, damp tile. At first he'd thought the presence had been a sorcerer, but the more he thought about it, the more he became convinced that what he had felt was a lingering hint of magic. A lingering hint of the stone spell.

Each day that passed, the spell's power grew in strength, ready to claim him. He could not let that happen, and he knew what he had to do to prevent it. 'Twas past time he forced Katie to face what simmered between them.

His mind drifted back over the day's events. After

Frances and Heather had said their goodbyes, he and Katie had worked inside the old house for many more hours. He'd enjoyed every moment of their time together, especially the way her gaze had repeatedly glided over his body with longing. But she never asked for his touch. Nay, she merely asked him more questions about his past.

How had the curse come about? she'd wanted to know.

He explained how he'd been abed—although he hadn't explained that he'd been with Maylyn. A servant had rushed inside, happily shouting a man waited below and claimed to know who had killed his father. As Jorlan had searched for months with no results, he welcomed any information most eagerly.

He had vaulted from the bed without giving Maylyn a second's thought.

But in the next instant, Percen materialized.

Maylyn, splayed across the linens in all her naked glory, had smiled oh, so sweetly and used her sorcerer's power to lock Jorlan's feet in place. He'd known then that everything she'd ever done or said to him had been a lie, and he'd hated her. She'd been Percen's ally all along. He had reached for a weapon, but just as his brother had cast the stone spell. Jorlan's flesh instantly hardened, yet he had still heard, felt and saw everything around him.

Limping, Percen studied the stone from every angle. He laughed, the sound filled with more glee than humor. "I know you hear me." He trailed a fingertip down Jorlan's chest. "I've already killed the man below, for the answer to Imperia's greatest mystery will die with *me*."

Percen uttered a long, drawn-out sigh laden with false sorrow. "Do not worry, my brother. There is hope for your freedom. When I think you've suffered long enough as stone, I will allow Maylyn to kiss you. After that, you will have two cycles to win her love." He laughed, the sound like shards of broken glass grinding together. "Just imagine. She betrayed you, and yet you will have to court her or lose your freedom forever."

Katie had listened intently, had even hugged him close afterward. But when he questioned her about her past, about her life, she turned away, suddenly busy. She'd done the same thing all these many days they'd spent together. He thought he understood her reaction, even if he didn't like it. Sharing of oneself created a bond and opened wounds mistakenly thought healed. But she would learn, just as he had, that they couldn't deny their pasts.

She would also learn that she couldn't deny her future.

WHILE JORLAN BATHED, Katie set the stage for his seduction.

Her fingers shook nervously as she lit jasmine-scented candles on her dresser. The flames flickered lazily in the darkness, dancing shadows and light together and casting a lacy canopy over the room. She wanted the atmosphere to evoke a mood of sublime promises and carnal need, where every shadow held a hint of the coming pleasure. True to Nick's advice, she wore nothing beneath her robe. The condoms, rope, handcuffs and lubricant were on the small round table beside the bed.

The atmosphere was perfect.

Just a few more finishing touches…

The flowing water tapered to quiet sooner than she'd anticipated.

Katie froze.

One minute ticked by. Then another. And another. From the far corner of her bedroom, she watched Jorlan emerge from the bathroom. A white cotton towel was wrapped around his waist as tendrils of steam wafted above him, curling up toward the ceiling.

She gulped, steeled herself. *I can do this. I can.* "Jorlan?"

Footsteps resounded from the freshly cleaned floor as she watched his approach. He stopped in her doorway. The candlelight snaked from her room to the exact place he stood, paying him nothing but tribute, making his skin glow to bronzed perfection. His gaze raked her slowly, deliciously. She didn't say anything, just waited. Then his gaze collided with hers. He must have guessed her intentions because he inhaled sharply, causing his nostrils to flare. Suddenly he possessed the patent stillness of a predator, just before attack.

In the next instant, his features were unreadable. "You know, Katie," he said smoothly, "I have been thinking." Looking as though he possessed all the time in the world, he leaned into the door frame. "We have talked about my life, my past, but we have never discussed yours."

"Oh?" She glanced away, guilt etched in every curve and hollow of her face. "What do you want to know?"

"You may start by telling me what qualities you desire in your life-mate."

Her gaze snapped back to him. "Are you asking me to marry you again, because I—"

"I am simply curious."

She wanted to make love to him, and he was curious about her future husband? Angered, she gave him more of the truth than he probably wanted. "I want a man who loves me for the woman I am, not the woman he wants me to be. And I want a man who will love me forever."

"I see."

Such an easy reply disappointed her. On some level, perhaps, she'd hoped he'd say *I can be that man.* "What about you? What are you looking for in a wife? Besides a means to an end."

"A woman with spirit and courage. A woman who fascinates me and makes my body throb with unquenchable need…a woman who makes me forget."

Cords of jealousy were already working a path down her spine. She didn't want to think about this faceless female who would one day be his life-mate. Katie only wanted to think of here and now. "I don't want to talk anymore, Jorlan."

His brows arched. "What, then, would you have us do?"

"Make love. All night." She reached out and beckoned him over. "Until neither of us can move."

Instead of racing to her and swinging her into his arms, he replied, "Are you sure this is what you want, *katya?*" There was an edge to his tone that suggested she agree, and as he waited for her answer, his eyes turned to cool slate, the crystalline light that usually danced within them subdued to dark sapphire. "You have refused me so many times."

"I'm positive I want this. I even bought us some things." She motioned to the side table with a wave of her arm.

His expression still unreadable, he eased into the room. He didn't come to her. No, he sat at the edge of the bed, just in front of the table and inspected her purchases. Lips twitching, he tested the strength of the rope then set it aside. He held up the handcuffs. "What do you plan to do with these?"

"Lock you to the bed." Her heart raced at the thought, her toes curled, and her nervousness increased.

"Mayhap I will lock you to the bed." He paused, then grinned slowly. "Aye, I like the sound of that. Having you subject to my will." He replaced the handcuffs on the table surface and fingered a box of condoms. "What is this?"

"Condoms."

His brow puckered in confusion.

She explained the consequence of unprotected sex.

Half grinning, half resolved, he uttered a sigh. "I could only give you a child if we were life-joined, *katya*. 'Tis the way of the Imperians."

"Really? So I don't have to worry about that?"

He gave a slight shake of his head, sending several strands of dark hair over his brow.

"Well, then," she said, gently brushing the inky locks from his eyes and fighting a rush of nervousness, "you have my permission to proceed to the next level."

"Not just yet, I think." He swept the box to the floor. He raised the tube of lubricant and studied it from every angle. "And this?"

"It's to help—" No, that wasn't how she wanted to explain. "It eases—" No, that wasn't it either. "It's to make a woman wet."

His grin faded completely. "*I* make a woman wet, *katya*," he growled. "What a ridiculous concept. This—" he eyed the tube with disgust "—is not needed." He didn't give her a chance to reply. He tossed the tube over his shoulder and beckoned her closer with a crook of his finger. "Now come here."

This is it, she thought. *I'm giving myself to him.*

Suddenly an unexplainable calm settled over her. This was right. So right. In fact, it was as if she'd always existed for this exact moment. For this man. She could no more deny that than she could deny her lungs air.

Filled with a heady mixture of need and anticipation, she closed the remaining distance between them. His hands anchored at her waist, easing her between his thighs. Warm and sweetly scented with mint, his breath kissed the V of her robe.

"I might have been in a hurry to get to this moment," he said, his voice laced with determination, "but now that it has arrived, I am going to take my time with you, savor every touch. Every sound." His eyes glinted with an emotion she couldn't name. "I do not want any games this time. Only you and me."

"Yes." The words escaped on a breathless sigh. "Just you and me."

"Later… We will play later." His gaze slowly slid

up her body and then he was gazing right into her eyes. Heat and longing and passion all blazed in those baby-blue depths.

A heartbeat passed, a mere whisper of time, before his lips touched hers. His tongue moved inside her mouth with drugging slowness, exotic and consuming. Each time before he had been molten lava. Now he was a well of water, and she was parched, living for every ounce of him that he offered.

"Do you know," he said, pulling back to watch her through the thick shield of his lashes, "that when I felt the stone dissipate, 'twas not vengeance or home that I first craved. 'Twas you."

Those words washed over her, gentle, wonderful, and oh, so beguiling. "I wanted you, too."

He uttered a soft chuckle. "Had we followed our instincts, we would have saved ourselves much frustration."

"I'm sure we would have made love over and over by now. In the garden, the truck, the bathroom."

"The rented chamber," he added helpfully. His hands slid languidly up her sides and cupped her jaw. He planted breathy little kisses and nips over her nose, eyes, her chin. "You know, of course, that I will not be satisfied until I have you in all of those places."

Warmth skidded along her spine. "Do you promise?"

"Oh, aye. You have my word, and my word is my honor."

He gently tugged her face down for another kiss. While his tongue worked its magic, he urged her onto his lap, spreading her thighs and hooking her legs around his waist until she straddled him completely and cradled his erection. His mouth never left hers.

In their position, she knew he was impossibly aroused, that he was huge and thick and hard—and *she* had caused this reaction. She, a woman who was too tall, too bossy and lacking in feminine graces, had brought this seductive man to such potent arousal. That knowledge gave her power, power that was very, very intoxicating.

On and on the kiss continued. Jorlan explored her leisurely, prolonging her pleasure, making her burn for so much more. He let his tongue trace the outline of her lips, leaving fire in its wake. His hand splayed over her collarbone, so warm, so inviting, a heartbeat away from dipping inside her robe and cupping her breast.

But that strong, masculine hand remained in place, teasing, taunting. Tormenting.

As one minute ticked by and then another, her nipple puckered in expectation and rasped against the cotton fabric of her robe. Her body began a constant ache for the heat of his hands—any part of his hands. His fingertips. The pad. The calluses. Something, anything except the waiting, the needing. She already knew an invisible cord stretched from her nipples to her clitoris, and if he would only touch her intimately the throb between her legs would spring and uncoil, giving her release.

She pulled away from their kiss. "Jorlan…"

"Kay-tee." He took possession of her mouth again, smothering her words. His fingers traced a path down the middle of her robe, and she thought, *Yes! This is it.*

He's going to give me what I need. But he merely traced the seam back up again, never once touching actual skin.

She'd been aroused one too many times in the last few days without receiving a reward. Her body was demanding that reward now. Immediately. She bit the cord of his neck and said, "Please." He just let his fingers blaze the same unhurried path they'd taken before, always remaining a breath away from where she craved them most. He paused sometimes to simply look at her, or tell her something naughty, but he always left her untouched and wanting, aching. She loved his kiss, she truly did. Never had a man kissed her quite so perfectly. But she was becoming more and more desperate for skin to skin, full body contact.

"Jorlan?" She strained against him. "You're killing me here."

His lips curled with wicked amusement. "Did you not once say you wished to die of pleasure?"

"I didn't mean it literally."

"So you wish me to do more to you?"

"Hell, yes!"

"Hmm," he said, tormenting her to an even greater degree. "Not just yet, I think."

Oh, he would pay for this later. His tongue licked and sucked the exposed skin of her neck and chest. He kneaded her butt. She writhed, she pressed against him, she tried to place his hands where she needed them most, but he always ruined her efforts by returning his palms a safe distance away.

"Damn it, Jorlan, I'm seriously considering tying you up and taking over."

His laugh was a low purr. Then—finally!—his hands dipped inside her robe. But instead of cupping and squeezing as she so desperately craved, he teased a fingertip around her nipple. The action only increased her frustration, her need.

"Tell me what I do to you," he commanded softly.

"You make me ache." She meant the words as a complaint, but they sounded more like a plea.

"Where exactly do I make you ache, *katya?*"

"Everywhere."

"Where specifically? Here?" He grazed the tip of her waiting nipple.

Her hips jerked, and she almost came right then. "Yes, there." He licked the same path his finger had taken. "Oh, God. Right there! Do that again."

He gave her other nipple the same treatment—a light grazing, followed quickly by the heat of his tongue. Her lower body arched into him. Just one more touch. One more.

"Where else?" he demanded. All touches ceased. She shimmed against him, causing her robe to part, and he sucked in a sharp breath. "By *Elliea, katya,* you are magnificent."

His words washed over her like a bold caress, making her groan and squirm. Beyond desperate now, she reached between their bodies and yanked at his towel. He caught her hand and brought it to his lips. "I asked you a question. Where else do you ache?"

She was too aroused to be embarrassed by her admission. Liquid warmth was whirling in her stomach, and lower. "Between my legs," she told him passionately. "I ache between my legs."

Watching her face intently, he tunneled her pale curls with his hand, almost reaching where she craved him. But just when she rocked forward, he darted away.

She followed.

Over and over he teased her, giving her a glimpse of pleasure, only to stop. He touched her briefly. Her head fell back, and she cried out, "Yes. Right there. No, come back. Oh, yes, there. No!" As the dance continued, her breath came in short, erratic pants. "I have another rule," she managed to croak.

"And what is that?" He was beginning to lose his playful air. In fact, the teasing light had completely abandoned his eyes, and now he watched her with a deep intensity. "What is that?" he demanded again, this time a rough edge to his tone.

"When engaged in lovemaking—hurry!"

His eyes darkened to a deep sapphire-blue. "My adjustment is simple. I will hurry, but only when I want to."

She ripped off her robe, hoping her brother's advice would not lead her astray. "If you don't hurry up, I'm going to break every one of your fingers."

"How fortunate I am, then, that I am ready to hurry." In the next instant, she found herself flat on her back. While on his knees, Jorlan jerked her to the edge of the bed, spread her legs and kissed the hot wetness between her thighs. At the first lick of his tongue, she exploded. Fire, joy, pleasure all rocked her, sending thousands of twinkling lights through her mind. Her head reeled. She lost touch with where she was, who she was, only feeling an incredible shiver race through her again and again. And when she thought she might die from the sensation, Jorlan kissed her again with his heavenly tongue until she could only gasp his name. He tasted her, sucked her, made her want him all over again. He expertly maneuvered his tongue and fingers in a way that made all her fantasies pale in comparison.

Suddenly he was standing up over her. His hair seemed darker than the night sky that framed her window, and his eyes...his eyes were blazing with passion, bright and crystalline. He gazed down at her body, at her spread legs and wet arousal.

"You amaze me," he said, his voice strained.

Jorlan knew at that moment he had never seen, nor would ever see, so beautiful a sight again. Katie's cheeks were flushed. Her eyes were brilliant and wide, her lips swollen and parted from his kisses. Her nipples were as ripe as pink berries and her woman's flesh was damp with arousal *he* had caused.

Muscles bunching, he crawled over her. They both cried out as skin met skin. He'd wanted to prolong the moment, to prolong their pleasure, but he wasn't sure how much longer he could last. He rocked himself against her, careful not to enter her yet.

"Just like that," she panted.

So he did it again, gliding back and forth in the slick V of her thighs while she rubbed herself wantonly against him. Finally, Jorlan had pushed himself to the edge of his control. He wanted this woman too desperately and for too long to stop himself now. He kissed her breasts, dragged his teeth over her nipples and positioned himself for entry.

He didn't push inside immediately.

"You have said no so often, I need to hear your assent once more before I go further."

She had been so bold about everything else; he yearned for her boldness in this as well. Her eyes were the warm color of honey and passion misted in their depths. Yet they had been so glazed before. When he took her, he wanted it to be with her cries of acquiescence in his ears. When she remained silent, looking up at him through her thick, spiky lashes, he teased her opening with his cock. "You have to say the words, *katya*. Say the words."

Another heart-stopping pause, then, "I want you to fuck me, Jorlan." Her voice was so sweet he was taken aback by the contrast of her words. "Now," she commanded, no longer so sweet, but a vixen aroused to the point of pain. "Do it now."

"My pleasure." He grinned slowly, wickedly. She was a warrioress through and through, even in lovemaking, and that fueled his desire as never before. "'Tis indeed my pleasure."

He plunged inside her.

She cried out as her virginity gave way, as her sleek tightness encased him. He stilled. Her nails deeply scored his back as she uttered expletive after expletive.

"*Katya*," he gritted against her ear, struggling not to go over the edge, and struggling even more to give her time to adjust. This bold, passionate woman was—nay, had been—untouched. He was the first, the only man to ever fill her this completely, to ever be a part of her, and the knowledge very nearly felled him.

How had this enchanting creature gone so long without knowing a man's touch?

Were the men of her world fools? Jorlan shook his head in wonder, for aye, they were. For what manner of man left such a prize untouched? Delight, wonder and awe all wound through him. *He* was no fool. He had wanted her, needed her, and so he had taken her. He was the only man to have ever seen Katie so flushed, the only man to have heard his name on her lips. What a sweet gift she had given him, a gift he would cherish all the days of his life.

"We're not done, are we, Jorlan?" she asked hesitantly. Her teeth chewed at her bottom lip.

He gave a strained chuckle. "Nay, my *katya*. We will not be finished for a long while yet."

"Oh." Her legs wrapped around his waist, sending him deeper inside of her. She winced.

He almost groaned at the exquisite sensation. "Did I hurt you?"

"No."

But he knew he had, and he knew, as well, that she needed more time to adjust to his size. He'd never taken a virgin before, so he did not know exactly how long he should wait. Not long, he hoped, for sweat was already beading on his forehead. His muscles were already clamoring for more. But he was determined to finish as slowly as he'd begun.

"Tell me when you are ready," he ground out. His restraint was quickly breaking, and he was fast losing his control.

Her breath fanned across his cheek. She moved her leg experimentally, sending him even deeper inside.

The movement drove him nearly mad with his needs. If she pulled back now, if she said no more, he wasn't sure he would be able to stop.

"Jorlan?" The tone of her voice did not bode well for him.

"Aye."

"Move," she said.

Dread speared through him, desperate and achy. "Just give it more time. You'll feel better and become used to my presence. Just give it some time," he repeated almost savagely.

"No." She chuckled, a rich, husky chuckle that poured over him like thick, sweet honey. "I don't want you to move away. I want you to move *inside me*."

Comprehension dawned, and with it, his movements spurred into action. Like a dam that had burst, he sank into her, then pulled back, over and over thanking *Elliea* for sending him to this woman. At that moment he might have thanked even Percen. He hooked her knees over the corner of his arms, spreading her wider, pressing against her center. She purred like a sweet little kitten.

He reached between their bodies and circled the center of her desire with his thumb. She gasped, cried out. He felt her inner walls tighten and spasm against him, and he moved faster. Harder. Deeper. Only when he heard his name rip from her throat did he spill inside her.

When the last pulse subsided, he remained as he was, surrounded by her essence. Silently, he gazed down at her. Katie's eyes were closed, and she appeared to be asleep. That had been the most intense, satisfying experience of his life, but he didn't have the strength to examine why just yet. By *Elliea,* he was not sure he would be able to move ever again. Still, he didn't want to crush Katie during the night. Careful not to wake her, he leaned slightly to the side. After a while, his eyes began to grow drowsy, the sounds of their breathing filling his ears.

"Jorlan?" Katie asked softly.

"Hmm?"

She paused. "Nothing."

Silence enveloped them like a thick blanket.

Katie lay still, unable to sleep as she waited for him to say something, even though she hadn't asked him anything. She couldn't help it; she craved words of praise. She knew she'd been good. After all, her body would not feel so sated if she hadn't rocked his world as he had rocked hers. But just as he had needed to hear her acquiescence, she needed to hear his adulation. Yet minute after minute dragged by and he remained quiet.

"Jorlan?"

"Aye, *katya.*"

Again, she paused. "Nothing."

His warm, silky breath fanned her ear, and he sat up, suddenly wide-awake and smiling. "Say what is on your mind or neither of us will sleep this eve."

"That was wonderful, Jorlan."

The corners of his lips faded to a frown of disappointment.

Feeling her blood begin to freeze, she gazed over at him with wide eyes. "You didn't think it was wonderful?"

"'Tis not that..." He settled at her side. "I had thought you were about to speak your love for me."

"Oh."

A long sigh escaped his lips. "Mayhap you still need some persuasion, which I will most happily provide once your body is not so sore."

She waited for him to say more. When he didn't speak again for a long while, she asked, "Is there anything else you want to say to me?"

"Good eve."

She jolted upright, hitting his chin with the top of her head in the process. "Good eve? Good eve! Well, you can shove your good eve right up your as—"

In the next heartbeat she found herself flipped over and pinned to the bed. Jorlan loomed over her. "Did you wish to hear something from me, little witch?"

Mutinous, she glared up at him.

"You were more than I could have ever dreamed," he said softly.

Well, that was better. "And?"

"And what?"

She slapped his chest.

He chuckled. "You owe me money, *katya*. I should like to collect my payment now."

She gasped. "I'm not paying you for sex, you...you gigolo. In fact, I was so good, *you* should pay *me*." Oh, my Lord, had she really just said that?

He blinked. "You misunderstand. You owe me a quarter for every time you spoke a foul word." His lips stretched in a grin. "The closer you came to your peak, the more profanities you uttered. And I—" he kissed her softly after every word "—loved every moment of it."

Her features softened. "Well, I've decided I'm not

going to quit cursing and I'm not paying. It wasn't working out for me, anyway."

"And I have decided you may quit. Later. Right now you still owe me, and I will allow payment in trade."

That sounded intriguing. "What sort of trade?"

"You will listen to my next words without com ment."

Curious at his sudden seriousness, she nodded. "All right."

He waited a moment to assure himself she listened. "Never have I experienced a joining like ours. You captivated me, amazed me and stole the breath from my lungs. Had I known you tasted so sweet, I would have sampled you that very first night, and every moment since, even without your approval."

Katie didn't know what to say. His confession was more than she'd ever dreamed, headier than a kiss. Then he began touching her once again and the added sensation made her purr.

Oh. Oh, my. Oh, yes.

CHAPTER SIXTEEN

WHAT WAS I THINKING, Katie wondered dreamily, *to deny this man so long?*

Most of the candles on her dresser had long since ceased burning. She lay atop Jorlan, her head cradled protectively in the hollow of his neck. The rest of her was draped over his body like a winter quilt. They had just made love. Again.

Right now, he was absentmindedly caressing a hand down the curve of her spine, making her shiver with delight. If she'd only known how delicious actual lovemaking would be, she would have demanded he take her that very first night. She knew now, however, and she would never let him out of bed.

Oh, she felt so unbelievably wonderful. The things she'd done, the things she'd said, didn't embarrass her. She reveled in them and the power they had over such a dominating man. Outside her window the stars twinkled brightly, like little diamonds scattered across black velvet. The world seemed to have slowed down. Everything, including the air and the softly chirping crickets, was quiet with the reverence of the moment.

Her fingers stroked Jorlan's chest, rising and falling with the ridges of his muscles. On each side of his ribs, four parallel welts slashed downward. She liked that she had put them there, a subtle reminder of her presence. She sighed, a breathy sound that rumpled what little chest hair he possessed. For the rest of her life, she would recall this night. Recall every sound, every scent, every sensation. Lord, she already craved more of the orgasms, the intimacy, and the afterglow. They were everything she'd never known she needed, and they were branded inside her memory in a way that no other man would ever compare.

Forget First Date Syndrome. She now suffered from Comparison Disease.

Katie couldn't summon the energy needed to worry about it, though. Lying in his arms was weaving a slumberous spell around her brain. Jorlan's heat seeped into her, drugging, comforting.

Her eyes had just closed completely when Jorlan said, "Now, little witch, we will talk."

"About what?" Her voice was raspy and lethargic, and she didn't open her eyes.

He rolled her onto her back and stared down at her. "About why you did not mention your untried state."

Her eyelids popped open. She absolutely did not want to have this conversation, but he seemed so intent, she realized there was no way he'd leave her alone until she confessed. "At what moment was I supposed to blurt out that I was a virgin?"

"After our first kiss. After we almost made love on the bathing chamber floor. During our trip to see Mon Graig."

"Okay, so I had the opportunity."

"Aye, you did."

"I just didn't want to seem inexperienced."

He nodded his understanding. "But why me?"

"I'd never met the right man until you."

His expression became thoughtful. "That is part of the answer, I think, but not the whole."

He was too perceptive, damn him.

"Has no man of your world ever courted you?" he asked.

"Well, yes. Some have tried."

"And failed." Pure masculine pride laced his tone. "Were they lacking in some way?"

He meant the question to be rhetorical, she could tell, but she answered him anyway. "The problem wasn't with the men I dated. The problem was with me. Something was lacking inside me, and they just didn't fill the need."

His brows smoothed as he pondered her words. "What was lacking in you?"

"Interest."

Slowly, he smiled.

"I just…well…I wanted a man who was taller than me."

That smile of his continued to grow. "I am that."

"And I wanted a man who made me *feel* like a woman, not just one of the boys."

He kissed her eyelid as soft as a butterfly wing. "I do that."

"Yes, you do." But she wasn't finished. "I wanted a man who desired me despite my height, despite my temper, small as it is, and despite my unwomanly interests."

Lightly he pressed his lips to hers. "I desire you *because* of those things."

"Do you?" Her heart flip-flopped. "Do you really?"

"How can you doubt me?" He planted his elbows on either side of her head. She felt his erection press between her naked thighs, though he didn't enter her. Her body instantly responded, heating and rushing blood through her like an awakened river. But still he did not ease inside her, didn't touch her more intimately. He became pensive. "We will not proceed until you tell me about your life."

Her lips pursed. So he'd caught her reluctance to share, had he? Lord, she wished he hadn't. Especially now. She wanted so desperately for him to continue thinking of her as a woman, a sexy, ravishing female. If he knew just how unfeminine she was, he might stop lusting for her.

"I'm tired. Why don't we continue this conversation in the morn—"

"Nay. You will speak of what I wish. Now."

"Or what? You'll pummel me?" Her challenging air quickly became breathless arousal. The feel of him so near her entrance, yet not quite inside her was exciting and frustrating. Then he brought his fingers into play, teasing her in a way guaranteed to propel her toward mindlessness.

"I will not pummel you, *katya*. I will beat you. Most soundly." His lips twitched, completely undermining his threat. "You claim you desire a man who truly sees you, but how can I do that if you will not share your life with me?"

How could she deny this man anything? She sighed. "What do you want to know?"

"Everything," he said, mimicking her response to the very same question.

So Katie told him about her life. He listened intently and chuckled every so often at her childhood antics. She told him about her fears, her hopes and dreams. At one point, he became so silent, so serious, she almost ended the conversation, but she decided to confess the worst of it before she lost her nerve.

"I don't like hair ribbons, or frilly dresses with bows. I don't like long fingernails because they're a nuisance. I *do* like tools and football games, fast cars and jeans." She drew in a deep breath. "When my truck breaks down, and I mean the engine and transmission, not just the tires, I don't have to take it to a mechanic. I do the repairs myself."

There.

Now he knew all of her unfeminine attributes.

She waited for him to laugh, to crack a joke at her expense.

He didn't.

"Come here," he said. He tugged her to her feet and ushered her to the body-length mirror on her right wall. He moved behind her, his palms on her shoulders.

Blushing, she tried to pull away. He held her firmly in place.

"Look, *katya.* See what I see."

She didn't want to look. How embarrassing! She didn't want to study her flaws while he watched. "No."

"Look," he beseeched. "Look."

Because he asked so sweetly, she did.

"Do you see how graceful your legs are? How pink

and ripe your nipples are? And the curve of your hips excites me every time I gaze at you." Each place he named, he touched—a featherlight touch that caused her breath to hitch. He whispered all sorts of things in her ear. Hot things that made her ache. Erotic things that made her blush. Sweet endearments that made her weep.

Then he began speaking in his native tongue, a lilting language that floated over her, arousing her in a way she'd not imagined. His hands were all over her—hands she could feel and now *see* as well. Her legs shook with the force of her desire.

"What do you feel when I touch you?" he asked, never removing his hands.

"Fire," she panted. "Pure fire."

"'Tis the same for me. Think you a woman lacking feminine graces could heat my blood so thoroughly?" That said, he parted her legs and took hold of her waist. Then he entered her from behind, slowly pushing all the way inside, making her cry out in bliss.

Even through her passion-glazed mind she understood the impact of his words.

My God, she thought, suddenly panicked. *I truly could fall deeply and irrevocably in love with this man— only to lose him.*

HEATHER MERCER LAY on her small twin bed, shivering with cold. The thin, ragged blanket covering her did little to keep her warm. The night air was tepid and laden with summer scents, so there was no reason for her to feel so chilled. But lately, nothing seemed to make her warm. Not coffee or hot chicken soup. Not thick flannel jackets or black leather gloves. The coldness came from too deep within her.

Trying to distract herself from her shivering, she allowed her mind to drift. Tomorrow she would begin working with Katie James, a prospect Heather loathed almost as much as she was grateful for. She needed the money, but the thought of spending hour after hour with the too-perfect woman made her stomach knot. How many reminders did she need that some people were blessed with happy, normal lives—and some people were not?

Around Katie, Heather always felt dirty and used. Like a cheap piece of furniture in a room full of glorious antiques. Katie had everything. Money. Talent. Love. Jorlan looked at her as if she were gold, and Katie spoke of her brothers as if they were gods.

Perhaps if Heather had had a brother, he would have protected her from her father. Would have protected her from the long string of men who had used her over the years as she searched for someone, anyone, to make her whole. Rolling to her side, Heather clutched her pillow to her body, pretending the soft down was the heat of a man, a man who considered her more important than a six-pack of beer. A man who thought she was worth more than what rested between her legs.

After a while, her thoughts tapered off and she slowly descended into darkness. A minute passed, or maybe an hour, when her mind shouted for her to awaken. She was toasty warm. So deliciously warm. The sound of a deep, male voice chanted quietly in her ear, and she stretched languidly, loving the depth of her dream.

The man spoke again, and this time she understood him. He uttered a single word: *Awaken.*

Her eyelids fluttered open. A strange man hovered above her. Fear sparked to life inside of her, an old familiar fear she'd endured her entire childhood. She tensed, tried to jerk away, to cry out, but the man chanted something else, something that lured her to relaxation. Everything around her slowly became hazy and distant, like a new, wondrous reality. Peace she could not explain settled over her.

Slowly breathing in and out, Heather totally and completely relaxed. Her arms and legs felt shackled to the bed, but as she gazed down at her body, she saw that she was free. Why then could she not move? Oh well, it didn't matter. She didn't want to move. She was happy right where she was.

"You're dreaming," she heard echo softly in her mind.

Yes, she was still dreaming, a glorious dream she never wanted to awaken from. Hadn't she just wished for a man to warm her? Yes. Yes, she had, and her wish had come true in the form of this twilight apparition. An apparition that felt strangely familiar to her. Sighing, she settled into the firm male chest and stared up at his face. Her breath snagged in her throat. He was so beautiful; his features were strong, chiseled and classic perfection. Such physical perfection unnerved her, and she didn't like it. But she didn't try and pull away. He was keeping her warm, after all.

"Who are you?" she whispered.

"Percen." The low timbre of his accent, an accent very much like Jorlan's, made her shiver with feminine awareness.

"Percen," she repeated, liking the sound on her lips.

"I've come for you," he said.

Her eyes widened with surprise. "Me? I don't understand."

"You belong to me." His eyes bored into her, making her shiver as currents of heat continued to race inside her veins. "Only me. You will never belong to Jorlan again."

She liked those words too much to correct him. Yes, she'd wanted Jorlan at first, maybe to hurt Katie, or maybe because she'd thought Jorlan was someone else, someone who could help her overcome her past. She felt nothing for him, though, and she certainly hadn't ever belonged to him. But this man…this man she wouldn't mind belonging to. She'd been many things in her twenty-two years, but never a woman who belonged.

"Since I'm yours to do with as you please," she said, "what are you going to do with me?"

He remained silent for a long while, as if debating within himself. "Tonight, I will simply hold you. Do you want me to hold you?"

"Oh, yes." She was so warm. Warmer than she'd ever been. "Hold me and never let me go."

"Soon I will make you mine in body. What think you of that?"

"I think I've never been happier," she said truthfully.

He reached out and reverently traced the curve of her cheek, slid his finger up and over her eyebrow. She didn't cringe as she usually did. She didn't feel her mind burst with nightmares. She felt cherished. Worshipped. Here in the twilight, the impossible stirred in the air like magic. This wasn't a room, and they weren't lying in a bed. This was a secret haven far away from civilization and they were lying in a hidden grotto while birds and insects chirped around them.

"Promise me you'll stay with me," she whispered. "Please." She rested her head on his chest, praying this heavenly dream would last all through the night.

"Worry not, angel. I will stay."

CHAPTER SEVENTEEN

MIDMORNING SUNLIGHT PEEKED through the curtains, bright and luminescent. Jorlan lay flat on his back, one hand bracing his neck as he stared up at the ceiling. Katie was asleep and nestled deep in the crook of his arm. He'd meant to leave her alone this dawning, to allow her body time to heal, but the rope had beckoned and he'd longed to introduce her to the many ways of lovemaking. So he had, and she had welcomed the introduction most eagerly.

Now however, when he should be sated, his thoughts refused to settle. For a man who valued control, he felt very…uncontrolled. He was moved to the core by the intensity of what happened each time he joined his body to Katie's and could not wrap logic around the emotions still coursing through him. Simply saying he and Katie coupled did no justice to what occurred. Tupping was a pleasure, sometimes gentle, sometimes raw and carnal, a hunger that could be quenched by any number of things.

What he'd experienced with Katie had been as intense and consuming as a third-season wind whirl. And by *Elliea*, he wanted to experience it again and again. The pleasure he felt with her was staggering, and no sooner had his pulse calmed than he had begun to feel the nagging need to possess her again. He hadn't known he could get hard that often and that quickly.

He knew how rare, how special, his encounter with Katie was. But did she? His little witch had no basis for comparison, for she had remained untouched until his possession last eve. He was not complaining. The knowledge that no other man had ever touched her body still awakened a possessiveness within him that defied reason. Yet virginity was not prized, nor expected in Imperia. Women reveled in their lovers just as men did. In fact, the more lovers a female took, the more prized she became, for her knowledge in heightening her partner's pleasure was greatly increased. Besides Katie, every female he'd ever tupped had been experienced in the art of pleasure and some, like Maylyn, had even possessed more experience than he did.

Katie was so different from anyone he'd ever known. His desire for her went beyond the physical, and now, more than ever, he wanted her to belong to him, with him.

Forever.

He could not deny it any longer. That he had once wanted her on a temporary basis seemed somehow foul to him now. Aye, she was mortal and he half sorcerer, but he was not concerned with that fact. He might very well age as the mortals did. He did not know for sure. But he knew cursed well that he could not tolerate life without Katie at his side.

He cared for her, aye, he'd known that for a while; but he also admired her. He admired the way she stood her ground, the way she raised her chin and overcame whatever challenges were placed before her. He admired the way she never wavered in her beliefs, never raced away from his anger. She always faced him, square on, and never flinched. She was strong. Capable. Courageous. There was underlying steel in her backbone. Her bravery far surpassed that of any warrior he'd ever encountered. She did not need a keeper, was in fact well able to take care of herself. He favored that about her, as well, even while he craved the responsibility of protecting her.

Careful to leave her undisturbed, he shifted, propping himself up on his elbow and gazing down at his bed-mate. In sleep her features were relaxed, giving her an almost childlike beauty. Stroking a finger across the curve of her cheekbone, he listened as she muttered something unintelligible. Contentment, so subtle yet so compelling—and a long time in coming—filled him.

What were her feelings for him after their night of loving?

He'd finally taken her, only to discover his own feelings had deepened. Had hers deepened, as well? He prayed that it was so. Another day had already been lost to him.

Katie lay naked, not an inch of covering over her body and he vowed to keep her like that for the rest of their days. Glossy, pale locks surrounded her head in a tangled mass. Her lips were slightly swollen from his kisses. Pink scratches lined her breasts, stomach and thighs from his beard stubble. She looked sexy and completely sated. One seductive touch, however, and he knew an intense ache would ignite within her.

He grinned, recalling how wantonly she responded to his touch.

As if she knew the direction of his thoughts, Katie stirred in his arms. Slowly, she cracked open her eyes. Seconds ticked by. The sleepy mist surrounding her completely evaporated. Color bloomed in her cheeks. Memories of what they had done danced in her eyes, making the brown rims deepen to a rich, golden bronze. She looked tousled, as though she had just awakened from a vigorous bout of loving. Exactly how he wanted her to look every dawning.

In that moment he knew he would not rise from the bed until he had her again, for having a woman had never felt so important. So *necessary*.

"Good morning," she said, her voice tinged with sleep. "Well, good afternoon, I should say."

"Aye." He smiled. "'Tis indeed a good dawning."

"I, uh, guess I should make breakfast or something. I believe I promised you a seven-course meal the day we made love."

Made love, she had said. His heart drummed in his chest. 'Twas close to what he needed to hear, but not exactly right. "You are wrong. You promised me a seven-course meal the day you allowed me to massage your hair."

She returned his grin. "I'm sure you did that sometime during the night."

"That and more. But unless death is imminent," he told her, "we will stay here a while longer."

"Okay. What do you want to do?" She traced a fingertip up his chest.

He remained silent for a long moment, studying her

every second of it. Her gaze sparkled through thick, spiky lashes. "You are too sore for bed sport." But he knew he would do whatever was needed to make her ready.

To his relief, she said, "I'm sore, but never *too* sore. I doubt I'll be able to jog today, so I need *some* sort of workout. And I've been wondering…" Sweet and innocent, she blinked up at him. "How do you feel about being the slave of a queen?"

"I think I would enjoy it. Immensely."

"Oh, you'll do more than enjoy, slave. You'll pleasure your queen until she can take no more."

And he did.

AN HOUR LATER, Katie sat at her kitchen counter, a fresh protein shake in front of her. *I'm a wildcat,* she thought happily. She and Jorlan had made love so many times she'd lost count. She simply could not get enough of the man, and to her surprise, he couldn't seem to get enough of her.

A secret grin curved her lips and she shifted in her seat. The action made her grimace. Her body was sore from the night's excess, sorer than she'd realized. But she didn't regret a single twilight—or morning—experience. No, she rejoiced in the fact that she had plunged headlong into all the pleasures he offered.

She took a drink of the cold liquid and closed her eyes in surrender. Perhaps orgasms caused women to experience things more clearly because suddenly, her senses were more attuned. Her shake had never tasted so delectable. The air had never smelled as sweet. Her clothing had never felt so delicious against her skin.

If only she could spend the entire day abed, but she simply had too much to do today. Since Jorlan's arrival, she'd gotten sorely behind schedule. The Victorian needed to be painted, inside and out, and she'd hoped to have that done by, well, yesterday. Yet she hadn't even begun.

Before they left, though, she wanted to watch Jorlan eat breakfast. Only twenty minutes ago, she'd done something she'd sworn she would never do again: she'd cooked for a man. Surprisingly, she hadn't felt like a forgotten servant, hadn't wanted to use toilet water or drop his toast on the floor. No, she'd worn a genuine smile while she baked, and now the fully cooked, sanitary meal waited atop the stove for his enjoyment.

Jorlan sauntered into the kitchen, naked and unabashed. "Something smells wonderful," he said, his voice husky with slumber. The moment he spotted her, he gave her a look she now recognized as carnal. That wasn't what gave away his arousal, however. What gave him away was the erection straining long and thick between his legs.

If Earth men had been so lusty, women would never leave the bedroom, she thought, or the kitchen counter...or the living-room floor.

He stood behind her, leaned down and nuzzled her neck. "I think 'tis you, *katya*."

A sigh of tenderness swept through her, and she was reminded of a special treat she had for him. She swiveled her chair around to face him. "I have something for you."

"Hmm, I like the sound of that." He leaned down to nibble on her collarbone.

"Not that." She laughed and swatted him away. "Open your mouth."

Though he hesitated, he did as she'd instructed. Hiding a secret smile, she reached out, lifted a Hershey's bar from the counter, and snapped off the tip. She placed the little square onto his tongue.

"Close," she said.

His lips snapped together. Then his eyes widened as the sweet taste coated his mouth. *"Katya,"* he breathed, his tone heavy with ecstasy and awe. "We must cover your entire body with this magnificent concoction."

Three hours, much chocolate and loving, breakfast and a shower later, they finally drove to the Victorian. Frances and Heather were already there, waiting on the porch. Had she known they planned to start early, she wouldn't have allowed Jorlan to seduce her again. Well, she added after a moment's thought, she wouldn't have allowed him to seduce her so slowly.

"Good afternoon," she said.

Frances gave her an eager smile filled with enough light to rival the sun. "Good afternoon, yourself."

"I hope you haven't been waiting long. Jorlan and I were…busy." Unbidden, her blush told them exactly how busy they'd been and with what they'd been busy doing.

Both of Frances's brows furrowed together, and she blurted, "I thought he was off-limits." Her weathered cheeks colored to a brighter shade of red than Katie's own boasted.

"He is to everyone *except* me."

He smiled at her oh, so sweetly for such a confession.

Heather stood silently against the porch wall, old wood at her back. Surely the lumber splinters were digging through the pink fabric of her sweater, but she acted as if she was leaning upon soft, fluffy clouds.

Something was different about the girl today. Something softer. There was a glow to her skin that Katie had never noticed before. Most puzzling of all was the fact that Heather never spared Jorlan a glance. In fact, she was pretending he didn't exist.

Wondering just what thoughts were spinning the wheels inside Heather's brain, Katie led the group inside. Behind her, Frances gasped. "Oh, this place is lovely, Katie." She paused. "Or it will be when everything is fixed."

"Katie will make this a spectacular residence," Jorlan said, a note of pride in his tone. He flicked her a gaze. "She is good at everything she does."

The waitress gave him a strange look, as if she'd never heard such praise from a man's lips.

"Heather," Katie began, "your mother mentioned that you have a talent for gardening."

Heather eyed her hopefully. "I guess I do."

"Great. You can start weeding and fertilizing the garden out back. Once that's done, you can plant whatever flowers you want."

Brown eyes stared up at her with fragile optimism—optimism that seemed fresh and new. Had she never experienced the emotion before? "I'll need a hoe and a mini shovel."

"All the necessary tools are in the shed." That settled, Katie turned her attention to Frances. "While Heather works out back, I'd like you to work in the front."

"Really? I get to garden, too?" Practically jumping with excitement, Frances clasped her hands together. "What do you think of morning glory, lilies and lavender all around the porch edges? And maybe a trellis by the north wall?"

"I think that sounds wonderful. In fact, why don't you take my truck and go buy whatever you need at Garden Warehouse? You can put it on my account."

"Really?" Frances asked again.

"Really."

Beaming, Frances said, "I can never thank you enough for this, Katie." With that, she accepted the truck keys and skipped out the door.

"Me, too," Heather said so softly Katie barely heard her. Then the girl left in the opposite direction.

"What shall I do this day?" Jorlan asked.

Katie's first impulse was to say, "Do me. Do me." In his jeans and too-tight T-shirt, Jorlan was more appealing than any man had a right to be. However, too many chores needed her attention first. Her body could wait. Barely. "Why don't you go with Frances," she suggested. "That way, you can help her carry the heavy items."

A pained expression creased his features. "If I have to listen to one of her man jokes, I will not be responsible for my reaction."

Katie chuckled. "Just go, before you miss her."

"I will go," he conceded, "but only because it is my wish to please you."

Had a more perfect man ever been created? "Do not mention that you're from another planet, okay? We'll both be locked away if you do."

At the words "locked away" he brightened.

"We wouldn't be locked away together," she explained, still grinning. "Now get out of here."

Instead of heading to the door, he strode to Katie and planted a fierce kiss on her lips. Only when she was breathless with longing did he walk away.

ALONE IN THE HOUSE, Katie taped the baseboards and upper trim of the main bedroom wall, preparing each section for painting. As she worked, she decided not to use the paint sprayer. She wanted a more personal touch for this house, a lingering print of her presence. Forty-five minutes later, she was popping the top of the taupe paint when Jorlan trudged up the stairs and entered the room on a scented cloud of lavender and lilies.

"What do you think of these?" he asked. His expression was tolerant, but exasperated as he held a posy of flowers in each hand. "Frances would like to know."

He looked so domesticated just then, like a man from her planet. Like *her* man. Her heart flip-flopped, and she realized with the speed of a bolt of lightning and the intensity of a clasp of thunder that she wanted him to be her man. Permanently.

Oh. My. God.

What had she done? What the hell had she done?

Katie fought a wave of rising panic. *I haven't done anything,* she assured herself. *Everything will be all right.* While she cared for Jorlan, desired him, she hadn't fallen in love with him. That meant he couldn't leave her yet, that he had to stay here with her a while longer. Her shoulders instantly relaxed. *See, every-*

thing will be all right. She ignored the twinge of guilt that drifted beneath her thoughts.

"Jorlan—" she began.

He must have caught the trembling in her voice because he set the bouquets on the floor. His gaze never left her. "What has placed that look of terror in your eyes?"

"I just—I don't…"

His brow arched, and he crossed his arms over his chest, revealing that stubborn streak of his that had so irritated her at the first meeting but now filled her with calm. "What are you trying to say?" He came to her then, glided a fingertip across her cheekbone. His touch was so gentle, so reassuring. "Whatever it is, I will help you."

She took him by the shoulders, her nails digging deep. "Just kiss me. Kiss me now and make me forget."

Without a word, he lowered his lips to hers.

PERCEN GLARED DOWN at the embracing couple, both enraged and joyous. Joyous because Jorlan did not desire Heather. Enraged because Jorlan would not suffer now that Percen had claimed the gentle temptress as his own.

For the moment, he concentrated on his joy, a completely foreign emotion to him. An emotion he attributed to Heather. Since leaving her this dawning, he'd thought of little else. And he'd wondered…could she be the one his mother spoke of? The one woman who could see past his scars and see the man he truly was?

Yestereve, she hadn't seemed all that impressed

with his beauty. Nay, she'd craved only his warmth, his presence. Two things he could give her, ugly or gloriously handsome. Percen gazed up at the white ceiling above him. Did he possess the courage to try and win this mortal woman's heart? Did he even want to, now that she was no longer needed to punish Jorlan? The answer came swiftly and unequivocally. Aye. He wanted her more than he wanted his leg untwisted.

He'd spent only the one night with her, and yet she stirred feelings inside him he'd never thought to experience. There was happiness, aye, but she also made him feel content. 'Twas ironic, really, that he felt so deeply for a mortal when he'd often hated his mother for doing the same.

Standing there in the silence of his thoughts, Percen began to plan. He would go to Heather this night. He would take her in his arms, make love to her over and over again. He would show her his true self, and she would…

He did not know what she would do, and at the moment, he realized the answer didn't, *couldn't* matter. He could never have lasting happiness with Heather as long as Jorlan still lived.

Percen forced his thoughts back to his brother. 'Twas past time he finished the war between them. But how? He didn't want Katie, couldn't bring himself to try and win her affections. And it wouldn't do just to turn Jorlan into stone again. Where was the suffering in that? Mayhap…

Oh, aye, he thought, his eyes narrowing. Mayhap the pain he sought for his brother was not the jealous rage that he himself constantly battled. Mayhap what he should do, must do, *would do,* was *physically* hurt the woman who so clearly claimed Jorlan's affections.

Percen's lips twisted into a cruel smile.

JORLAN JERKED AWAY from Katie, abruptly ending their kiss. A sense of magic was enveloping him, a bit stronger than before. He had not cast a spell, yet power hummed all around him just the same.

"What's wrong?" Katie asked, startled. Her lips were still parted with desire and swollen now from the force of his mouth.

His gaze scanned the area around them. There was no one save he and Katie in the chamber. There was no furniture, either, where someone might hide. Only paint tins and brushes were scattered about, and some sort of transparent material covered the floor.

Katie gripped his forearm. "Jorlan? Tell me."

"There is…" His words tapered to a close, for the magic evaporated as quickly as it had appeared. Curse it, what was going on? Was he being watched, or was the stone spell trying to claim him early?

He froze, nearly fell to the floor with the force of his panic. He had not considered the possibility of losing his freedom before his two cycles had passed. Desperation twisted inside his belly. A cold sweat broke out across his brow. He pierced Katie with a glare. "Do you love me?" The words left his mouth in an explosion.

"I—" She shook her head, her eyes filled with sorrow and regret. "No, not yet. I'm sorry."

More panic. More desperation. There had to be a way to gain her affection. "Your brother mentioned a family gathering on Saturday."

She nodded, flowing with the swift change of subject. "That's tomorrow."

"I would like to go." What better way to win her than to prove himself to her family? Aye, 'twas it, the answer he craved. Slowly, his muscles relaxed.

Her eyes widened, and her jaw went slack. "You want to meet my dad?"

"Aye."

"Are you sure you want to meet my dad?" she asked again, yet hope was dancing in the depths of her tawny-colored eyes. "He's bossy and arrogant and even throws tantrums upon occasion."

"I would still like to meet him."

"I'll think about it," she said, but she was smiling brighter than he'd ever seen her.

That smile proved to be his undoing. He pulled her back into his arms and didn't let her go until they were both panting with desire.

CHAPTER EIGHTEEN

KATIE DIDN'T HAVE TO THINK long about whether or not to take Jorlan to the luncheon. Yes, yes, yes! was the answer. She'd never before introduced a man to her father, but for some reason, she wanted him to meet and love Jorlan.

At the moment, she and her alien were in her truck, speeding along the highway. Jorlan had no idea what he'd gotten himself into, of course, but she'd tried to warn him. His determination to spend the day with her family was startling in its intensity, and made her care for him all the more.

"Will there be 'lick her' at this family gathering?" he asked. He tugged at his seat belt, still uncomfortable with being locked down.

"Yes. To be honest, I don't think my brothers can tolerate each other without it."

Misunderstanding her dry tone, Jorlan reached around her and sunk his fingers into the base of her neck, massaging. "You have nothing to fear, *katya*. I will not harm your siblings."

She chuckled. "What if they deserve it?"

"Even then."

"Well, they need to pay for what they did to us the

other night, and I brought the means to do that." One
sandy brow arched and the corner of her lip elevated
with smug confidence as she patted the bag at her side.
Oh yes, her brothers were going to pay.

Before long, her father's house came into view. It
was the house of her childhood, an unusual house,
high and sprawling, redbrick, with a tall, cathedral
roof. She couldn't say the structure was to her personal taste, but the memories she had built there more
than made up for any architectural failure.

Five cars, each a different make and model—depending on the owner—were parked in the winding
driveway. She kept her truck close to the entrance, not
wanting to be blocked in with no escape. Bracing herself, she turned to Jorlan. "Are you ready for this?"

"Aye."

"I just want to warn you again. My dad is a
very…opinionated man."

"I wonder how his daughter became so pliable,
then," Jorlan teased.

"Ha, ha. Very funny." Instead of leading him to the
porch, she grabbed the plastic bag she'd brought and
strode directly to Nick's sedan. He was going to be her
first victim.

She raised the hood. Jorlan peered over her shoulder, casting a shadow over the engine. "What are you
doing?"

"Getting our revenge." With that, she clasped a container of baby powder and dumped the contents into
the ventilation system. She did the same to all of her
brothers' vehicles. "When they turn on their air con-
ditioners, they'll be blasted with the powder."

Jorlan slowly grinned. "Remind me never to make you angry."

They walked hand-in-hand to the porch. The front doors were oak and had elongated silver handles in the shape of the number eight. Music blared from speakers, fast-paced and without a noticeable rhythm. Not bothering to ring the bell—who would have heard her anyway?—she led Jorlan through the house. Every piece of decoration, from the floral print ottoman to the cream-colored lace curtains, was positioned exactly as her mother had liked them.

Everyone was in the backyard playing basketball. Even her dad had donned shorts and a bandana for the occasion. The dark blue kerchief wrapped around his head made him look like a slightly older version of her brothers, instead of an aging heart patient. Sunlight streamed down, hot and dry; unfortunately, no breeze meandered by to cool them off. The yard was flat, mostly light grass that had long since turned dry and weedy. All of the roses and azaleas that had once lined the fence were withered.

"Katie," her dad called when he saw her.

As one, all of her brothers halted in different stages of play and glanced over at her. Nick raced to the patio table and turned down the music as her dad's long strides closed the distance between them. He kissed her cheek. "How've you been, girl?"

Just peachy, she thought. *I'm sleeping with an alien and a curse hangs over our heads.* "I'm great."

"Good, good." His golden-brown eyes lit on Jorlan. He frowned. "Who's your friend?"

"Dad, this is Jorlan en Sarr. Jorlan, this is Ryan James. My father."

The two shook hands. "I've heard about you," he said, and judging by his tone, the information hadn't been good. "You may call me Detective James," he announced in his no-nonsense voice.

"Dad, you're no longer on the force," she reminded him. But she knew it would do no good—he made everyone, including her upon occasion, call him Detective.

"Doesn't matter." He wiped his sweaty cheek with the back of his wrist. "I earned the title and still deserve the respect that comes with it. Boys, say hi to our guest so we can get back to our game." Just like that, Jorlan was dismissed.

So far, things were not going well.

None of her brothers had been expecting her, obviously, because they stood all in a row, staring at her, waiting for her to reveal how they would be received. They all wore equal expressions of guilt and shame. Well, except for Nick, who was grinning as if he was having the time of his life.

"Hey, Jorlan," Erik finally said, ignoring her altogether.

"Hey," all the others called. Gray even gave Jorlan a stiff nod.

"Good dawning to you," Jorlan said. Of all of Katie's brothers, he liked Gray the best. The man had a way of intimidating everyone around him, a fine quality for any warrior to possess. Not that he intimidated Jorlan, however. Or Katie for that matter. In fact, the hard lines of Gray's face softened every time he glanced at his sister, ruining his I'm-about-to-kill-you frown.

How pathetic, Jorlan thought, his high praise for Gray evaporating. Couldn't the man remain outwardly unaffected while dealing with the opposite sex?

Katie chose that moment to glance at Jorlan. A smile grew on her lips, warm and intimate. He knew those lips felt like heated satin against his skin. He knew they tasted like the sweetest *gartina* petal.

His features relaxed.

The James men were hard and golden, yet Katie was soft and fair. Each man present could have easily passed for Imperian warriors. Katie, though, would not have blended with the men *or* the women of his world. She was too exotic-looking, too opinionated and commanding. If he introduced her to his warrior friends, they would surely string him alive, fearing such a spitfire would embolden *their* women. But ah, what fun he and Katie would have!

For some reason, all of the James men were lined up side by side, now staring at him with hard expressions. He crossed his arms over his chest and stared right back at them.

"Are you having fun yet?" Katie whispered in Jorlan's ear. She turned her attention back to her brothers. Knowing they would soon be drenched with baby powder put her in a forgiving mood. "Well," she said, hands on hips. "Are you going to greet me or not?"

In a snap, sweaty male arms and chests enfolded her. "Enough," she laughed.

"Glad you came," Gray told her, then kissed her cheek.

"Don't smother the girl," her father barked. "You all smell like a locker room and I don't want you to gag her to death. God, no wonder she lives alone and refuses to marry a decent man. You've all given her a bad impression."

"Don't get all tense, Dad." Katie pointed a finger at his chest. "It's not good for your health."

"Well—" he blustered.

"Besides, the James brothers can't help themselves. I'm irresistible."

"That you are," Jorlan whispered against her ear.

In the sudden silence, everyone overheard. Gray rolled his eyes at the sweet entreaty. Nick chuckled. Her dad watched them with narrowed eyes. "Who's ready to finish the game?" He grabbed the ball from the ground. "Katie, go sit by Denver's friend. You gals can cheer for me. Jorlan, why don't you be on Nick's team?"

For the first time, Katie noticed the lone woman perched beneath the bright-yellow patio umbrella. Dark-brown hair spilled around her shoulders. She wore a lightweight, strappy sundress made of light-blue fabric and somehow managed to look cool and sophisticated amid the crackling heat.

"Jorlan doesn't know how to play basketball." Katie swiped her sweat-beaded brow with the back of her hand.

"What red-blooded American doesn't know how to play basketball?" her dad roared.

"He's not American."

"Doesn't matter. He's red-blooded isn't he?"

Actually, she didn't know.

"I know the game," her alien lover said. "Over the spans I have watched several of them played. I will play, but I would like Katie to play, as well."

"Girls shouldn't play sports, son. They can get hurt." This was, of course, said by her father as he gave her a pointed look that conveyed the message: don't disappoint me by stepping beyond feminine boundaries yet again.

She just arched a brow. "I'm your sixth son, Dad. I can take anything you dish."

"Fine." Ryan threw his arms in the air, as if he'd been pushed to the last level of his tolerance. "But I'm not willing to take a chance that you'll get trampled. We'll just take turns shooting from the line."

"Oh, I like that," Nick said with a sly grin. "First one to miss has to tell everyone his best pickup line. Maybe this way, we can teach Gray something about women."

Gray slugged him in the shoulder.

Katie rolled her eyes. "I'll sit this one out, boys, but I do thank you for the offer." While she would have loved playing with Jorlan, she had a much stronger desire to watch him. She skipped to the shaded umbrella table and introduced herself to Denver's friend. "I'm Katie. The sister."

"Madison." Madison wore big sunglasses that covered half her face. This close up, her dark hair appeared glossy, like chocolate tinted silk. She was pretty in a delicate, pixieish sort of way.

Shading her eyes with her hand, Katie plopped down in an available seat. "How long have you and Denver been dating?"

"A few weeks." Madison's tone was cool, and she offered no more information.

Katie got the hint. She also realized that Madison was the usual type of female Denver dated—a woman who needed icicles surgically removed from her veins. When would her brother find someone at least partially thawed?

Without another word, she turned her attention to the men. They were all lined up in front of the goal, taking turns shooting the ball. When Jorlan's turn arrived, a look of such intense concentration masked his face. He studied the goal, weighed the ball in his hands, then finally shot. The ball swooshed through the net.

Five rounds later, Nick missed.

"Let's hear your best pickup line. Maybe I can learn something—not to say," Gray finished with a laugh.

Nick's mouth twitched with amusement. "I prefer a direct approach. Something like this. Nice legs." He wiggled his eyebrows. "What time do they open?"

Madison gasped.

Katie chuckled.

All of the men burst into laughter, including Jorlan. Her heart warmed at the sight. How wonderfully he was interacting with her family. And he wasn't even hammered! Her smile slowly faded. Why, why, why couldn't she keep him?

Life was so unfair.

Erik was the next to miss. "You've got two hundred bones in your body. Want one more?"

Again, Madison gasped. "That's disgusting," she said scathingly.

On and on the boys played until she'd heard everything from, "I'd really like to see how you look when I'm naked." To, "You know, if I were you, I'd have sex with me." To, "Wanna play army? I'll lay down and you can blow the hell out of me."

Madison had spewed her glass of water over that one.

Jorlan finally missed. Everyone, including Katie, stared at him in expectation. Just what constituted an Imperian come-on? As she watched him, she noticed his eyes were crinkled merrily at the sides. Oh, he was having fun, and she wanted to throw herself in his arms because of it.

Another second passed, then another. He had them all on the edge, waiting.

Finally, he said confidently, "Get thee to my bed, woman."

All of Katie's brothers frowned. "That's not a pickup line," Denver said.

"It's not even funny," Nick added.

"But it works," Jorlan added with a smile. "Every time."

Male chuckles abounded, some a deep tenor, others a husky baritone. Still, she could distinguish Jorlan's chuckles, like a deep, honey-rich caress.

"I'm starved," Gray suddenly announced. He dropped the ball and let it roll onto the grass. "Someone get into the kitchen and make me a sandwich."

Half a dozen male faces peered at her and Madison. "I am not fixing anyone anything," Katie retorted, popping to her feet.

"Don't look at me," Madison ground out. "I'm ready to leave."

"Katie," her father began, entreaty woven into the deep timbre of his voice. "You and Madison are the only women here. While we've been busy, you've been sitting. Fixing us lunch is the least you can do."

"We have this argument every time I come over." When her mother had been alive, hamburgers, hot-dogs, casseroles and fresh fruit punch had abounded. Since Hannah's death, however, the only food to be served was what Katie prepared. "You're a big boy, and if you get hungry, you can cook."

"Cooking is a woman's job, young lady."

"Then I guess all the big bad men here will have to starve."

Jorlan came to her, put his arm around her waist. His masculine scent filled her nostrils, raw and primal. "No woman of mine serves those who are ungrateful."

Everyone stilled, awaiting an explosion from Ryan.

"Ungrateful!" Ryan roared. "I'll have you know—"

"Uh, why don't I order a pizza?" Erik clasped a hand on his dad's shoulder.

Katie barely acknowledged her brother. She was too shocked by Jorlan's pronouncement. He wasn't demanding she obey; he was supporting her, helping her. Caring for her. An undeniable sense of peace and rightness settled deep inside her.

Jorlan read the disbelief on Katie's face.

He did not like her family making her feel so unimportant. He liked even less that he himself had often done the same. Did they not see she possessed the fire of a warrior? The courage? The boldness? She belonged at a man's side, not behind him. Not serving him.

"Can I speak to you a moment?" Ryan locked his hands behind his back and braced his feet apart, looking every inch the detective. It was a war position. His mouth was firm, with grim lines at the corners.

Jorlan nodded. Katie opened her mouth to protest, but he gave her a slight shake of his head. "I will speak with him."

"His health isn't great, so try not to make him mad, okay?"

"For you…anything," he said, and he realized surprisingly that he meant every word. He placed a soft kiss upon the sensitive skin of her wrist, then followed the older man inside the house. A cool blast of air enveloped him, welcoming him and drying his sweat.

In the next instant, Ryan rounded on him. "Just what are your intentions toward my daughter? The boys say you're leaving her soon." His eyes, identical to the light amber-brown of Katie's, were narrowed with fatherly concern.

Jorlan crossed his arms over his chest. "Katie asked me to be gentle with you, thus I will ignore the disrespectful tone you continue to use while addressing me."

Ryan stared at him in silence. Slowly, his expression softened, until finally, he settled down onto the couch with a plop, grinning widely. "You still set on leaving?"

"Mayhap."

Ryan nodded. "You're strong. Won't take any crap."

What was the man getting at?

"By damn, you're just what she needs. She runs roughshod over everyone else, but you, I think, will have a chance of corralling her. She's my only daughter, you know? My baby."

"I know."

"Looks just like her mother. A bit taller, though. She gets that from me," he said proudly.

Jorlan didn't respond. Ryan was lost in his memories, and he hated to disturb him. But more than that, he wanted to learn about Katie as a little girl. He could very well imagine her with chubby pink cheeks and long pale hair in wild disarray as she raced along a pebbled path.

"Katie's always been such a stubborn girl. Likes to keep me on my toes." The detective launched into a tale about the time Katie had stuffed her dress full of frogs and tried to sneak them inside her room. "Calls herself my sixth son."

"Yet you treat her as a servant."

Ryan lost his soft edge. "I never mistreat her."

"You do. Every time you command her to serve you."

A lengthy pause ensued. Then, Ryan expelled a deep breath. "Maybe you're right. But damn, son, women are gentle creatures and in need of protection. And men, well, we're in need of coddling."

Jorlan finally decided to answer the detective's initial question. "My intentions toward your daughter are honorable." He slid his tongue over his teeth, not liking his next confession. "I want to make her my lifemate, yet first I must convince her to accept."

"Life-mate? Has Katie heard you say that?" He chuckled. He pushed to his feet and slapped Jorlan on the shoulder. "Good luck, son. You're going to need it." He was still chuckling as he strolled outside.

CHAPTER NINETEEN

HEATHER WENT TO BED early that night, as she had the last two nights, hoping for another appearance from her dream man. She didn't have to wait long. Just as he had the other times, Percen materialized beside her as quickly as if she'd flipped on a light switch—as if he couldn't wait to see her.

But this night, as she gazed at him, she couldn't deny that she was awake. She wasn't dreaming, yet there was he. She'd suspected that he was more than a figment of her imagination, but now she knew for sure.

He was real.

The realization didn't frighten her, however. He made her feel too good to fear him. She couldn't explain his presence, but that didn't matter. All that mattered was that he was lying beside her, enveloping her with his warmth. Whoever he was, *whatever* he was— a ghost or vampire or a dream come to life—she wanted him with her just the same.

He'd told her she belonged to him, and Heather wanted those words to be true. She wanted to be his. Totally and completely. Yet he hadn't made love to her yet, hadn't touched her in a sexual way. She yearned for his body inside of hers, making them one being.

Silently, she studied this man she had known only a short time, but had somehow managed to become so important to her. As she took in each of his features, a frown tugged at her lips. Tonight Percen looked as if he were wearing some sort of mask. His usually flawless skin, almond-shaped eyes and straight, even nose appeared…too perfect. He was beautiful still, in a dark sort of way, his skin wonderfully tanned, his muscles hard as stone, but something wasn't right.

Maybe he had always looked this way, and she was only just noticing. Or maybe he truly was different. She saw a vulnerability about him now, a deeply ingrained vulnerability that seeped from every part of him. He reminded her of herself, wounded and weary, and that knowledge wrapped around her like a long bolt of silk. Did he possess the same bone-deep hurts that she possessed?

"You're back," she whispered into the darkness.

"Aye. I am back. I cannot stay away."

"I've thought about you all day," she admitted. "Every moment I worked, every moment I *breathed* all I could think about was you."

He paused, as if he was scared to utter his next words. "What were your thoughts?" Each syllable emerged stilted and hesitant.

"I thought of the way you hold me, the way you make me feel so warm."

He didn't respond. She began to curse herself for her hasty confession. What if he liked the challenge of winning a woman? What if her easy surrender drove him away?

Then he spoke. "I like that you think of me, angel,

I truly do, but I am not the man you think I am." The admission came reluctantly, and she noticed that every muscle in his body was tense, as if preparing to bolt. "You would not consider me so sweetly if you saw my true appearance."

Her chin cocked to the side. "I don't understand."

"What you perceive me to be is only a mirage. A mask of the man I can never be." His tone was dark and gritty, accusatory. "I cast a spell that causes you to see only what I want you to see."

"You're a witch?" she asked. "A warlock?"

"I know not those words."

"Someone who uses magic."

"Aye, I am a sorcerer, the Druinn High Priest, and I do wield magic."

As a teenager, she had dabbled in the supernatural to escape the terror of her life. She knew outside forces existed all around her, and didn't doubt his claim of magic. How else could he appear and disappear at whim? "Whatever you are and whatever you can do, I see a man who is good and decent. You have to be. How else could I feel so safe with you?"

He didn't comment on her words. Instead, he softly caressed a hand over her cheek. Though his hand looked smooth and unblemished, it felt rough with calluses and scars. Strange. Yet the sensation caused a soft tingling to work its way from the back of her neck all the way to her toes.

"Percen?"

"Aye."

"Is the spell responsible for the warmth I feel every time you are near? For my...desire?"

Again, he hesitated. "Nay," he said truthfully, his eyes slowly widening with surprise. "Nay. 'Tis not."

"Then it is you who makes me feel so alive. You." She realized then that she wanted him to stay with her, not just during the night, but during the days, as well. Every day. Every night. How could she give up this warmth, now that she knew it existed?

"I—I do not know what to say."

"Say you'll stay with me." She cupped his cheeks in her hands. "Say you will stay with me always."

"Heather, I am... I cannot... You will not understand," he ended, suddenly angry.

She fought a wave of panic because she felt him mentally and emotionally withdrawing from her. She needed him in her life; somehow, in only these three nights, he had become the center of her existence. She wanted them to have a normal life together. The storybook life she'd always desired, but always found just out of her reach.

"At least give me a chance to understand. Please," she added desperately when he didn't acknowledge her words in any way. "Please."

A knock sounded at the door.

"Heather?" her mother called.

Before she could utter a protest, or even clamp an arm over his abdomen to hold him in place, Percen disappeared. Fighting a wave of desolation, Heather stared down at the bed sheets, at the indentation and wrinkles where he had lain. Her stomach lurched, and she wanted to weep as cold chills raked her from head to toe.

He was gone.

Shaking, she caressed the lingering warmth his body had left.

Another knock, this one louder and more intense, jolted her into awareness. "Are you okay?" her mother asked.

"I'm tired," she said listlessly. "Just leave me alone."

A pause. Muffled footsteps as her mother walked away.

Tears pooled in Heather's eyes and for a moment, she couldn't see, could only make out the blurred silhouette of her room. Would Percen return to her? She didn't think so. He was angry with her for a reason she didn't understand. She had pushed him too far, perhaps. Or asked too much of him.

A quiet sob tore from her throat. It was a sound only a wounded animal would make, deep and gut-wrenching.

"Why do you cry?"

Percen!

"You came back." She swiped her eyes with the back of her wrist. When she focused, she found he was in the exact position he'd adapted before he left. Of their own accord, her arms wrapped around his neck, holding him close, holding him tight. Holding him to her. "Don't ever leave me again," she sobbed, suddenly warm again. "Don't ever leave me again."

How long she held him like that, while she cried in his arms, she didn't know. She only knew that being with him was necessary for her survival. She didn't care if it was magic or chemistry that linked them together. The feelings were there, crackling between them.

"Look at me, Heather," he beseeched. His tone was softer than she'd ever heard it. "Look at me. Really see the man I am."

Slowly, keeping herself firmly against him, she pulled back and gazed up at his face. A gasp congealed in her throat. No longer did Percen have the flawless skin and features she'd come to know. His face was now marred with scars. His left eye drooped lower than his right, and his nose was bent at an odd angle. His body was broken and twisted.

Heather didn't doubt that this was Percen; she knew it was him because of his eyes. The same glint of vulnerability was hidden in their light-blue depths.

At her continued silence, his face darkened with rage. "Do you wish me to stay with you now?" he growled. "I tried to warn you, tried to make you understand that you would not want me."

Her father had been a very handsome man, yet his beauty had hid the beast within. "I don't care about your appearance." Realizing she spoke truthfully, she took his hand in her own and beckoned him to rest his head upon her chest.

Shock, disbelief and incredulity flickered over his expression. "You are not frightened?" he asked softly, hesitating only a moment before burrowing his face in the hollow of her neck.

She held him to her, clinging to him as much as he clung to her. His twisted body shook with his effort to control his emotions. Or perhaps the shaking came from her. "I could never be afraid of you."

He glanced up, and the look of utter worship he gave her would have felled her had she been standing.

His gaze flicked longingly to her lips. A deeply in-grained hunger danced between them. Her mouth parted in invitation. He leaned completely into her, leaving no part of her body untouched, and then he began kissing her, loving her body in a way she'd never dreamed possible. Making love to him felt right, clean and pure. She felt worshipped as he kissed her breasts, her belly, her thighs.

When he entered her, bits and pieces of her soul began to heal. *This* was the reason she was alive. *This* was the reason her attempts to rid the world of her ex-istence had failed.

Afterward, they stayed in each other's arms, both lost in the rightness of the moment. He began telling her the details of his life, his childhood, how he'd been aban-doned and forgotten. Heather felt a deep kinship with him, for although her father had not abandoned her, he had betrayed her. And as Percen spoke, she began to think that maybe, just maybe, they could save each other.

"Jorlan did nothing to you, Percen," she told him gently. "Why do you wish to kill him?"

Percen jolted up, glaring at her. The soft dreamlike haze was destroyed, replaced with the fury she had witnessed only moments before. "He did everything! Had he never been conceived, our mother would have come for me. She would have missed me."

"No." Heather shook her head sadly. "Your mother made her choice long before Jorlan was born."

"Why are you saying this?" He slammed his fist against his hand, then quickly began to reclaim his clothing. "Why are you hurting me like this? I thought you accepted me, wanted me with you always."

"I *do* want you with me. I *do* accept you. Can't you see I'm trying to help you? If you kill Jorlan, you'll be hunted. You'll be taken away from me and locked inside a cell."

"I am not bound by the rules of your world. Besides, if I were captured, no mortal cell could hold me."

Maybe not, but he was still just a man, a man who could die like any other. She couldn't allow him to risk his own life. "Please rethink this, Percen. Do you truly want to risk your own life simply to hurt Jorlan?"

"Aye, I do. I will risk anything, *anything* to watch my brother suffer."

"Even me?"

Something cold and hard glittered in his eyes. This was not the man she'd come to know. "Aye, I will risk even you."

Oh, those words hurt. Yet she still clung to her belief that she could save Percen on her own. "I'll tell him," she said. "I'll warn Jorlan of your presence."

Percen's eyes narrowed. He cupped her chin in his hands. "If you tell him anything, I will never warm you again. Do you comprehend what I am saying?"

Everything inside her withered. He'd named the one thing she would never risk. Slowly, she nodded.

"Try to understand." His tone became soft. "I cannot release what has driven me for so long. Until Jorlan is destroyed, we cannot have the life I dream for us." He pushed to his feet, once more the stranger she did not recognize. "Stay away from Katie's home. Do you hear me? Stay away from her home."

Heather nodded again, this time almost imperceptibly. Satisfied, he waved his arm in the air and disappeared.

CHAPTER TWENTY

KATIE BURROWED deeper into Jorlan's arms, her mind too active to sleep and her body too sated to move. Twilight filtered through the window and cast a luminous spell around her bed, a canopy that kept the real world at bay. She'd enjoyed watching Jorlan with her family today. She'd enjoyed even more how he'd swooped in to her defense.

A girl could get used to that.

She wondered what was going through Jorlan's mind right now. He'd been silent with his thoughts the past hour, and she'd been loathe to disturb him.

Sighing, she lightly traced her fingers over his chest. Right now both she and Jorlan were sticky with a light sheen of perspiration, and she thought longingly of a warm bath and all the things they could do inside that warm bath. Perhaps in the morning they could—

"I want you as my life-mate, Katie. Not for a time, but forever."

Jorlan's voice sliced through the silence, startling her. Surely he hadn't said... Surely he didn't mean...

"I don't understand." Shocked, afraid to hope she'd heard him correctly, she didn't know what else to say.

"I want you in my life, now and always." His arms

tightened around her bare waist, locking her in place. "Do you understand now?"

"Yes." Joy burst within her chest then raced along her nerve endings with the force of an earthquake. "Are you sure? I mean, this is a big step."

"Aye. I am sure." Absolute conviction filled his eyes, making the blue appear deeper, darker than any ocean.

"I can't believe this is happening. Sure, you asked me before, but that was temporary and this is… God, I don't know what to say."

"Start by telling me your answer, woman."

This gorgeous man wanted her as his wife. Now and always, he'd said. What shocked and thrilled her the most, however, was that he was going to stay with her. She hadn't asked him, yet he was going to stay of his own free will. A smile brimming with happiness curved her lips. She should have had to think about it, but she already knew her answer. "Yes! Yes, yes, yes!" A laugh bubbled past her throat, and she wrapped her arms around his neck, holding him close.

His entire body relaxed, though she hadn't noticed that he'd tensed. He breathed a long sigh of relief, smiled and adjusted their bodies so that he could gaze down at her. His glorious weight pinned her in place. "I feared you would say nay again."

"Are you kidding me? I've never been happier than I am at this moment." She smiled. "Do you want to have a church wedding? That's what the couples of my planet do. Oh my God. I'm still in shock."

"Say it again." His hands tangled in her hair, forcing her to continue looking up at him. "Tell me your answer again."

"Yes. I said yes."

The awed expression he gave her washed over her body with the smooth richness of a caress. He gently laced his fingers through hers, bringing her hands up to rest on each side of her head until they were palm to palm. His expression was warm and tender. "You will not regret this decision, *katya*. You will love my world as you love your own, and I will devote my life to making you happy."

Katie froze.

Jorlan continued, lost in his own thoughts. "Tell me you love me. I need to hear those words, not simply because of the curse, but because they come from you."

The delight dancing through her withered. Comprehension dawned, and she was suddenly left bereft and cold. "When you asked me to marry you, you assumed I would be coming with you?"

He blinked. "Of course."

Of course. She laughed, but the sound held no trace of humor. No, the sound emerged as a painful whimper, like an animal trapped by a snare. "Jorlan, I assumed you would be staying here."

"Katie—"

"You have to understand. My family is here." Tears burned her eyes. She held them back. She loved her family too much to leave them, but for Jorlan's love she just might do it. She might pack her bags and go with him to the ends of the galaxy. Lord, she just didn't know. "Do—do you love me?" It was the hardest question she'd ever asked, because she both feared and craved an affirmative answer.

For a long while, he hesitated, some sort of war brewing in his expression. Then, "Aye. I love you."

What did that hesitation mean? Was he lying now? Finally compromising his honor so that she'd admit she loved him in return? Could she risk her heart, her life, her existence on words he might not mean?

"You have to stay here with me. Please. Stay. Just stay."

"My family is there, and I have been gone so long. Too long. I have to know what happened to them. I have to know who lives…and who has died." Pain etched every curve and hollow of his face. "I cannot stay."

She squeezed her eyes together so tightly her tears were forced to fall. Her chin trembled. "Then I'm sorry. My answer is no."

JORLAN SAT before a small, picturesque window, nestled in a private alcove within Katie's bedchamber, gazing out at the moonlight. Stars twinkled across the heavens like the jewels of a king's crown. If only he possessed such riches right now that he might present them at Katie's feet. Yet he did not for a moment think that such an offering would change her mind—but he hoped. And hope was what drove him.

She'd asked if he loved her, and he'd thought *love her?* Did he truly, could he possibly love her? Care, aye. Admire, aye. But love? And then the truth of it had danced through him, a culmination of victory and defeat, yet so undeniably true it pounded through his heart with the force of a magic spell. He loved her. He loved Katie with all of his being. Nothing else explained why he wanted her so desperately, why he *needed* her for eternity.

This feeling of love did not resemble the type of love he'd felt for Maylyn on any level, and mayhap that was why he'd taken so long to discover the truth. This feeling was deeper, more intense. Real. What he'd felt for Maylyn hadn't been love, he realized now, merely a healthy dose of lust.

He wouldn't have cared if Maylyn had said no to his proposal. Yet hearing Katie say nay cut deeper than the sharpest talon. Her refusal might have been easier to accept if her reasons had been different. He could have easily soothed her had she worried that the sting of age would overcome her, while he remained as he was. He did not know how he would age, so why worry until they knew? He could have easily soothed her had she worried that he might one day wish to possess another woman, for he knew that to be untrue. Katie held his heart, his desire.

But he could not discount her love for her family.

At the moment, Katie was lying on the bed, sleeping soundly. He thought again how in slumber her features relaxed, softened, giving her a delicate quality, almost angelic. Strands of her hair surrounded her face like a pale halo. Yet he knew that awake and aroused, she was anything but celestial. Nay, she was carnal, like the very devil, taunting him, teasing him.

Tempting him.

In the last hours he'd taken her over and over again hoping to prove to her just how much she needed him. Instead, she had held fast to her convictions. Winning

Katie was proving the greatest challenge of his life, and he knew not what to do next.

THE SORCERER KNOWN ONLY as Mon Graig was coming for Jorlan, coming to take him home. Percen sensed the old sorcerer's magic drawing nearer, and knew the man would soon appear to Jorlan, would wait until Jorlan's curse was completely broken and then take the warrior to Imperia. Percen could not allow that. He needed more time, just a little more time. So he waited at the man's tiny dwelling, shadows surrounding him, scepter drawn.

By the new dawning, Mon Graig was trapped inside his own stone casing.

"HEATHER STILL ISN'T feeling well."

Katie lowered her paint roller from the wall and gazed over at Frances, who stood at the Victorian's threshold. Midday sunlight streamed around her, mingling with the overhead light. Katie was careful to keep the thick mauve liquid from dripping onto the plastic floor covering. She didn't want to track the stuff on her shoes. "Is she okay? She's been sick all week."

"I hope so." Concern darkened Frances's hazel eyes. "I can't help but worry about her, though. She lies in bed all day and all night. She doesn't want to eat or sleep; she just stares up at the ceiling. Sometimes she even talks to herself."

"If there's anything I can do, just let me know, okay?"

"I will. Thanks for understanding." With a shaky smile, Frances left to continue her work outside. The

little slice of light cut away as the screen door banged
to a close.

Half of the day was gone already, Katie realized. It
had melted away as quickly as the week had. Frowning,
she dropped her roller into the tin. Her arm muscles
ached from pushing it up and down the downstairs walls.
She wondered how Jorlan was doing upstairs. Had he
finished painting the bedroom yet?

With each passing day, he'd grown more and more
restless, more and more reserved. He no longer smiled,
no longer teased her. He almost seemed...sad. Every
day he told her he loved her, and every day he asked
her if she loved him. Her answer remained the same.
No. She was unwilling to love a man she could not
trust completely. While part of her believed him every
time he spoke those wonderful words, a part of her still
felt disbelief and suspicious of his intentions.

Time was running out, though, and she couldn't
allow him to return to stone.

What was she going to do?

Katie didn't know. She did know that she needed to
see him and assure herself that he was still here, that he
was still the flesh-and-blood warrior who held her each
night. She marched up the stairs. Her tennis shoes
squeaked with every step, and she made a mental note
to wedge a few nails between the plank seams and at last
end the squeaking. When she entered the bedroom, she
stopped and silently observed. Jorlan had his back to her.
He was shirtless. Natural light flooded through the un-
adorned window, caressing his muscles, making his skin
glow a golden brown.

Her nerve endings hummed to life as she watched

him stroke the roller up and down just as she'd shown him. His shoulder muscles were tense, but not from painting. He knew she stood behind him, and he was determined to ignore her.

I will not be ignored. Her steps clipped, she closed the remaining distance between them, jerked the roller from his grasp, and rolled it down his face. Ha! Ignore that.

At first, he remained completely still.

"You will pay for that," he said softly. But instead of punishing her, he wiped his eyes clean and grabbed the paintbrush at his feet. He dipped the bristles into the paint tin. Then he smeared the pale-yellow liquid onto the walls. His face took on an I-must-concentrate-because-the-fate-of-the-world-rests-in-my-hands expression. Up. Down. Up. He put his entire body into the experience, making his muscles strain and flex.

Even while ignoring her, the man was passion incarnate. His physique came from many years on the battlefield, she surmised, but looking at him did not evoke images of blood and gore. No, looking at him made her think of silk sheets and sweaty bodies.

"I need more paint," he finally said, though he didn't glance her way.

"To paint me?"

His jaw tensed. "To finish painting the wall."

It took a moment to register what he'd said, and when she did, she snapped out of her lustful haze. "I gave you enough to cover the Great Wall of China."

"And yet my tin is empty."

Not sure what to expect, Katie leveled her gaze onto the wall. It looked perfectly fine. She rotated and surveyed the wall behind her. Her gasp echoed in the sudden quiet. "Oh my God. What did you do?"

"I painted." Three empty paint cans occupied one corner of the room. "With a bit of magic," he reluctantly admitted.

"You opened and used other colors." Her voice whisked out in a horrified whisper, but soon picked up in volume. "I only gave you one color. One. One!"

"Those were available, thus I made use of them." He motioned to the row of paint tins she had organized according to color. He'd taken one from each row. "If they were not to be used, this should have been mentioned."

"Not mixing colors is common sense."

"Do not paint the floor, you said. Do not paint the side trim, you said. Do not use circular motions, you said. Well, I did none of those things."

"You're right." Hell, he was right, and she couldn't chastise him for her own mistake.

The wall looked horrible, though. Absolutely hideous. Like a smeared, discolored rainbow. Several places were bubbled with…good God, was that mud? She stifled a groan. How was she going to fix that wall? With four years of experience, she'd never encountered this sort of problem before.

"Have I not done as you wished?" he asked, his expression mutinous—and comical because of the streaks of yellow paint running down his cheeks.

Now, on top of everything else, she'd hurt his feelings. Wonderful. Just freaking wonderful. "You've done fine."

"I will hear your thanks, then."

He would hear her thanks? *He would hear her thanks?* A red cloud descended over Katie's eyes, eradicating her previous benevolence. He had ignored her all day, had ruined her wall, and now he would hear her thanks? "Why should I thank you when you missed a spot?" With that, she reached out with her roller and drew it down his nose.

He paused only a brief moment, but then returned the favor.

She gasped as the cold liquid coated her skin. "Do *not* do that again," she growled. But even as she said the words, she was reaching out and smearing him with another coat.

He grabbed her in the next instant, looking like the playful, teasing lover she'd come to know. "Think you can paint me?"

She chuckled. "Yes, actually, I do."

"Then let us see who wields the mightier brush." In a heartbeat of time, he had her pinned to the ground. Slowly, very slowly, he painted her hair, her collarbone, her legs.

Toward the end, she was laughing so hard she couldn't rebuke him. Finally, he tossed his brush aside. He stared down at her with a serious glint in his pale-blue eyes, watching her for a long, silent moment. Then, he kissed her, a languid kiss that went on and on and made her wet with arousal. Instead of making love to her, however, he pulled away and, without a word, swiped up his brush and went back to painting the wall.

Turn away from her, would he? She dumped the remaining paint over his head.

He stood stunned for a long while, yellow rivulets

dripping from his head and face. His eyes narrowed. "You will pay for that, *katya*."

"You have to catch me first," she taunted, darting away.

"Oh, I will catch you. Doubt it not."

Smothering her laughter with her hand—it wouldn't do to give away her location so easily—she slipped into the next room. But she had only taken three steps when the wood cracked beneath her feet. Without warning, she tumbled down, down, down. Something sharp sliced at her body. Katie screamed, anticipating impact.

When she hit, she hit hard, like brick against brick. She tasted the metallic tang of blood in her mouth, grasped for a breath, but couldn't drag in the smallest bit of air.

Jorlan shouted her name, the sound anguished and desperate.

Darkness claimed her.

CHAPTER TWENTY-ONE

JORLAN RUSHED DOWN the steps, taking three at a time as the horrifying scene replayed over and over in his mind. Only seconds ago he had watched Katie tumble from his sight. Then he had gazed through a hole in the upstairs floor and seen her body lying so still, so broken, trickles of blood flowing from her mouth and body.

Time ceased to exist, and yet an eternity passed before he reached her. He skidded to a halt, bent down, and gently folded her in his arms. She didn't make a sound, didn't move. Didn't flutter her eyes. "Katie? Please open your eyes."

Still, no response.

Pieces of wood protruded from her body, causing her blood to mingle with the paint she wore. Jorlan knew this was no accident, knew that the wood had not splintered from natural causes. Magic coated the air. He had attempted to paint Katie's wall with his powers, only to cause the thick, gooey liquid to explode. Could he have also weakened the house's flooring?

By *Elliea,* his woman was hurt, in danger of dying, and every protective, primitive instinct he possessed surfaced, fueled by fear and anger and impotence. He went cold all over. He needed her too desperately to lose her now. Saving her wasn't an obligation, wasn't a duty or an effort to save his freedom; it was necessary for his sanity.

If he used his magic to help her, would he cause her more harm?

There was a chance he could help her, and because of that chance, he had to try. If he did nothing, she would surely die.

Closing his eyes, he harnessed every ounce of power he possessed. He'd never attempted anything like this, shouldn't be attempting it now, yet he could not sit idle, helpless.

"Help me, Druinn," he muttered. "Help me. Please."

A door slammed shut. Footsteps.

A woman gasped. "What happened?" Frances. He knew 'twas her.

He did not expend any energy speaking to her or even facing her. He simply kept his eyes closed and concentrated on Katie, on his magic. Soon his hands began to burn, and he felt another power, someone else's power, mingle with his own. Whose? He didn't know. Didn't care. Consumed by his desperation, he ran each of his palms down Katie's body, from the top of her head to the bottom of her feet.

Mayhap 'twas his desperation. Mayhap 'twas his love for Katie. Or mayhap 'twas whoever helped him. Whatever the reason, he knew beyond a certainty that he was at last wielding his mystical abilities to their full potential.

Very distantly, as if she stood in a tunnel, he heard Frances demand, "What are you doing?"

Still, he ignored her.

"Your hands are glowing." Her tone was shrill. "Now *Katie* is glowing."

With that, he heard a loud thump, like that of a body hitting the floor. A sound he now knew all too well.

His power was waning, his strength weakening. He collapsed at the waist and remained hunched over, barely able to breathe. Had he saved her? He had used his magic like a true sorcerer, but had it been enough? With much effort, he opened his eyes. The first thing he noticed was that Katie lay completely still, oblivious to the world around her. Next he saw that Frances had indeed fainted. Her body was sprawled on the floor.

One heartbeat passed. Then another. Katie moaned. Her eyelids fluttered open. "Jorlan?" she asked weakly.

She was alive. She was well. So glad was he to hear her voice he used what little energy he had left to answer. "Aye, *katya*."

"You look terrible. All splotchy."

He gave a weak chuckle. He'd almost lost her. *Lost her!* That she was whole and awake did little to improve his horror and fear, emotions that had nothing to do with his curse. Had he the strength, he would have howled. He wasn't sure when the curse had ceased to matter, when Katie had become all-important to him; he only knew that his life, his very freedom, meant nothing without her. A wave of dizziness assaulted him and he closed his eyes.

"Are you okay?" she asked. "Do you need a doctor?"

"I am fine." But he wasn't. His body felt weak and irreparable, as if he would never again regain his strength.

Gingerly she sat up. "Ouch. That hurts a little."

"What?" he asked, immediately distressed.

"If you must know, my butt."

The only area he had not touched, he thought wryly. "I will massage away the soreness when I have regained my energy."

"What happened to you?" Concern dripped from her voice, and she glanced to her right. "What happened to Frances?"

"Fainted."

"And you?"

He managed a shrug.

As if sensing their scrutiny, Frances moaned and shifted, slowly coming to consciousness. "Wh-what happened?" In the next instant, remembrance flooded her features. She jerked upright, starring with morbid fascination at Jorlan, and then Katie, and then Jorlan again. "He, he—" Her gaze continued to flicker between them both as she pushed with her heels and scooted backward, widening the distance between them. She looked so frightened, so shocked, and she began babbling about lights.

Jorlan had lost the ability to speak. He couldn't reassure or comfort her. She would not have believed him anyway.

"Frances?" Katie said, her own confusion evident. "What's going on?" Slowly, grimacing all the while, she eased to her feet. Bloodstained wood chips were scattered about her. Frowning, she took a step toward the waitress. With a shriek, Frances bolted out the door. Seconds later the sound of crunching gravel erupted as a car sped away.

Kate threw Jorlan a glance over her shoulder. "Jorlan, this is beginning to scare me. Tell me what's going on."

He managed another shrug. Darkness was threatening to overtake him. He needed to stay awake, however, to assure Katie's full recovery. He could not allow her to sink into a decline. But he could not fight the lethargy, either. He was too weak and only growing weaker...weaker.

Darkness finally conquered him.

BREATHING DEEPLY of the stale, unscented air, Percen hobbled across Heather's bedchamber carpet, his body so tense his left leg dragged painfully behind him. Here, with Heather, was the only place he'd ever found a shred of inner peace. He needed that peace now, yet it remained hopelessly out of his grasp.

"What's going on?" Heather asked. A thin, ragged blanket was draped around her shoulders. She sat at the edge of her bed.

He longed to sink to his knees, burrow his head into the hollow of her stomach and tell her all of his troubles. She'd listen. She'd understand, but then she would talk again of forgetting the past, of forgiving. So he remained standing, unwilling to lose himself in her just yet.

"Percen," she said, opening her arms to him.

Her allure proved too heady. He went to her and dropped to his knees. He cupped her face in his hands.

"When this is over, angel, tell me you want to begin a new life with me."

"I do." Her sensual lips curled in a bright smile. "I really, really do."

Those words sparked something to life inside of him, something he couldn't yet name. "I need only a few more days, then I give you my blood oath we will be together."

The sparkle in her eyes dimmed. "Why can't you just forget about Jorlan? Please, Percen. Forget about him and think of me. Of us."

"Don't you see?" With everything inside him, he beseeched her to understand. "If I leave him now, I will never be able to give myself wholly to you. Part of me will always belong to Jorlan."

"But what if you fail?" she whispered, her expression a mixture of pain and longing.

His teeth clenched so tightly he feared his jaw would snap. "I will not fail again. Katie might have escaped, but she will not next time."

Heather drew in a sharp breath. Her fingers clutched the fabric of her blanket until her knuckles looked pale and brittle. "You tried to kill Katie? Why? You said nothing about hurting her."

"Both she and Jorlan must suffer. 'Tis the only way."

"No, that's not true."

Watching her, Percen stopped mid-step. "Why these hysterics? You hate her as much as I do."

"I never wanted to see her harmed. She's been good to me and my mom."

"Good or no, she is Jorlan's lover and *that* makes her my enemy. Yours, as well."

Slight tremors shimmed down Heather's small frame. From cold? Or disappointment? Was he losing her already?

"You were right when you said I don't know who you are," she told him softly. "I don't. I don't know how you can make me feel so warm inside, yet speak so cruelly of murder." She gazed at him through wet lashes. "How are you so cruel?"

"How am I so cruel?" Scowling, he clenched his fists. "I am so cruel because there is nothing inside me except hate. Nothing."

"That's a lie, Percen." She looked past him, past the window. "You have given me back my dreams. Leave with me now, and I will do everything in my power to give you back yours."

Percen wanted so desperately to believe her, to believe that they could live happily ever after and forget the past. Yet how could he ever truly pry the sharp talonlike fingers of the past from his heart if he did not first destroy the hand that bound him?

In the next instant, Heather's mother shoved open the door and flew inside. "Heather," she panted, "you won't believe—" Her gaze fastened on Percen, who promptly disappeared, and she dropped in a dead faint to the floor.

Heather leapt down and gathered her mother into her arms. She cooed soft words of concern, Percen all but forgotten.

He materialized just in front of them. "I will not kill Katie, if you do not wish me to."

Heather's head jerked up. She watched him, silently. Hopefully.

"But I must use her if I am to destroy Jorlan."

"Percen!"

With a wave of his hand, he disappeared once more. Long did the memory of her stricken expression, like a woman betrayed, linger in his mind.

JORLAN SLEPT FOR TWO DAYS. In fact, since he'd fainted, he had not stirred. He hadn't even moaned, hadn't uttered a sound. Such stillness frightened Katie all the way to her bones.

Even now she regarded his sleeping form. She'd managed to work streams of water down his throat. Had cleaned him and somehow managed to change his clothes, but she hadn't been able to move him. He was still lying on the hardwood floor of the Victorian. Damn it! She needed some sort of affirmation that he was alive and well. So many times, she'd almost picked up the phone and dialed 911. But what would the paramedics say to her? Your alien is ailing? No telling how Jorlan was fashioned inside. His heart might very well rest in his ass. Who knew?

Maybe she should call her brother, Brian. He'd fly in and examine Jorlan; he'd also demand answers she couldn't give him. Katie rubbed her temples. One more day. She'd give Jorlan one more day before calling in reinforcements.

As it did every time she was around him, her gaze sought Jorlan. Now more than ever he looked every inch a hard, wary man. His body was laced with scars, evidence of the difficult life he'd led. Yet, at times, he was so tender and gentle with her. She toyed with a lock of his hair, running the midnight strands between her fingers.

The clamor of her heart echoed in the quiet of the room.

She wasn't exactly sure what had happened. She recalled falling through the wood, then waking up with Jorlan cradling her head in his lap, his eyes darkened with fear.

Katie knew she'd fallen. The gaping hole in the living-room ceiling was proof enough of that. But she must have sustained more damage...the bloody wood! Lord, she'd been stabbed by sharp pieces of wood; they'd pierced her flesh, sharp and biting. A fall like that, combined with the bladelike timber, should have crippled her—if not killed her outright. Yet she possessed not a single bruise or cut. Her rear end was still a bit sore, but that was the extent of the damage.

Jorlan had used his magic to heal her.

That was why Frances had run away as if the IRS was after her.

Everything made sense. Everything *except* Jorlan's continued slumber.

Another hour passed, yet his condition remained the same. Katie glided her fingertips over his cheekbones, along his jaw. A soft, almost undetectable moan slipped past his lips.

Hope burst inside of her.

Determined to wake him by any means necessary, she strode to the kitchen, snatched a cup and filled it with water at the sink. Seconds later, she stood over him, about to toss the entire contents in his face.

He woke up on his own.

"Katie," he said, slowly smiling as if he hadn't scared ten years off her life.

"Oh my God." Her knees went weak. She almost collapsed. "Welcome back, Jorlan. Welcome back." She stood just where she was, simply watching him, drinking in the sight of his masculine beauty. With each second that passed, he looked stronger, healthier. All the color was quickly returning to his cheeks.

They simply watched each other.

Finally, she said, "Don't ever do that again. You nearly scared me to death," nearly choking with the force of her relief.

"Then I must make amends." Never taking his eyes from her, he stretched out his arms. "Come to me."

She didn't even hesitate. He was alive, and that was all that mattered. Dropping her cup, she threw herself into his embrace. "Don't ever, ever go to sleep again." Unnoticed, water pooled around them.

"I will not, if you will not ever fall again."

"Deal." Then, "God, I need you." She breathed the words into his neck. "Do you have the strength?" She needed to reaffirm that they both lived, that they were together.

"Aye. Tell me what you need. Tell me and it is yours."

She captured his face in her hands. "I want you inside me, a part of me all day. I want to fall asleep with you deep within me and wake up with the taste of you in my mouth."

"Then take me," he rasped.

Katie did just that. She removed her clothing, then his, until they were both gloriously naked. Inch by inch she moved down the length of him, stopping at the object of her fascination. "Jorlan?"

"Hmm?" His breath emerged unsteadily.

"I meant what I said. I plan to taste you."

He gave a little chuckle. "I will stop you not, *katya.*"

She took him in her mouth, took the bulbous head all the way to the back of her throat. Up and down, she stroked the length of him, savoring the thickness, the heat. He tasted of male and warmth, and Katie couldn't get enough. She didn't know the way of it at first, but she soon caught on.

"Katie," he called hoarsely. "Katie."

When he could take no more of her sweet torment, he grabbed her by the shoulders and wrenched her up. He kissed her then, and oh, sweet God above, then he entered her in one long, swift thrust.

Breathless, Katie closed her eyes. Because she was on top, she controlled the depth of his penetration and she arched her back, sending him deeper inside. Softness met hardness in one glorious burst of sensation. At first, she rode him slowly, deliciously, and not quite taking the full length of him.

"Take me deeper," he commanded. Sweat beaded his brow.

"No, I want—" Oh, right there, she thought, finding a place that made her shake with an intense torrent of pleasure. She wanted to prolong this moment, make it last forever. So she continued to take only part of him, riding the waves of sensation.

Jorlan took her by the hips, urging her on. "Faster. Please, *katya.* Please. Deeper." He made a low sound in the back of his throat. She'd never heard a sound so full of need and promise and desperation, and she realized she wanted to fill her ears with that sound all night long. "Aye, just like that. By *Elliea*, you are mine. My woman."

She bent down and sucked his nipples. She soon heard that moan again.

"Say it," he commanded. "Say the words."

Through heavy-lidded eyes, she watched him; her body continued to arch against his. The only sounds she made were gasps of pleasure. In the next instant, he rolled her over, pinning her against the cold hardness of the wood. She gave a light intake of breath, an exclamation of wonder really, that somehow they managed to stay connected. But now, he was no longer moving. He remained still, gazing down at her, his expression hard and unflinching.

"What are you doing?" She tried to move, to finish what they had begun, but he kept her immobile.

"I want to hear you say the words that bind you to me. You are mine. No exceptions. Say it."

No exceptions? If she were one hundred percent sure of his feelings for her, she'd tell him anything and everything he wanted to hear. But trust didn't come easy for her. She was a creature who demanded proof in all things. So far, he'd only managed to prove he needed her, not that he loved her. "I can't say what you want to hear."

"You can."

"No!"

"You will say the words, Katie, and thus you will cease acting as if you will not be my life-mate. Think you I would let another have you? We belong together. I almost lost you, and I never wish to experience such a fright again."

We belong together. Oh how she wanted to believe him, wanted to give him everything he desired. A part of her still held back, unsure. "I'm sorry," she found herself saying. "My answer is no."

"Curse it!" He pumped into her once, twice, harder each time. "Say you are mine."

"I won't commit myself to you like that." She arched her back, taking all of him that he would give. A gasp pushed past her lips. Oh, he felt so good. "I won't," she said again, more for her benefit than for his.

He slipped his hand between their bodies and pressed against the core of her desire. She groaned in pleasure, in exquisite pain. "So you are refusing me yet again?"

No, I just want to survive emotionally. "Yes."

"Then perhaps, my little witch, I will have to convince you otherwise." His voice was a husky ripple purring against her skin. The wicked gleam in his eyes did not bode well for her sanity.

"What—what do you mean to do?" she asked.

He flexed and surged inside her at the same moment his fingers circled her.

"Oh, Jorlan." Her breath grew ragged as he moved within her again, and again, harder and harder. So hard, in fact, she leaned up and bit his collarbone.

His ragged moan echoed in her ears. "Again. Bite me again."

She did.

He roared his approval, gave her more of his cock. Her head thrashed from side to side with the intensity of her pleasure.

"That's right, Katie. Your body needs mine. Can you feel yourself tighten around me? Can you feel how your body cries out for me?"

"Yes." She gasped. "Oh, yes."

"Say the words. You know what your body is telling you, now listen to your heart."

"No."

"I accept not your answer, *katya*. You belong to me. Soon you will realize just how much."

God help her, he was a man of his word.

JORLAN STOOD OUTSIDE under the darkening sky. A storm was brewing, the scent of coming rain thick in the air. The garden where he had spent so many spans loomed in front of him, but he did not enter. 'Twas a place he would as soon forget. A phantom breeze swirled around him, there one second, gone the next. He could not sleep. He could feel the magic inside him, growing and deepening, churning for release, as if he'd at last unlocked the door to his true abilities.

He possessed the power to open a vortex. He knew that as surely as he knew he loved Katie. At last, he could go home. And yet…

Katie was sleeping soundly on the pallet they had made on the floor.

He could not leave her here alone.

He would not take her away from all she knew.

Neither of which had anything to do with at last breaking the curse, but everything to do with the woman herself. Aye, the curse was readying itself, preparing to strike. For some reason, he was no longer panicked by that thought. Nay, he was more concerned with Katie. If he was to become stone again, he wanted her to be protected by his name and his powers. The only way to do that was to at last make her his woman.

In her stubbornness, she continued to refuse him.

'Tis past time I took the decision from her, he thought suddenly. *Irrevocably.*

Determined, he strode inside the house. Murky light bathed her sleeping form, like fairy dust illuminating a magic circle. Gently, he shook her awake. He positioned himself just above her, his elbows on either side of her shoulders. "This is very important, Katie. Awaken."

Her eyes fluttered open. "What is it? Are you okay?"

"I need you to repeat after me," he told her.

"Not now," she yawned and closed her eyes again. "I'm too sleepy."

"Katie." He shook her a bit harder. "This is very important."

"Why?"

"Please, Katie."

She uttered a sigh and faced him. "Okay. I'm awake."

"Repeat after me." He uttered a string of words in a language she didn't understand. But something inside her demanded she do as he said and repeat every word exactly.

So she did.

He said the words again.

She repeated them again.

Then he nodded. "It is done." With that, he removed his clothing and surged so deeply inside her she wasn't sure where she ended and he began. Lost in passion, she forgot to ask him just what she'd said.

THE EVENING CAME upon them with a vengeance. Rain pounded against the windows. Wind whistled like demons of the night coming to take their chosen to hell.

Only a few hours remained. Jorlan knew it. Felt it.

Katie stirred beside him and yawned. "Good morning." Her eyes were heavy-lidded, slumberous. She gave him a sweet smile, the yawn clinging to the edges.

"We must talk." His expression grave, almost desperate, he helped her to a sitting position.

She frowned and furrowed her brows. "Let me wake up first. I need a protein shake or something."

"Nay. You will listen to what I have to say."

Her arms raised over her head as she stretched. She winced at her body's soreness. "What do you want to talk about?"

"Hours ago—" his heart drummed erratically "—I made you my life-mate."

She froze. All traces of sleep abandoned her features. "You did what?"

"I made you my wife. I spoke the words of binding, as did you."

"You're joking, right?" But Katie knew he wasn't. His eyes were a dark slate, no longer light and twinkling. Her stomach knotted together, and dread clamped around her like shackles, making her breath burn in her lungs. "I told you no."

"I told you aye, and I meant it."

"Did you think I'd fall to my feet and vow to love you forever?"

"Nay, I am prepared for the fate that will soon befall me. What I did, I did for you."

She'd heard that rationale her entire life. *I know what's best for you, Katie. You're a girl. I'm a man.* She'd expected better from Jorlan. "This changes nothing. I won't love a man who doesn't truly love me in return."

"How can you say that? I love you with all of my heart."

"Oh, really? How can I believe that when you ignored my wishes and enforced your will over mine?" The last escaped as little more than a whisper. Hurt was pulsing through her with a consuming, racking force.

"You are mine, *katya.* 'Twas past time you realized that." He gave a sharp shake of her shoulders. "Do you understand? Mine. You belong to me and I belong to you. There is no choice in this matter. It is done. Meant to be."

Fighting through her hurt, Katie thought back to the day she first stumbled upon his statue. She had already decided not to buy the house. There had simply been too many renovations needed, and she had been searching for a smaller summer project. Yet she had seen Jorlan's statue and had known, *known* the house belonged to her.

They did belong together. That didn't mean he had the right to marry her without her consent, however.

"I did not mean to hurt you, Katie, or take away your decision, but I did what I thought was right. You said the words. That is all that matters. You bound yourself to me of your own free will."

CHAPTER TWENTY-TWO

KATIE STOOD in the kitchen, drinking from a glass of water. *I'm married,* she thought. *Married.* Already prongs of delight were disabling her anger. By noon, she realized she *liked* the thought that Jorlan was her husband. She *liked* the thought that she was his wife.

Lord, what was she going to do?

Since Jorlan had confessed what he'd done, he had followed her like a lost little puppy, never ceasing his talk of love and commitment and his need to see her protected.

She was beginning to believe him.

She had only to speak words of love...and yet something always held her back. A sense of dread, fear even, that everything he claimed to feel for her was merely a delusion, and that he would lose interest once he got what he wanted.

"Katie," he began.

Just then, the front door swung open, spraying a fine mist of rain into the living room.

Heather and Frances raced inside and closed the door with a snap. Startled, Katie remained in front of the kitchen sink, mouth agape, water glass positioned midair, and watched them. Frances approached her side, careful to avoid Jorlan, who stood in the corner, observing them all. "Heather convinced me to come. I don't know what happened here, and I don't want you to tell me. I'm just going to do my job, and I don't ever want to talk about what happened."

Katie nodded and set her glass aside.

With that settled, Frances disappeared out the front door.

Heather remained in place, wringing her hands together. "Katie, I— Well, how are you doing?"

Katie blinked. "I'm fine, thank you. How are you?"

"Better." The girl gave a half smile, hesitant but authentic. "I'm better. I've spent the last few days thinking about my life, and I—" Again she halted whatever words she wanted to say.

Something had changed about Heather. Something for the better. "Would you like something to drink?" Katie asked her.

She shook her head. "No, thanks. I've got a lot of work to do out back. If you still want me to work for you."

"I do."

"Well, then, I should probably get started." Heather took a few steps away, before pausing and glancing over her shoulder. "I meant to ask—when did you get the new statue?"

Katie's brows slanted over her eyes. "What new statue?"

"The one that's standing on the platform that used to be empty."

"Used to be…" Oh. When Jorlan had come to life, he'd left an empty dais, the only empty dais in the pleasure garden. Even Nick had commented on it. Still, Katie hadn't had time to replace the statue. "Are you sure there's a statue there?"

"Yeah. It's kinda hard to miss because it's different than all the others. It's not meant for pleasure."

Dread churned in her stomach because she didn't exactly know what this new development meant. She knew it wasn't Jorlan; he still stood a few feet away from her. "Will you meet me there in five minutes?" she whispered.

Though she wore an expression of puzzlement, Heather nodded.

Until she knew what was going on, Katie didn't want Jorlan knowing anything about the new statue. She marched to him, told him she had to use the bathroom and she'd break his fingers if he tried to follow her.

"Then we must talk, Katie," he said. "I do not have much time."

She nodded slowly. Yes, they definitely needed to talk. There was a lot they needed to work out, something she needed to tell him, her fear be damned. With every step she took away from him, she felt his gaze bore deeper into her back. In the bathroom, she locked the door and, like a teenager, sneaked out the window. Rain pelted her body the entire time.

Thunder boomed as she strode to the center of the garden. Heather was there already, waiting quietly. Neither of them had bothered with an umbrella, and they were both soaked to the skin in mere seconds.

"This is it," Heather said.

Katie drew in a breath. Dark clouds hovered over

white stone that formed the rounded curves of a woman. She wore an opulent robe, and a large, circular locket hung at her neck. She was beautiful, as beautiful as Jorlan, yet her beauty was breathtakingly feminine.

Katie's heart raced with a staccato beat, and she wiped the rain from her eyes. "When did this arrive?"

"I'm not exactly sure. I noticed it from the road as we were pulling in the driveway."

Shielding her gaze, she stared up at the statue, wondering what to do. This stone woman seemed eerily similar and had the same vibration of power Jorlan had had. Should she kiss the blasted thing? Before she could place her foot on the ledge to climb up, Heather gasped, drawing her attention. "What's wrong?" she asked, even as she realized a strange man stood only a whisper away.

"Percen," Heather said, conveying all sorts of emotions with that one name. Dread. Happiness. Fear.

The man ignored her; the storm swirled around him, and his pale, unsmiling gaze swept over Katie. Katie knew she should run, should grab Jorlan and demand he protect her, yet she also knew she couldn't have run if her life depended on it. And it may have. Something cold and hard gleamed in the stranger's eyes.

"Come to me," he said, his hand outstretched.

"Percen, don't do this." Heather barked the order with a fierce determination she'd never before displayed. "You promised not to do this."

"I vowed I would not kill her. I said nothing of hurting her. And after I make this concession for you, what do you do to me?" he ground out bitterly. "You choose Jorlan, but then, I knew you would. What woman would help me when she could help Jorlan?" He faced Katie and beckoned her with his fingers. "Come."

Yes, she thought. Yes. Heedless of anything except his summons, she did as instructed. She was vaguely aware of Heather pulling on her clothes, trying to stop her.

"Katie, listen to me. He's doing this to destroy Jorlan."

Katie couldn't make herself care.

"You will lose me if you do this," Heather cried to the man. "You will lose me."

For one second of time, he wavered, and a look of pure torture etched the lines of his mouth. His features hardened. "Did I ever really have you? Go get my brother," he said, his voice cruel.

CHAPTER TWENTY-THREE

A FEMALE SCREAM TORE through the house.

Jorlan reacted immediately. He reached for his weapon and raced from the chamber. Was Katie hurt again? Nay. Nay, he had watched her hawkishly all morn, and right now she was in the bathing chamber perfectly safe.

Just then, a single, terrifying thought suddenly slammed into his mind. What if the lingering effects of his magic had splintered the wood inside the bathing chamber? Fingers of dread clutched at him, chilled his blood, and he cursed himself for allowing Katie a single moment away from him.

At the chamber, a dark wood door barred his entrance.

"Katie," he shouted.

She didn't answer.

He kicked the wood with his foot and timber shards went flying. The small room was empty. The window was open, allowing rain to trickle inside. Heather raced through the hallway, then stopped abruptly. Water dripped from her clothing. She whipped around and faced him, her features etched with panic. "Jorlan," she cried. "You have to help me. Please. Come quick."

Katie? Where was Katie?

He must have spoken the question aloud because the answer rushed from Heather's mouth. "Percen has her. He's going to hurt her if we don't do something."

Jorlan clutched his weapon with all his might. There was no time to question how Heather knew of Percen. "Where is she?"

"I'll take you." Tears streamed down the girl's face leaving a glossy trail. "I should have told you sooner, but I wanted him in my life. But he doesn't deserve me. He doesn't," she rambled.

They flew into the garden, and Jorlan welcomed the rain. The cold kept him alert and ready. Yet, in the center, Jorlan stopped midstride, frozen. In a flash as powerful as the lightning above, he realized his mother peered down at him through white stone eyes. Shocked, horrified, he dropped his weapon and sank to his knees. He hadn't seen her in so long, so very long, and now to see her like this...

"What are you doing?" Heather cried, tugging at his arm. "We have to hurry."

Jorlan knew 'twas Percen's doing, for no other sorcerer could perform the stone spell quite so expertly. How could his brother curse their mother to this life that was no life at all? He had to save her, had to help her in some way.

"You helped me, didn't you?" he asked her. "You helped me save Katie. Now I must save you." But there was no time. His first duty was the protection of his life-mate.

"Hurry, Jorlan." Heather's voice cut into his thoughts. "We have to find them."

"I am sorry, Mother," he whispered, slowly standing. "I will come back for you."

"No need," a smug voice laughed. Percen materialized a few feet away, Katie just in front of him.

Jorlan's eyes narrowed. Katie's clothing was plastered to her body and partially undone. The sorcerer had his hands on her shoulders, stroking her like a kitten. Her amber eyes were glazed with vague detachment. The bastard had entranced her with a spell, Jorlan realized, and he feared if he attempted to snatch her from his brother's grasp, she would fight him. Still, relief that she was alive washed over him in a crashing tide.

"Release her from your snare." He longed to rush his brother, to cut the bastard down before he could harm Katie, but in doing so, Jorlan feared he would hurt his life-mate. "Must you hide behind a woman?"

"Nay." Percen's lips pursed. "I need not hide. I simply thought you would enjoy watching as I destroy your one chance of gaining freedom."

"I do not care about myself. I care only for her."

"Do you speak true? I wonder…" Still grinning, his brother cupped the weight of Katie's breast, and Katie's eyes closed in surrender. "Would you still care for her if she gave herself to me?"

Heather gasped at the sight. "Stop! What are you doing?" Tears continued to flow like a river down her cheeks. "I thought you loved me."

Percen's angry mask slipped for a moment, revealing devastation and hurt, but then his eyes narrowed and he returned his attention to Jorlan.

"You will die for this," Jorlan told him. "You realize that, do you not?" All the hatred he felt for his brother surfaced. "If you are brave enough, let us at last end our feud."

"Percen," Heather sobbed.

His brother hesitated for a long while. Then he nodded. The fire in his eyes roared to life with molten promise, and he shoved Katie aside. "Aye, 'tis time we at last ended this, and what better way than death."

Jorlan didn't give him time to react. With an unholy roar, he sprang into action like a panther who had just spotted his evening meal. Almost too quick for the eye to see, he drew back his elbow and planted a fist into his brother's jaw. Percen's head snapped back. Blood trickled from his mouth.

Jorlan struck him again.

Percen uttered an unholy screech and flew at him. They grappled to the hard ground, fists and legs flying like two wild beasts.

Heather's scream pierced the air.

"I cursed Mon Graig," Percen taunted, half in laughter, half in rage. "Even if your woman loves you, you cannot go home now."

"You are wrong. So wrong." Jorlan thrust his fist smack into his brother's face again. "I can take myself."

Katie slowly came to her senses. When she did, she wished she had not. Shock froze her in place, and there wasn't anything to soften the reality of what couldn't, *couldn't* be happening around her. But the sound of crushed bones and pain-filled moans assaulted her ears as she watched Jorlan and Percen beat at each other. This was all too real. While Percen lacked Jorlan's strength, his magic more than made up for it and placed power behind his blows. If she lived to be two hundred years old, she would never forget the terror and desolation of this moment.

Though she hated to leave him even for a second, she raced inside the house. Her fingers trembled as she grabbed the phone. It took her three times to dial correctly, but she finally managed to call Gray's cell phone.

The moment he answered, she rushed out, "I'm at the Victorian. They're killing each other. You have to hurry." She didn't give him time to respond. She simply threw down the phone and rushed back outside.

Jorlan landed a blow to Percen's mouth. Blood and teeth flew from the man's parted, swollen lips. He fell onto the new statue, causing his blood to mingle with the white stone. A crimson stream trickled along the woman's feet.

Slowly, the stone disappeared, leaving a beautiful, dark-haired woman in its place. Katie paid her no heed. Jorlan was in danger. She had to help him, had to make the fighting stop. She glanced around for some type of weapon. Found nothing.

"You cursed me, you bastard," Jorlan growled. "Then you cursed our mother and tried to kill the woman I love."

"You cursed me the day you were born. She loved you. Always you." There was a wildness to Percen's tone that she'd never heard in a human voice before.

On and on the fight continued. Finally, she heard the comforting blare of police sirens. Soon, red-and-blue lights flashed all around the garden.

"Katie!" Gray shouted a moment later.

"Hurry." She shouted the demand in a voice that shook with terror. "In the center of the garden."

In seconds he and Steve Harris were there, kneeling, guns drawn. "I've already called for backup," Steve said.

"Jorlan, put your hands up and move away," her brother commanded. "Do what I say before I'm forced to shoot you."

Percen chose that moment to unsheath a long, lethal-looking dagger.

"Put the weapon down," Gray shouted. "Put the fucking weapon down *now*."

As if in slow motion, she watched Jorlan and Percen lunge for each other.

The woman who had changed from stone to flesh shouted "Nay," and sprang forward. But she didn't go to Jorlan; she went to Percen.

Heather screamed and rushed in front of Percen.

Katie jumped in front of Jorlan.

Four shots rang out.

Both the strange woman and Heather collapsed at Percen's feet. Katie remained standing. Percen gazed down at the two bodies surrounding him, eyes wide, and dropped his blade.

Heather slowly sat up, wiping tears and rain from her eyes. "My shoulder," she said, shock making her sound hoarse. "My shoulder is bleeding." The other woman didn't move. Blood seeped from her chest at three separate wounds.

Katie whipped around. Jorlan stood frozen, as if he couldn't move. "Jorlan!" Horrified, she watched as his beautiful skin began to turn white. Oh my God. She knew exactly what was happening. "Jorlan, I love you," she shouted over a clap of thunder. "I love you. I do. I love you."

Her confession came too late.

He gazed down at her, his lips curling up in a smile and his eyes warming with love. "You have made me the happiest of men, *katya*. Never doubt that." And then, the stone consumed him completely. He spoke no more.

What had she done? Katie sobbed silently. Horror wrapped around her like a thick sheen of ice. Too long. She'd waited too long, and now her unwillingness to believe in this man that she loved had caused her to lose him. She'd wanted proof of his love. He'd just given it to her.

"I've loved you since the beginning," she whispered brokenly. "I was just afraid to admit it, even to myself. I don't think I ever really doubted your feelings for me. I just couldn't allow myself to believe. If I had, I would have had to go to Imperia with you or let you go without me. I couldn't let you go."

Behind her, Steve rushed at Percen, wanting to cuff him. Percen caught the action and brushed his hand swiftly through the air, creating some type of invisible shield no one could penetrate. The sorcerer sank to his knees. "You saved me," he said to the unconscious woman. "You saved me."

Sirens echoed in the background. The Dallas PD was arriving in torrent. Katie didn't care about anyone except her husband. She stood on her tiptoes and placed a soft kiss upon his lips. "Please, Jorlan, come back to me. I love you. I swear I do."

He remained as he was.

"Damn you, why won't you come back to me?"

Her brother was at her side in the next instant, trying to pull her away from the statue. She clung to Jorlan with all her might, shaking him in the process. "I need you. I need you so much." So many times she'd imagined their parting, but now that it was upon her, she knew she couldn't live without him. She'd go wherever he wanted her to go; she'd take him on any terms. If only he would come back to her.

"I'm your little witch and I command you to open your eyes." The words left her mouth softly, quietly, as another round of thunder boomed overhead. Maybe Percen could help her, she though hopefully. "Percen?"

He ignored her.

"Percen, God damn you, cast a spell! Do something to save him."

He acted as if he didn't hear her. Maybe he didn't. He was focused solely on his mother, gently gathering her into his arms. "Why?" he asked brokenly. "Why did you do that? You could have saved Jorlan, but you chose me." He gave a violent shake of his head and raised his fists to the heavens, cursing all the while. But then, suddenly, his shoulders slumped. "I have done this to you." He hung his head and sobbed.

When he quieted, he gazed up beseechingly at Heather. "Help me, Heather. Please help me. I'm so sorry for all I've done to you. Give me a chance. I'll make it up to you. I swear by the ancient Druinn laws I'll make this up to you. Do not leave me now. I need you too desperately."

Wincing in pain, Heather dropped to her knees behind him and took him in her arms. "I'm here. I'll always be here for you."

He closed his eyes for the briefest moment and nodded. Then, he waved his hand through the air and the trio disappeared.

In that moment, images flashed through Katie's mind. Images of Imperia, of the billowing white grass, the crystal castles and the high-flying dragons. Jorlan would never reach his home, the place he'd always longed to be.

Her knees crumpled and she floated to the ground in a rain-soaked puddle.

A week later

DUSK WAS QUICKLY SETTLING over the horizon, leaving a violet and golden glow in its wake. Wind swirled around the two figures atop the cliff, lifting their robes in a primitive dance. The air was laced with silvery droplets of moisture that swept from the cliff all the way to the white sands of Druinn, creating a cool, damp haven.

Despair and shame beat inside of Percen for all the pain that he had caused. However, hope and joy proved tenacious because of the woman at his side. His mother was dead and he knew an eternity could not wipe away his guilt.

With a bit of help from his magic, Heather's shoulder had healed enough that it no longer gave her any pain. She wrapped her fingers around his right palm, giving him strength for what he was about to do. In his left hand he held his mother's amulet. Imperian custom demanded he destroy that which had been the heart of his mother's magic. Yet he could not bring himself to destroy this last reminder of her.

And so, he stood above Artillian Mer, the largest body of water on Imperia, to pay his mother homage and give her essence back to the powers that created her. His fingers trembling, he raised the amulet to his lips and placed a soft kiss upon the center. He drew in a deep breath. Let it out. Tears began to slide down his cheeks. "I love you," he whispered brokenly. He removed the left stone, the smallest of the three, then tossed the necklace into the churning amber liquid.

He watched the amulet sink, slowly at first, then disappearing altogether in the depths. Silence stretched for a long while. Neither he nor Heather moved away.

"Thank you for coming with me," he told her softly. "I just wish you could have known her."

"I knew the most important thing about her. She loved you."

"Aye, she did. She truly did, and yet I am responsible for her death."

Heather's fingers tightened around him.

"I could take you back to your world if you wished." His gaze never left the water. He didn't want to face her yet, for fear of what he'd see in her eyes.

She answered without hesitation. "I want to stay here with you…if you'll have me."

The viselike grip clamping around his muscles eased. He turned his chin to stare at her in wonder, awe and happiness. "I am glad, so glad. I do not think I could survive without you."

She gave him a half smile. "You're stronger than you think, Percen. We both are."

He took her face in his hands, loving the feel of her skin. "I have to go back for a little while. I cannot tamper with Imperia's time, for the magic here will not allow what has happened to be undone. But I *can* manipulate another world's time within a season of my last departure. While that will not save my mother," he whispered sadly, "it will allow me to do something for her." He closed his eyes and pressed his forehead against Heather's. "I must try and right the wrong I have caused Katie and Jorlan."

"I know, and I'll be here, awaiting your return."

He placed a soft kiss upon her lips. She wrapped her arms around his neck. Behind them, Imperia's three suns finally descended.

KATIE WHIPPED her truck into her driveway. Two weeks had passed since Jorlan had returned to stone. Two miserable, horrible, wretched weeks! She'd been racked with grief every day, grief that only grew, never lessened.

Gray called her every morning. The first week, he'd been in shock from what he'd seen. But he and Steve had agreed not to speak of the things that had happened. Who would have believed them, anyway? Now Gray and the rest of her family simply wanted to know how she was doing.

How was she doing?

Horribly.

She wanted Jorlan back in her life, in her arms and in her bed. He was her husband, after all. How could she have ever been so stupid as to think she didn't love him? So stupid to think he didn't love her? She'd invaded every library and Internet resource she knew, but hadn't even found a cross-reference to a stone spell.

Tears spilled down her cheeks, and she rested her head against the steering wheel. The future looked so bleak and pale without him. What was she going to do?

What was she going to do?

What if she never found a way… No, she couldn't allow herself to think like that. She *would* find a way to save Jorlan; she had to believe that. Determined, she wiped her tears away with trembling fingers and emerged from her truck. She strode inside her house. Fighting great waves of depression, she tossed her jacket on the floor and went into the kitchen.

Without Jorlan beside her, everything just seemed *wrong*. Like her soul wasn't complete. She sniffled, dangerously close to tears again. Pressing her lips tightly shut, she went into the living room and flipped on the television. She squeezed her eyes closed and tried to clear her mind. She hadn't slept at all in the past weeks and soon felt herself drift away into fitful oblivion.

A few hours later, she awoke to a man standing over her.

Percen.

She jolted up, fury pounding through her. "You!"

She lunged at him, intent on killing him for all the things he'd done to Jorlan.

He didn't try to fight back, just let her beat at him, as if he knew he deserved every punch, scratch and kick.

Finally, her strength deserted her and she collapsed on the couch.

Percen remained in front of her, though he watched her cautiously. "I've come to help you," he said.

"Why should I believe you?" she snapped, but hope was a silly thing and was already unfurling inside her.

"You shouldn't," he answered simply. "All you can do is allow me a chance."

"Can you free him?"

He hesitated only a moment. "Nay. I cannot. I created the spell so that not even I could undo it."

Her shoulders slumped. What good was he to her if he could not grant her fondest desire? "Get out of my house, Percen. I don't want you here."

"What I can do, however, is teach *you* the stone spell."

He could teach her the... Katie sat up straighter. Yes. Yes! Why hadn't she thought of that before? If she turned herself to stone, she could be beside Jorlan forever. She didn't have to think about her answer. "Yes. Teach me the spell."

"Are you sure?"

"Yes. Damn you, yes!"

"Then you will need this." He placed a small blue stone in her palm.

Warmth tingled up her arm, and power hummed at each of her fingertips.

"Come," Percen said. "I would like to see him." Together they walked to Jorlan's statue.

Each time she saw him, Katie was filled with love and tenderness and desperation for this man she had so long denied.

Percen stood, gazing at his brother. "Why did I not release my anger sooner?" His deep baritone dripped with longing and pain. "Why?"

What a pair they made, Katie thought. Jorlan's brother unable to let go of the past. She, unable to grasp the future. "We all have our reasons for doing the things that we do. We can only learn from them, and go on."

"Heather says the same." Percen sighed, the sound an echo of his inner torment.

Lord, in her grief, she had all but forgotten Heather. "So Heather is well?"

"Aye. I have made her my life-mate, much to the distress of the Druinn. But I am High Priest, and they can do nothing to usurp my law." His gaze skidded away. "I—I am sorry for all the pain I caused you, Katie. So sorry."

She thought about all the things she could have said just then. *I hate you for what you've done. I hope you feel as much pain as I do.* But she realized that she truly didn't want to say those things. She couldn't. It took only one look at Percen's blue eyes, eyes so much like Jorlan's, to see that he suffered, too. She took in a deep breath and sighed. "You are...forgiven. I have to forgive you," she rushed on, before she stopped herself. "This is my fault as much as yours. Had I not been so stubborn, so selfish, Jorlan would never have returned to stone."

A look of disbelief sprang into Percen's eyes. "You truly forgive me?"

"I think even Jorlan has forgiven you," she added. "The grudge you bore each other brought you nothing but pain."

Percen all but sobbed, "Nay. It brought us love, as well."

For a long moment, the only sound was birds chirping nearby. Katie didn't think she could respond to such a statement. Her love for Jorlan was killing her.

As if it hurt to look at her, Percen moved his gaze to the fading sunset, and said, "I have freed Mon Craig. If you decide not to utter the spell, and wish to visit Imperia, go to him and he will take you."

Her lips trembled, and she managed a nod.

"Jorlan can hear us, do you know that?"

"Yes," she whispered. "I know."

"I want him to know who killed his father. 'Tis my gift to him, though I know it can never make up for what I have done." He faced the statue. "It was…it was our mother. Do not blame her though," Percen rushed to add. "The king asked her to do it. He hated being old while she was so young."

The knowledge shocked Katie, and she knew it had shocked Jorlan, as well. "How do you know this?" she asked.

"I divined the truth the same day 'twas done." Percen paused, sucked in a breath, as if to bury the past. Unable to talk about it any longer, he said, "And now, my gift to you. Are you ready to learn the spell, Katie?"

She didn't hesitate. "Yes."

"Know first, that if you do this, you will be trapped inside, unable to respond. Nothing, not even a kiss, will set you free."

"I understand." She curled her fingers more tightly around the jewel she held, suddenly recalling the first psychic she and Jorlan had visited. *You have the power within yourself to go home.* Home was with Jorlan, and

Katie would use every ounce of power she possessed to be with him. Even as stone.

Percen conjured a yellowed tome and handed it to her. "As you hold the stone, say these words...my sister, and know that I am eternally grateful for your forgiveness." With that, he disappeared.

Katie spent the next hour tying up the loose ends of her affairs. She wrote a letter to the bank, telling them to give the deed to the Victorian to Frances. She wrote a letter to each of her brothers, explaining how much she loved them and expected them to always follow their hearts. Last, she wrote a letter to her dad. It was the hardest to write, and she often had to pause to wipe away her tears. When she finished, she signed, "Love, your sixth son."

She left the letters on the table, knowing her brothers would search for her in a day or two. She just prayed they would understand.

With nothing left to do, she placed herself next to Jorlan, wrapped one hand around his and held the azure-colored jewel in the other. She was about to give up her freedom, her family, and her life, but oh, she was gaining so much more in return. If she couldn't have a life with Jorlan, she would spend eternity beside him. After a deep breath, she began to utter the spell. Seconds later, she thought she felt the breeze kick up. She even saw a few leaves drop to the ground. But nothing happened to her.

She uttered the spell again. Still, nothing. She was as flesh-and-blood as always. Realizing she didn't have the power to make it work, she leaned against Jorlan's arm, closed her eyes and began to cry. Not a sobbing, gushing cry, but a salty trickle that flowed slowly down her cheeks. God, she missed Jorlan so much.

Katie's palm began to burn. The jewel burned like debris from a spewing volcano. She felt something shift beside her. Then…nothing. "I love you, Jorlan," she said, because it seemed there was nothing else to say. The spell hadn't worked.

"Ah, *katya*," a male voice said, rich with promise, "I will never tire of hearing your confession."

Shocked, she jerked her head to stare at the man standing beside her, at the bronzed skin she loved and had missed so much.

Jorlan stood, smiling down at her. Lord, he was here and real and with her. Truly with her. Now tears of joy and hope and love slid down her cheeks in the torrent she denied herself before. She became a blubbering slob and she didn't care.

Jorlan held her through it all, and brushed away her tears. "It feels so good to hold you again."

"But how?" She gave him a watery smile. "How are you standing here, Jorlan?"

He chuckled. "'Twas not a stone spell you uttered, but a wishing spell. 'Tis something that works only with a supreme act of unselfishness. When you spoke the words, your willingness to join me gave you your fondest desire."

"You," she breathed. "It gave me you."

"It seems I owe my brother a debt of gratitude." He caressed a finger along her jawbone. "You were right, you know? I have forgiven Percen. How could I still hate him when he has given you back to me?"

Suddenly overcome with the force of her joy, she

threw her arms around his neck. "Oh my God," she said in between kisses. "You're real. You're real. You're real."

He breathed in the scent of her hair. "I am real, and I will be with you, here, always."

Frowning, she pulled back just a little. "You don't have to stay here, Jorlan. Mon Graig can take you to Imperia. And if you'll have me...I'd like to go with you."

"I will have you, *katya,* but I will have you here. *This* is my home. Besides, I am well able to open a vortex on my own now. Mon Graig is not needed."

"But you haven't been back, haven't seen your family or your—"

"*You* are my life-mate, my family. The other half of my soul. I realized over the last days that Imperia is my past. You are my future."

With those words ringing in her ears, Katie felt whole and complete again, fulfilled. Jorlan had come back to her and wanted to spend his life with her! What had she ever done to deserve this much happiness? A smile of contentment curved her lips, then slowly faded. "I'm sorry about your mother, Jorlan. So sorry."

Sadness flickered in his eyes. "She has joined my father. I know she has found her rightful place, and I must be content with that."

"I love you," Katie whispered.

He kissed her softly. She clung to him. When he pulled back, they were both panting with need.

"I can't believe this is happening," she said. "I mean, what are the odds of you and I ever meeting? Of all the planets in all the galaxies, your mother sent you to mine."

"I did not come here by chance, little witch. We were always meant to find one another. I love you, and I will always love you. Will you let me stay with you, be your life-mate and your lover? I will help you with your houses and love you all the days of our lives. If you will let me."

She blinked up at him innocently. "As long as you agree to one more rule."

He arched a brow, and his lips twitched. "And what is that?"

"Ravish me at least once a day."

At that, he grinned. "That is one rule that needs no adjustment. Now take me inside, little witch, for I have need to obey this rule immediately."

EPILOGUE

"You look soooo sexy."

"I've never seen anyone look so hot in satin and lace."

Katie chuckled. She just couldn't help herself. Gray had lost their bet—the bet they made the day Jorlan entered her life. Only one month ago, she'd sold the Victorian to her husband for five thousand and one dollars over purchase price and renovation costs.

Because he'd lost, Gray was wearing a dress at their dad's luncheon.

Now her entire family was gathered in her dad's backyard whistling and complimenting Gray on his attire. Even Brian had flown in from New Orleans for the event.

"The pink really does flatter your coloring, Gray," she told him, settling more deeply atop Jorlan's lap.

"Smart-ass," Gray grumbled. He stood over the steaming grill, flipping hamburgers and hotdogs. "Jorlan, come over here and help me with this."

"Nay. You are doing well enough on your own, and I like where I am at the moment."

All of Katie's brothers—except Gray, of course—chuckled.

Jorlan massaged the base of her neck. Relaxed and in love, she sighed. Ah, married life was more satisfying than she'd ever imagined. Jorlan took care of her in every way possible. He made love to her daily, pampered her, played basketball with her and even helped around the house. He saw to her every need.

He truly was her Prince Charming.

She'd kissed his lips and set him free, but it was he who had truly saved her.

His hand slid from her neck to her belly, and a greater sense of contentment filled her. Their first child was due in less than a month. Even her dad had softened with thoughts of welcoming this first grandchild.

"Well, I for one am tired of waiting. I want to eat." That was from Frances, who stood next to Katie's dad.

Katie and Frances had developed a bond over the last months. Most surprising of all, however, was how Frances actually liked and accepted Jorlan for what he was, even if she didn't understand it.

Ryan turned his attention to Frances. "You're tired of waiting? You're tired of waiting? Then get your little butt over there and help. It's a woman's job, after all."

Frances's eyes narrowed. The sparks between the two of them were almost visible. "I'll tell you what a woman's job is. It's building her self-discipline so she doesn't kill every man she sees."

Ryan snorted.

Katie chuckled. Oh, great things were in store for Frances and her father; she just knew it.

"I love you, *katya*," Jorlan whispered in her ear.
"And I love you."
Life had never been better.

* * * * *

AUTHOR NOTE

If you're like me, you find the thought of a half-naked warrior immensely appealing. Even better is a half-naked warrior who must obey your every command. Meet Tristan ar Malik, the hero of my next romantic fantasy *The Pleasure Slave*. He is a slave to women's desires; his only purpose to attend to the pleasure of his mistress. Poor baby. Also, I have an exciting new series in the works, the first of which features Mia Snow, Alien Huntress. She is the leader of an elite task force that stalks the night, hunting and killing predatory aliens. For more information about my upcoming books, visit my Web site at www.genashowalter.com.

Don't miss Gena Showalter's sexy new story

THE PLEASURE SLAVE

Coming from

HQN™

February 2005.
Please turn the page for a preview.

PROLOGUE

Imperia
The 5th Season

"I WANT YOU AGAIN, TRISTAN."

Waves crashed against the cliffs outside, their lulling rhythm floating upon the sea-kissed beams of moonlight filtering through the arched windows. The sweet scent of *gartina* and *elsment* filled the chamber, a palpable omen of magic few could comprehend or even acknowledge.

Zirra leaned naked against the window frame, the exact place her lover had taken her moments ago. When he failed to respond to her words, she seductively arched her back and skimmed a hand down the flat plane of her stomach. "I want you again, Tristan," she repeated, a husky edge to the words. Her body still hummed from his touch, but she needed more of him.

She *always* needed more of him.

The darkness of his hair hung in wild disarray over his shoulders as he fastened his black warrior *drocs* around his waist. He eyed her with amusement. "You know I must go, *nixa.*"

"Why?" Annoyed, Zirra abandoned her pose of relaxed beckoning and stalked to the bed. She didn't bother covering herself with the silky white sheet, but left the plump mounds of her breasts bared for his view. "Why do you deny me the pleasure of your touch?"

He closed the distance between them and eased atop the bed, mere inches from her reach. "You know I must journey to the palace for instruction from Great-Lord Challann. A rebellion brews in Gillirad."

"But I—"

"I cannot disobey a direct command from my sovereign. This you know, as well."

Her brow knit in annoyance. Tristan acted as if her nakedness no longer tempted him.

Mayhap it didn't.

Tendrils of fury kindled inside her. Earlier she had kissed and licked a path down his entire body, had taken him deep into her mouth as she'd never done for another man. When she finished, he had slid himself inside her, pumping and sliding erotically, giving her a rapture so complete she had begged for mercy. Yet he had yawned. Yawned!

Her fists clenched so tightly her knuckles whitened, and her long, oval nails dug into her palms, cutting deeply into the skin. She had given Tristan everything she had to give, and yet she, a priestess of the Druinn, had failed to truly satisfy him. And because of her failure, she would soon be discarded like a worthless piece of garbage.

That image burned in her mind, and the urge to hurt Tristan, to destroy him in some way, coursed through her. For eight cycles he had come to her bed, giving her incomparable pleasure, and for each of those eight eves he had left her here afterward, alone in the vast emptiness of her bed, desperate for more of him. Dying for more of him.

He must suffer as I suffer, she thought. Yet...

Her need for his affection proved a vehement ache she could not ignore, and she found herself reaching out, gripping his muscled forearm. Even now, with his features drawn tight with annoyance, he exuded the sensual eroticism of a man who existed only to pleasure his woman. She wanted, *needed,* to be the one who obtained his eternal devotion. Mayhap then the constant ache inside her heart would be filled.

"We belong together," she said, her words emerging on an ethereal wisp of breath. "Life-join with me and I will give you more carnal pleasure than any other woman is capable of giving."

He did not even pause. "Nay."

"Treasures. I will give you treasures beyond your deepest imagination." With a desperate flick of her wrist, she tossed her long, black hair over one shoulder. "Even, if you so desire, a planet of your own to rule."

"Zirra," Tristan chided softly. Watching her, he lounged across the bed and propped his weight on his elbow. "Best you recall my words before I ever came to be your lover. I told you I would never be more than a passing fancy for you."

"Aye, I remember," she admitted through gritted teeth. But she hadn't let it stop her from having him. One look at Tristan's male perfection, at the way his pale violet gaze promised untold passion, at the way his hard, muscled body moved with sinewy grace, and she'd been lost. Lost as if her mind and heart were separate entities.

"Nothing has changed," he said. With a touch as gentle as his tone, he ran a fingertip down her cheek. "Nor will it ever. You are Druinn, and I am mortal, and permanent ties are forbidden. I am sorry."

Once again, fury blazed through her, hot and hungry for vengeance. No one treated her this way. No one. "I will give you but one more chance to bind yourself to me."

He pushed to his feet, uttering that husky chuckle of his that usually made her shiver with delight. Now the sound merely fueled her anger.

"Or you will what, *nixa?* Boil my eyeballs in water? Render my manhood flaccid for all time?"

"Oh no, my fine warrior. I will do much, much worse."

Not the least affected by her ominous warning, he lifted his gleaming silver blade from its inclined position against the wall and hooked it to a metal loop on his belt. He bent down and placed a quick kiss upon her cheek. "Mayhap later we will work off this energy you seem to harbor, hmm?"

Without waiting for a reply, he turned on his heel and strode to the door.

"You desire women above all things, Tristan," she said, "and now I will make you a slave to them." Scowling, she snatched up the jeweled trinket box he had given her mere hours ago and hurtled it at his head. It sailed past his ear and crashed to the floor, unharmed. She vaulted to her feet. "I will make you a slave to *me*."

Tristan spun and faced her. His expression no longer boasted of easy confidence, but of incredulity, and just a little fear. "What are you doing, Zirra?"

A rush of excitement pooled between her legs, for *she* had made this mighty warrior afraid. "No one refuses me," she told him, her body remaining taut as she stood in all her naked glory, fury and indignation her only cloth. "And you, my handsome mortal, shall pay for doing so."

"Mortals have vowed never to destroy your people's Kyi-en-Tra Crystal, and in return the Druinn have sworn never to use their powers against us. You yourself agreed to this, and if you break your oath you will break the Alliance between our people and war will erupt. You *will* honor your word. No sorcery. I forbid it."

"You, a mortal? Forbid me? I think not." She chuckled, yet the sound lacked humor. "How will your Great-Lord ever discover what I have done to you if you cannot tell him?"

"Zirra—"

"Beg me to become your life-mate, and I will swear never to harm you."

Lavender fire instantly blazed in his eyes. "I will never beg you, or anyone, for anything."

"Then you have brought this on yourself, Tristan ar Malik."

Dark brows arched in mocking salute, she raised her hands in the air, palms up.

He growled low in his throat as he advanced, his intent to immobilize her evident with every step. A simple wave of her hand froze his feet in place.

Surprise flashed across his features a split second before he glared at her with such hostility she shivered. She refused to allow a mortal to frighten her, so she closed her eyes, splayed her fingers wide and began to chant. "From now until love finds you true, a woman's slave I shall make of you."

Wind howled in swirling procession, thrashing and clawing throughout her spacious chamber, whipping the white gossamer cloth over her windows and rattling the very foundation of her floor. Energy erupted and glowed all around, striking like bolts and war spears. A rumbling boom echoed in her ears. She raised her arms higher.

"Into a trinket box you shall rest, answering each summons as it suits best. This I bind, this I speak, your will matters none. So said, let it be known. So said, let it be done."

One moment Tristan stood before her a strong, virile man, the next he was gone. Only the small jewel-encrusted box she'd thrown rested on the floor. Grinning slowly, she hopped from the bed, bent down, and clasped the box in her hands. A wave of giddiness swept through her. Tristan now belonged to her—only to her. And over the next thousand years or so, she would enjoy letting him make up for his behavior today.

He would learn well his mistake in refusing a priestess of the Druinn.

On sale now

girls' night in

21 of today's hottest
female authors
1 fabulous short-story collection
And all for a good cause.

Featuring *New York Times* bestselling authors

Jennifer Weiner (author of *Good in Bed*),
Sophie Kinsella (author of *Confessions of a Shopaholic*),
Meg Cabot (author of *The Princess Diaries*)

Net proceeds to benefit War Child, a network of organizations
dedicated to helping children affected by war.

Also featuring bestselling authors...

Carole Matthews, Sarah Mlynowski, Isabel Wolff, Lynda Curnyn,
Chris Manby, Alisa Valdes-Rodriguez, Jill A. Davis, Megan McCafferty,
Emily Barr, Jessica Adams, Lisa Jewell, Lauren Henderson,
Stella Duffy, Jenny Colgan, Anna Maxted, Adèle Lang,
Marian Keyes and Louise Bagshawe

www.RedDressInk.com   www.WarChildusa.org

Available wherever trade paperbacks are sold.

If you enjoyed what you just read, then we've got an offer you can't resist!

Take 2 bestselling novels FREE!
Plus get a FREE surprise gift!

Clip this page and mail it to MIRA®

IN U.S.A.
3010 Walden Ave.
P.O. Box 1867
Buffalo, N.Y. 14240-1867

IN CANADA
P.O. Box 609
Fort Erie, Ontario
L2A 5X3

YES! Please send me 2 free MIRA® novels and my free surprise gift. After receiving them, if I don't wish to receive anymore, I can return the shipping statement marked cancel. If I don't cancel, I will receive 4 brand-new novels every month, before they're available in stores! In the U.S.A., bill me at the bargain price of $4.99 plus 25¢ shipping and handling per book and applicable sales tax, if any*. In Canada, bill me at the bargain price of $5.49 plus 25¢ shipping and handling per book and applicable taxes**. That's the complete price and a savings of over 20% off the cover prices—what a great deal! I understand that accepting the 2 free books and gift places me under no obligation ever to buy any books. I can always return a shipment and cancel at any time. Even if I never buy another The Best of the Best™ book, the 2 free books and gift are mine to keep forever.

185 MDN DZ7J
385 MDN DZ7K

Name	(PLEASE PRINT)	
Address	Apt.#	
City	State/Prov.	Zip/Postal Code

Not valid to current The Best of the Best™, Mira®, suspense and romance subscribers.

Want to try two free books from another series?
Call 1-800-873-8635 or visit www.morefreebooks.com.

* Terms and prices subject to change without notice. Sales tax applicable in N.Y.
** Canadian residents will be charged applicable provincial taxes and GST.
All orders subject to approval. Offer limited to one per household.
® and ™are registered trademarks owned and used by the trademark owner and or its licensee.

BOB04R   ©2004 Harlequin Enterprises Limited